FLOOD TIDE

FLOOD TIDE

AN LT NICHOLS MYSTERY

ALBERT WAITT

Praise for Flood Tide

"*Flood Tide* will sweep you up, throw you into a whirlpool, and have you gasping—not for air—but for the truth. LT Nichols, police chief of Laurel, Maine, cares about the truth. But there are those who will stop at nothing to keep it from being revealed. Suspenseful and surprising, Albert Waitt's book will catch you like a riptide and pull you to a fully satisfying ending."—Sarah Bewley, author of *Burning Eden*

"*Flood Tide* is smalltown politics and power, where appearances are more than maintained. This novel ripples with the dark undercurrent of life and crime in a New England town."—Gabriel Valjan, author of the Shane Cleary Mystery series

Chapter One

I was staring at the ceiling when the phone rang. All summer a fisher cat had been hunting the woods behind my house. Its predatory howls— imagine the scream of a teenage girl being horribly attacked—never failed to jolt me from sleep. Since it had awakened me an hour earlier, I'd been contemplating a relationship I feared was headed into the ditch. I reached for the receiver. The alarm clock glowed five-thirty.

Fran Pickey was on the line. She'd been radioed by her lobsterman husband with instructions to roust me. Ed Pickey could occasionally be level-headed and had all the imagination of a potato, so when she told me that Ed thought there was a body on Stage Island, I tossed back the sheets and got rolling. Since I'd been chief, we'd had great white shark sightings, a tidal wave warning, and reports of a Russian submarine lurking offshore. None of which had held a drop of truth. I hoped that run of luck would continue as I lead-footed to the pier.

Laurel, Maine, despite having miles of jagged coastline, three beaches, two municipal piers, thousands of summer visitors, and a harbor master who was a drunk, had chosen to ignore my annual request to purchase a boat for the department. Rick Schoefield, whose job it was to oversee these piers and should have been escorting me on his town-funded Boston Whaler, was nowhere to be found. I'd had to commandeer whatever was available at Cape Laurel Harbor. That was Gus Brown's ancient dory. We chugged toward Stage Island, blue smoke pouring from the engine. I could have swum faster.

Gus steered left as we came out of the harbor. We passed the automated beacon and hooked around the red can following it. The sun was rising on the horizon, and gold reflected off the flat, black-green water. Spiky peaks of shoal rose beside us like dinosaurs' backs.

"Beautiful out here this morning," I said.

Gus's eyes rolled under thick, white brows. I'd just asked to run the lights and turn on the siren. He handed me a pair of binoculars. Stage was the size of a football field, with a half dozen scraggly pines sprouting from its center. It was the beginning of a series of rocky outcroppings that ran from the harbor north to Gray Gull beach. An anchor line held Pickey's lobster boat in place off the island's western shore. The deep V of its bow pointed to the Atlantic, its open deck behind. Ed's eyes were fixed on a splash of white on the black stone.

Gus came around to give me a better look at what held Pickey's attention. A brick began forming in my stomach. He had not been hallucinating. A man in standard summer finery of khaki pants and collared white shirt sprawled face down on the shore. Water lapped at the rocks inches below him. It could be that he'd slipped off the deck of a passing yacht headed Downeast. Or maybe he'd had one too many martinis at the Sea Squall and taken one too many steps while stargazing on the jetty, mistaking a black emptiness for solid ground.

We didn't have many drownings here, if that's what this was. Laurel's coast was sheltered by a series of shoals and scattered small islands like the one in front of us. Rather than creating a surf, they protected the shore. Vacationers who showed up with their boards were sorely disappointed, and the riptides that dragged people to their deaths on Cape Cod only surfaced here in stories reported by The Boston Globe. We were known for our safe beaches. There were, of course, exceptions to every rule.

Gus pulled up alongside Pickey's boat. I thanked him and jumped onto Ed's deck.

Ed looked at me, then nodded toward the island, twenty feet away. "What the hell, LT?" he said. LT was short for Little Timmy. A fellow third grader had called me Tiny Tim while we were watching *Mr. Magoo's Christmas Carol* in school. I broke his nose with a punch. My brilliant classmates came up with "Little" as a less antagonistic alternative. It stuck, eventually getting reduced to initials for ease of use.

"Can we get closer?" I asked, my eyes on the body. The back of his head was matted with sandy blonde hair. His feet were bare.

"Can't," Pickey said, shaking his head. "Rocks under the surface."

"I'll get the state police. They have a Zodiac that can get right in there. We can gather what evidence there is before we move him," I said.

"Evidence?" Ed said, the pitch of his voice rising. "Don't you think he just drowned?"

"You can't assume, Pick," I said. My mind had gone to the worst-case scenario by default—that this wasn't an accident. Most likely, Pickey was right. But likely wasn't always reality. Even in this postcard of a town, one couldn't take anything at face value. "How do you think he got caught there?"

"He's a piece below the high-water mark. New moon last night. Shit goes everywhere in a flood tide like that. Probably dropped him on its way out." He tucked his hands into his overalls. "Lucky, or who knows where he'd be." Pickey nodded to the unending expanse of water on the horizon. The sun was rising full red. Red sky in morning, sailors take warning. Even I knew that one.

"Yeah, lucky," I said, reaching for my walkie-talkie to call the station and request the state police Zodiac.

"I don't think you want to wait on that boat, LT," Pickey said.

"Why is that?"

"Tide's coming in. He's floating again in twenty minutes."

"So how do we get him?" I asked. Sometimes, I spoke before I thought, a habit I'd nearly given up trying to break.

"Don't look at me," he said, happy not to be the police chief.

I stripped down to my boxers and climbed onto the stern.

"How deep is it?" I asked.

"Right here, eight feet or so," he said, pointing behind us. He then pivoted toward the island. "But there's no telling where the rocks start at this tide. They can be closer than they look."

I dove in. While the weather in Maine can change from one minute to the next, the water is always cold. I came up to the surface. Some would have called it refreshing. I was not one of those people.

"Be careful not to clip yourself," Pickey yelled. "You know about blood in the water." He tossed me a life preserver to put under the body, the irony lost.

Fifteen strokes around the boat and I was finding my footing next to the body, the water to my waist. I got my breathing under control and told myself to take a clinical look before I moved him. I placed my hand on his neck, where a pulse would have been if he'd had one. His gray skin was rough like a roofing shingle. I gently turned him toward me. The brick that had been forming in my gut solidified.

We had three thousand people who lived in Laurel year-round, willing to tough out the winter and the quiet. In summer, things were different. On a given day, we could have that many again flooding our beaches, downtown shops, and bed and breakfasts. Then there were the seasonal folks, another few thousand, most of whom were working people from Massachusetts and southern New Hampshire who owned small, neat cottages. We also had a good number of professionals from Boston and down along the northeast corridor: lawyers, doctors, and financial professionals who kept our contractors busy with remodels. Of the entirety of these residents and visitors, there was only one I would call important: Randolph Grimes of Darien, Connecticut. He lorded over a spit of family land just north of here called the Compound. After spending ten years in the House of Representatives and launching something called the Competitive America Foundation, he'd been appointed Secretary of Commerce by President George H. W. Bush. It was his son, Alex, who lay dead in front of me.

Chapter Two

If I weren't shivering from the cold, I would have been sweating. A purple bruise covered Alex's left eye as if he'd been beaned by a Roger Clemens fastball. When I checked it, I could have been pressing into a rotten grapefruit, a clear fracture. The rest of him looked okay, considering. His shirt was untucked and buttoned. His pants were twisted. The dishevelment could mean he'd dressed in a hurry, though it could have resulted from being tossed around in the Atlantic. I found two items in his pockets. Neither surprised me. The first was a matchbook from the Dockside. Everyone in town drank there, including me. Accompanying it was a small one-hitter. Even well-heeled young professionals from important families smoked pot. But I'd never seen anyone drown because of it.

I cradled him as if handling a baby, one arm under his neck to keep his head in place. He was shorter and stockier than his athletic father and must have weighed close to two hundred, having fifty pounds on me. I focused my energy, exhaled, and lifted him from the rocks, placing his back onto the life vest. I strapped him in and swam toward the seaward side of the boat. It felt like I was towing a loaded barge. We came up alongside the cutout where Pickey pulled his traps. He watched me tread water.

"Ed, you goddamn well know I can't lift him onto the deck from here. Help me out."

"He's dead, LT." This, from a guy who'd worked all spring with broken ribs. "I ain't touching him."

"Since when have you been a lily of the valley?"

I could see him working it out on his long face. He sighed and leaned over, and I pushed Alex's shoulders up. Pickey yanked him in. Alex's right foot caught me in the jaw. It wasn't exactly a love tap. Maybe he'd wanted to disappear out there, and I was getting in his way. When I climbed in, Ed was pressed against the opposite rail. He'd dropped Alex Grimes in the middle of the deck.

"Thanks," I said.

"That isn't G-One, is it?"

"It sure is."

Around town, Alex and his older sister Abby were known as the Gold Dust twins, shortened to G-One and G-Two. The Grimes family were scions of a manufacturing empire that produced everything from cardboard boxes to ammunition. It was this industrialist background that had paved Randolph's path to Washington. The family had a long heritage here, owning their land since before prohibition. Randolph and his wife Violet took no airs and, to the delight of many townspeople, were gracious in public and notably generous to servers and bartenders. Randolph even used to fish with my father, whose highest political office was that of town selectman and whose height of industry reached owning a downtown tourist shop. While the elder Grimes would put smiles on faces when they entered an establishment, Alex and his sister's presence elicited groans. If there were drinks spilled, an ass grabbed on a dance floor, or a waitress bursting into tears, odds were a Grimes offspring or someone in their party was involved. Rather than signs of appreciation, the Jacksons and Franklins G-One and G-Two slapped into hands on their way out the door were payments on the rope they'd been given—and insurance on it being available again. Blood money, the bartenders called it. I'd received plenty of late-night pleas from managers worried they'd be held responsible if one of the Grimes kids wrapped their car around a tree on River Road. If the voice on the phone sounded desperate enough, I'd make some calls and arrange to have them driven home. It wasn't a long shot that Alex, on his own, could have managed a long drunken walk off a short pier and cracked his skull in the process.

"Holy shit," Pickey said. "You think the old man knows?"

"Do you see the Coast Guard out here?" I asked.

"I need a damn beer," he said. He threw me a towel spotted with oil. It was just six-thirty. While he could dream of getting drunk, I dried off feeling midnight tired. It wasn't the lack of sleep that was bothering me.

"What time would the tide have hung him up like that?" I asked.

"Maybe eleven because he ain't nearly at the high point, not with the moon."

"What way do the currents run?" I asked.

"They swirl in and out around here."

"Really, Pick? You've fished here your whole goddamn life, and that's all you got for me?" They might have heard me all the way to shore.

"Jesus, LT," he said, looking down. He took a breath, and his head wobbled. I almost felt the need to apologize. "If you're asking if G-One could have floated up here from the Compound, yeah, he could've." He shrugged, glanced at Alex, and looked away like he'd put his finger in a light socket.

"Great," I said.

"But to be honest, he could've drifted up here from anywhere on the river, even from Gray Gull. The wind was southwest last night."

"I found this in his pocket." I showed him the matchbook from the Dockside. Pickey nodded. If Alex had been there last night, I'd have plenty of witnesses to tell me what happened. I didn't produce the pipe. There'd be enough chatter around town, and many would suspect on their own. The family wouldn't need that.

I radioed the station. I told Estelle Maynard, our dispatcher, to roust my sergeant, Cole Crowley, and get him to the Cape pier. Then I told her to contact Nate Trout, one of my former officers and now head of security for the Compound, a position that had become necessary once Randolph Grimes assumed his Cabinet post. My instructions were that he grab Randolph and meet us right away. Sometimes, Nate, who was my best friend as well as someone I'd once fired, operated on his own clock. I made sure she let him know not to stop for breakfast.

Chapter Three

I had to give Crowley credit. He beat us to the pier, in uniform, taking less than fifteen minutes. His cruiser sat in front of the dock, which he'd apparently cleared. A dozen men waited in the parking lot behind it. This did not reflect careful foresight on the possible seriousness of our cargo but was simply true to character. Crowley relished his authority. He wouldn't care if he was holding up ten working boats. Trout always claimed that the next traffic warning Crowley gave out would be his first. A year away from retirement and with all the pliability of marble, he was better now than when I had first taken over as chief ten years earlier.

"You keep this quiet, Pick, you hear me?" I said, as he swung into the dock.

"Believe me," he said, "I'll be drinking to forget." He gazed up at the Rusty Bullet Tavern on the other side of the pier. I tied us off at the stern and hopped over to hitch the bow. I told Pickey to go find his beer. He raced past Crowley, head down. He hadn't moved that fast since his days as a high school hurdler.

"Friendly," Crowley said, shaking his head. His six-foot-two, two-fifty frame rattled the planks of the gangway as he came down to the boat. His eyes found the blue plastic tarp that we'd used to cover Alex. "What do we have here, another seal assassination?"

"Not quite," I said. "Alex Grimes."

"That dandy shot a seal?"

"No, he's under the tarp."

"You're shitting me." Crowley looked at me and raised his aviators, then stepped across the deck and pulled up a corner of the plastic. Alex hadn't gotten any more appealing since coming out of the water.

"Go figure," Crowley said.

"His skull's fractured."

"What happened?" Crowley said. "He tried to not act like an asshole, and his brain exploded?"

If there was someone in town who disliked Alex more than our bartenders, it was Crowley. He'd pulled him over a few years ago for OUI. The kid wouldn't submit to a field sobriety test and refused to take the breathalyzer. When he'd dropped a, "Whatever you think this is, my father will have your job and get me out of it," Crowley cuffed him and threw him in the back of the cruiser. Then he called me, which was smart. Crowley locked him up in one of our cells, and I called Randolph. While Alex sat swearing to himself, we met with Randolph in the station's conference room.

"I know the kid's a brat," Randolph had said. He shook his head. "And I'd have done the same thing that you did, Officer Crowley. I don't blame you one bit."

"I appreciate that, sir," Crowley said. Then he turned to me. "Should I get the state police here for a blood test, so we can make some kind of determination?"

"I don't think we need to jump right on that," Randolph had said. His grave look would have been frightening on the floor of Congress, never mind in our small station. "Can I be honest, men, and keep it in this room?"

Of course, he wanted to get his son out of it, for us to give him a pass. It's what any father would have done, including mine. Randolph had explained that Alex was about to start a position in Washington, and an arrest could jeopardize that. And Randolph, then a US Representative, had a dogfight of an election coming up. He didn't need this to be an issue. What he didn't do was threaten a lawyer, which surely wouldn't have been one of the yahoos from around here. He didn't tout his position or outline the shitstorm he could create for us. He showed respect and asked for help instead of demanding special treatment. Outside of Crowley, we tended to give people a break, especially if they were one of our own. With the annual speech Randolph gave at our Independence Day parade and his generosity around town, he was close enough. If it were Ed Pickey's son or one of the local girls home from college who'd had one too many, we'd have had them park it and gotten them home. Of course, they would have known better than to threaten us, but that wasn't Randolph's fault. Crowley looked to me to make the decision and managed to hold his temper when I gave Alex the break Randolph was asking for.

After being released and talking to his father, Alex apologized to us. Randolph had stood behind him, drilling steel eyes into the back of his head. We warned him that this would be his one and only chance. He'd listened, as far as drunk driving went. In his new position, Trout got a lot of late-night chauffeuring calls. But that wasn't my problem.

Crowley and I looked at each other across the deck of Pickey's boat. Both of us were shaking our heads.

"I'm counting on you," I said, "to be diplomatic when Trout brings Randolph here."

Crowley nodded. "I'll make it a point not to mention that if the kid had ever learned there are repercussions for actions, he might not be lying there under a piss-stained tarp."

"I appreciate that, Cole." I couldn't help but feel that he had a point, even if a fraction of it was directed at me.

Chapter Four

The black Suburban rolled into the parking lot at a reasonable speed. Trout managed to park it at an angle, taking up two spaces. The Secretary apparently had his requirements. No crowd witnessed this, however. I'd let the lobstermen get to their skiffs and go to work.

"What's going on, LT?" Trout asked, stepping out of the car and looking around for the reason that he and Grimes had been summoned. "Estelle's on the phone like the town's on fire." He stood with his arms folded across his chest. I exhaled and looked to Randolph. In pressed chinos and a golf shirt, he appeared to have been hijacked from an early round at the Cascades. A Rolex shined on his wrist, and his still-black hair was pushed back and perfectly combed.

"I'm sorry, Randolph," I said. "It's Alex."

"What did he do now?" he said, taking off his tortoise shell Ray-Bans and sliding them into a pocket. He had a good six inches on my five-seven, and even in his sixties, and logging hours of desk time, his posture was perfect. He folded his arms to match that of Trout. I'd been ready to explain how we'd found Alex on Stage Island, but it was clear they weren't aware he'd been missing. That changed my tack.

"When was the last time you saw him?" I asked.

"Yesterday afternoon," Randolph said. "He and a friend are staying with us. Riley Stevens took them out on the Mako after lunch. I think they were headed downtown. Stevens had the boat back by three, and I imagine Alex and his lady friend came in well after Violet and I called it a night."

"I'm sorry. We found Alex this morning on Stage Island."

"What do you mean, found?" Trout said, his voice dropping.

"Washed up on the rocks."

"Drunk?" Trout asked, his voice on the edge of disgust. Grimes stood there like granite.

"Dead," I said, looking at Randolph. "I'm sorry."

From the dock, Grimes's eyes went to the island, a far-off gray line with a splash of green. He brought his gaze back to me. "Are you sure it's Alex?" He put his hands on the dock rail to steady himself.

I nodded. "He's on the boat."

I turned but didn't have to point. The blue tarp on the deck was impossible to miss, Crowley standing next to it. Randolph started down the planking, his legs taking long strides. As we followed, Trout grabbed my arm and raised his eyebrows, questioning. I nodded.

"Secretary Grimes," Crowley said, straightening to attention as Grimes boarded the lobster boat. Crowley looked at me, and I gave him the go-ahead. He got down on one knee and folded back the top of the tarp.

"Jesus Christ," Randolph said. He widened his stance. His eyes didn't leave his son.

"I'm sorry, sir," Trout said. He turned. "You found him on Stage?"

"Ed Pickey spotted him this morning on his way out. He had his wife call me."

"And he was gone?"

"He was hung up on the rocks. The outgoing tide must have dropped him there last night."

"He was a hell of a swimmer at Hotchkiss," Randolph said. "I don't understand."

"I hesitate to say, Randolph, because we don't know when it happened. But that bruise over his eye, he took a real blow either before or when he went into the water. He might not have even been conscious." Not to mention that he wasn't wearing anything resembling a bathing suit. It wasn't a late-night swim that did him in.

"God damn him." The anger in his father's voice left little doubt that Randolph held Alex responsible for his own death.

Crowley stood impassive. Sweat broke out on his forehead.

"He was a good kid," Trout said, his eyes going from Grimes to me. I could feel the small brass pipe in my pocket.

"He wasn't a kid," Randolph said. He shook his head. He didn't have to finish the thought—whatever escapade resulted in this tragedy, it shouldn't have happened. He looked over at me, his face grave. "When Alex *was* a kid, he gravitated to our breakwater like it was a playground. He clambered over that thing like a mountain goat. I told him to knock it off a thousand times. Dangerous. One slip. He'd stop for an hour, then get back on it. Not the beach or the tennis court or the boat; those rocks were his spot. He still sat on that damn wall, thinking about who knows what, looking at the ocean as if it was going to tell him the secret of life. He was out there last night, and he fell head-first into those rocks."

"You saw this?" I said, confused. Why, then, had he been surprised to see Alex on the boat?

"I don't need to have to know what happened. He was drawn there, especially when he'd been drinking. And it's no secret that he was probably off his ass." His eyes found the island, then returned to his son.

"Did you hear them come home last night?" I asked.

"No, unfortunately. I sleep rather soundly up here. A curse, in light of this."

"Could Mrs. Grimes have heard or seen him? Did she mention anything at breakfast?"

"She sleeps even more deeply than I. But no, she did not say a word. We assumed that he and his lady friend were sleeping in, as usual."

"The kids are well down the hall from the Secretary and Violet," Trout said. I hadn't known him to be so formal. "A bomb could go off over there, and they might not hear it."

Grimes adjusted his feet as if he'd taken a blow, then squatted down and covered his son with the tarp. He stared at the blue plastic. All we could do was wait. After a few minutes, he stood and took two steps toward the stern. His eyes locked again on Stage, then he shook his head and turned to me.

"Thank you for bringing me here. I'm grateful his mother won't have to see him like this." He shifted his gaze to Trout. "Nate, what's that funeral home on Summer Street, the one in the old Captain's house? Can you arrange to have them take him and clean him up before I have to bring Violet and his sister there?"

"I'll get right on it," Trout said.

I looked from Trout to Crowley to Randolph.

"I'm sorry, Randolph," I said, regretting having to say the words, "but I'm not sure that we can do that."

"Excuse me?" Grimes said. His voice had hollowed, but his face remained stone.

"I don't know that I can release the body."

"Release? I'm his father."

"It's procedure," I said. "We don't know the cause of death, or the circumstances. We need to determine those things before we can release him. I'm going to have to notify the Maine State Police. They'll need to examine him and get him to the medical examiner."

"Oh, like hell, Nichols." Grimes's tone ratcheted up. "We are not putting his mother through that."

"I'll do what I can to expedite the matter, sir," I said, mindful to not sound antagonistic. "But until we know what happened, I can't allow you to take possession of him. The state police will make that call."

"That is not satisfactory. To have Violet see him like this would be nothing short of cruel. We know what happened."

"Come on, LT," Trout said. "You know who you're talking to. Make some allowances."

"With all due respect," Crowley said. "He can't, no matter how understanding we'd like to be."

Grimes's gaze shifted to Cole. He didn't want to hear another word from him.

"You can see how hard this is going to be on the family," Trout said. "Now is not the time to worry about some bullshit technicalities."

I exhaled and shook my head. I couldn't even look Randolph in the eye.

"Did you not say that he was found on the rocks?" Grimes said, his voice deflating as he pivoted to me. "Doesn't it make sense then, that's where his bruising comes from? A face-first fall off that breakwater. What else could it be?"

"That could be it, sure. But we need to be certain. What if that isn't what happened? What if he was involved in an altercation? That skull fracture could be the result of a blow. Someone could be responsible for this."

"Please," Randolph said, shaking his head. "Someone is responsible, and it's Alex. He was a lot of things, but he was no brawler. He'd never been in a fight in his life. He spent the day with a friend and his sister. He probably couldn't sleep and wandered out to those damn rocks like he'd done a thousand times. We all know how unlikely it was that he was sober. He slipped the way I'd been fearing he would since he was four."

"The point is, we don't know that."

"What do you think happened, Nichols? He got mugged? Downtown Laurel isn't Times Square. Or maybe he went to the Rusty Bullet and challenged the biggest jughead in the place? What is it?"

"Believe me, Randolph," I said, shifting on my feet, "I hope that you're correct and that this was an accident. But that is yet to be determined. I'll do whatever I can to see that the state police crew works as quickly as possible. It shouldn't be difficult to verify, if that's what happened. But they're going to need to do their due diligence and find out."

"There are things we know about Alex," Grimes said. "He couldn't handle his alcohol, which he indulged in to a great degree. But he wasn't violent, nor did he associate himself with those who were. Whatever happened, I'm certain he brought it on himself. He did something stupid. Knowing that he fell off the breakwater or jumped in on a whim and hit his head won't bring him back. This will devastate Violet, and I'm not about to see my family pay the emotional price while you drag it out. It's terrible enough. You shouldn't want that, either. If I, his father, am accepting of calling this an accident, which, in fact, must be the truth, then Chief Nichols, you should be, too."

"You know that isn't how things work here. The state police will take charge of this. I couldn't let you remove him, even if I wanted to."

"The hell with that," he said.

I'd known Randolph since I was a kid. I looked up to him, as had my father. The speeches he made and the graciousness he showed shaking everyone's hand at the town's annual Fourth of July celebration were something out of a World War Two movie. He and my father had occasionally brought me along on their fishing trips, and he'd slip me a twenty for baiting his hooks. That was a fortune back then. When I was older, he let me know that if I had an interest in Annapolis or West Point, he could help. When I confessed that I didn't have the grades, he waved that off and told me those guys had sticks up their asses anyway. He'd always done the right thing. While I wished I could have let him take his son, he had to have known that I couldn't. Maybe after thinking of other people so often for so long, he felt owed some leeway for his own family. I understood that, even if I couldn't act on it. No matter how much sense it made, the possibility existed that Alex's death had not resulted from a drunken misstep.

"We don't even know," I said, "if Alex returned to the Compound last night. Please let me do my job. I'll get a jump on things and start looking into it even before the staties get here. I'll see that the investigation is managed as quickly and respectfully as possible."

Randolph looked like he wanted to slap me, then his face relaxed. "You've helped us out before. Frankly, I'm disappointed that you're taking this line under these circumstances."

"This is not Alex having too many kamikazes and getting behind the wheel."

He shook his head. "Your father was always there for a friend." His tone indicated that if I had a kid who wanted to attend a service academy, he or she would be getting in on their own merit.

"He didn't have the official responsibility that I do. I'm only doing what's expected of me, what I expect of myself. And if I let you take the body, the state police would have a real issue with it."

"You let me worry about the state police," he said.

"I'm sorry," I said. I refused to look off his glare. "I can't."

Randolph grimaced and sighed. He didn't let his eyes fall on me when he turned to the parking lot.

"Trout," he barked and leapt from the boat.

"One minute, sir," Trout said. He came up to me, panting as if he'd just run up a hill. "Let me tell you something—"

"Trout," Grimes bellowed.

"Listen," I said to Trout. "Out of respect for Randolph, I'll give him time to talk to Violet and Abby. But I'll be notifying the state police and then heading to the Compound myself. I'm going to need to interview everyone who was there last night and with Alex yesterday. As head of security, I'm expecting you to keep them there and make them available. I'll give you an hour."

Trout's face reddened as if he were holding his breath. His flaring nostrils indicated that he wasn't.

"You do realize," I said, "that if you let me do my job, it might not take me long to prove that it was an accident, if that's actually what happened. Then I can put the staties onto it."

"Wise up, jackass," Trout said, then left.

"Wow," Crowley said, raising his right eyebrow. "That went well."

I wondered where I'd have been if Grimes's security man wasn't a friend of mine.

Chapter Five

I'd radioed the station and requested the state police crime lab team be sent to the pier. Then I drove home, again leaning on the gas. As I rolled past green August lawns, my mind returned to where it had been when I'd first seen Alex's body. I couldn't assume, no matter how convenient and logical that it might be, that Alex's death was an accident. We had to be sure, regardless of Randolph's unwavering belief. That meant eliminating other possibilities. It shouldn't prove a monumental task. Laurel was small enough, and everyone knew the Grimes. People would have seen and recognized Alex as he'd moved through town yesterday. We'd only have to follow that trail and see where it led.

The brass pipe in my pocket edged my mind in a different direction, however. I hadn't mentioned it to Randolph, but he had correctly evaluated his son. If a toxicology report indicated that Alex had been using drugs, even pot, that would certainly look bad. Grimes wouldn't want his son's legacy tarnished. Or, if one thought cynically, a habit I seemed to have picked up in recent years, neither would it look great for a Cabinet member. But it may not matter to Randolph how Alex got into that state of mind. It wouldn't change anything. We just needed to determine how Alex Grimes and his fractured skull came to be floating out to sea in a flood tide.

There were things that could have tied Alex to a violent end. I don't think it would have surprised anyone if he had been using something stronger than pot. In Laurel, the characters likely supplying him wouldn't be carrying Uzis and AK47s. But they might not hesitate to swing a Louisville Slugger. Or if Alex had goosed a waitress's bottom, a nearby boyfriend might not have found it as humorous as G-One did. It wouldn't take much to find out if such things had happened. And if we could eliminate those scenarios, it would indeed be likely that it was Alex's inability to steady himself on a breakwater he'd scaled for twenty years that caused his death.

As soon as I walked through my door, I called Rick Pettibone, the state police detective for our county. He was their best, and I was sure he'd be placed in charge of the investigation, especially considering Randolph Grimes's position. I wanted to let Pettibone know what he was getting into and that I'd be starting in on it myself. He and I thought along the same lines, and he'd been invaluable in helping me investigate the missing Connolly sisters a few years earlier. He wasn't at his desk, however. While the barracks did assure me that the lab team was on its way to the pier, they didn't know if Pettibone was accompanying them.

I found no reason to sit on my ass and wait for guidance. I changed out of my damp clothes and into my uniform. If the morning's conversations were an indication, jeans and a Red Sox t-shirt did not project sufficient authority for what needed to be done. I assumed that, eventually, Detective Pettibone would catch up with me. I grabbed my keys and headed to the Compound.

Chapter Six

The new security gate was down. Behind it, a five-foot blonde stood in front of a yellow VW Bug with a gray left fender. She was trying to raise the gate's black and white-striped metal arm and failing. So much for Trout making sure that no one left. If she had known there was a release in the guard shack opposite her, she would have been gone.

I parked at the end of the driveway and walked over to her. "Having a problem with that?"

She put her hands on her hips and cocked her head. Her eyes were puffy and red. "Obviously."

Then she noticed the blue pants, white shirt with the badge and gold schooner sleeve patch. She leaned back against the hood of her car and put her head in her hands. She shivered. She couldn't have been cold. It was seventy-five and sunny, and she wore thick gray sweatpants and a black sweatshirt proclaiming, "The Channel, Boston's Best Live Rock."

"Trying to get out of here?"

"You're a smart one," she said, the hands coming down.

"I'm Tim Nichols, the chief of police here in Laurel. And you are?"

"Getting out of your fucking town."

"How about a name?"

"Sally Strummer." She was able to focus enough to see my eyebrows rise. "I'm a musician."

That, she assumed, explained it.

"I take it you've been informed about Alex Grimes?" I asked. She nodded. "He was a friend of yours?"

This was answered by another nod. Her hands returned to her face. A sob escaped. She looked to be in her mid-twenties. This, I assumed, was the "lady friend."

"Can I ask you another question?"

She crossed her arms in front of her. She had a small nose and a sharp chin. Inside the red of her eyes were dark blue irises. "I just want to get home."

"Where are you from?" I asked, coming around the gate.

"Boston."

"Were you with Alex yesterday?"

"Yes." Tears poured. She wiped her eyes with the sleeve of her shirt.

"All day?"

"Yes."

"When's the last time you saw him?"

"Last night."

"What time?"

"I don't know. We came home from that bar. I don't think it was too late, but it was dark when we left. I went to bed. I don't know what he did." She shuddered.

"You didn't go to bed together?"

Something flashed in her eyes, a look of panic. She reached for her stomach. I didn't need med school to diagnose a hangover crossed with emotional turmoil.

"We're not like that," she said. "Friends." That defined it. I considered asking if she wanted to go back inside and talk. But she wouldn't even look at the place, and she was already answering my questions. I decided I had a better chance out here where we were alone and unbothered.

"Had he mentioned any plans for later in the evening?"

"I don't know," she said, throwing up her hands. "I was plastered. I don't remember shit."

"That bad?"

She scowled. "The last thing I remember is Alex having his boat guy carry me out of that awful bar. That's how bad I was."

She couldn't have weighed much more than a hundred pounds, and Alex and Abby's endurance at local watering holes was legendary. It made sense.

"Who was at the bar with you?"

"It was me, Alex, Abby, and Will Ranford." She said the last name like I should know it.

"Who is that?"

"He owns clubs in Boston. He's Abby's friend."

"This bar you were at, was it the Dockside?"

"I don't know the name. It was in the middle of town on the river. We got dropped off by boat. Then the same guy came later and picked us up with a car, I think."

"Did anything happen there?"

"We drank." She coughed. "To excess."

"Did you or Alex have a problem with anyone?"

"No."

"An incident of any kind?"

"No, why are you asking that? He fell off the rocks out there." She waved behind her. But she wouldn't look in that direction.

"Did you see him on the breakwater? Was he headed there when you were going to bed?"

"I have no idea. You know what a blackout is?"

"Then how do you know he was on the seawall?"

"That's what his father told me. I'm not even sure how I got to bed. Alex must have carried me."

"Okay. Is there anyone who can verify your condition last night?"

"Sure. Abby, Ranford, the boat guy, and everyone at that bar."

"How did you know Alex?" I thought I'd redirect and come at her from a different angle.

"We went to Brown together. We've been friends since freshman year."

"But not romantically?"

"No. Not ever."

"If you can't remember anything after dark, what about before? Had Alex mentioned plans for later? Going somewhere after the Dockside? Meeting someone else? A late-night swim? Anything?"

"I can't remember. I'm not lying. I just want to go home."

She'd found five different ways to tell me she'd blacked out. While believable, it seemed a convenient explanation if she wanted to distance herself from Alex's death.

"I'm guessing," I said, looking down at my notebook, "that Sally Strummer isn't your real name."

Miss Strummer was actually Beth Davenport, and she lived in a loft on Kneeland Street in Boston. She even had a phone with a real number. She'd grown up in Lowell, her father owned a dry-cleaning business, and she was the front person for a band that I'd never heard of, the Clap. They were named after the venereal disease, not the applause. They had a few records out, and at one time, they'd been in some sort of rotation on MTV. She'd come up for the weekend to support Alex because he was going to tell his father that he was quitting his job, one that his father had procured for him and he hated. He was planning a move to Los Angeles to get back into acting. That's how they knew each other at Brown, from the drama department. According to her, he'd yet to mention his desired career change to his father. He had planned on doing it today before he returned to Washington. It was a moot point now.

"Can I go?" she said once she'd finished explaining all that.

"Just a few more questions," I replied. "How did Alex and Ranford get along?"

"Fine. Ranford's a cheap prick with a lot of money. Unlike Alex, who was a generous prick. But that wasn't a point of contention."

"Is there anything you can remember about yesterday that could be important?"

"Yeah, I never should have come here," she said, breaking down into tears again. She waved at the main house.

"Did you and Alex have a disagreement?"

"Not anything like you're thinking. I told him to quit that fucking job a year ago. It was killing him. Soul-crushing work for some conservative think tank. But I wouldn't push him into the water for not listening to me."

"That's not what I was thinking."

"Good for you." She nodded her head back at the house. "They all just spent a week at that Nazi convention in Atlanta. My band ridicules that shit. I don't know how he could stand it."

"You're talking about the Republican Convention?"

"I am. Alex was a good person. I can't tell you how many times he's been there for me when I needed help. But how these other people, his family, live and think, it's corrosive. There's a reason he could drink a gallon of vodka."

"Was Alex using drugs yesterday?"

She looked at me, took in the uniform again. "Of course not."

"I thought you were a musician."

"That's not funny, stereotyping like that."

"It will come up in a toxicology report."

"Maybe he got stoned at some point. But if he did, it wasn't my dope. I don't like it. You can search my car if you want."

"Do you think the drinking and pot may have had something to do with what happened?"

"Jesus," she said. "Have you been listening to me? These people are different. It's not even like real life. And the worst thing is, if I hadn't gotten caught up in it, maybe this doesn't happen."

"What do you mean?" I wasn't trying to get more out of her. I simply couldn't follow her train of thought.

"I don't know, really. Someone normal has a job they don't like, they quit. But Alex couldn't do that. There was all this pressure on him, and expectations. It was a lot. This environment, it's not fucking healthy. Rum punch and some dope aren't the reasons he's gone. They're just the symptoms."

"That's what I'm looking for, the immediate reasons."

"I can't help you then."

Sally Strummer stopped talking and took a deep breath. She ran over to the grass next to the guard shack and dropped to her knees. Her back rolled as she got on all fours and retched a string of yellow bile onto the well-manicured lawn. I got some paper towels out of the Bronco. As I brought them to her, Nate Trout came speed-walking down the long driveway, his arms swinging. I handed Strummer the towels and waited.

Sally stood and wiped her mouth. Spots of puke dotted her sweatshirt. By the time Trout reached us, he was out of breath.

"I didn't know you were leaving, Sally," he said. He wouldn't look at me.

"Can I go now?" she asked. I walked over and handed her my card and let her know that the state police would want to talk to her, as well. I told her that if she thought of anything that might shed any light on what had happened, to please let me know. She was not a murderer. She barely served as a functional witness.

I opened the door to the shack and flipped the latch. The gate slowly rose.

"I'm sorry about your friend," I said. "Drive carefully."

She climbed into the car without looking at us. We watched her pull out and slowly head down the road. As shaken as she was, it'd be lucky if she didn't get in her own accident driving back to Boston.

* * *

"I almost missed her, Nate," I said, not bothering to hide the irritation in my voice. She shouldn't have been allowed to leave.

"It's chaos up there, LT," he said. "Abby, Violet, the boyfriend. They're all in tears. Even Tracey in the kitchen. Everyone's devastated."

"Sally claimed that she was not Alex's girlfriend," I said. "Is that true?"

"I don't know," Trout said. "Probably. She had her own room. Abby and her guy were shacked up, so there's that." He took a deep breath and gathered himself. "I don't know what the hell's got into you today. When a man like Randolph asks you to help him out, you do it. He works for the fucking President. He's in the White House on the regular, for chrissakes."

"A little help and what he's asking are two different things. The staties would have had my ass for it, and you know it."

"You don't think something happened, do you?"

"Something did happen."

25

"You know what I mean," he said, waving me off. "He was probably up on the breakwater getting high after drinking enough to paralyze a rhino."

"What if he wasn't? It will be easy enough to find out if he was running around town and someone cracked his skull. Randolph could be right. But we don't know that yet."

"He was a pain in the ass, that kid. But he's no Boom Boom Mancini."

"As far as you know."

"You don't know anything, either."

"Exactly," I said, nodding. "Sally also told me that Riley Stevens drove them home last night. Isn't that your job?"

"It's his when I'm off."

"Riley's here?"

"Yes, I told him what happened when we got back."

"So he'll be taking a boat out in the next five minutes?"

"I didn't know she was trying to leave."

"Why would you? You're just the head of security."

"You're being a real dick today, LT. No fucking joke."

I couldn't disagree. Sometimes, it went with the job.

Chapter Seven

The main house lay at the end of the peninsula, one hundred yards away, surrounded by a sea of green lawn and then the ocean. A breakwater of granite boulders surrounded the property and protected it from the Atlantic. Halfway down on the right was the boathouse, twice the size of the Cape that I lived in. A wooden staircase led from it down the rocky bank to a dock that extended in an L into the cove between the Compound and the road that curved along the coast. A twenty-two-foot Mako with a gleaming black Mercury outboard, the fishing boat, was tied to one side of the dock. Across the planking was Randolph's pride and joy, a forty-five-foot Hinckley sailboat called *Steadfast*. Long and sleek, with plenty of teak and brass, it reportedly had been featured in some yachting magazine as one of the country's finest vessels. Before it could be brought here, Randolph had to have the inlet dredged so it could draw enough water to float at low tide. Despite being a former America's Cup sailor himself, he'd hired a captain for it, a local Maine Maritime grad, Riley Stevens. He was nowhere to be seen as Trout and I drove past.

We parked in front of the garage, further up on the left, and walked over the cobblestones to the sprawling New Englander estate. It rose two stories and was nearly as wide as the spit of land it sat on. The faded cedar shingle siding contrasted with the dark green trim and shutters. Trout paused on the front landing and shook his head.

"Who do you want to see first?" he said, exhaling. The drop in his voice was another way of telling me that he didn't think this was a good idea.

"Let's begin with Abby and her boyfriend." They, being the other two people who'd spent the day with Alex, seemed like the place to start. Hopefully, they had not been as compromised by alcohol as Miss Strummer.

"It's not easy in there right now," he said.

"It would be strange if it was," I said, eliciting a soundless snarl in response.

"I'll do my best," he said and went in. I tried to watch seagulls riding the wind over the cove. What my eyes found was Stage Island. Randolph and Violet would see it every time they looked out a south-facing window.

"Nate said that you could probably use some coffee." I hadn't heard the door open but didn't miss the "you're-an-asshole-for-doing-this-and-I'm-doing-your-friend-a-favor" bite in Tracey Bolton's tone. She worked as domestic help for the Grimes during the summer. She was much friendlier when she manned the cash register at Bartley's Store the other ten months of the year.

"I could, thank you. If I—"

"I know how you like it," she said, raising her hand as if stopping traffic.

"Before you get that," I said. "Can I ask if you were here yesterday?"

"I don't know anything, LT."

"That's not what I asked you."

She wiped her hands on her plaid apron and placed them on her hips. "Yes."

"When was the last time you saw Alex?"

"I made lunch for him and his friend; then they went into town on the boat."

"Did you work last night?"

"I did." She looked at me, her lips open just enough to let some air in, eyelids low, and her wide nose flaring at its bottom. She could have easily told me what I wanted to know, something a fifth grader would have sensed. While Tracey might have been obstinate, she wasn't stupid. I'd remember this in the fall when she'd cut through Forest Street at forty, like everyone else in town, ten miles over the limit.

"What time did you leave?"

"After I cleaned up from dinner. Must have been around eight."

"Had Alex and his party returned by then?"

"Nope."

"Who was here when you left?"

"Just Secretary and Mrs. G."

"What were they doing?"

"Mrs. Grimes had retired for the evening."

"And Randolph?"

"I'm not sure. He may have been in his office. I'm not required to check in and out. There's a level of trust with some people."

I let that go.

"Did you hear anything at lunch that might be of interest, like plans for last night? Or if anything unusual was going on?"

"I barely saw them. I prepared their rooms. I served them lunch. The kids don't tend to run their plans by me."

"Any tension in the house?"

She sighed. "There's plenty. A son is dead."

"I meant prior to the event." I tried to keep my voice down. "Yesterday, for example."

"Of course not. This family contains some of the most gracious people on earth. My heart breaks for them."

Apparently, the domestic help was treated differently by Alex and Abby than those who worked in town.

"You know," Tracey said, "the sooner you stop bothering me, the sooner you get your coffee. It looks like you could use it."

"Thank you for being so thoughtful," I said in my nicest voice, hoping she wouldn't miss the sarcasm. I knew that might erase the chance of actually getting the coffee. But I was done taking flack for doing my job.

Footsteps sounded on the stairway behind the door. I rose to my full height. Trout came through first, followed by Abby, who was somewhat engulfed by her boyfriend, a tall, slight fellow in orange tennis shorts and a faded blue alligator shirt. His black hair was cut short over his ears but long in the back, like a musician. His eyes peered out behind a pair of thick-framed black glasses. Despite the youthful accents, lines at the corners of this mouth made it clear he was a dozen years older than Abby. She had her face buried in his shoulder.

"The chief has some questions for you two," Trout said after introducing us. He then moved off to the side. Apparently, he was sitting in on the interview. I assumed he'd been instructed to do so. "He knows this is a very difficult time, and I'm sure he'll be brief."

"I'm sorry for your loss," I said.

"I had the impression that you didn't care much for my brother," Abby said, turning to look at me full-on. She was my height and athletically built like her father. She also had her mother's chestnut hair and fine features. A black t-shirt hung over the top of her faded jeans. "Or me."

"That's not the case."

"Right," she said, with a puff of air. Even with her eyes red and haggard, she was a stunner.

"I understand that you were at the Dockside with Alex and Miss Strummer yesterday."

"We met them there. We came straight from Will's in Boston."

"I'm in nightclubs and had some business to take care of before we could leave," Ranford said.

I was glad for the clarification. Without it, a rube like myself would have surely assumed that he just hung out, rather than owned them. The what-were-supposed-to-be-ironic Clark Kent glasses had been a good indication that I wouldn't be impressed.

"What time did you get to the Dockside?"

"We met them around two," Abby said.

"That would be Alex and Sally Strummer?" I asked.

"Please," Abby said. "Her real name is actually completely banal, Beth Dipshit, or something."

"You're not a fan?" I asked.

"Her band sucks, and she creates more drama than *General Hospital*."

"She did take this as hard as anyone," Ranford said, adjusting his glasses.

"Hand her the fucking Oscar." Abby gave him a look.

"What happened?" I asked.

"She was throwing herself around the house this morning like Ophelia, as if she'd lost the love of her life. She wouldn't even fuck him, and who knows what kind of music scum she's screwed. That moron Stevens had his tongue dragging over the deck of the Mako because she was flirting with him."

"When was this? I didn't think you were on the boat with them."

"Oh, you got us." She rolled her eyes. "My brother noticed, of course. Maybe she was trying to sell records. Who knows? A big lunch topic was how long it took that creep Stevens to run up to his room and jerk off to her album cover. Is that of interest to you?"

I let that one go untouched.

"Did it appear that she knew Alex was missing this morning?"

Trout took a step into our circle. "I don't think she was aware of anything. The Secretary sent Tracey to wake her up and bring her to his office this morning. That's when he told her. She screamed like a banshee."

"Just the start of it," Abby said.

"What do you mean?"

"She ran around saying that we could all go to hell, how we'd fucked him up, and she didn't know how we could live with ourselves. As if we had teased the shit out of him since college. As if he had no control over what he did. How she couldn't wait to get out of here, and we would all burn in hell, blah, blah, blah."

"Do you know why she was carrying on like that?" I asked.

"Jesus Christ," Abby said. She looked like her father when she was speaking dismissively, gazing down her long, straight nose. "I think my brother being dead might have something to do with it."

"That's a safe assumption, officer," Ranford said. I wanted to remind him that I was the chief here, but didn't want to get off track. I focused on Abby.

"Your father said that Alex liked to sit out there on the seawall and think. Did he still do that?"

"He did. But that's generous, if not disingenuous. He went out there to get baked and tried not to think."

"What did he try not to think about?" I asked. That would explain the pipe in his pocket. The one I hadn't mentioned to anyone yet.

"Jesus, did you really just ask that question?"

"It could be helpful," Ranford said.

"He hated his job," Abby said. "Let's start there. He hated Washington. He hated the people he worked with. This slut that he moped over since college, she wouldn't fuck him. Even drunk off her ass. She probably passed out before they left the parking lot. I suggested he have Stevens take her home and put her to bed; then he could come with us to the Squalor. He'd have better luck there with the bored yuppie housewives than he would with her. He should've listened to me. He might still be here."

"What time did you get home?"

"Must have been one-thirty."

"Did Riley Stevens come pick you up?"

"I don't drink," Ranford said. "I drove. Don't hit your own supply, as they say."

I had to concentrate to not groan.

"Did you notice anything when you got back?"

"Yeah," Abby said, "there were tons of moths on the porch lights."

"That's it?" I asked.

"Look, Chief," she said, her eyes and voice tired. "I imagine he came back and watched her sleep, wishing that she'd wake up and put his dick in her mouth. But even if she'd wanted to—which she didn't—it would have been too much for her in her condition. That's what a lightweight she was. She had to be carried out of the Dockside. So it's my guess that he got his stash and his pipe and went out to his damn rock and got fried. The rest, you know."

When we'd finished, Trout opened the door, and they went back inside. He shook his head, and I watched him turn away once his eyes landed on Stage.

"The kid was upset," he said. I wasn't sure which one he was referring to.

"It seems this could be the last place that anyone saw him, though no one actually saw him."

"You're overthinking it," Trout said, low enough that even if anyone was listening, only he and I could hear it. "Pissed off, blue balled, and baked. Probably was out on those rocks and wobbling like a Weeble."

"You ever see him sitting out there?"

"All the fucking time."

"Where?"

"Usually off to the left. They got a rock shaped like a car. He called it the Cadillac. It's his spot."

"Let's go take a look," I said.

We walked beside the house on a lawn that would make many golf courses jealous. The peninsula itself, half as wide as it was long, was perched on a rise of granite. At some point in the line of Grimes who had owned the land, one of them had commissioned the rock wall fortifications. I'm sure they weren't just worried about the saltwater killing the grass but had come to the conclusion that a bad Nor'easter or the occasional hurricane could send the Atlantic over the spit and start the house on its way to Europe. Car-sized boulders were brought in and placed at the base of the natural bank and then stacked to form a double-wide, chest-high wall around the property. They weren't fit together like bricks, but landed wherever the crane operator dropped them. They rose to a height that allowed anyone in the house or on the grounds a view of the ocean. The top of the wall was at least ten feet over the ocean, even at high tide. If one were to fall off the top, there would be plenty of opportunities to crack one's skull on the way down.

Nate pointed out one boulder that had a rise in the middle like a car's cab. That was the Caddy. It was angled forty-five degrees to the land, and as I stood on it, if I had chosen to dive in, I would have had to propel myself out only a foot or so to avoid the granite below it. But if I stepped off without looking and went head over tail like Shemp Howard, it was quite possible to land headfirst on the rock below it. It was also likely that I may have only clipped a hand or a foot. We knew the ocean was calm that night, so it's not like a roller would have launched him back into the wall. I don't think a physicist could have stood with me and reached any certain conclusion.

I got down on my haunches on the flat of the hood and looked around. It was easy to see how Alex could have kicked back and leaned against what would be the windshield, his legs resting in front of him. If he had set himself in the middle of the Caddy, there was a hollow to the right. There was ash in it. I scooped it into a Baggie. I assumed it was from marijuana but would have it sent to the lab. We were a long way from hard-core drug areas, but not on another planet. It could have been treated with angel dust or been some super-toxic hash. I climbed down to the boulders below. I combed every inch of stone but found no trace of blood or a patch of skin that could have deemed this an accident. Of course, with a flood tide, the ocean could have swept it away had Alex left some piece of himself behind.

"Well?" Trout said when I returned to the lawn.

"Some residue. Nothing that would indicate he fell." It would have made all our lives easier if I'd found a chunk of his forehead hanging from a jagged edge. I pulled out the pipe. "I found this in his pocket on the island. And a matchbook from the Dockside."

"So that practically verifies he was out here getting stoned," Trout said.

"It means he could have been, and it doesn't mean it was last night."

"There ain't going to be no smoking gun or witnesses. You realize that, right?"

"I guess if it were up to you, I could just punch out and call it a day then?"

Trout shrugged and looked out to the boathouse.

"You going to put that pipe in your report, LT? It's one thing if we know he's a head, but that's not something we'd want to get out, considering."

"Are you turning political, Nate?"

"I know who signs my checks. And I like this family."

"You think I should ditch it."

"What good is it going to do if it leaks that he had some reefer in his system? It'd hurt Violet, and Randolph doesn't need that circulating Washington. It's only pot, for chrissakes."

"The autopsy will tell us what it is."

"Like one of those has never been blacked out," Trout said, in a quieter voice.

"I'd like to talk to Randolph again," I said.

"He's with Violet. It's horrible in there."

"I'd like to talk to her, too."

"I don't think he'll allow that right now, anyway. She's in bad shape."

"I don't think that's his choice, Nate."

"You heard what the Secretary said. Violet doesn't know anything. Most nights, she goes to bed right after dinner."

"And how early is that?"

"Usually around eight."

That's what Tracey had told me. I shook my head. I didn't know anyone not in elementary school who hit the sack that early. There was much here that they were expecting me to take at face value. I found it hard to believe that the Compound possessed some magical quality, as if it were the most tranquil, relaxing house on the coast. Everyone slept like the dead. Sound didn't travel. No one had seen or heard anything. The thing was, even in summer, this was a quiet town. There was no hum from traffic or buzz from industry. Sound carried. Things like car wheels on asphalt, an outboard motor, even a twig snapping traveled a good distance. But not on this peninsula.

Pettibone would be here soon enough to sort things out with Randolph and Violet. By then, maybe something would come to them as they tried to pull themselves together. I could let them alone for the time being.

"You don't mind if I talk with Riley Stevens then?" I said, although I was questioning him regardless of Trout's answer.

"By all means, your excellency," Trout said with a bow. "You know the way."

We marched back across the grass.

Chapter Eight

"Captain," I said.

"Coach," he said and continued to polish the Hinckley's aft rail as if he hadn't seen or heard me coming down the stairs.

I'd known him since he was in Little League. I'd been drafted to take over the coaching of his team when his brother Scooter, a former Division One pitcher at UConn who had been managing, caught a fishing job in Ketchikan that he couldn't pass up. While Riley shared his brother's talent, it seemed that he only played because it was expected of every boy in Laurel, especially one from his family. Whether he'd gone three for three or one for three (I don't ever remember a game that he didn't hit), he'd have the same blank look on his face. For him, baseball was something to be endured. When he cracked a bases-clearing double that made us district champions, he was the only kid on the team not jumping up and down, only breaking into a hint of a smile when his teammates mobbed him. I asked him about it when we were packing up. He'd said that now the season would go on another week, and knowing that I was coaching, we'd have practice every day. He'd rather have been out on the water. No amount of encouragement had been able to fire him up. It was as if he and excitement were mutually exclusive. When I told him that he was just as good and could go as far as his brother had, he'd replied, "Who would want to?" We lost States in the semi-finals, falling to Lewiston as their pitcher threw a two-hitter, both singles by Riley. He was one of the few boys on the team who hadn't been in tears.

"You got a minute, Riley?" I asked.

"I guess." He carefully laid the rag over the rail where he'd stopped, then took time to screw the top back on the can of Brasso.

"You heard about Alex, I take it?"

"Mr. Trout told me." The placid look on his face indicated that this was no more impactful than a weather report.

"What do you think?"

"What do you mean?" He adjusted the black Mercury Outboard ball cap he was wearing. His eyes were hidden by a pair of Vuarnets.

There were two types of royalty in Laurel. The Grimes, with their wealth and prestige, of course, were one. But there was a second: Families who'd been here forever and had distinguished themselves in one way or another. The Stevens were one of those clans. Pictures of Riley's ancestors standing in front of sailing vessels with harpoons in their hands lined the walls of the town hall. His grandfather had rescued a gaggle of Roosevelts when their yacht began to sink on its way to Campobello, his picture making it onto the front pages of newspapers across the country. His father was an undisputed champion when it came to fishing of any kind—salt or freshwater—and had accompanied the great Ted Williams on fly fishing trips to Canada. Scooter was recognized as the finest athlete in the history of Laurel, even without being a state champion like I had been as a mid-weight wrestler. He'd been all-state as a quarterback and power forward, but baseball was his true sport. He'd pitched a long line of shutouts his senior year and batted five hundred, which got him drafted by the Cleveland Indians. He opted instead for a full scholarship, where his coach blew out his elbow as a sophomore pitching an ungodly amount of innings in the College World Series. That derailed his baseball career and with it any desire to spend time in a classroom. Instead of returning to Laurel bitter, he took over one of his father's boats and set up a co-op for the town's lobstermen. Everyone profited. Then, he started catching tuna and shipping them to Japan. That brought in serious cash, which he spread around town. He probably had more drinks bought for him than anyone in Laurel. He was that kind of guy.

Riley was not short of his own accomplishments. All he'd done was go off to Maine Maritime, graduate, and work as an officer on a merchant ship. He'd seen the world for a few years and returned at twenty-five to captain one of the most prestigious yachts on the East Coast, Grimes's *Steadfast*. But where Scooter couldn't walk down the street without being greeted, grabbed, or hugged, Riley seemed to pass as if invisible. He hadn't inherited the charisma that came naturally to the rest of the Stevens. He may have even actively avoided it.

"I heard you spent time with him and his friend yesterday," I said.

He nodded. "I took them out on the Mako. He had me show her the coast, up to Gray Gull, south to Bishop's, downriver up to where the new condo development's going in, then into Laurel, where I dropped them at the Dockside."

"What time was that?"

"We shoved off around two, I guess. Left them there at three."

"What did they have to say?"

"That Merc isn't running too smoothly. It's kicking up some noise. I need to look at it. So, I didn't hear much."

"You're with them for an hour but don't catch any conversation, even when you're trolling the rivers?"

"They were meeting Abby and some guy. He was cheap, according to Sally, and older, but supposedly some big shot in Boston."

"Alex have anything to say about that?" The more connections, the greater chance for conflict. That was just the law of averages.

"I tried not to listen to his bullshit, ever."

"So, nothing?"

He shook his head. I get lied to frequently. Sometimes, it comes as straight denial, and other times, it's by omission. Riley had just nailed a perfecta, one of each. He'd had to have heard something after an hour with Alex and Sally, especially when I knew that he'd talked to her. He'd also failed to mention that he'd driven them home later that night.

"You say anything to Alex's friend, the singer?"

He nodded sharply. A real smile crossed his lips. "She was great. Unbelievable. Her band is fantastic. I'm a huge fan. So yeah, I asked her about their albums and some of their songs. She was cool about it. Not everyone who comes around here is down to earth like that, believe me."

"Did you get an autograph?"

"No," he said, his face reddening, an indication that he'd thought about it. "I had to focus on doing my job."

"That includes driving Alex and Abby when Trout is off duty?"

"It does, if they're drinking in town and I'm not out on the boat."

"Which is often?"

"I work for their father." His answers were not as non-committal as he thought. Especially when he was shaking his head ever so slightly, and the corners of his mouth tightened.

"You ever have a problem with Alex?"

"Every job has its pluses and minuses. You know their nicknames."

"Is there a reason you're not answering my questions?"

"Look, I feel bad the guy died. But he was a dick, and he did plenty of dumbass shit without any help from me."

"Do you know anyone who had a problem with him?"

"How many bartenders and waitresses are there in Laurel?"

"Did you see him sitting on the breakwater last night after you brought him home?"

"I can't say that I did, but I've seen him out there plenty of times. Including at night."

"Did you ever see him smoking dope?"

Riley raised his hands on each side in a "What do you think?" pose.

"Have you seen him doing anything else of that nature?"

"We didn't exactly hang out."

"Is there a reason you're not telling me that you drove them home from the Dockside?"

"It's no big deal. Any number of people could have told you already, including your buddy Trout."

"But you didn't, and I'd like to hear about it."

"Alex called around quarter to nine. I took the Suburban and left right away."

"And?"

"I picked them up. I had to go in and carry Sally out."

"So they weren't in great shape?"

"She was shitfaced. Alex wasn't too bad, for him."

"You helped her into the car?"

"Yes."

"Not Alex?"

"You could say he supervised. He got her up, and I took it from there. She tried to thank me, I think, but it didn't come out in actual words, just some mumbling." He blushed. "She patted my cheek."

I seemed to remember some Seventies detective show where one of those guys maintained that it was always about a woman.

"What was Alex doing?"

"Being himself. He told me not to get any ideas, as if I would mess with any of them. Then he went around and tried to get her seatbelt on. She was a rag doll. Once he got her situated, he sat back and said, 'Drive on, George Eastman.' Don't ask me who that is because I have no idea."

I'd never heard of the guy, either.

"Do you think Alex was upset with you being friendly with his girlfriend?" I knew that they weren't an item, but wanted to see if Riley did.

"He was never happy about anything. And she wasn't his girlfriend."

"Did he tell you that?"

"She did."

"And on the way home? Don't tell me the engine was so loud you couldn't hear anything."

"He had me turn on 'BLM. Alex and I don't talk if I can help it. She was passed out. It was probably lucky she didn't throw up. I would've had to clean it."

"What happened when you got back?"

"He said, 'I got this, Eastman.' I'd driven the car up to the house because we were going to have to carry her. Alex told me to wait and brought her in. He came out after a couple minutes and bitched me out for my behavior that afternoon. Apparently, me talking with someone who actually enjoyed answering questions about her band was objectionable to him. Or maybe I didn't kiss his ass enough. I don't know. Then he told me to beat it. So I parked and went up to my apartment."

"You didn't have anything to say about that?"

"About what?"

"Him giving you a hard time."

"He's always like that, and if I let it bother me, I wouldn't have lasted here."

"Anyone up when you got back?"

"I live alone."

"At the main house? Any lights on? TV playing?" He'd had to have known what I'd meant.

"There may have been lights on, but like I said, I didn't go in."

"What was Alex wearing, by the way?"

"I don't know. His usual shit, khakis and a shirt. At least he wasn't in those stupid-as-fuck whale shorts."

I nodded. I also didn't understand why men would wear pink chino shorts with little whales on them.

"Did he ask you about you taking him back out to meet his sister and Ranford at the Sea Squall?"

"No."

"Did you hear or see anything after you dropped them off?"

"No," he said, shaking his head. "I went to bed."

"At what, nine-thirty on a Saturday night?"

"I don't drink like a fish," he said. "I actually have things to do around here."

"Did you hear Ranford and Abby come home?"

"No. I must've been asleep."

"Did you hear anything after you went back to your place?"

"I had the stereo on. Sally's band. So, no."

I didn't like what I'd heard. He hadn't volunteered that he'd driven them home. He didn't think much of Alex, and Alex hadn't been pleased with him. They both thought highly of Sally or Beth or whatever we were calling her. There was the classic triangle on top of a natural animosity. If she had been nice to Stevens, which seemed to be the case, it may have dug at Alex. And Riley wouldn't have liked getting dressed down in front of her. Many a fight had broken out at the Port Tavern over less. But Alex had never been known to mix it up. And Riley barely had a pulse most of the time. The likelihood of those two going at it seemed small. That didn't mean I didn't look at his knuckles, which were unblemished. What I did know was that I couldn't name another twenty-five-year-old in town who called it a night at nine-thirty on a Saturday. That would have been rarer than an accidental drowning or a knock-down, drag-out.

The gate above us at the boathouse slapped shut. Trout was coming down the stairs. Another man tailed him. I turned back to Riley. Our time was short.

"You don't have any out-of-town trips planned, do you?" I asked.

"With a boat?" Riley took a step back. His eyes narrowed, but he didn't look away.

"Or otherwise."

"I'm taking the Hinckley to St. Johns in October."

"Good," I said. "Stick around."

As soon as the words were out of my mouth, Trout and Biron Wisterman, the state police captain in charge of York County, were crowding us.

"Where's Detective Pettibone?" I asked. Wisterman was Pettibone's supervisor, though he was a fraction, and a very small one, as effective as his underling. He frowned as his combed-over, thin rows of hair got tussled by the breeze.

He cocked his head before he spoke, a clear signal that the words spouting from his sea bass-like mouth would be of grave importance. At least to him.

"What, exactly, are you doing, Chief Nichols?"

"What?" I said. It should have been fairly obvious, even to someone dressed in gray slacks, a red and white checked shirt that impersonated a tablecloth, and a brown sports coat.

"I assume you think you're questioning a witness?"

"That's right," I said. Score one for him.

"No, no, no." He shook his head on his turkey neck. "I'm sure you realize what an important case this is, given Secretary Grimes's political standing."

"I'm aware." I looked over to Trout. He grimaced.

"Considering Secretary Grimes's position, this is not something that your department will be handling. Or should I say mishandling. I'll be taking this one myself, at the request of Secretary Grimes and Governor Brennan."

It was standard for local departments to step aside and have the state police take over capital cases. It was also usually the local outfit that called for help, which I had done hours earlier and that Wisterman seemed to have forgotten.

"What does the Governor have to do with this?" I asked. Apparently, amidst the tragedy and chaos, Randolph had managed to make a call. Pragmatic, certainly.

"He runs the state, if you haven't heard. He and the Secretary are well acquainted, and they would both feel more comfortable with our experience and resources on the case—and with you and your department staying out of it completely—unless, of course, we need some traffic control. We are aware that you've already mishandled aspects of it."

"Like hell," I said, starting to count to ten in my head to defuse a desire to see what my knuckles would look like after landing one on his recessed chin. I was guessing that my reluctance to not immediately deem this an accident as requested had sparked Grimes's judicious use of his phone and connections. As far as I was concerned, I'd done nothing wrong, other than I hadn't yet questioned Violet Grimes.

"You moved the body," Wisterman said, shaking his head, as if I'd made a mistake a hall monitor would have avoided. "We could have brought out the Zodiac and had our team handle it according to proper crime scene protocols. Maybe you're not aware of them. You just grabbed Alex Grimes and tossed that man's body onto the deck of a vessel strewn with fish guts. Do you know how much evidence you may have destroyed?"

"The tide was coming in, Captain. I could have waited and let you try to track him down once it took him again, which would have happened within a few minutes of my arrival."

"Enough of this," he said. "I understand that you've given the family members and guests the third degree, including a woman who then left. Why that was allowed is beyond me. I'd like a full report on that, and every interview conducted, your so-called recovery of the body, and anything relevant to the events of this morning. And I'd like it today."

I would have been glad to produce such a report if I knew that Rick Pettibone was going to run the investigation. He would have actually read it, and I could have trusted him to get to the bottom of things, no matter what. It was true that most departments like mine weren't equipped to handle things like this, with or without state police help. But I'd proven myself in difficult spots in the past. The Woodman's Village case, which I had broken, had started with two missing sisters and turned into something worse. I'd only known Wisterman to surface after his men had done the work, and it was time for someone to step in front of a camera.

"Can I get back to my job?" Stevens asked.

"I'll be talking to you, son," Wisterman said. He turned to me. "I'll be expecting that report on my way out of town today. Thank you, Chief."

Trout gave me the slightest of shrugs and held out his arm to lead me toward the boathouse. I would be walked off the property by my friend. What choice did I have? The Governor had spoken. I hadn't known that he could have picked Laurel out on a map.

"So, I guess that's that," Trout said, following me all the way to the Bronco.

"Quite impressive that Randolph was able to fight through his grief to get Brennan on the phone and have me pulled from the case."

"You were giving this up anyway. So don't get all butt hurt. This isn't two missing backwoods girls that no one cared about. He's a national figure. They can't take a chance and leave an investigation like this with someone like you."

He must have noticed the tightness in my jaw. And the redness on my face wasn't coming from the sun.

"I'm not saying that you couldn't get to the bottom of it, but the Secretary can't risk something going wrong."

"By going wrong, do you mean maybe finding out that Alex didn't fall off the rocks?"

"You know what I mean. The staties are just better equipped to deal with this, that's all."

"Come off it. Wisterman's here to be a rubber stamp for Grimes."

"Aren't you the one who says the most obvious thing is usually what happened?"

"That doesn't mean you shouldn't take the time to eliminate the other possibilities."

"You don't think Stevens did anything, do you?" Trout said, opening the door of the Bronco for me. It wasn't a bad question. He'd been the last one to see him, and they weren't the best of friends.

"I coached him in Little League," I said. "I like him. And, for the record, no, I don't think he did anything. But that doesn't mean you don't look."

"He was an Eagle Scout, for crying out loud."

"Did you ever go to bed at nine o'clock on a Saturday night?" I asked, leaning back against the fender. I'd worked a lot of cases talking things through with Nate Trout.

"He ain't like us," Trout said, waving me off. "You're outsmarting yourself. We got ourselves a dumbass who liked to sit out over the water on some slippery, craggy rocks, drunk as a skunk and stoned off his ass. What does your common sense tell you?"

"I know. But Randolph admitted that Alex being out on the rocks was only conjecture."

It was the scenario that would be easiest for the family to accept, emotionally. Maybe that's why Grimes so badly wanted it to be true. I knew him to be upstanding and honest, and I'd never had reason to doubt anything he'd said prior to this. But this was what he guessed had happened. He hadn't seen it. That bothered me.

Policing in this town that people saved all year to come to for a week or two in July, with hardly any violent crime, void of the trouble that plagued officers in Boston or New York, had changed me. I'd trained myself to be more suspicious and, as a result, less trusting. That was an occupational necessity. But as I considered that perhaps Grimes was right and that I'd gone to extremes, another thought entered my consciousness: that no one on this spit of land had seemed inclined to give me a straight answer. I should have been happy that I was being removed from the case, because along with it would go the stress that was already tightening my shoulders and shooting up my neck. If I thought that Wisterman would actually work to rule out other scenarios, I might have been able to walk away without being miffed about it.

"Look at it this way," Trout said. "Now you won't be pissing off an honorable, powerful man who you've known since you were a kid."

"Great. I wouldn't want anyone mad at me. Because that's never happened before. I just couldn't live with myself."

"This ain't about you, LT," Trout said, shaking his head and digging a toe into the ground. "It's high stakes down there in Washington. The Secretary and his family have a certain reputation. You should see the way he got his ass kissed down at that convention. By millionaires, maybe even billionaires, for all I know."

"This is less trouble for them if it's an accident?"

"Who do I look like, Walter Cronkite? I don't know. You and I are small-timers. We can't hope to understand such things. But no one wants to see their family dragged through shit. Not me and not you, and the Secretary's no different. Luckily, it's been taken out of your hands, so you can stop worrying about it."

"Luckily," I said. Trout knew as well as I did that my thoughts on the case wouldn't be burning off like fog in the morning sun.

Chapter Nine

I was working on Wisterman's report when Estelle buzzed me on the intercom. A reporter from the Press Herald was out front. I sighed, assuming he wouldn't be asking about upcoming Labor Day tourism. Mike Sawyer was one newsman that I'd never met. Outside of the Woodman's Village case, we'd done little to garner statewide coverage. Occasional bar fights and beach right-of-way disputes didn't cut it. Sawyer wasn't a kid just out of college, either, which is usually the type they sent. Gray at his temples and that he was wearing a necktie had me placing him around forty. I asked him to take a seat, not having gotten up from mine.

"I understand that you found the body of Alex Grimes this morning," he said. He opened his well-worn notebook and pulled a clear Bic pen from his shirt pocket.

"That is correct," I said. There was no use denying it. It would be officially logged soon enough by the state police.

"Where did you find him?"

"Can I ask how you heard about this?"

"I have sources," he said calmly. "I'd rather not say."

"Strange that you heard so quickly." This wasn't the Pentagon Papers, just a complication that we all could have lived without.

"I'm a professional reporter, Chief," he said, tapping his pen.

"He was found on an island outside of Laurel Harbor," I said.

"Dead?"

I nodded.

"Cause of death?" he said, his pen scratching across his notebook.

"I'm not the medical examiner, Mr. Sawyer. Also, I'm not in charge of the case. I can direct you to Captain Biron Wisterman of the state police. He's handling it."

"But you recovered the body, right?"

"Yes."

"And you have reason to believe that it was of an accidental nature?"

I wondered if Secretary Grimes had time to call him, too. He seemed to know quite a bit, for someone who'd just rolled into town.

"No comment," I said.

"Do you believe there's reason to consider the death of a suspicious nature?"

I stared at him. The pen resumed tapping.

"I have no comment."

"You recovered the body yourself, but have no idea what happened?"

"I won't be quoted on that, but, off the record, that's correct."

"Would you rule out foul play?"

"Sorry, but I'm not making any determinations. It's the state police's case. Maybe you should talk to them."

"You're not being very helpful, Chief Nichols." He smiled. His teeth were yellow and crooked.

"Would you prefer that I make up something?"

"I guess not."

As soon as he left, I grabbed my Rolodex and got Rick Pettibone's number. I wanted to know why he wasn't out there with his boss. I was halfway through dialing when Wisterman walked in unannounced. I was glad to see that he'd straightened out his hair.

"You got yourself a problem, Chief," he said, helping himself to the chair that Sawyer had just vacated. He slipped one leg over the other, crossing his feet.

"I'm guessing you're not talking about the shot muffler on my Bronco."

"I was referring to Mike Sawyer. He can be a real pain in the ass."

"I didn't say anything, other than to tell him it was your case."

"Yes, he's aware." He clasped his hands together and placed them on his lap.

"You didn't spend much time at the Compound," I said.

"Those people aren't going anywhere."

"I haven't finished your report." I'd just started it, to be exact.

"I wouldn't think so," he said. "I'll pick it up tomorrow. I'll be back."

"I hope the Governor wasn't too upset this morning."

He laughed, missing the sarcasm.

"He did not call me directly. But his wishes were clearly communicated. You can be glad you're off of this. Very high profile. Very high pressure."

"So you'll be putting Pettibone on it?"

"I don't see the need. It's fairly obvious, what happened." He shrugged, and his face twisted with his body. "But I'd like to hear straight from you how you found Alex Grimes's body on that goddamn island in advance of your report."

I told him everything from Fran Pickey's phone call to the luck involved with Alex getting snagged on Stage. I handed him the Polaroids from the deck of Pickey's boat.

"That's quite a shiner."

"The impact was just over the eye. His skull is fractured."

"How'd you fit in medical school with all your duties here?"

"I touched it. It moved."

I didn't mind being given a hard time by someone who was competent. Wisterman only qualified if he wanted to critique how the stacks of forms were arranged on my desk. Instead, he spent twenty more minutes getting further details. I explained how I'd proceeded and who I'd talked to at the Compound. Wisterman sucked in his lips as he listened, his small eyes pinballing from the photos to me as if we were moving targets. Unlike the reporter, whom I'd barely told anything to, he didn't take a note.

"I did converse with Secretary Grimes," he said, finally. "He's certain that the boy fell off that rock wall. It makes a lot of sense."

I told him that I'd gone out to his rock, but only discovered ash and residue. I put the baggie on the desk for him. And the pipe, which I told him I'd found on the body.

"Hmmm," he said, nodding. "I understand the son was a bit of a card."

"That's one way to put it," I said.

"A lot at stake here. Important family. I'm good with the current explanation. Everything we've learned suggests it."

"Suggests isn't the same as proven."

"No one saw shit, Nichols. We're never going to be sure. What we need here, and what we have, is *most likely.*"

"Aren't you going to check things out? Go by the Dockside and see if anything happened while they spent the afternoon there? What if he went out to buy dope, and some shit went down? You can't ignore that those things may have happened."

Wisterman chuckled. "I was doing police work while you were watching Bugs Bunny in your PJs. The answer is right in front of us. And it's supported by some very powerful people."

I shook my head. I knew why Pettibone wasn't on the case. He wouldn't have been satisfied being the Secretary's lackey. He would have actually wanted to do his job.

"You can leave the pipe and the residue out of your report," Wisterman said, scooping them up and placing them in his jacket pocket.

"Why would I do that?"

"They no longer exist," he said. His thin lips turned down. "So just do it."

I stared back at him. I didn't know what to say.

"What about this Strummer girl that was there, highly intoxicated?" he said. "Where does she fit in?"

"She was a friend of Alex's from college. Not romantic." I drummed my fingers on the desk. "Drunk is right, however. She said that she doesn't remember much. She was throwing up this morning and had to be carried out of the Dockside by Stevens last night. I think she was being honest. I can go by the Dockside and verify that easily enough, if you want."

"I don't want, Nichols. You do not do jack shit on this case. Is that clear?"

"I apologize a thousand times for offering to help."

"It's evident that he brained himself on those rocks. Everyone calls him and his sister the Gold Dust Twins. It follows, doesn't it?" Wisterman must have spoken to Trout, too. And he wasn't lying when he'd said he'd talked to Randolph. He had the approved story down point by point.

"If you found someone like that out behind the Dockside, your first thought wouldn't be that he tripped on a rock and fell."

"But that's not where you found him. He left there upright."

"We know he wasn't out for a swim. Maybe Bannon, our esteemed medical examiner, can tell you more. It's only conjecture at this point."

"You're trying my patience, Chief." Wisterman made a sucking sound with his tongue and cocked his head again. He looked like a game bird trying to see over tall grass. "Trust me, you don't want to be a problem on this one. Do you get what I'm telling you?"

"I get it." It was crap. Even a small-timer like myself could see what was going on, and there'd be nothing I could do about it. At least not officially.

"Just complete that report," he said, pointing a long, bony finger at me. "And whatever you do, don't say a word to that bastard, Sawyer."

Chapter Ten

As soon as he left, I started typing. If I was out, I was putting this behind me as soon as possible. I could understand why Grimes might want someone with more experience leading the investigation, someone with direct access to the crime lab and forensic unit, and vast case experience. But that wasn't Wisterman. Wisterman wasn't even going to bother eliminating the other possibilities before confirming this was a drunk falling off a rock and hitting his head. I didn't understand the hurry. The legwork needed wouldn't take long. While it looked like Grimes truly believed that the breakwater had finally claimed his son, he should have wanted to be sure. Maybe he feared that verifying his theory would uncover Alex's involvement in things he wanted to keep quiet. Maybe it would hurt the family and only lead to more turmoil. I couldn't blame him for that. But no one seemed to care that if this wasn't an impaired doofus executing a slip and fall, then someone else would have had a hand in it. And that someone could be seated next to any of us at the Dockside or lounging on a blanket at arm's length on the beach. That wasn't a chance we needed to take.

As I pecked away on the report, I was sure the state police headquarters, or at least Wisterman's desk, might have had a computer. One was supposedly headed our way. I could only imagine what the ability to connect to databases or write reports without having to empty bottles of Wite-Out could mean for efficiency. But that technology hadn't made it to Laurel yet, like many other things.

So I typed. Detail after detail. Phone numbers and addresses. The position of the body. Likely level of intoxication. Alex's habitual practice of seating himself on the breakwater. The exact time of tides, high and low. "Expert" testimony on the currents around Stage. I included the matchbook and pipe found in Alex's pocket, and the residue found on the rock wall. If Wisterman wanted them removed, he could use his own Wite-Out. I noted Alex's reaction to and riding of Riley Stevens regarding his interactions with Sally Strummer. I called Bannon to get his initial impressions, so I could include those. He was either busy or not taking the call. I indicated that my own impressions were that Alex hadn't drowned and that the cause of death came from the fracture above his eye. I was writing the *Moby Dick* of incomplete and useless police reports. The case had been closed. Maybe that's why when I was finished, my shoulders were stiff, my jaw was clenched, and my temples were throbbing.

I called Crowley to let him know that the staties were taking over the Grimes case and that it had pretty much been decided that Alex had tumbled from the breakwater. His comment was succinct and in line with my own: "Assholes."

I went home to take out my frustrations with a run, though I doubted I was in shape enough to get everything out of my system.

Chapter Eleven

y workout calmed me down enough that I could enjoy the beer
I was drinking afterward on my front porch. In my depleted
post-run state, it took quick effect. I considered that I may
have overreacted. I'd defaulted to worst-case scenario as soon as I'd seen
Alex's body. It *was* quite plausible that his death had been as Randolph
Grimes believed. Randolph, knowing his son's habits, likely wanted to spare
his family the tumultuousness of an investigation that could uproot drug
use. Still, the idea that the accidental death should be verified by process of
elimination buzzed around my head like a swarm of black flies. Just as I was
about to crack another Budweiser, the phone rang. That was the second
time that day that a brick formed in my stomach: Suzanne.

"Where the hell are you, LT?" she asked.

"Shit," I said. "I'm sorry. I forgot." We had been invited over to her friends
Jerry and Diane Wentworth's for dinner. My mind had gone off the rails
with Alex Grimes. I was already a half hour late.

"You weren't at the station. My guess is you're sitting on your porch with
a Bud in your hand, trying to come up with a reason not to be here."

"You heard about Alex Grimes, right?"

"Oh, is he there with you now?" A great white didn't bite as hard as the
tone of her voice.

"Give me twenty minutes." That was greeted with a dial tone. I did have
an excuse: Alex Grimes being an all-timer if there ever was one. But that's
not what she was thinking. She knew that I thought Diane was a gossip
who pumped me for dirt on everyone in town as if I were running some

sort of East German surveillance. Jerry tried not to point out his many fine possessions but couldn't stop himself from doing so. As soon as I put the phone down, Nate Trout's pickup rolled into the driveway.

"I need to talk to you," he said, jumping out of the Chevy.

"Make it quick," I said.

"You're not going to offer me a beer?"

"I was supposed to be at the Wentworth's with Suzanne thirty minutes ago."

"And you forgot?" He laughed. "Because you were sitting here thinking about Alex Grimes?"

"Shut up," I said.

He shook his head. "You ain't ever getting married."

"I tried it once. You were there. It didn't go well."

"You ever consider that you may be the problem?" he said, chuckling.

"It's crossed my mind," I said. "Does this visit have a point?"

"It would be better with a cold one. You're pretty much screwed anyways."

I went in and got him a beer. Then he sat down across from me. The sooner he started, the sooner I'd get to Suzanne.

"Look, LT, don't get all wound up and listen to me for a minute."

I groaned.

"That's what I mean." He shook his head and took a long drink. "I know that you're probably pissed because Randolph went over your head and aced you out of this case. But I'm here to tell you—"

"That he wants this classified as an accident and found someone who'll do that for him, simply because he was told to. And that I need to rewrite the report and remove the pipe and residue."

"You shouldn't take it personally. There are larger things at stake."

"I get it. The fate of the country's commerce hangs in the balance."

Trout bit down on his lip and shook his head.

"You know I was with Randolph for nearly two weeks at that convention." He'd been back for five days and had managed to mention it to me a half dozen times, as well as tell me how the Secretary had dropped over a grand buying new suits for Trout to wear during the festivities. It had been all

I could do to ask if he'd been promoted from security to butler. "No one there did anything but show him the greatest respect. His ass was kissed for days by people who could buy and sell us with the change in their couch cushions. And you're treating him like he's one of those numb nuts who poach lobster pots."

"As a government official, he should be demanding that things go by the book. To set an example. He's supposed to represent the country."

"The book is for guys like us, not him, you dipshit. Do the man a favor and lay off. Who does it hurt? We both know that kid was a fucking dope."

"But we don't know what happened, for sure. If he didn't fall off those rocks and someone did that to him, that person could be out there right now next to one of your kids at the Tavern or Allie's."

"Enough," he said, shaking his head. "His son fucked up, and Grimes wants it to go away so the family can put it behind them. It's an accident, no matter what you say or do. So use your head for once and go along. It may benefit you someday."

"I could accept that if Wisterman would do some leg work and verify that nothing else happened."

"I'll make sure President Bush is aware of your dissatisfaction." Trout smiled. "You ain't exactly been level-headed these days, especially if you'd rather sit here arguing with me instead of getting your ass over to Suzanne."

I'd forgotten again.

"You know the Secretary's in a position to pull some major strings for you one day. Stay out of it and let him take care of his family."

"What strings do I need pulled?"

"How should I know?" Trout finished his beer and handed me the empty. He shook his head again. "You might want to leave Laurel someday and be a pain in the ass to some other folks."

"Sure, that's my career goal."

"Alex Grimes couldn't walk and chew gum, never mind smoke some reefer and navigate those rocks. Don't lose any sleep over it."

"We might never know, given what little evidence there is."

"That's my point. You ain't going to change anything. Accept that, and you might be a little happier." He patted me on the shoulder. "You also might want to take a shower before you head out. You stink."

I was finding it useless to argue about anything.

Chapter Twelve

I considered running the lights and siren on the way to the Wentworth's but showed a measure of restraint. A few more minutes couldn't make it much worse.

Suzanne popped out of the front door as soon as I pulled into the driveway. She was not smiling.

"Really?" she said before I could take a step. Her arms were folded across her chest.

"I had a long day," I said. There was no point in lying. "I got tied up in Alex Grimes and forgot. Then Trout stopped by to discuss something about the case. All I can say is I'm sorry."

"Do you know how embarrassing it is to sit here making excuses, with them looking at me like I'm some sort of dumb puppy waiting for my master to come let me out?"

"I know embarrassment."

"I grew up with Diane. She knows how I feel just by looking at me, and I don't feel great."

"They do realize what my job is, right? Things happened today that I couldn't walk away from, no matter what elegant wine from some exotic vineyard is being served." This was one of those areas that Jack couldn't stop babbling on about, as if Suzanne or I would have known the difference if they'd stomped the grapes in their basement.

"You smell like you drank a bottle of Scope. I've learned some deduction techniques myself. If it wasn't for the mouthwash, you'd be standing here reeking like a brewery."

"Jesus Christ, Suzy. I'm sorry."

"You said that, and your eyes are red." She took a deep breath. "I don't deserve to be treated like this."

"No, you don't."

She hadn't moved from the top of the sloped lawn. I was at the bottom of the driveway, parked behind her Subaru and the Wentworth's Audi. The house over her shoulder was something I'd never have. Natural wood siding with floor-to-ceiling windows overlooking the ocean in the back. A redwood deck that cost just short of the GNP of Costa Rica stood over the white sand. I could only smell the salt from my house, a half-mile inland. Dianne had found Jerry in Boston. She'd been smart enough to get out of town for college, only to return for this gem of a summer house.

"A spoiled dead kid drank too much and fell in the ocean like an idiot and cracked his head. You're sitting at home with your Budweiser mulling it over, and I cease to exist. I don't get it."

"I'm not here to make excuses," I said. "But you don't know what's been going on behind the scenes. It's complicated, not that it's an excuse."

"Are you going to stand there all night? We're starving."

"You didn't have to wait."

"But we did. Because it's the polite thing to do. Like calling if you're going to be held up. Not everyone is an asshole."

Two teenage girls rode by on bicycles in matching red gym shorts and Wade Boggs baseball shirts. They smirked, then looked away as soon as I glanced at them.

"Are we really having this discussion on someone's front lawn?"

"We wouldn't be having it at all if you gave a shit," she said, turning to the house. Then she stopped and reversed herself. "Just make sure to apologize."

"I don't need to be told how to act." It was out before I thought about it. Yes, I'd screwed up. But I wasn't devoid of manners, and I'd eaten enough shit for one day.

"Could have fooled me."

I don't think I'd ever seen her this mad—about anything.

"You know what?" I asked. "You can apologize for me. I'm not in a frame of mind for an evening like this."

"If that's the way it is," she said, "I'm not in a frame of mind for whatever we're calling this now." Her hand went back and forth between us.

"Duly noted." I climbed back into the Bronco. I slipped the key in the ignition and started the car. I counted to ten. There was a chance that if I calmed down, I could salvage things. Then Diane glided out of the front door in a flowing Stevie Nicks-gypsy dress and put her arms around Suzy's shoulders. She must have been waiting, the two of them anticipating the inevitable. I dropped the truck into reverse.

I drove home slowly, contemplating another failure. Suzanne and I had been together for two years. It had started as something easy and comfortable, as we'd been friends since elementary school. Our feelings had deepened. We'd become attached to each other. Though we'd both been burned by disastrous marriages, we'd committed. We shared much in the way of hopes and desires, and we weren't getting any younger. We decided to have a child together, but our biology wouldn't cooperate. The weight of that failure, along with my job and the distance I tried to keep between Suzanne and it, to spare her the heaviness, had worn us down. With the potential tie of a child untethered, there seemed to be less and less to keep us moving forward. Romantically, we weren't even the stuff of daytime television anymore.

When we looked at each other these days, whether we realized it or not, what we began to see was our own disappointment. If you look into a pair of pure green eyes that belong to someone you know is deserving of better and see your own failure reflected back, that's not going to work. We'd been fooling ourselves. I swore out loud, realizing I had once again reverted to a worst-case scenario. I thought of that Doobie Brothers album about vices becoming habits. My marriage to Analisa, the result of a whirlwind summer romance, hadn't lasted a year. Now this. I'd had the chance to back off, but instead found myself triggering the detonator. My shelf life in relationships only slightly outlasted a carton of milk.

Fatherhood had been a staple of my thoughts for so long. But that conceit now appeared gone. I'd watched Randolph Grimes, a man who seemingly had everything, stomach his son's death with a mixture of anger and disappointment. There'd been a detachment that couldn't be missed, as if it wasn't everything. That wasn't how I'd envisioned fatherhood. I wondered if he were sitting in his library now, four fingers of scotch in a tumbler, questioning where he went wrong with Alex, who one way or another, wound up dead long before his time. If the answer was that there was plenty he could have done differently, how would those thoughts ever subside? I'd been certain that I wanted a child of my own. Suzanne had shared that belief, and we were both sure we would make great parents. I was less certain now. It was too easy to picture myself on my same front porch, drinking yet another Budweiser, torches failing to keep away the mosquitoes, wondering where I'd gone wrong with a son of my own. Maybe never getting the chance to make those mistakes was better than making them. I considered what Alex Grimes would have to say about that.

Chapter Thirteen

I walked into the station at eight o'clock the next morning. Nate Trout, his face crimson, waited for me in front of the counter.

"What the fuck is this shit, LT?" He threw a folded newspaper at me. He knew there'd be a Coast Star waiting for me on my desk.

I nearly spilled my coffee, catching it. I saw that I now also possessed a Press Herald. Nate folded his arms and waited for me to open it. I tucked it under my arm and asked him to join me in the office. Estelle averted her eyes when I looked at her. He'd probably been bitching at her for fifteen minutes.

I spread his newspaper out over my blotter. The headline, in large block letters, answered any questions I might have had: "Son of Commerce Secretary Found Dead in Laurel." It was the sub-heading that was trouble: "Foul Play Not Ruled Out." I looked up at Nate.

"That's not what I said." I sighed and sat down.

"That's what they printed. That's not the goddamn Tourist News. I do believe they've got actual journalists who aren't in the habit of making things up."

"What I said was that no determinations had been made, that the state police were handling the case, and that I had no comment as to the cause of death."

"You already owed that family an apology, and now this. Do you know the kind of shit this could stir in Washington?"

"No. Do you?"

"We'll have reporters up our ass. Probably the Washington Post, the New

York Times, all those big papers. The Grimes are trying to come to grips with losing their son, and now they're going to have to deal with this media pressure."

"Doesn't that come with Grimes's position?"

"It wouldn't if you kept your fucking mouth shut."

"I didn't say anything."

"The nothing you said could have been a whole lot better."

If I had said something that indicated I thought foul play was the reason he'd died, I'd have been inclined to apologize. But I hadn't. Once again, I'd done nothing wrong and was catching shit for it. I respected Randolph. I hadn't meant to put him in a bad position.

"Maybe you should be talking to Sawyer," I said. "The reporter, or his editor who wrote the headline."

"His time is coming. Bet on it."

"And instead of sending you to yell at me, your boss should be prepping Wisterman to release some bullshit correction."

"Oh, we're on that. Jesus, LT, you were barely on this two hours and still totally screwed the pooch. This is a delicate business. I don't think you realize that."

"That skull fracture didn't look too delicate."

Nate sighed.

"What is this, anyway?" I asked. "That you came down to complain in person."

"I was sent to give you a message. The Secretary never wants to see you set foot on the Compound again."

"Tell him to do a better job of keeping his kids alive, and he won't have to worry about it."

"I can't believe you said that," Trout said. "You're not usually such a miserable bastard, but you sure could be a hell of a lot smarter."

I was pretty tired of hearing that.

"What's that?" I cupped a hand behind my ear. "I think your dog whistle is being activated."

"Oh, hell," Trout said. "I hope Suzanne wised up and dumped your sorry ass."

"She sure did."

That stopped him. He looked back over his shoulder. The look on his face indicated that was my fault, too. At least he was right about that.

Chapter Fourteen

"Chief?" Chelsea said, pushing her bangs out of her eyes. "Do you want one of your St. Louis coffees?"

Chelsea, the Dockside's best bartender, had read me perfectly. On occasion, I'd have a Budweiser camouflaged in one of the Dockside's ceramic coffee mugs. The edge did need to come off, but now wasn't the time. I shook my head and sighed. The deck surrounding the bar, twenty feet wide and running forty feet along the river, was a shit show of day-drunk tourists, even on a Monday. On the other side of the rail, customers could spill gin and tonics onto speedboats and day craft and wish one was theirs. The more ambitious could look downriver to Chip's Marina, where the sailboats and cabin cruisers were docked. The Abenaki Club was upriver around the bend, just out of sight. That's where the Grimes would likely host Alex's funeral reception.

They could tell me not to investigate Alex's death, but they couldn't dictate where I ate lunch. A few questions with my club sandwich couldn't possibly drop me any deeper in hot water. And I might end up with some peace of mind.

Chelsea slid an iced tea in front of me.

"You've heard about Alex Grimes?" I asked, emptying in a sugar packet. It was a silly question. I doubted there was anyone in Laurel who wasn't aware of his death.

"Yes," she said, dropping her eyes. "It's horrible. Not one of my favorites, but my God."

"Were you here that day?" I said, trying to act as if I were making conversation rather than digging for information.

She nodded.

"How were they?"

"The usual nonsense. They can put away Planter's Punches like it's their job, even that little blonde who was with them. I heard he fell off a pier or something, then I saw the newspaper today. Do you think something happened, like a fight?"

I shrugged to beg off the question. Of course, she'd read the Press Herald. Everyone probably had. But she'd also heard the accident scenario. That had to be coming from the Compound. They hadn't worked only on me. Maybe this level of politics did make for a different dynamic.

"Did anything unusual happen while they were here?" I asked.

"No, not really. They were at a table and not the bar, thank God. Katie waited on them." Chelsea called over a tall, red-headed waitress and introduced her. I didn't recognize her. She must have been summer help.

"You waited on Alex Grimes and his sister the other day?" I asked.

"Yeah, they were having a time," she said, shaking her head. "Not that great, I guess, with what happened."

"Anything out of the ordinary? Did they say anything? Do you know what they were up to?"

"It depends if you think putting away multiple bottles of Myers is ordinary. They were here all afternoon. G-One didn't seem too bad, drunk-wise. I mean, compared to that tiny blonde. She was blotto. I was going to shut her off, but she hit the wall before I could. The other couple didn't seem fazed. The older guy wasn't even drinking, so I assumed he was driving. I didn't think much of it. You know, we do get some professionals in here, and G-One and his sister were two of them. I don't imagine they stopped when they left, except for that girl."

"Anything you remember about them?" One never knew what could be important, so I didn't ask for information that could help. The less filter, the better.

"Typical shit," Katie said, forgetting about her sweating drinks sitting in the pick-up window. "They thought my name was 'Sweetie' or 'Baby.'

They were yapping about how great Boston was. I guess G-Two's boy toy owns some big club. Then Alex and his sister were bragging about going to London this fall, as if anyone couldn't just buy a plane ticket and fly there."

She took a breath and looked around, then lowered her voice.

"G-One thought it would be okay to grab my ass. I nearly lost a full tray of empties. They laughed. I was about to go off on him when Chels came and grabbed me." A look of horror crossed her face when she realized what she'd said. "Of course, I didn't. And then we were here late until closing. We went to an after-hours party at Bill Jones' place near Bishop's. Probably till three. Right, Chels?"

"That's true," Chelsea said. "We drove home together."

"Okay, okay," I said. I wanted to laugh but didn't. She'd realized she might have made herself a suspect. I'd been behind a bar for a time after dropping out of college. Dealing with assholes and not losing your shit was a job skill.

"If they had just cracked up a car or something," Katie said, "I wouldn't feel bad. But, damn, the guy wound up dead. That's crazy."

"Did they have a problem with any other customers?"

"Not at all. Kept to themselves. They were loud, of course, but it was busy. No one probably even noticed them."

"Did you hear anything while they were getting sauced?" I asked. "Plans for later, after they left?"

"No," she said. "Sorry."

"What time did they leave?"

"Around nine, right?" Chelsea said, looking at Katie. "Riley Stevens came and picked them up. He carried the girl out."

"Any trouble between him and Alex?"

"Alex was bossing him around, but Riley just seemed to shrug it off. He's a sweetheart, though; just rolled his eyes and dealt with it."

"Did Abby and her friend stay long after Alex left?"

"Maybe another round for her. I don't know if they were going to meet up with Alex, but I doubt his date would have made it. I stayed away after he put his hands on me. They left me sixty on two-hundred. Still not worth it."

Chelsea and Katie had confirmed what I'd been told. Sally had been blackout drunk. Alex and Abby had acted true to form. Then, another thought hit me.

"Has anyone from the state police been down here to question you?"

"Nope," they said in unison.

The official investigation that never started was over.

* * *

My next stop was the Sea Squall, where I heard the same version of the story that Abby had told me. She and Ranford had come in and closed the place. Alex had not made an appearance. It was becoming more likely that whatever had happened had done so at the Compound. That left two options to consider: One, Alex fell from the rocks. Or two, he somehow got into a fight with the passive Eagle Scout sweetheart, Riley Stevens, who managed to club him in the head—an altercation that Sally Strummer had no recollection of. The accident did seem like the most likely cause of death. I felt better about that. Maybe I would be able to let things go.

I went about the rest of my day. I sat at my desk and started going through my standard thrill-a-minute to-do list. I wrote the patrol schedule for the following week, returned a stolen bike to its owner at Bishop's Beach—and answered seven phone calls about the case from newspapers riding in the Press Herald's wake. I refused to say anything other than "No comment" and let them know that the State Police had taken over the investigation. Even though I knew he'd be pleased to see himself quoted in these various papers, I was kind enough to supply the reporters with Wisterman's number. Good luck to him.

Of course, this gave me the opportunity to dwell on my own problems. Suzanne and I were apparently through. It seemed like it had been inescapable, and yet, it left me with a stomach full of acid.

Chapter Fifteen

The second-to-last thing I expected that night was another call from Trout. It was ten o'clock when he reached out. The last thing I expected was an invitation to the Compound.

"Get out here right away, LT," he said. His voice was high with excitement.

"Don't you have something better to do than bust my balls?" I asked.

"I'm serious."

"What's this about?"

"You'll find out. I'll meet you at the gate."

I drove code one, no lights or siren. I assumed that they'd found some piece of evidence that proved the accidental death and wanted me to see it firsthand. I was a dog about to get his nose rubbed in it. Then, I'd be expected to grovel and beg for forgiveness. If I had missed something obvious, I'd be getting what I deserved.

The gate was up when I arrived. Two state police cruisers and a Lincoln that I didn't recognize sat in front of the garage. Wisterman's shit-brown Crown Victoria was at the boathouse. I drove in slowly, and Trout came out of the guard shack. He grunted hello and had me park behind it, then led me up the drive. He wasn't talking. Apparently, he was going to enjoy me getting my comeuppance. I didn't blame him.

"Okay," I said, my patience evaporating after ten yards. I wanted to be prepared for what I was walking into. "What's going on?"

"They solved the case," Trout said as we crossed the lawn. Light poured from every window of the boathouse. A sail had unraveled on the Hinckley and flapped in the wind.

"What do you mean solved?" I doubted that Wisterman could find his dick with both hands in his pants. And I hadn't missed anything on Alex's rock perch. I was sure of it. But there really was no other explanation.

"Grimes is a little smarter than you gave him credit for. He wasn't leaving it up to Wisterman. He flew in a US marshal from Washington. She figured it out. You're not going to believe it: Riley Stevens."

"Riley Stevens, what?" I asked.

"He killed Alex."

"Really?" Though I'd recorded the animosity between the two in my report, I hadn't imagined that they would've come to blows. It fit neither of their personalities.

"This fed got here before noon and was like a house afire. She questioned Abby and Stevens, then went over to the Dockside, talked to them. She came back and interrogated Stevens some more. She sent one of her men to that singer in Boston. Called Bannon and lit a fire under his ass. I don't know the science of it, but he concluded that Alex'd been hit, rather than fell. It seems like they had a real beef over Strummer. Alex had been giving him some serious lip, and he must've snapped."

"He told me he put up with it just fine." This had been confirmed by Chelsea at the Dockside, as well.

"Of course, he'd say that." Trout cocked his head and raised his eyebrows. "But you know that family. They aren't inclined to take crap from anyone."

"He's not like his brother, or his old man."

Trout shrugged. He wasn't buying it. I should have been pleased that I had been on the right track, indicating that conflict between them was a possibility. But I'd known Riley for years, and he'd never seemed to have any kind of fire in him.

Trout lowered his voice. "Wait'll you see this marshal. Holy shit."

The boathouse opened up into a lounge with a four-seat bar, paintings of America's Cup boats covering the wall, and some plush leather seating. It didn't take long to see what impressed Trout about the marshal, the only woman in the room. She was close to six feet tall, with long black hair in a shining ponytail. Her badge hung from the waist of a sharp gray suit. Even in dress clothes, she looked to be in better shape than the two troopers who flanked Stevens on the black couch, where he sat handcuffed. Wisterman stood off to the side. She commanded the room from in front of the bar. We stopped two steps inside. Her gaze shifted to us.

"Who the fuck are you?" she said. Her eyes ignored Trout and landed on me. I was coming to realize that I should stop leaving the house in jeans and t-shirts.

"I'm Tim Nichols, chief of police here," I said. I was not intimidated, though that was clearly her intention.

"Okay," she said. "You're the reason I'm here. If you'd followed up with Mr. Stevens the way you should have, I'd still be enjoying oysters in Chincoteague. Instead, here I am, working. Benita Salazar, US marshal, in case you were wondering."

"I wasn't," I said. I also wasn't going to complain that I'd been pulled from the case fifteen minutes into it. That would make me look like a whining incompetent instead of just incompetent.

Wisterman grinned. Salazar turned to him. "What are you smiling at, Captain? Secretary Grimes didn't trust you with the case, either."

At least she was an equal-opportunity ball-buster.

"I think we're done here," she told him.

"Okay, you two," Wisterman said to the troopers. "Take him to the barracks and put him on ice until we get there."

"On ice?" Salazar said, raising her eyebrows and shaking her head. She sighed. "Christ."

Riley had his head down and kept his eyes on the floor as he passed. Wisterman checked with the marshal to verify that she'd be taking her own car there, rather than riding with him, which he mentioned that he'd be glad to do as a service to her and Secretary Grimes. She stated that she was quite capable of driving herself. He, unlike Riley, shot me a nasty glance as he went out the door.

Salazar shuffled some papers on the bar into a manila folder, then looked over at Trout and me. Her eyes got big, apparently surprised that we were still there.

"I think you can go back to your clam flats or wherever it was you came from," she said. I could make out the bulge of her piece off her hip when her jacket pulled back. While she did possess some wit, she wasn't flawless. "Show's over."

"Come on, LT," Trout said. "Let's go."

"I thought you said you were the chief," Salazar said.

"I am."

"He just called you, LT, as in lieutenant. What is it, chief or lieutenant?"

"It's chief. LT's a nickname."

Salazar shook her head and zipped her briefcase.

"It stands for Little Timmy," Trout said. "Some kid called him Tiny Tim in grammar school, so he socked him and broke his nose. To be safe, they started calling him little instead of tiny, as he is kind of short."

"Fascinating," she said.

"Could you tell me what led you to Stevens?" I asked. I wanted to hear for my own edification, to see what I'd missed that should have put me onto him.

"I'm not running a clinic for small-town sheriffs," she said. "I'd like to get out of here and return to my vacation. And from what I understand, the press already walked all over you. I shouldn't even be talking with you in the room."

"If they needed comedy on this case, they could have left Wisterman in charge," I said, not moving from the doorway as she slid a folder into a soft leather briefcase.

"You've got me there," she said. She looked at her watch. "I'll give you five minutes. You do not open your mouth to anyone, either of you. We haven't made the arrest yet. Understood?"

"Good enough."

"Not good enough. Understood?"

"I get it," I said. "Understood."

She motioned for me to sit down. She looked at Trout but left him standing. Her boyfriend, if she had one, would have to be a drinker.

"I was notified by my supervisor this morning, early. He'd been contacted by someone in the White House. The Secretary did not have much faith in local and state law enforcement, which is not news to you." She gave me a fake smile. "He wanted to know what happened to his son, quickly, and he wanted it handled discreetly. He didn't think either of those benchmarks would be reached with you or your state police captain running the case. It's not my place to question that. So, if you're offended by my presence, it's on you."

"I'm a big boy."

She smirked. She towered over me.

"I arrived and talked to Secretary Grimes and Mr. Trout, who you are acquainted with," she said, nodding at the man she wouldn't let sit down. "I read your report, which wasn't entirely terrible. Very detailed, and you did note that tension existed between Alex Grimes and Stevens. Why no one dug into that is beyond me. I questioned him. I went to that tourist bar that serves as a floating frat party for white people. I talked to the same bartenders and waitresses that you did while you ate your lunch, though it was my understanding that you were not to be investigating this case." She tilted her head forward and cocked her eyes like a parent catching a kid coming home after curfew. "They saw Riley pick them up, help Strummer to the car, and then, presumably they drove off. Alex, apparently, was riding his ass the entire time.

"So I questioned Mr. Stevens again. He is a shifty little bastard. At least when he's answering questions that he'd clearly rather not face. His body language indicated evasiveness of the truth, which, of course, is not enough to solely base judgment on. However, we know this: He drove from the Dockside to here. He said he dropped them off at the house and returned to his apartment above. It wasn't difficult to put things together. Alex's sister and her boyfriend both stated they'd heard that Stevens was doting on Sally Strummer." She laughed. "Quite a name. He admitted to fawning over her, himself. She confirmed this, as I had her interviewed by one of my associates. It sounded like he was aggressively friendly, you could call it. She seemed traumatized by the entire episode. I don't blame her, being sandwiched by those two. She's probably overcome with guilt for passing out, which obviously further frustrated Alex, who was then inclined to march down here and call out Stevens for his behavior. Which is what led to the fatal altercation."

"That's what you think happened?"

"Obviously."

"How did you come to that conclusion?"

"One, they were the only two people awake on the Compound. Randolph, Violet, and Strummer, all asleep or passed out. Two, Stevens admits that Alex, after yelling at him at the main house, came to the boathouse and confronted him."

"He what?" I asked.

"Oh, he didn't mention that to you?" She smiled and shook her head. "You either didn't ask the right questions or asked them the wrong way. Or maybe you were a pussy about it and didn't push to expose what should have been in front of your face. Maybe that explains why you're you, and I'm a federal officer."

If she saw my eyes roll, she didn't show it.

"Anyway, Stevens admits to listening to one of Strummer's albums when Alex called him out. More gas on the fire, I guess. It gets violent. Stevens wins the fight, clocks Alex, and whether he intended to, or not, kills him. And now he's fucked."

"He's admitted to all this?" Shock sent my voice to a register I didn't recognize. Stevens had only told me about the abuse he'd taken at the drop-off. Salazar had uncovered the fatal conflict—something I hadn't been able to surface.

"He did not."

"You have evidence, then?"

"I checked the path from the end of the driveway right up into Alex's room, looking for signs of a struggle. In fact, after I interviewed Abby, that's the first thing I did. But I found nothing. So, I knew the altercation took place somewhere else. I went down to the dock, because if you were smitten and pissed off, wouldn't you go to where you were most comfortable? And you know what, there was blood on the deck."

"You see, there's a filleting station there," I said, pointing in the direction of the raised Formica board at the near edge. Did the blood happen to be below that?"

"Some was, and some wasn't. And not being a complete idiot, as well as growing up on the water in Miami, I'm familiar with the gutting of fish and other living beings. I'm having the blood tested. Wisterman is good for that." She folded her arms across her chest like a teacher with a slow class. "Did I fail to mention that I talked to another of your happy troop, the medical examiner, Bannon? He assured me that the wound on Alex's head came from a blow, that most certainly came from above, and as even you could see, with a solid object. You may have mentioned that possibility in your report. Riley Stevens is six-two. Alex Grimes was five-nine. There are plenty of objects around here that are potential weapons. They will all be checked."

"I'm not following how you came to this conclusion if Riley hasn't admitted to it."

"He's evasive; he withheld information—from you—that he didn't want to come out. I pried it from him. He admitted to a confrontation. And I'm supposed to believe that it just stopped peacefully? Not to mention that I'm sure we'll find the murder weapon, either on a boat or in the workshop out back here. There will be an exhaustive search that I'll supervise myself. As far as him confessing, the night is young." She nodded and picked up her briefcase.

"I'd like to be there for the interrogation," I said.

"I think not," she said, shaking her head. "I've given you the courtesy because I've heard you're a stand-up guy, and your report was marginally helpful. But if you had done your job correctly and followed through as you should have, I'd be sunning myself on Chesapeake Bay tomorrow."

"I know the kid. I could help."

"To be honest, I don't need you adorning the room like a potted plant. That's the way it is. And remember, I've asked you to keep quiet. I expect that to be respected."

"It will be," I said, having been dressed down by a professional. She was correct. I should have never let Grimes influence the investigation and steer me off course. I knew there was a point of conflict between Stevens and Alex and hadn't pushed enough looking into it. I'd remembered Stevens as a twelve-year-old ballplayer and not an adult in a pissing contest over a woman. I had no one to blame but myself.

"Very good." She nodded and walked out.

I looked at Trout.

"Tough woman," he said.

Smart woman, I thought. Riley Stevens was up against it.

Chapter Sixteen

As I drove to the station the next morning, my grip tightened on the wheel until my fingers were white. I'd been on the right track in not accepting that Alex's death was an accident. But as Marshal Salazar had pointed out, I had not followed through the way I should have. In the process, I'd given Riley Stevens the opportunity to hightail it to the Caribbean, Mexico, or any other place he'd could've run to. I was lucky he hadn't fled. I'd tried to be respectful of Randolph Grimes and had only disrespected myself as a result. Instead of doing my job the way I should have, Wisterman or no Wisterman, I'd let myself be boxed out. I looked like the dunce that Salazar and Grimes thought I was.

I didn't know if Riley had rolled up into a ball and confessed or told them to screw and asked for a lawyer, which is what his father and brother would have done. If I drove to the barracks in Limerick and tried to find out, they'd shut the door in my face. That much had been made clear. So, I worked on my standard "to-do" list. Twenty-five minutes in, I reached for the keys to a cruiser.

I took a ride through town. I wasted some time checking on Irene Mitchell, our rookie whom I'd assigned to patrol Bishop's Beach. She was the first woman we'd taken in for a seasonal officer. We'd given her a mountain bike, and she alternated riding up and down the road frontage with walking the length of the beach on the sand. Tan wasn't a color she did. With her red hair and freckles, all summer, she alternated between ghost white and sunburned. Though it might have been cruel given her complexion, she watched over some of the finest homes in town. This gentrification wasn't a bad thing. It kept our carpenters busy, which kept the bars full through the off-season. It was a good beat for Mitch in her first go-round. Her most dangerous incident had involved corralling an unleashed golden retriever running off with a kid's Nerf football.

Jack House, a muscular, crew-cutted former offensive lineman, patrolled Gray Gull Beach. That was my neighborhood, though I lived on a dirt road on the marsh behind it. It wasn't exclusive like Bishop's and hadn't changed much since I'd grown up there. Perhaps the large public beach made it somewhat less desirable. It was also our wild west of parking violations. House was having his lunch at the General Store when I caught up with him. He had already given out eleven tickets and appeared to be just short of suffering from writer's cramp. Unlike his colleague at Bishop's, he had a deep tan and was enjoying the weather. He asked me if there were regulations against dating someone who lived on his beat. He tried not to grin when I told him there was not. I didn't tell him that I'd first met my ex when she was a summer person. Who was I to step on a young man's dreams?

After leaving House I drove back toward town and turned toward the tidal pool at Cape Laurel. That's where Riley Stevens's father kept his boat, and his brother Scooter ran their cooperative lobster pound and fish market. That the open sign, red paint on a weathered shingle, hung out I took as a good omen. Maybe Salazar had found that Riley hadn't had anything to do with Alex and had been cut loose. If he'd been arrested, I was sure Scooter and his old man, Pop, short for Popeye and his muscles, would have been camped at the State Police barracks. Wisterman might have even called me in for that, as those two were probably worth four or five troopers if things got out of hand.

Scooter looked up as the bell over the door tinkled when I came in. He stopped wrapping haddock filets in wax paper for an elderly woman in a pink cardigan in front of the case.

"You've got some balls showing up here, LT," Scooter said. The woman didn't flinch when she looked over her shoulder and saw me in my uniform. I stood with my hands folded in front of me and waited until she went out the door. Scooter slammed the display case shut and came around to the sales floor. His expression told me that his brother was still in custody.

"Wait a minute," I said.

Scooter pushed his thick, brown hair off his forehead. At six-four and two-twenty, he blocked out the entire rear of the shop.

"That spoiled fuck brains himself falling into the ocean, and they're questioning my brother? Like he had something to do with it? It's bullshit." Scooter had heard the party line that spread from the Compound. And while they still held Riley, apparently, Salazar hadn't arrested him yet. He was either keeping quiet, or Salazar's evidence hadn't checked out like she thought it would.

"He was one of the last people to see him alive. It's standard to talk to him."

"Really? You spoke to him. You didn't lock him up."

"I got pulled from the case by the state police in the middle of questioning him. But if I were doing my job right, I would have probably brought him in, too."

"What the hell do you mean by that?" Scooter's face reddened.

"A US marshal is running the show now. They don't mess around. She must have her reasons."

Scooter's glance shifted to the lobster pool, where the chickens were clustered in one corner. The water sloshing through the overflow pipe competed with the droning motor on the circulator. The air was heavy with moisture.

"So you're with that fed? You think my brother had something to do with it?" He wasn't smiling.

"I didn't say that, either. They have to investigate everything. It's practically a national security issue. You know Grimes's job."

"Since when does grabbing waitresses' asses concern national security?"

"I don't think that's what they're worried about," I said.

"If anyone's stupid enough to get himself killed, it is G-fucking-One. What makes them think my brother's involved?"

"I couldn't say if I knew. I just stopped by to see if there was any news. I figured if it was bad, they'd have arrested him, and you wouldn't be open."

He sat down on the edge of the pool. "Do they really have anything on him?"

"I haven't seen all the evidence."

"What evidence?" The muscles in his neck tensed.

"There must be something, or they wouldn't be talking to him," I said, respecting Salazar's wishes.

"What do you know?"

"Not much."

"Don't bullshit me," he said, jumping up and slamming a fist on the pool, scattering the cluster of lobsters in the corner. He walked back behind the counter. "You're not here to buy fish. But I got some cod I was going to give the cat. You can take it over to the Compound with my compliments after I rub my dick all over it."

"Flying off the handle isn't going to help Riley."

"You know that kid, LT. He's a fucking mouse. All he cares about are those goddamn boats, and they're not even his."

"I knew him when he was twelve, Scooter. He hasn't said a dozen words to me since."

"You've dealt with me. And Pop. You've never had to do anything with him. That should tell you something."

"You and your father aren't exactly hardened criminals."

"And Riley is?"

"Stop putting words in my mouth."

"Then what the hell are they doing to him? Pop didn't get a call until this morning, and he went right out there with Ben Freeman from Milltowne. That joker couldn't get a snail out of a speeding ticket."

"You haven't heard from them?"

"No. I'm asking you one last time, LT. What the fuck is going on here?"

He must have seen the look travel across my face. If they hadn't released Riley, that meant that Salazar liked him for it and was still working on a confession. I wondered how much I could or should tell him. Scooter never refused to help anyone. He was a legend for it. But I'd made a promise to Salazar. If they found evidence that Riley had done it, which it looked like she was expecting, then there'd be little harm in telling Scooter what I'd found out on my own. Scooter could prepare his family for what they'd be facing—public pressure, a trial, jail. His brother was in real trouble.

"There was a girl staying over at the Compound, a friend of Alex's. A singer from some band in Boston that Riley was a fan of. Cute, little blonde. Riley took them out on the Mako and dropped them at the Dockside, then picked them up that night and brought them home."

"So what?"

"Alex wasn't happy with how Riley acted around her, and let Riley know about it after they got back to the Compound. Riley admitted that Alex was heated about it."

"Let me get this straight, LT. The kid likes this band, the singer of this band shows up with G-One, a monumental asshole, and my brother makes a play for her, and that somehow results in Alex Grimes being dead?"

"That might be the thinking."

"I see." He shook his head. "And the idea would be that they fought over her? The most violent thing G-One's ever done is grab a waitress's ass. And while Pop or I get into our share of scraps, you ever heard of Riley doing it?"

Someone started to come in the door. Before they could get it open, Scooter yelled that he was closed and to come back later.

"I don't know what to tell you," I said. "I'm not in on the investigation."

"So if Brooke Shields walks into your police station over a parking ticket, and you happen to get all tongue-tied and make googly eyes at her, that means you're going to pull out your piece and blast that tennis player she's screwing?"

"Look, Scooter, I'm just trying to give you an idea of why they're talking to him. I'm not saying he did it. If he didn't, there's nothing to worry about."

"That's a fucking lie, LT. You don't know what can happen with those people mixed up in it. They aren't us."

"Randolph Grimes is one of the most honorable men I know," I said. I could say that, even with the demands he'd made since we'd found Alex, though my conviction might be less than it had once been.

The bell on the door tinkled again.

"I said we're fucking closed." Scooter's face reddened. Vibrations echoed off the weathered siding.

Flo Stevens, the boys' mother, came in and stood next to me. She must have walked from their house up the road. She was breathing hard.

"It's your brother," she said. "They arrested him. Your father wants you in Limerick."

The three of us piled into the cruiser and took off. The thirty-minute ride was made in silence.

"Do you think it looks bad for him, LT?" Florence Stevens asked, as we pulled into the lot at the barracks.

"If they arrested him, I do," I said. "I'm sorry."

"That kid hasn't had a fight since third grade," Scooter said, leaping from the front seat before I could bring the car to a stop. "There's no way he killed that rich prick."

Chapter Seventeen

The barracks were fronted by a wood-paneled counter. No one was behind it when we came in. I told Scooter and his mother to wait and went down the hall.

Their makeshift conference room was a box-like office with two tables pulled together so eight people could fit. Ben Freeman and Pop Stevens were on one side of the table next to Riley. Wisterman and Salazar sat opposite them. None looked like they were having the time of their life.

"Who let you in here?" Wisterman said.

"No one."

"You should have waited."

"Riley's been arrested?" I ignored Wisterman and looked to Salazar.

"He'll be on his way to booking in ten minutes," Wisterman said.

Riley's head was at a forty-five-degree angle, cocked to the side. His lips were pressed together. His eyes focused on a random spot on the table. If not a specimen like his brother, he was a good-looking kid. I could see where Sally might have been glad to talk to him.

"Scooter and his mother are out front. Do you think she could see him before you take him away?"

Riley looked up at me, as if figuring what my angle might be in all this.

"They can talk to him after he's booked," Salazar said. "I'm assuming they know where this jail is?" Freeman rolled his head but didn't have anything to say. Scooter's assessment of his brother's lawyer had been accurate.

"You can't give his mother five minutes?" I asked.

"This ain't a nursery school, Nichols," Wisterman said. Two of his men came in and brushed by me. They went behind Riley and told him to stand. He did. He kept his eyes low and his face blank. I wouldn't have blamed him if he'd checked out. They cuffed him and left us in the room.

"You think this is right, LT?" Pop Stevens asked, stopping across from me in front of the door. He was not taking this well. His face was as white as the hair on his head. His lips were pulled back against his teeth like a dog about to bite. I'm sure he would've liked to take the room apart.

Benita Salazar stood. Her eyes went to me.

"I don't know what all the evidence is," I said, "but I'm sure they wouldn't make an arrest without cause."

"Fuck that," Pop said, his head going up with the first word and coming down with the second. He and Freeman followed Riley down the hall. Wisterman trailed them, leaving Salazar and me alone.

"Thank you for your support, Chief, though it doesn't mean jack, one way or another. The kid's dead to rights." She picked her briefcase off the floor and put it on the table.

"You got him to confess?"

"I did not."

"What am I missing?"

"Again: not to be shared. We found some evidence early this morning. A boat hook, which is a—"

"I know what a boat hook is," I said.

"Well, this one's five feet long, made of hickory with a brass end that matches up quite nicely with the cave-in on Alex's skull. It was in the cove, ten yards from the dock. Probably as far as he could pitch it after tossing the body in. Only it sank into the mud. When we went out there this morning, it was low tide, and we spotted it under a few inches of water. We were able to get some prints off it, anyway. Those prints belonged to Alex Grimes."

"He ran the boats. Wouldn't that make sense?"

"Oh, it would. But one, it meant that he'd used it recently, or they wouldn't have been matchable after being submerged in salt water. And there aren't many reasons a captain would toss one of his tools away. It's lucky we found it when we did. The lab boys have been busy."

"And Riley's alibi is that he went to sleep?"

"That is a fact," she said, nodding. "Of course, there's no one who can corroborate. He claims to have told Alex to calm down and then went up to his room. We did find that girl's album on his turntable. We also found a size nine footprint, a Topsider, in the blood on the dock. They were there."

"The blood was Alex's?"

"Unfortunately, it was that of mackerel. Bait, I'm told. Would you like to hazard a guess as to what size shoe our boy wears?"

"That could have happened anytime."

"Motive: We know Stevens has a thing for the singer. Alex, who I hear was pretty much of an ass, was giving him a hard time. Alex comes down to confront Stevens over him hitting on the chick, who is already a source of frustration for Alex. Riley admits that. But instead of walking away and going up to his room, he retreats to where he feels safe—to one of his boats. Alex keeps pushing him until he snaps. He grabs the hook and wham, it's over. There are no other signs of a fight. Stevens panics. Alex goes into the high tide, which Stevens knows is on its way out and will take the body away. The murder weapon follows. Alex travels further. If he doesn't get hung up, we don't know what happened."

It made sense. All I could do was stand there and shake my head. If I'd had the chance and been doing my job, I should have been able to pull the relevant information out of Riley. I should have reached the same conclusion. But I wasn't sure that I would have. I'd just accepted what he'd told me because I knew him as a kid. It was a disgraceful performance on my part.

"Did I forget to mention that Riley admitted to asking Miss Strummer if she'd like to talk about her music when they got home? What a line. That was when he dropped them off at the bar in the afternoon. I would have been upset if I were Alex, too."

"You've got a dead body, a murder weapon, fingerprints, and a kid who admitted that he had a verbal altercation with the man who wound up dead hours later."

"Succinctly put," Salazar said.

"Why would he admit to that confrontation and then expect you to believe that it went nowhere, knowing what happened?" The admission defied logic, especially if Salazar's narrative was accurate.

"I've been told he's a college graduate, but I don't think he's got the common sense of a stone crab. And you know—well, maybe you don't—that criminals are not always the clearest thinkers. Prisons aren't full of Ivy Leaguers."

"I appreciate the information. Always great to see where I fucked up. Really enjoy it."

"I don't know what to tell you." A confused look came across her face. She might have thought I was more pathetic than she'd originally determined.

"If you're tight with that family, you can tell them that if their lawyer has a goddamn brain in his bald head, he better start thinking about a confession and a plea deal."

"I coached that kid in Little League. I never thought he was capable of something like this."

"No one is a killer at that age. A woman, an asshole boss, and you men reaching puberty can really fuck things up."

"Secretary Grimes is okay with this scenario? When I was looking into it, all he wanted was an accidental death determination."

"I was brought here to run an investigation," she said. "When I laid it out for him last night, he accepted it. He was the one who spotted that the boat hook was missing this morning."

"Shit," I said.

"Tell the kid's family to look for a plea deal. It's his only way out."

Chapter Eighteen

"I know when things get tight, you don't eat," Suzanne said. She stood on the other side of the screen door. I opened it and let her in.

It had been forty-eight hours since Riley Stevens had been arrested for the killing of Alex Grimes. I couldn't walk into a store or restaurant without being asked about it or told that Riley was too nice a boy to have done it. I'd also "no commented" a host of television crews and reporters, including my friend Sawyer from the Press Herald. He'd had the balls to ask for my thoughts on the case after he screwed me the first time around. Riley still hadn't confessed.

Suzanne's eyes took in the living room, then went over my shoulder to the kitchen. I should have been embarrassed about how different it looked than when she'd been staying here on a regular basis. It wasn't that when we were together that Suzanne took care of these things. I'd been motivated then to clean and organize like an adult. Lately, I hadn't seen the point. I'm sure she saw the dishes piled in the sink, the food wrappers on the table, and the half-open bag of chips on the counter. The living room wasn't much better. An Afghan was clumped on the couch. Magazines and beer bottles competed for control of the coffee table.

"Let's sit on the porch," I said, so I wouldn't have to watch depression set in as she realized my current state of existence.

She was wearing faded jeans and her Blink's General Store work shirt, having come after closing at nine o'clock. I got two beers out of the refrigerator, and we sank into the Adirondack chairs. I left the lights off to keep the bugs away. Months earlier, we'd sat there and talked about how the flat driveway would be great for a toddler on a Big Wheel. That wasn't going to happen now.

"Roast beef," she said, handing me one of Blink's specialties.

"Did you bring one for yourself?" I asked, before unwrapping it. With food in front of me, I became hungry.

"I have sense enough to eat at regular hours."

I shrugged and took a bite. They baked their own bread at Blink's and there had to be a half-pound of rare beef to go along with two thick slices of white cheddar and horseradish mayo. At least with my mouth full, I didn't have to talk. Maybe she'd anticipated that. We watched two bats flying around the bird feeder hanging on the oak. She let me get a quarter of the way in before a question came out.

"Pop Stevens came in today to grab some lunch. He looked awful."

"It doesn't look good for Riley."

"I didn't know what to say."

"Pop came to the office yesterday, too."

She looked at me with her big green eyes. She was going to wait me out, knowing I wouldn't make her ask.

"He asked if I thought Riley was guilty." I took a long hit off the sweating brown bottle. The swallow tasted randomly bitter. "I told him that I didn't know, but that I didn't want him to think that it was a commentary on his kid. I laid out the evidence for him and tried to explain how it was substantial."

"And?"

"You know you can't repeat this." I felt like a fool airing that out, having recently been on the receiving end of a similar warning and knowing better. Suzanne and I had been together for two years. She didn't have to be told. If there was anyone in town I could trust to keep quiet, it was her. A cloud passed through her eyes.

"Before I could get started, Pop stopped me. He said he knew the evidence. What he wanted to know was what I thought. I told him it wasn't my job in the process to determine guilt. He wasn't having it. I had to tell him that based on the evidence, I would have arrested Riley, too."

"Jesus," she said, both hands gripping her bottle.

"He said that he knew his son, and that he didn't do it. And that I should know it, too. Then he asked if they'd brought in Marshal Salazar because I thought Riley hadn't done it. I had to tell him that I just hadn't pushed hard enough on him.

"Then he asked me if I thought Riley should take a plea deal. I told him to think about it, that they could argue self-defense."

"You think he's screwed, don't you?"

I nodded and put down my sub.

"You can't do anything?"

"I told you that I was removed from the case two hours into it. That marshal from Washington, she hasn't missed a thing." I should have been grateful that Grimes had brought her here. Wisterman wouldn't have figured this out, and I wouldn't have had the chance. Riley Stevens could have done it and walked.

"So you're just going to let this happen?"

"What if he is guilty? That's what the evidence suggests."

"You should know better." Her arms crossed in front of her chest.

"It doesn't matter what I think. I'm the smallest fish in this pond, and they've kicked me out of the water. I don't have a say."

"When did that ever stop you from doing something?"

"I don't think you understand my place in the hierarchy."

"I thought this was your town, and we were your people. Flo's about to have a nervous breakdown."

"It's tough on everyone," I said.

"That's all you can say?" The tone she'd found on the Wentworth's front lawn reappeared.

"Given the evidence, I don't know how I could've reached a different conclusion than Marshal Salazar. I would have never thought that Riley could do something like that. But it looks like the night went sideways on him."

Suzanne looked away, out to the road, and put her legs up on the porch rail. The thin lines that came out around her eyes did not diminish her. She flicked away a mosquito with the back of her hand.

"So you think he did it."

"I didn't say that. What I said was there's evidence that indicates it."

"What do you think?"

"He told me one story, and he told Marshal Salazar a different version. There's physical evidence. There's circumstantial evidence."

"If that's the case, then why don't you just come out and say it? You think he killed Alex Grimes."

"Because I'm not one hundred percent sure, and he's claiming he's innocent."

"The kid's not a murderer, and you know it."

"I don't know it. That's what I'm saying."

"If there's a chance he's innocent, you need to do something."

"I told you, there's nothing I can do. I'm out."

"What if he were your kid?"

"That's different."

"How so?"

"Because I wouldn't be able to think rationally about it."

"You're making excuses."

"I'm trying to use my head."

"I can't imagine," she said, looking me in the eye, "what either of those sets of parents feels like right now. One child gone, the other might as well be. Unless you do something."

"Do you think maybe it's a good thing we weren't able to do it?" I put down my beer and leaned forward, elbows on my knees. She knew what I meant. I didn't need to spell it out.

Her head whipped around. Her first instinct had been to say no. Her eyes narrowed as she stopped to think.

"I don't know if I could take it," she said. "Although I can't imagine a child of ours being mixed up in something like this."

"I don't think any parent does. It's not like either the Grimes or Stevens are bad people. Who knows why things happen the way they do?"

"Do you think a kid would have kept us together? Or would it be like we are now, with them ping-ponging between us?"

This was a question that neither of us really wanted to explore, never mind answer.

"We're talking, at least," I said.

"That's because we took time to let things cool." She patted my arm. "I'm worried about you. You don't have anyone. Your parents are gone. You have cousins you never see. Your best friend growing up comes back once every ten years. You and I, done, sorry to say. Outside of work, the only one you spend any time with is Trout, who doesn't know his ass from a bologna sandwich."

"I've got a whole town," I said.

"That's usually a one-way street," she said. "Going the other way."

"It's not always like that."

"Then where does that leave Riley Stevens?" she said before I could think of an example.

"You're really giving it to me, Suzy," I said, trying not to sound aggravated, angry, or hurt, all of which were in play. "I have a conscience of my own, you know."

"Maybe you should turn it up a bit, then."

"I'm glad to see that you're not bitter or anything."

"That has nothing to do with it," she said.

"I know." She was telling the truth.

"I'm only one beer in," she said. "A few more, and I believe I could work up to it."

"At least you left me with furniture. That didn't happen with Analisa."

She reached over and patted my arm, leaving her hand resting over mine. Our eyes met. She smiled. We started leaning in, fractions of an inch at a time. The corners of her mouth turned up. The phone rang. I started breathing again.

"I'm going to need to get that," I said. It was a welcome excuse not to travel down a road that we probably knew would lead us off a cliff. She arched her eyebrows and watched me bolt into the house.

"Chief, you better get out here." House's deep voice crackled over the line.

"Where are you?"

"The Sea Squall. There's trouble." As my mind started processing what that could be, the moment I'd just shared with Suzanne vanished. It didn't make sense. The Squall's servers wore ties and dress pants. A steak cost thirty bucks. They carried wines that most people couldn't pronounce. This wasn't the Port Tavern or the Rusty Bullet, full of drunks ready to bust loose.

"Give it to me quick," I said.

"That marshal and Scooter Stevens are about to go at it."

"Have you called Sergeant Crowley?" I said, grabbing my keys.

"He's here. He's the one who told me to get you."

I hung up and ran out the front door. I only stopped when I realized that I was in the driveway and that Suzy was still on my front porch, hands on her waist.

"I've got to run," I said.

"I see," she said.

I started the Bronco and turned on the blues that flashed from my grill. I whipped the rig around Suzy's Subaru and hammered it, shooting a river of gravel behind me. I took one quick glance at what I was leaving behind and reached for the roll of breath mints I kept on the dash, then for the thirty-eight in the glove box.

Chapter Nineteen

I went through the Squall's employee entrance in the back. I came out of the kitchen into an empty dining room set with white tablecloths, clean plates and silverware, and sparkling wine glasses. As I stepped into the lounge, I wasn't expecting the quiet that hit me. Benita Salazar had her back to me at the edge of the room closest to the rear, as if the others had tried pushing her out of their space. Opposite her, standing in the front, fifteen feet away, was Scooter Stevens. The aisle separating them was cleared out like Main Street in Dodge City. My two officers, Crowley and House, stood between them but off to the side in front of mahogany wine racks that held hundreds of bottles. Frank Consentino, the owner, was behind the bar that ran the length of the room. He was with his bartender, Maureen DiGiovani, who everyone called Mary Queen of Shots. I could have used one. Maureen was chewing gum like it was on fire. Finn Sampson and Sal Robins, two of Scooter's running buddies, were seated on bar stools. Their backs were to Maureen and Consentino, watching the action. An army of empties was deserted behind them. All eyes were on Salazar. It must have been her move in whatever this was. That a gun wasn't drawn seemed like a miracle.

No one acknowledged me as I came up behind Salazar. She either had complete focus on Stevens or confidence the size of Canada to ignore my Nikes on the hardwood. The quiet didn't last.

"I told you, Mr. Stevens," she said, "it would be in your best interest to let these officers walk you out. Because they know you, they'll be really nice and won't kick the shit out of you when they bring you in. It's no small thing to threaten a federal officer."

"I'm not moving until you tell me why you're railroading my brother. Who is he taking the hit for? You answer that and I'll let you walk out of here."

She laughed, shaking her head. I moved past her into the space directly between them.

"Did I miss last call?" I asked.

"Give me a fucking break," Salazar said after a beat. She took her eyes off Stevens and put them on me. "I hope you're here to babysit your men, because they're somewhat confused as to what their job is. Mr. Stevens, of those Stevens, has threatened a federal agent. That, I have told them, is a felony. But for some reason, they seem to think it's not worthy of arrest. Would you care to explain?"

It was obvious they were trying to avoid all hell breaking loose, and she knew that.

"Scooter, what the fuck are you doing?" I asked. I figured to start at the top and work my way down.

"I'm finding out why my brother's getting set up by Mrs. Tubbs. And I'm not getting answers. It's pissing me off."

I didn't look to see if the Miami Vice slur had further angered her. The brawl potential had my legs shaking. Scooter was a handful by himself. I'd seen him clean out the Port Tavern when some of the Jackals, a bike gang from Lewiston, thought they could take some liberties with standard barroom pool table etiquette. Four guys with their colors up over their heads as if they'd lost a hockey fight, blood pouring from their noses, were lying in the parking lot by the time we got there. Sampson and Robins had big hearts, larger muscles, and small brains. If Scooter wanted to go for it, they'd back him and worry about consequences later. This, despite knowing Crowley and me personally. And the marshal did not look any less capable than the character they'd named her. I stepped toward Scooter.

"You need to go home. Now. This is not the place. Crowley, House, open the door so I can escort him out."

Scooter turned to the two officers beside him. "Don't touch that fucking door. I'm not leaving until I get answers."

Apparently, this was another situation where logic or reasonableness was not going to work. I was pleased to see Crowley showing unusual restraint, because usually someone telling him not to do something was the best way to get him to do it. This was only getting worse. I needed the civilians out.

"Frank," I said to Consentino. His eyes kept going from Scooter to Salazar to the thousands of dollars in wine on the wall across from him. "Why don't you and Maureen go upstairs? Or, better yet, call it a night."

"They have tabs going," Maureen said, nodding at Scooter and his backup.

"They'll settle tomorrow," I said and nodded at Consentino to get moving.

Frank, slick with sweat, pointed to the cash drawer. Maureen pulled it, and they walked past Salazar, back to the office. I waited.

Salazar laughed and turned to me. "Now, why don't you take your minions the fuck out of here and let me handle this?"

The answer to that was, because you'd get your ass kicked, even if you're quick enough to pull the fancy Glock on your hip. I didn't think there was anyone I couldn't handle myself, and that included Scooter. I'd taken down bigger men, and I hadn't slacked on working out. But there were three of them, three of us, and the marshal. Anything could happen. Crowley was capable, and House's name befitted his size. We could do it, but it wouldn't be easy, and people would get hurt. There was also a chance that a gun comes out. The only way this could be avoided was to stop it from starting.

"You two," I said, pointing to Sampson and Robins. "Out right now." They didn't move, unless one counted turning their heads to Scooter for direction.

"Wow, the respect you have amongst your townspeople is impressive, Chief Nichols," Salazar said.

"Crowley," I said. "Open the door."

My sergeant moved around Scooter to the front of the building. I turned to Stevens. "You want these guys going to jail because you're acting like a moron? That's okay with you?"

"It's okay with us," Finn Sampson said.

"You shut the fuck up," I said.

Scooter flicked his head toward the street.

"Come on, you two," Crowley said, in something less than his usual bark.

House opened the door.

"Let's make sure that our friends decide to enjoy some of that cool night air," I said. "Crowley, you stay out front. House, you go around and keep an eye on the back."

"Got it." The two townies shot me a look on their way out, as if they were as tough as their friend. I returned it with one of my own that let them know they weren't. Sampson opened his mouth to say something.

"Think again," I said. He didn't like it but kept quiet as they left. I waited until they were out of sight and Crowley was alone on the sidewalk.

"I'll be taking you out next, Scooter," I said, taking a step toward him.

"With all due respect, LT, the hell you will."

"Do you think this ends well for you?" I asked. "Ms. Salazar is here at the request of the federal government. Play this out a bit. What do you think is going to happen?"

"You think my brother's a killer?"

"I'm not getting into that."

"I told you that I'm not leaving until I get answers. He's taking the heat for something he didn't do."

"This isn't the place."

"So, you're with Mrs. Tubbs?"

"Right now, yes."

"Enough," Salazar said. Apparently, she must have skipped the federal seminar on de-escalation.

"Look," I said to both of them, "we don't need more shit piled on top of what we already have."

Scooter still had a locked-in stare. Right on Salazar.

"He's broken I don't know how many laws," Salazar said. "And you're treating him like he's the fucking mayor. Chief, get the fuck out of my way. I'm taking it from here."

"Yeah, LT. Take a walk, and let me and Mrs. Tubbs settle this."

"Shut up, both of you," I said. She hadn't given me the chance to defuse the situation. He somehow thought there was a way that this turned out okay for him.

I turned and looked at her. She stared back and flashed a fake smile, her white teeth gleaming in the dim lighting of the bar.

"This is an arrest situation, Nichols," she said. "That it hasn't happened yet means you're either stupid or corrupt. Regardless, you're in the way. Leave. He might find that he likes getting his ass kicked by a Cuban."

"You're not helping," I said.

"I'm not here to coddle a hick who threatened me and whose brother killed a man over some bimbo. It's gone on long enough."

I heard the movement behind me, a hand brushing against fabric. Scooter's eyes got big.

"Of course you need a gun, you snatch," he said.

His words reached my ears as my eyes found the pistol in her hand, pointed past me at him.

"You see where this is going?" I said to Scooter.

"I'll get to her before that stops me," he said.

I could have explained that it wasn't her fault that his brother was in jail. That anyone in law enforcement would have come to the conclusion that she did. But I might as well have been speaking French and talking to the wine bottles.

"Turn around and get the fuck out of here, Scooter," I said, shifting sideways between them.

"Fuck that," he said, and took a step forward.

"Out of the way, Chief," Salazar said.

I didn't have much choice.

"Put that gun away before I take it from you," I said, as nasty and dismissively as I could, turning to her.

"Oh, hell no," she said. Scooter snickered.

As soon as I heard it, I spun and took a jab step toward him. On reflex, his arm came up in a defensive position. I whipped behind Scooter, placing my left leg in front of his, and at the same time, brought my arms up under his shoulders, forcing a vise behind his neck. I took him down face first. I ground him into the hardwood to neutralize his bulk. He was stunned.

"Cuffs," I yelled, hoping Salazar was carrying some or I was loud enough for Crowley to hear.

She had hers in my hand in an instant. I had them on him before he could move. The side of his face was scraped red.

"Damn, Nichols," Salazar said.

Crowley burst through the front door. Scooter was fuming but subdued. I had Crowley and House take him to the station to lock him up. He could cool off, and I could take time to decide how hard I needed to go on him. At least gallons of expensive grape juice had been spared from mixing with blood on the wide plank floor.

Chapter Twenty

"How the fuck does this happen?" I said once she and I were alone. Consentino had come out, and I'd sent him back to his office. Then I helped myself to a beer. I didn't think Salazar deserved one.

"I arrested his brother. Something you should have done."

"If I'd had time to carry out an investigation."

"I hope that's the truth," she said.

"No one may have told you this, but I was pulled because I wasn't willing to call it an accident. Not to mention that the state police run most capital cases in this state."

"Riley Stevens could have been halfway to Tahiti by the time you figured it out."

"I'm aware."

"Maybe you're just a man of action. That was a slick take-down."

"It wouldn't have been needed if you'd let me de-escalate the situation."

She laughed. "That wasn't happening. You saw the look in his eyes."

"You're wrong."

"Skip the psychology and stick to what you're good at. A lot of marshals I know couldn't handle a guy like that."

I grabbed another beer, then decided to try a different approach. I held out a glass for her and she nodded. I poured.

"So, what happened?" I asked.

"I was in here having dinner. I'm stuck in this town until the grand jury. That's come down from the top. Even though there's not much for me to do, those are my orders. They don't want this case fucked up. I heard this was a decent place to eat. Then Pretty Boy Floyd's brother came in with his friends. Sat across from me. Tried to stare me down."

"And you refused to ignore them."

"Where I'm from, if you want to intimidate someone, you pack an Uzi. A couple of fishermen on a beer bender are a joke. They annoyed me. And when the object of my annoyance doesn't go away, I get angry."

"You asked them what their problem was."

"Maybe you do have a head on your shoulders."

"And then the place cleared out like in *High Noon*?"

She nodded. "It took a while, but yes."

"And someone called my men?"

"Your men were scared of him."

"My men have more sense than to start a brawl in a place full of civilians."

"I'm sure that's it," she said, laughing. Then, a thought passed through her face, deflating her smile. "Hey, that was a dig."

"Maybe you have a head on your shoulders."

"You are arresting him, correct?"

"We'll let him sit in a cell for a few days and see how it goes. His family's been through plenty."

"Because one of them is a murderer."

"That's the problem. Scooter doesn't think it's possible."

"No one should ever get away with threatening an officer. If I see him on the street and he opens his mouth, I'm not being nice. I didn't get to finish my halibut tonight, and let me tell you, it was fabulous."

"I believe it." I quaffed my beer and left the empty glass on the bar. "Do you need a ride back to wherever it is you're staying? I can drop you on my way to the station."

"Thanks, but I'll walk." She finished her beer and placed her glass next to mine. "Can I ask you something?"

"Sure."

"Why do they think I'm railroading the brother? The evidence is clear."

"He grew up here, an Eagle Scout. Everyone loves the family. You'd have to turn over a lot of rocks to find someone who liked Alex Grimes."

"Luckily, I'm not a geologist," she said.

Chapter Twenty-One

Scooter Stevens was a bit less agitated in the morning. He was on his back on the bunk, legs crossed, Big Tuna ball cap pulled down over his eyes. He could have been sacked out in a Hilton, as comfortable as he looked.

"Wake the fuck up," I said, whipping the door shut on the adjacent cell. It sounded like a car crash. That got his legs straightened. His hat came off as he rolled upright.

"Fuck off, you sneaky prick." He did not sound angry.

"How you feeling today, hot head?"

"I've woken up in worse places."

"You should be proud of yourself," I said. "You haven't done anything stupid in the last ten hours. That's real progress."

He swung his legs off the bunk and faced me, leaning back against the wall. The top of his left cheek showed a series of burgundy lines from kissing the floor.

"Am I getting out?" he said, smiling slightly.

"Not quite," I said. "Let's take a walk."

He rose from his seat and stretched his neck, rolling his head. "You're not going to try another sneak attack, are you? Because I'm not falling for it again."

I laughed and led him to my office.

I don't know how many times I've sat in my chair and recapped a laundry list of dumb things that someone had done. I'd had to tell Sam Rooney that stealing his neighbor's bike, spray painting it, and then riding it past his house indicated that he should not be considering a career in crime. Wes Draper had learned that using his brother's front-end loader to block his neighbor's beach right of way by depositing boulders the size of ponies—in broad daylight—was not a viable way to settle a dispute over who could use its path. I've also had occasional real criminals whose outcomes required them to spend time with the state. But I'd never had a combination quite like this. Scooter Stevens was a guy, though on the wild side, who'd gone out of his way to help a good number of people in Laurel, and yet, he'd displayed a nearly incomprehensible lack of judgment in threatening a fed. Not a brilliant move, regardless of the trouble his family was experiencing.

Scooter sat in the chair, hanging his head. I probably didn't need to itemize his list, but did anyway. He deserved to hear it. I began with the idiocy of tracking down a federal marshal with the purpose of antagonizing her. I followed that up by questioning what he expected to happen, as there was a less than zero chance that even if she had railroaded Riley, she would admit it in a barroom full of witnesses. I also pointed out that she was trained in hand-to-hand combat and, as he had seen for himself, carried a gun. I then asked if he had been lucky enough to land a punch without getting shot, how that was going to make his brother look less guilty. And I asked what the fuck he was trying to put his parents through. They had one son in jail for murder. Another for threatening a law enforcement officer would not help matters.

"I know, LT," he said when I'd finished. "I was a fucking idiot."

"We can agree on that." He had enough sense, at least, not to rationalize his behavior.

"So what now?" he said.

"Marshal Salazar wants you booked. I don't see where she is wrong."

"Man," he said, elbows on his knees, burying his head in his hands. He took a deep breath, then sat up. "Are you going to do it?"

"I haven't decided."

That widened his eyes. It was the truth.

"So there's a chance I won't wind up in a cell with Riley?"

"He might have been through enough."

"I can't believe you'd joke about that."

"It's not about him. I'm talking about you, the guy who ignored me when I gave him a chance to walk away."

He sighed, his body slumping. "You know Riley didn't kill that asshole."

"I hate to say this, but I don't know that. From the evidence I've seen, I can't make an argument."

"He was an Eagle Scout, LT, literally. You coached the kid. He couldn't even be bothered to steal a base, and now he's a killer? The hell with that." Scooter got up and walked over to look out the window, then turned to me. "You saw the idiocy I was capable of. You know my dad had his day. The old man never walked away from an argument. I bet you and Crowley have broken up some of his scraps yourselves. I lived from one sports season to the next. My father boxed. Why the hell do you think my sister moved to Seattle? She'd had enough of us bulletheads. But Riley, he's not like us. He played soccer, for chrissakes. He lettered in sailing at Maine Maritime. How is that even a sport?"

"Anyone can lose their shit, Scooter. He was the last one with Alex. He admitted they had a disagreement. His fingerprints were on the murder weapon."

"That doesn't mean shit. I know who he is. Freeman said they were making a big deal because he had that chick's record on the turntable. And he was fawning over her. Maybe he just liked her music. Did you ever think of that? Is that a crime? That kid loved his bands, and let me tell you, some of those bands suck. You probably wore out *Night Moves* on your stereo. Does that mean you want to fuck Bob Seger?" He sat back down in his chair and ran his hands through his hair.

"Did you talk to him?" I asked.

"They gave me fifteen minutes."

"Did he tell you he didn't do it?"

"Of course, because he didn't."

"On top of everything, he has no alibi. No one's buying the 'going to bed at nine-thirty' story."

"If there is someone who would, it's Riley. You know any other kid his age captaining a Hinckley?"

"I don't. That's the only one I've ever seen."

"You need to help the kid, LT. That's all there is to it. Or he's going away, because that's what Grimes and that marshal want. I know he didn't do it."

"People can surprise you, and not always in good ways."

"Someone you've never had to give a thought to in his twenty-five years hauled off and cracked a guy over the head because he got mad that he was checking out his chick? Come on. And don't give me that murder weapon bullshit. Do you think Riley said, 'Stand here, Alex, while I run over to the boat and grab something to bash your brains in?'"

"It could have been on the dock."

"Did you look at the kid's room? Did you see anything out of place? Or a speck of dust?"

"Thanks to Marshal Salazar and the state police, it doesn't matter what I think."

"You did question Riley that day, right?"

"That afternoon."

"But you didn't arrest him, did you?"

"It was hours after I found the body and the beginning of the investigation. Eventually, if I were doing my job correctly, I would have come to the same conclusion that Salazar did."

Scooter shook his head and adjusted his cap. "Will you go to Brookeville and talk to him?"

"Why?"

"Because he's innocent, and you don't want that on your head. If he really killed Alex, would he have told you that he had an argument with him?"

"He didn't tell me they had an argument. He mentioned that Alex had sniped at him after he'd brought Sally in. In fact, he failed to tell me that Alex later went down to the boathouse and confronted him. Salazar got that out of Riley. I didn't dig in the way I should have, because I did give him the benefit of the doubt. And he wasn't straight with me. When Salazar went after him, objectively, she pushed like I should have and shook out the truth. I look like a jackass. Riley played me."

"No, you were right to do what you did. You knew in your gut that he wasn't involved."

"I don't know that now, and I didn't know it then."

Scooter shook his head hard enough that his hair moved.

"So you won't go talk to him?" he said.

"I don't think so."

"Don't you want the truth?"

"Have you considered that Salazar has arrived at the truth, and it's just one that you don't like?"

"You think I don't know my brother?"

"Give it up, Scooter. We need to face reality when it hits us in the nose."

"You're wrong, LT. About my brother. I'm asking you to go talk to him. As a favor. Let him explain it better."

"I owe you a favor?" I asked. "After last night?"

"I know. I was an idiot. Let's put that aside."

"When I questioned him, he wasn't very forthcoming."

"He'll have smartened up by now. Please, just give him fifteen minutes, and I'll leave you alone about it."

"You don't have much of a choice in that."

"You're not letting me out of here?"

"I don't want you bothering Marshal Salazar again. She won't mind shooting you, and one dead man this week is already over my limit. You're staying here."

"For how long?"

"I don't know. We'll get you lunch from Blink's," I said, rising. "That'll give you something to look forward to."

"That's a sorry excuse for you to spend a few minutes with your girlfriend."

"She's not my girlfriend," I said. "Anymore."

"Man, maybe you really are a dope," he said.

Chapter Twenty-Two

Dope seemed like an accurate description. That afternoon, I found myself driving to the county jail in Brookeville. It wasn't Scooter's pleading that sent me there, nor was it my gut. Something was bothering me. Suzanne had asked me if I was positive that Riley had killed Alex. I couldn't admit that I was, though it sure looked that way. The evidence was substantial. But if Riley had killed Alex, why would he have told Salazar that they'd had a confrontation, knowing it would only point to his guilt? To Scooter's point, his brother had been a model citizen, accomplishing much at a young age and assuming responsibilities that belied his years. Of course, anyone could snap if pushed far enough. What would Alex have done to push Riley over the edge—if he even had an edge? If that's what happened, I wanted to know how and why. Then, I might be able to explain it to his family. That was as much help as I could offer.

Salazar's ability to get answers, when I had not, also ate at me. I'd taken Riley at his word when he said he'd walked away from what he'd painted as an everyday rant from Alex. The marshal had seen something that I'd missed. Maybe that's what allowed her to pull the truth from him. I'd been too accepting when what I'd heard should have compelled me to dig deeper. I wanted to see if the things I'd missed were still there to be noticed.

The Brookeville lock-up wasn't a soul-sucking pit of despair. But that didn't mean it wasn't depressing: concrete walls painted pale green, black iron bars, clanking locks, and fluorescent lighting that never stopped flickering. The stench revealed an ongoing battle between piss and Clorox. I sat on a plastic chair on one side of a table in an interrogation room and waited. The second hand on my watch crawled.

Riley was brought in by a guard who told me he'd be right outside should I need him. Riley's jail pants and shirt were rough cotton, pale blue with a number stamped on the chest. His five o'clock shadow looked like goose down. He sat. His eyes went to the wall behind me.

"How're you doing, Riley?"

"What do you want?" he said, sounding less than aggravated, but not happy.

"Your brother asked me to talk to you."

"Why?"

"Because he thinks you're innocent."

He slumped in his seat while shifting his gaze to meet mine. "I didn't kill that jerk."

"That's what Scooter says."

"What does he think you're going to do about it?"

"Help, if you really didn't do it."

"My brother's problem is that he has a million-dollar heart and a ten-cent head. You're on the other side of this."

"That's what I told him."

"And I already told you what happened."

"No, you didn't."

"What do you mean? I told you I took them out on the boat and dropped them off at the Dockside. I brought them home in the Suburban. Alex gave me shit when I offered to help Sally into the house." He ran a thumb over the delicate growth on his chin.

"That you did, but the omission of the complete truth might as well be a lie. You made it seem like Alex just chewed you out, and that was it. You failed to mention that he'd come down to the boathouse after you'd parked the car and gone to your room. That you two had a real problem with each other. You did mention that to Marshal Salazar."

He dipped his head and took a breath. "When he came to the boathouse, it wasn't anything different than he'd said before. Nothing came of it, so what difference does it make?"

"A dead Alex Grimes is what came of it."

"Not from him being at my place."

"So why tell her and not me?"

"You don't know what it's like to have her on you. It was as if she knew there was more to it, and she wasn't going to accept anything less. No offense, but you, Coach, you're just a guy. She's a force. I don't mean any disrespect."

He'd missed the mark with that. "Is there a reason I shouldn't walk out of here right now?"

"Because I didn't do it. That's why I told her everything. I didn't think the truth could hurt me. To be honest, I didn't have much faith in you being able to see the big picture. I thought you'd be on him coming down to badger me like a striper on chunked mackerel, like you did just now. I counted on the marshal being able to sift through it if I told her the truth. That backfired."

I drummed my fingers on the table as I considered leaving. It wasn't his fault I didn't like what I was hearing. He was being honest. I signed on for a few more questions.

"Tell me what happened that night, starting with when they called you to come get them."

"I told you already."

"I want to hear it again. This time, I want every detail."

He told me the same story I'd heard on Monday. Between what I'd learned from Salazar and my own poking around, I'd already been able to verify most of the details. It was hard not to sympathize with having to put up with Alex and his condescension. But I'd already fallen into that trap once.

"You had problems with Alex prior to this, correct?"

"If you can find someone from Laurel who's been around him and hasn't had a problem with him, that would take some real detective work."

"Did it ever come to blows before this?"

"No, and it didn't this time." He'd sidestepped that rather nicely.

"What would he do to you, specifically?"

"He was a spoiled brat, which I'm sure you know. He'd go out of his way to be a pain in the ass."

"Meaning?"

"If he scheduled the boat to go out at two, he'd show up at three-thirty, then smirk as if it were my job to wait around for him. He'd call for a ride and have me sit in the parking lot for hours. And he always had a name for me like Champ or Sport. Or Eastman, whatever that meant. He liked to make it known who was in charge and who was the help."

"You never did anything about it?"

"I let Secretary Grimes deal with it."

"You let him know when Alex was bothering you?"

Riley chuckled. "No. Getting dicked around by him and his sister went with the job. If he wanted to do something with the boats that I didn't think was a good idea or conflicted with something Secretary Grimes wanted me working on, then I'd mention it. That would put a stop to it."

"Tell me what happened when he came down to the boathouse. What were you doing?"

"I was going to bed. I told you that."

"Anything else?"

"What do you mean by that?"

"You didn't have the Clap on your stereo?"

"I did. That band is unbelievable. I've said a million times that I was a huge fan. That doesn't make me a killer. Have you heard them?"

"No."

"Of course not. They might be a little, I don't know how to say this, smart for you. I don't mean that you wouldn't understand them; that's not it. You're probably just too establishment."

"Establishment?" I asked. "You're an Eagle Scout."

"All kinds of people are Scouts," he said. Then he took a pause to think about it. "And we generally care about those around us, unlike those jackasses who only sing about beer or cars or girls. The Clap are socially conscious. They're outsiders. Sally's songs are important and vital."

"And you relate to them?" I had no idea what he was trying to tell me.

"I'm from bumfuck Maine, and I spend my days on a million-dollar yacht or, at worst, a fifty-grand sport boat. I'm wintering in St Thomas. For months at a time, I'm the only one around who doesn't have a stockbroker and a trust fund, other than your boy Trout or Tracey. I don't know anyone around here who thinks about the things that I do or at the level that I see them. How regular people live and survive in this world. The Clap cares about that, as a band."

"What are you talking about?"

"Let me put it this way," he said. "You saw Sally?" He waited for me to nod. "She's lovely, isn't she?"

That was not my impression of her. Of course, I hadn't seen her at her best, nor had I become entranced by her music.

"I didn't meet her in the best of circumstances," I said, "as can be expected when one wakes up in a friend's house and finds out that he's dead."

His eyes darted back to my face.

"You had a thing for her," I said.

He took a deep breath. "Not like you're thinking."

"Explain."

"If you want to understand what she's about, go over to my place. You can borrow my records. It might be good for you." He exhaled and shook his head. "The point I was trying to get at before you went off track was that she was a real person. Not a privileged fuck like Alex or Abby, and that was even though she was famous."

If he were trying to deflect suspicion from himself, he was clueless. A love triangle, even if only based on desire, was trouble. Especially with one of the parties being a dismissive prick.

"If you weren't hitting on her, what were you doing?"

"Before we got on the Mako, she asked about the *Steadfast*. It is practically a work of art. I showed her the boat, and she thought it was beautiful. When I mentioned that her boyfriend didn't really appreciate it, she corrected me."

"Where was Alex?"

"He'd run back up to the house to grab some beer. He'd decided that he wanted me to give them a tour of the coast before I dropped them at the Dockside. And that couldn't be managed without his usual Heineken supply."

"Did you mention to her that you were a fan?"

"Of course."

"And you weren't fawning all over her?"

"You sound like fucking Alex. It wasn't like that. I try to be professional. If she hadn't been talkative and willing to answer questions about the music, I wouldn't have gotten into it. The stiffs I show around for Secretary Grimes don't interest me. I don't care if some guy owns a chain of banks or has a monopoly on meat packing in Kansas. She was the first person to come through there that I was glad to meet. And you know how that turned out."

"What happened when Alex came down to your apartment?"

Riley sighed and rolled his shoulders.

"I don't think you know the level of embarrassment Alex and Abby enjoy dishing out. You can ask Trout or Tracey if you don't believe me."

"I will." I'd been on the receiving end myself this week.

"He stood outside on the walkway and screamed for me to 'Get my ass out of that fucking shack and get down there.' And he kept yelling until I came down."

"What were you doing?"

"I told you, going to bed and listening to music."

"Do you think he heard it?"

"Probably."

"What happened after that?"

"He called me a pathetic asshole and said that I was lucky that he wasn't going to kick my ass—which is a complete fucking joke—and that I'd be lucky to have a job when I woke up in the morning."

"And you told Salazar that?" Information he hadn't seen fit to mention to me and that didn't help his cause.

He nodded. "She had sensed that something had gone on between us. But I thought she'd see that from my perspective, it wasn't a big deal. Alex had threatened my job plenty of times, especially if I told him 'no.' His father wouldn't listen to him, ever. He knew he was a pain. He'd told me never to worry about Alex. That I worked for him. I told Salazar that, too. Alex coming down and pitching a fit wasn't the big deal you think it is. Your eyes are bulging out of your head."

"So, what did you do?" It was a big deal: head-to-head conflict, which looked like it led to hand-to-hand combat.

"I told him to stand still. Then I went down to the Hinckley and got the brass boat hook. Then, I asked him to move over to the bait station. Then I stood on a stool and cracked him over the head with it. Then, instead of loading him into the kayak and attaching him to one of the eight anchors we have in the boathouse and taking him out to Harper's Shoals, where it's two-fifty deep on the lee side, I just went over to the end of the dock and pitched him into the outgoing tide. Oh yeah, and then I tossed the boat hook into the water on the other side of the Mako. Because I'm a complete fucking moron." He held up his hands as if he were giving up.

He had a point. But it didn't mean anything.

"People lose their shit every day," I said. "They do dumb things and then compound them with panic."

"Why would I lose it over Alex? I never cared a gnat's balls about him."

"Because he dressed you down and embarrassed you in front of a woman you wanted to impress."

Riley frowned and shook his head. "I had no illusions that she'd have any interest in a guy like me."

"You're telling me that his actions didn't bother you more than usual, even with Strummer there to see them?"

He sucked air in through his teeth, then exhaled. "They did, for sure. But not enough to do what you people think."

There are signs you can look for that indicate when someone's lying. Their appendages, away from their body, will move. They will adjust their base. Their hands will touch other parts of their bodies. But in telling me this, Riley had remained still and looked me in the eye. If he wasn't exactly comfortable, he did not appear stressed.

"What did you do when he was down there yelling at you?"

"I told him to shut the fuck up and go to bed."

"How did he take that?"

"That's when he said that he'd have my job."

"That didn't piss you off?"

"Please. I turned to go back inside. Then he threatened to kick my ass. I laughed and went in, locking the door behind me so he couldn't follow and I wouldn't have to throw him in the cove."

"You considered that?"

"If he tried to put his hands on me, I would have had to do something. But you know him. All bluster. He didn't have the guts to throw a punch."

"You realize that if he had come after you, it would be easy to explain that you were forced to defend yourself. Maybe you tossed him in to cool him off, and his head accidentally clipped one of the boats."

"I'm sure they've checked everything with a fine-tooth comb. There's nothing to find. Because that's not what happened. And, anyway, I wouldn't have chanced damaging the Mako, never mind the *Steadfast*." He stared across at me. "That was a joke."

"Not funny," I said, though I'd had to stop myself from grinning.

"I'm trying to be honest here, and all you're doing is twisting what I'm telling you into a story that makes me look guilty. That's police work?"

"I bet you were pretty steamed when you went in."

"Sure I was."

"And you went right to sleep?"

"I did."

"When I have something bothering me, I don't nod off as soon as my head hits the pillow. Someone threatening my job might be one of those things that would keep me up."

"I don't have that problem," he said. "I sleep like a rock." His feet were shuffling, and his right hand went from his thigh to adjust his collar, then ran through the bangs on his forehead. That was the kind of movement that indicated what he was saying was making him uncomfortable.

"You went to bed. What did Alex do?"

"I don't know. That's the question, isn't it?"

"Was anyone else around to see this?"

"Who would be?"

"You didn't look out the window to see if he went back to the house?"

"He didn't have the stones to come in after me, and I'd locked the door, remember?"

"You didn't check?"

"No. I assume he went home. But I don't know."

"Were there lights on across the way?"

"I don't remember, honestly," he said.

"And this is what you told Marshal Salazar?"

"It is."

"You didn't hear anything after he left?"

"No. Like I said, I went to sleep."

"That's a lie," I said, only to prod him. He repositioned his feet and slid further back, straightening up in the chair. The statement had bothered him. He would have heard something had someone else come to the Compound. But he'd claimed that he hadn't, even when doing so would have helped his case by creating another potential assailant.

"No, it isn't." He wasn't taking the bait.

"What if Abby and her friend called you for a ride after that?"

"I don't sleep so well that a phone won't wake me up. But I didn't have to worry about it. Her boyfriend didn't drink."

"Did you hear them come home later?"

"No. I must have been asleep."

"You have no idea what Alex did after he threatened you?"

"Why do you put it like that? He couldn't do anything to me. Secretary Grimes had made it clear that Alex wasn't anyone that I needed to worry about. He was an idiot. He could have gone back into town. He could have fallen off the rock where he smoked his dope. That's what Mr. Grimes thought until that marshal started railroading me."

"Who else was at the house that night?"

"I don't know who was up there, other than Sally and Secretary and Mrs. Grimes. They don't keep me abreast of guests unless I'm expected to take them out on the boat."

"Did Alex ever have late-night visitors?"

"I'm sure he did."

"Who would that be?"

"You know Torch. He came by every now and then. Alex used to hang out with some assholes from Ogunquit. People he knew from college or Washington."

We'd busted Torch Harrison for dealing pot a few times. We'd caught him once with a bale in his trunk that he'd try to tell us was alfalfa. Reportedly, he'd cleaned up and was washing dishes at Allie's Restaurant. I'm sure that didn't preclude him from dropping off a bag to a former client.

"But you wouldn't know if any of them came by that night?"

"I don't."

"And how do you think that hook got into the cove?"

"I didn't put it there. The last time I saw it, it was on the Hinckley."

Of course. What else would he say?

"If Alex did come at you and you were forced to protect yourself, Freeman could plea you down to something like involuntary manslaughter. No one would blame you for protecting yourself, especially with Alex pushing you. A jury here would understand."

"That's all well and good, but it's not what happened."

"You know you're the only twenty-five-year-old in the state who claims to go to bed early on a Saturday night in the summer."

"Apparently," he said, "there are worse things happening after nine-thirty than sleeping."

"You're not offering a lot of help for yourself."

He shrugged, but his voice rose. "I've been honest the whole time—or at least tried to be. I didn't kill him. I shouldn't have to worry about getting convicted. I shouldn't be in jail. But here I am."

I sighed. I must have shaken my head, because he sat up in his chair.

"You think I did it, don't you, Coach?"

"Do you know that the most obvious answer to a question is usually correct? And if the question is who is most likely to have killed Alex Grimes, that would be the person whom he had a disagreement with, who had access to the murder weapon, who was the last one to see him, and who had been constantly demeaned and humiliated by him in front of someone he'd wanted to impress. Maybe you were pushed further than you'd ever been pushed. You weren't thinking straight. It's understandable."

"That would be a tough one," he said, "if half of your assumptions weren't wrong. A dope like Alex was never of consequence enough to push my buttons, Sally or no Sally. She probably saw through him, like looking through a window. And I wasn't the last one to see him. Whoever killed him was, if he didn't manage to do it to himself, which is definitely possible. The most critical part of your supposition is wrong: I didn't kill him. How many times do I have to say it?"

"That's what Scooter has been telling me."

"He doesn't even know who I am, but he's right about that."

"Who do you think did it, if you didn't?"

"How should I know?"

"What about Sally?"

"She could barely speak and couldn't even stand. I wouldn't look there."

"You're with Alex up until the last; you live fifty yards away. And you've got no ideas?"

"I don't. He doesn't live there. He only visits."

"That's not helping your case."

"I'm only telling the truth. It's your job to find out who killed Alex, not mine."

"They took me off the case. It's in Marshal Salazar's hands."

"She's got it wrong."

"You're not doing anything to help yourself."

"I'm being honest."

"You left things out, talking to me."

"I'm sorry," he said, shaking his head. "It was a mistake. I should have known better. I thought you'd screw it up. I was wrong, okay?"

I'd never thought of myself as overly intelligent, but I wasn't the simpleton that Riley considered me. He was right in that if he'd told me about Alex coming down to the boathouse, I would've gone hard on that, just as Salazar had. And it would've been the right thing to do. Maybe Riley wasn't as sharp as he thought he was. His sitting behind bars gave that impression. But I knew differently.

"If you had killed Alex," I said, "you would admit it?"

He looked down and then up at me. "Yes."

Easy to say.

"And this is one of those times I'm supposed to believe you?" I cocked my head.

"I'm innocent. Someone needs to realize it and do something."

"The evidence suggests otherwise."

A shadow crossed his face. His mouth tensed at its corners and clamped shut. "If you're off the case, then what are you doing here?"

"I want to know for myself."

"So, you're not helping Marshal Salazar?"

"She wouldn't let me if I wanted to. This was deemed too big for me from the start."

"You can help me, then?"

"That's not exactly my job, either. And, as you pointed out, I'm just a guy. I don't know what you could expect from me."

"You have to know that I didn't do this." He looked at me, mouth open. "Jesus, Coach. Find out who did. Please."

He heaved a deep breath. His bottom lip quivered. I sighed.

"I'll see if there's anything I can do," I said. Then I called for the guard.

In a town like Laurel, I'd come across plenty of people who would lie their ass off just to escape a speeding ticket. Here, Riley could have said plenty to cast doubt on himself, but he wasn't voicing any of it. Instead, anytime he opened his mouth with his version of the truth, it only worked against him. He also refused to consider framing Alex's death as a result of having to defend himself, solid footing for a lesser charge or perhaps acquittal. None of this meant he was innocent. But it left me with questions. The least I could do was bring them to Salazar. And maybe try to answer a few on my own.

Chapter Twenty-Three

"Really, the Clap?" he said, eyeing me as if I were the one wearing a blue mohawk, flannel shirt with cutoff sleeves, and leather pants. Apparently, a uniformed police officer asking for a punk album deserved suspicion. It used to be that we elicited trust. "Did you miss the new Journey release over there?"

"I'm trying to expand my musical horizons," I said. "You listen to them?"

He stopped punching numbers into his register. His eyebrows raised. I'd asked a dumb question.

"What do you think?" I asked.

"They're one of the only American bands that matter," he said. His sour expression lifted in a moment of conscience, as I was buying music that he thought highly of. Maybe I wasn't the moron that my uniform indicated.

"They only had one hit, from what I've heard," I said.

"Their dumbest song, too." His eyes rolled. "If you're looking for "Green Jello Girl" it's not on this cassette. That's the *Young Republicans* album. Is that the one you want?"

"I was told this one is better." I'd recognized the cover from Salazar's description of what was on Riley's turntable.

"They should be so much bigger than they are." A disgusted look crossed his face. "The hordes who are listening to Styx and Foreigner are wasting their money."

"Who is into this band, then?"

"You might be the only cop in the country," he said. "They don't have a high opinion of the status quo and our institutions." He paused as he slipped the cassette into a bright orange bag. "Bonus, the lead singer is hot as hell."

"Is that why they were on MTV?"

"Unfortunately, yes. The average caveman can handle a moderate amount of wit and intelligence in lyrics if they can see a blonde chick in a bikini in Jello. Unfortunately, not enough people bothered to buy the freaking album, and less probably listened to the words."

I thanked him and started out to the Bronco, then stopped. The remark that Alex had dropped on Riley popped into my head, and this guy had a grip on the culture that eluded me. I returned to the register. "Have you ever heard of someone called George Eastman?"

His face scrunched in thought.

"Do you mean Montgomery Clift's character in *A Place in the Sun*, which is based on *An American Tragedy*? We do have movies." He pointed to the back wall, which consisted of shelves of VHS tapes.

"Do you have that one?" I wondered how many more references would be made that I didn't get.

"Unfortunately not," he said. "I could order it for you. We should carry it. It's a classic."

"What's it about?"

"Let me give the Montgomery Clift's notes version," he said.

"I get it. The guy from *Red River*." I did know my Westerns.

He nodded. "It's like this: Working class stiff gets a job in his long-lost relative's factory. Rises through hard work. Gets a girlfriend and knocks her up, that's Shelley Winters. Then, he falls in love with Elizabeth Taylor, the factory owner's daughter. And who can blame him? Then, he accidentally kills Shelley Winters and loses it all. He gets the electric chair."

"Sounds like a good time," I said. It hit the mark. To Alex, the actor, Sally Strummer would be Liz Taylor, and that would make Stevens Montgomery Clift.

"It's outstanding class commentary," he said, flipping his mohawk, "while at the same time being entertaining as hell. Brilliant writing and acting."

I thanked him and headed for home with the Clap in my cassette deck. The drums sounded like synchronized M-80s. Then the guitars came in. They buzzed like tuned-up electric razors. When Sally's voice emerged, it was a throaty roar with a deep resonance that contrasted with the chaos behind it. It grabbed you and brought you in. The small girl had a big presence, and it powered through the wind buffeting the cab. You could hear the lyrics, and I—despite being a Bob Seger and Rolling Stones listener—agreed they were good. Bullet-Head Rock ridiculed oversized college football players. Poseur Posse skewered wanna-be musicians who worked at record stores. I could relate to that one. Pleistocene Beach humorously claimed that we hadn't evolved beyond shellfish, another hard-to-argue point. The best song was Boo Boo Kat, about a boyfriend whose major attributes—the ability to procure cocaine and letting the singer drive his Porsche—outweighed a lack of competency in the bedroom. The songs were funny, but they had a bite. I got it. The last track was a Who cover, a song I knew, "The Real Me." But instead of Roger Daltrey's anger, there was a level of quiet desperation. I wondered if that was the one that Riley related to most. He'd claimed that Scooter didn't know him, and he didn't deny that he was different from the rest of his family. Whether that made him someone who would bash another person's head in and not let it bother him, or someone who truly believed that his innocence would speak for itself, remained to be seen.

Chapter Twenty-Four

I called Trout at the Compound when I got back. He didn't sound happy.

"What do you want?" he said.

"I just talked to Riley Stevens."

"Now, why would you do that?"

"As a favor to his brother."

He laughed. "I heard you broke out one of your championship moves on him. Salazar was impressed."

"Could have fooled me," I said.

"You ain't letting him out, are you?"

"Not yet."

"Salazar will kick your ass from here to Cuba." He laughed. "She's stuck in Laurel until Riley's locked up for good, and I don't think she's thrilled about it. Why are you doing Scooter a favor?"

"The family is hurting," I said.

"That family? You want hurting, come over here. Violet hasn't left her room for days, and she's got Tracey running bottles of wine up there nonstop. Randolph's buried himself in his office. Abby couldn't stop crying, and then two days ago, she just took off. They can't find her anywhere, and they're spreading Alex's ashes at sea tomorrow. It was his wish, I guess. So I don't want to hear no sob story about that idiot Stevens clan."

"They got Alex's body released already?" My mind had stopped at ashes.

"Everyone around here's got a great deal of respect for the Grimes, it seems, except for you."

"I don't think that's the case," I said.

"What did you want?" he said. I could picture Trout patting down the tufts of hair over his ears, which he did when he got anxious. He was in his office over the garage. The wheels on his desk chair squeaked as he rocked.

"I have some thoughts I'd like to run by Marshal Salazar."

"About what?"

"What if Riley didn't do it? There are things that don't add up."

"Don't even go there. I hope you're not buying that Eagle Scout bullshit. It's no different than that Father Gregory and the altar boys up in Waterville."

"Where can I get a hold of her?"

"No way. You want me to lose my job?"

"Then why don't you come over tonight, and I'll run my doubts by you? You can judge for yourself and tell me how wrong I am."

"You don't keep your beer cold enough for me to sit through that."

"I'll buy some ice," I said.

"You couldn't get me there if you brought down the whole North Pole," he said, then hung up.

Chapter Twenty-Five

I tried to watch the Red Sox game on television that night. Naturally, I couldn't enjoy it. My mind kept returning to Alex Grimes, Riley Stevens, and Marshal Salazar. On the surface, I could not deny that Stevens was a likely suspect. He had opportunity. He and Alex had been together, and he'd been the last person to admit seeing him alive. He had motive, after being badgered and humiliated by the victim. He'd confessed that there'd been some sort of altercation. His fingerprints were on the murder weapon. And if one wanted to go into psychology, his calmness in the face of these accusations was eerily odd. I couldn't see where Salazar had made an obvious error. But the more I considered the flaws that Riley Stevens had pointed out in her narrative, the pricklier they became.

This didn't come from my gut or Scooter Stevens's blind faith, but from simple logic. It was hard to believe that Riley would have told Salazar about Alex marching down to berate him, if it had led to a fight that resulted in his death. When I first interviewed him, he didn't even tell me it had happened. However, by the time he spoke to Salazar, he'd had time to think through what that admission would mean in an investigation. Still, it came forward. That was either complete honesty or incredible stupidity, and I didn't think Riley was oblivious. Other things bothered me, as well. I tried to think of how best to present this to Salazar. I couldn't have her reaction be an uncontrollable urge to pistol-whip me. I didn't even know the score of the ballgame when the phone rang.

Abby Grimes had returned for her brother's service. Unfortunately, she hadn't made it past the Dockside. That was another problem.

Chapter Twenty-Six

The tiki lights at the water's edge cast a hazy glow over the empty deck. Chair legs reached for the sky, set upside down on tables, waiting for the planks beneath them to be hosed down. Chelsea waved from behind the bar. Behind her, Abby Grimes sat with a drink. Her head was down. She stared into her vodka or gin or whatever was in the glass, as if it would soon reveal secrets like a crystal ball.

"Even if she were willing to leave," Chelsea said, bouncing a bank bag against her thigh, "she shouldn't be driving." Chelsea shook her head and made a circle with her index finger next to her ear, the international sign for crazy. "She shouldn't even be talking."

I skirted around and pulled up just short of Abby. Her eyes didn't leave the glass.

"How's it going, Abby?" I said, giving my voice a light, hopefully, unofficial-sounding tone.

She looked up and tried to focus. "Oh, it's you," she said, then returned to her cocktail.

"Can I give you a lift home?" I asked.

"I don't think so. I'm not done drinking."

"The bar's closed, Abby. Why don't we call it a night?"

"Don't you have some pull around here?" She released a smile from the hair that fell about her face. Her dark blue eyes had a watery sheen. I assumed that losing her brother had taken a toll, one she was still paying.

"I'm on duty," I said, hoping she wouldn't place my jeans and t-shirt.

"I didn't think that mattered to you."

"Come on," I said. "Up and at 'em. I'll get you to the Compound. I can have one of my guys get your car later."

"Tell the girl to get me another Absolut and tonic, and I'll consider it."

The girl was almost her age and had been waiting on her for years. From the scowl on her face, Chelsea didn't like the term any more than I did.

"They're closed," I said, giving Chelsea a sympathetic look.

"But you can do anything you want. You're a big man in Laurel, so to speak." She laughed at her own joke.

"That's not how it works," I said.

She looked at me as if I were a ghost and she was having a hard time believing I was there.

"You're not in uniform," she said. "You can have one."

"Her brother's service is tomorrow," I said quietly to Chelsea as a way of trying to explain this behavior and my tolerance for it.

"This is G-Two at her finest," Chelsea said, shaking her head. "If it will get her the fuck out of here, I'll give you both one."

Abby cocked her head. That hadn't gotten by her. She slapped her hand on the bar. I don't know how they put up with this on a regular basis. In my younger days as a bartender, I couldn't have taken it. I'd have had her by the collar and the belt, and she'd have been pitched into the river. And I'd probably have had to go in after her. Chelsea poured a beer for me in a coffee mug and made a weak drink for Abby. She slid them in front of us. I told her she could lock up and call it a night, that I'd put the glasses behind the bar. If there wasn't a bartender present, Abby couldn't ask for another drink.

"Thanks for coming, LT," Chelsea said, giving me a shrug as she strode toward the main restaurant. "Good luck to you."

I took a deep breath and took the stool next to Abby.

"You're upset about Alex," I said.

She looked over, snarled, and sipped her drink.

"It must be tough to lose someone you were so close to."

"You didn't like him," she said.

"He was okay. I didn't really know him." She was right, but I wasn't about to get into it. Honesty was not always the best policy.

"He was a spoiled asshole," she said.

I shrugged. Correct again. She was doing well for someone so shitfaced.

"It's okay. I'm one, too. Though at times, I do try not to be."

"You could try harder," I said, stopping short of pointing out her treatment of Chelsea.

Her head snapped toward me. Her eyes got big, and she was pretty when she smiled, even as the lid of her left eye became lazy and slid down into her pupil—a result of her drunkenness. She chuckled.

"I blame genetics," she said, waving her hands to encompass the world around her. "For all of this."

"An easy target." I saw no reason that she couldn't handle a bit of truth. I was not going to let her think that this stunt was something to be repeated. Even with a dead brother.

"It always starts with the parents," she said. "Haven't you taken a fucking biology glass—I mean class?"

"I have. But I don't recall parenting coming up with the fruit flies and frogs."

"Well then," she said, straightening up. "Maybe you should see an analyst and let them tell you. It's always the parents. But they probably don't even have shrinks up here."

"Maybe we don't have the need."

"Let me enlighten you." She leaned forward into me. I slid my stool back before she fell into my lap. "My father, as I'm sure you know, is a raging donkey. You've seen that, have you not?"

"I can't say that I have. I've seen him donate his time to provide us with a speech every Fourth of July that many people appreciate. And anytime he's out in town, he and your mother are always gracious."

"That's a fucking show, you gullible moron," she said, giggling and reaching out to my shoulder to steady herself. "Jesus Christ."

"Well, he is a politician," I said, thinking that maybe humoring her might get us out of here before sunrise. "That's his trade."

"Maybe you're not so dumb," she said, smiling. "But you're wrong if you think it's harmless."

"Are you sure you want to spill family secrets?" I took a drink, unsure of what she meant and positive I did not want to hear it. Until this week, Randolph Grimes had only shown respect to me and the people of Laurel.

"Ha. The only difference between us and every other fucked up family is that we have a shit ton of money. You can't put on a show without a backer." She laughed even louder.

"If you say so."

"Then there's my mother. She's a drunk. Did you know that?"

"I did not." Violet Grimes looked at least ten years younger than she was. Her family was related to the Remingtons and involved in firearm manufacturing. As a result, she'd taken to target shooting and was rumored to have received an invitation to try out for the 1968 Olympic team— comprised of men at the time. In an only slightly poorly lit room, one could have ridden the cliche and asked if she and Abby were sisters. I was beginning to think that Abby was toying with me for sport.

"Let's call it a night," I said.

She ignored me.

"It's nothing to be ashamed of," she said. "Or I'd have to be disappointed with myself, and that's not healthy."

"I'll take your word for it."

"Well, thank you Officer Friendly." She took a long pull on her straw. The liquid hit the midpoint of the highball glass. "Old Violet hasn't made it an hour past dinner this entire summer. Maybe that's because she starts her Napa Valley tour at lunch. 'It's only wine,' she says. She was a drinking buddy of Betty Ford, you know. Not even kidding."

I sat back and took a hit of my beer. This information made sense, regarding Alex's death. It explained why Violet would have been useless as a witness, as well as something Randolph wished to keep hidden. Trout could likely verify, if there was a need.

"And then there's my brother," she said. "The reason that we're all here." She wasn't gone enough to miss my eyes focusing on her. "Oh, that's of interest to you."

"What about him?" I asked.

"He's a brat. Let's start there. You know all about that from his not-a-DWI that Father pried him loose from." She laughed and shook her head. "Not entirely unrelated, he was also a gigantic pussy. In every aspect of his life. Finally, he stands up and does something, even if it was over that tramp, and it gets him killed. The Short Happy Life of Francis the fucking Mule."

"Excuse me?" I had no idea what this had to do with a talking movie donkey.

"Oh, never mind. He was not too happy about Captain Steubing trying to run a Love Boat into his singer. Alex has been whipped on that girl since Brown. You should have seen him at lunch. He was giving her so much shit about Stevens, you'd think that she'd blown him. I think he was actually hurt."

Some might have found this to be an ethical dilemma. Here was a potential witness who knew more of her brother's death than she realized. But she was only communicating it because she didn't know that I cared. I wasn't inclined to stop her, however. It did seem to be helping her, getting these things off her chest. And I'd be returning her home safely. Questionable arguments, for sure.

"Does it make sense to you," I said, "that Alex went down to the boathouse to have it out with Riley Stevens?"

"I don't know," she said, slurping her drink. "I can't picture him taking a swing at someone, even someone as basic as Stevens. That's not who he was. He could bitch for hours or slice and dice you with that mouth of his. Alex was world-class at that. He probably dressed that jackass up, down, and sideways. But I doubt he'd throw a punch."

"Could he have been vicious enough to make Riley Stevens snap?"

"Sure, but that depends on Stevens, doesn't it?"

"What do you think of him?"

"I haven't fucked him, if that's what you're asking."

"I wasn't," I said.

"Then I'll say this. He is a bit of a hunk, but so, so, so boring. Other than kissing my father's ass, all he cared about were those fucking boats. Have you seen me in a bikini? He's never looked twice."

She got up and spun around, her hair flowing like in a beer commercial. She was lean and fit in white painter's pants and a sleeveless black top. Her features had straight, clean lines, unlike her rounded brother. Reportedly, no one at the Abenaki Club could touch her on the tennis court. She steadied herself by grabbing the back of her barstool and slid back onto it. It was easy to imagine the heat she'd generate in a swimsuit.

"Maybe Riley Stevens didn't want to do anything that would complicate his job."

"Let me tell you," she said, dipping her head, "it would have been worth it."

"Don't you have a boyfriend?"

"Debatable. Ranford tries to fuck every nineteen-year-old that sneaks into his clubs, especially the blondes. He thinks I'm unaware, which I am certainly not. What you give is what you get."

"Could your brother have been upset about him treating you like that?"

She bellowed a string of laughter that required her to support herself by grabbing the bar. "It's every man for himself in our house."

She paused and took another draw from her cocktail, now down to a quarter.

"You know," she said, "who my brother should have taken his frustration out on, don't you?"

I shook my head.

"Our dear father," she said, laughing. "He started fucking up Alex when he was a kid and never stopped."

"What do you mean?"

"You've seen my brother? He's not gifted in the ways of the athlete, like the rest of us, including my mother, a most graceful and coordinated alcoholic. Alex couldn't hit a ball, whether it was lobbed at him underhand or placed on a tee. He'd rather cut his dick off than get on a tennis court. Hated guns. Throws like a girl. You name it."

She paused to take a drink.

"I have no actual useful skills," she said. "I'm not quite beautiful enough to trade on looks, nor am I smart enough to get by on brains. I slap my shit together and get by, even if it doesn't leave me thinking too highly of myself. But my brother. He was an artist. Full of useless passion. He could paint. He could draw. Watch a movie with him, and he's pointing out camera angles and shadows and what they mean and how the director is trying to do this and say that. He was a damn fine actor. I saw his college plays. He would've had as good a chance as anyone to make it. But my father was on a mission to stomp that out of him. It wasn't a career for a Grimes, he said. Can you imagine telling a ten-year-old that his drawings were worthless? Or that being in a play was a waste of time? Or that the girl you've pined over for the last eight years was a mutt who looked like an Irish terrier? Because that happened last weekend. That is my father. I couldn't hit a tennis ball well enough to make All-American. That only brought disappointment. But my brother faced open hostility, just for trying to make the most of what talent he had. And the great Randolph beat it out of him. Alex hated that fucking job he had in D.C. But it was business, the family heritage. You think that might fuck you up? Do you?"

"And this frustration got aimed at Riley Stevens?"

"My father may have been the original catalyst that started this, but it wasn't my brother who killed Stevens. It was Stevens who killed him. Don't you fucking forget that."

"Sorry," I said. The frustrations that spilled out on Riley stemmed from more than Sally. Maybe to the point that Alex had gotten physical, despite what Abby thought. It could have been that Riley was defending himself. Which he also denied. My mind was chasing its tail.

"Alex never talked to your father about wanting to quit his job?"

"Of course not. He whined to me about it, and to Sally, of course. Maybe even to my mother. He would have liked to burn that think tank down. But he didn't have it in him to take it to Randolph."

I shook my head.

"Your father is one of the most reasonable men I've ever met," I said. This was true, even considering his requests once we'd found Alex's body.

"Try living with him." Abby gathered herself. "Did the great Randolph Grimes shed a tear when you showed him my brother's dead body?"

"He took it quite hard from what I could see," I said.

"That's not what I asked you."

"No, he didn't cry."

"I bet he thought that Alex had brought this on himself."

She was right about that. Of course, none of this pointed me to an alternate suspect. As Abby had just reminded me, it wasn't Alex who had clubbed Riley. He was the victim.

"Could anyone else have been at the Compound that night, other than you and your family? Did Alex ever have friends over?"

"That freak from town with the ZZ Top beard used to come by, and my brother knew some douchebags from Ogunquit who occasionally visited, more dreadful Brown people. But I haven't seen them for years. Thankfully. And if Alex had anything planned, he never mentioned it. Ranford and I didn't return until one. And it was quiet. I hate it here." She sat bolt upright. "You're questioning me."

"I'm just trying to understand what happened."

"I was beginning to think you were okay," she said, slapping her palm on the bar. "But you're just another lying creep."

Nailed. I shrugged.

"You're not quite as dopey as you look," she said.

"I'll take that as a compliment," I said.

"Stevens killed Alex. I loved my brother, but—and it sickens me to say it—he might have ridden that jerk too far. The thing is, what brought Alex to this didn't start with Stevens making eyes at Sally fucking Strummer. It started a long time ago, and the real tragedy is that guilt isn't an emotion my father possesses. Because he'd be drowning in it."

I didn't know what to say. That Randolph was not what he seemed in public shouldn't have surprised me. He was a politician, and even the selectmen who ran our little town were not immune from posturing and putting on airs. With his position, Randolph was someone who had reason to protect his reputation. Maybe I'd caught a glimpse of Abby's Randolph when he'd tried to influence my investigation. My father had taken a different approach in raising me. While he'd been disappointed that I didn't want to take over his tourist store downtown, he'd conspired with Chief Dederian to get me to consider a position on the force.

Abby raised her head and looked me in the eye. "Are you really trying to understand or are you trying to get Stevens out of it? We know he's one of your own."

"I'm covering my bases." She had tagged me again, but only to a point.

"That sounds like bullshit," she said. "If you've learned anything, it should be that people are all the same. Everyone only wants to cover their ass. Randolph, you, that bitch of a marshal. I only wish that my brother had taken it out on our father instead of his lackey. The old man would have lost his shit, which would have been entertaining as hell, and, more importantly, my brother would still be alive."

I didn't know what to say. I wasn't sure I could believe everything she'd told me. Until this week, her father had been nothing but gracious, a fishing buddy of my father, a regular guy even if he ran half the businesses in Connecticut. If all that had been a show, it wouldn't be hard to determine where Alex got his acting talent.

"I'm sorry," I said.

"Of course you are," Abby said. "You and every other stiff think Randolph is a few lucky breaks from Mount Rushmore. But you haven't seen him in action. Not really. He's the fucking Wizard of Oz, the small man behind the big curtain. Why don't you ask me why I never had friends from college visit? Because it would make me sick the way he'd parade around in a smoking jacket like he was Rock Hudson, acting as if they were dying to fuck him. Pathetic. I wasn't afraid to call him out on it. Of course, he denied it, and I got put on the shit list. It's no wonder my mother drinks."

She sucked the last drops out of her cocktail. My eyes must have gotten big.

"You think I'm making this up. Don't be an idiot. If you take me to the Tavern for last call, I'll keep talking. I'll give you some real stories."

"Sure," I said. "Let's go."

I took her glass and mine and stowed them in the sink behind the bar. I walked behind her as we moved to the parking lot. She swayed more than one should, though short of looking ready to topple.

"You know I don't do civil servants, if that's where you think this is going," she said, climbing into the Bronco. She smiled as we pulled out of the parking lot. "I just need another drink."

"That's okay," I said. "I've never considered myself to be in the Rock Hudson category."

She laughed and reached over to touch my shoulder. I turned right onto River Road, away from the Tavern and toward the Compound. She shook her head.

"Dick," she said. "I should have known."

She was out cold in less than a half mile.

Chapter Twenty-Seven

The spotlights over the boathouse were just bright enough to get fractured in the fog. The Mako and Hinckley were ghost ships. Yellow smudges in the white mist marked the entrance of the main house. Outlines of luxury sedans crowded the driveway in front of the garage. Friends and family, I guessed. I parked at the head of the cobblestone walkway. I didn't think throwing Abby over my shoulder and ringing the doorbell would be great for either of us. She'd be the second woman returning here like that in a week, and it hadn't worked out the first time. I left her belted in my passenger seat. Her head rested on one of my sweatshirts pressed against the window. The drool wouldn't hurt it much. No harm would come to Abby, either.

Tracey answered my knock, a scowl on her face. She was in an actual maid uniform, black with a white apron. I reserved comment and asked for Trout. His pickup had been parked at the guard shack.

"In regards to?" she asked.

"Go get him."

While she stomped off, I listened for the signs of activity: footsteps, ice clinking in glasses, conversation. There was nothing. I hadn't believed the early night on the evening Alex had died, and I wasn't buying it now. If I were them, I wouldn't be in a hurry to get to tomorrow when I'd be tossing my son's ashes into the ocean he'd been found in.

Trout was shaking his head and appropriating Tracey's scowl when he appeared at the door.

"No, LT," he said, straining to keep his voice from rising. "Not tonight, goddamn it."

"Calm down, Nate. Abby's passed out in the Bronco. I just grabbed her from the Dockside."

"You? The whole federal government's out looking for her."

"Those geniuses should have tried a bar."

"Thank you," he said, exhaling and sounding like he meant it.

He followed me to the truck. He stopped short when he saw her snoozing.

"What does it look like inside?" I asked, nodding to the house. I hoped Trout could carry her through the kitchen and up to her room without anyone noticing.

"The old man is up. The relatives just went to their rooms. How bad is she?"

"Overwrought, but south of comatose."

Trout opened the door a few inches, hesitating to go further should she tumble out. "Abby?" he whispered. "Miss Grimes?"

"It's going to take more than that," I said. A screen slapped behind us. Trout eased the truck door shut. Randolph Grimes strode toward us, brushing something off the chest of his blue blazer. Tracey must have alerted him. Even this late, his hair was perfectly in place.

"What now, Nichols?" he said, his tone exposing a red line of aggravation. It might have been a timbre Alex had been familiar with.

"It's Abby," Trout said. "She was at the Dockside."

"For chrissakes," Randolph said. He gazed at her, then shifted his look to me. "At least one of them is safe thanks to you."

There was a chance he hadn't meant that as a dig. Still, I wondered how much trouble I'd find myself in if I dropped a high-ranking government official with a right cross.

"Nate, why don't you go in and fetch her cousin Stella to help you with her. She's in the blue bedroom. I'm sure she's awake. I'll let Violet know in a bit."

Nate nodded and jogged off. If Abby had been telling me the truth, Violet Grimes would have long been asleep, which explained why she hadn't been summoned. The Secretary looked down at me, evaluating my refusal to drop his stare.

"You look like you could use a drink," he said. I couldn't tell if it was an insult, a lousy joke, or an offer.

"Tough times," I said, as noncommittally as possible. He nodded.

Trout and a woman who looked Abby's age came out the front door. Her grim smile turned into a dropped jaw when she spotted her cousin.

"Abby, goddamn it," she said. Stella rapped her knuckles on the window. Abby's eyes fluttered open, and her head came off the sweatshirt.

Abby looked at her and rolled down the window. Then Abby's gaze shifted over to me. She giggled. "Stella, quick, it's the cops. Stash the blow." She burst out laughing.

"I don't know what she's talking about," Stella said, turning to me, wide eyed. "She's joking. Obviously."

I stepped between them and opened the door to the Bronco. Abby slid off the seat to solid ground with the style of a gymnast. Not a bit of sway in sticking the landing.

"Nate," the Secretary said, "can you help Stella get her to her room? It's going to be an early morning, whether she likes it or not."

"You bet, sir," he said.

The Secretary turned to me. "Now, let's see about some scotch."

I had no idea what he saw in me as a drinking partner. But I didn't think it was going to be enjoyable, no matter how old the liquor was.

* * *

He led me to his study in the back corner of the house. The red beacon south of the harbor diffused to pink. Somewhere north of there, lost in the fog, was Stage Island. After listening to Abby for the previous hour, I wondered if I'd accepted only for the chance to pick up on the Randolph she'd told me of, the one I was unsure existed. He motioned for me to sit in the leather chair in front of the desk.

"I don't think whiskey is going to cut it," he said. "Do you like cognac, Chief?"

"Sure," I said. He looked me over, eyebrows riding up. I'd surprised him. I had spent time behind a bar and knew my liquor. He poured two snifters from a crystal bottle of Remy Martin that sat on a liquor cart in the corner and handed me one. He leaned back in his seat, carrying the glass to his nose before taking a drink.

"To be honest," he said, "it isn't making a dent."

"Understandable."

"Abby dropped out of sight three days ago, but I knew she'd come back. The weight of this loss has been incomprehensible, as I feared."

I nodded and sucked in the warmth rising from my snifter. He'd failed to recognize that she hadn't made it all the way to the Compound. For a reason. But I didn't see the wisdom in sharing that detail.

"You're an only child," he said, "if I remember correctly."

"That's right."

"You'll never know what it's like to lose a sibling."

"I did lose my parents before their time," I said. "Not that this is a pissing contest."

"Well put." Grimes nodded. "Apple of your father's eye. Goddamn, he was proud. A state champion son."

I took a sip of Remy. It warmed its way to my stomach.

"Alex could have been a champion," he said, gazing into the copper liquid. "If he gave a shit about anything." His eyes landed on my face. I had to say something.

"He probably thought he'd have more time. Like we all do."

Grimes nodded.

"When he was younger, he wished to be an actor," Grimes said. "But this family's business is business. He had a sharp mind. He was doing good work at the Institute."

I nodded. Randolph remained unaware of his son's disdain for his job. Abby was correct when she said the subject hadn't yet been broached.

"We all have our time," I said.

"Until we don't." He poured himself another few ounces and returned the bottle to the cart. "Is this your time, Chief? Doing what you think is right, even when most people don't give a damn. You're one cop of how many hundred in this state, thousands in this country, yet you keep on as if it matters. Is that enough for you?" He swirled the cognac in his snifter. "Or was it that state championship?"

"I've never given it much thought," I said. "I guess I'm day to day."

"Simple," he said, a slight smile crossing his face. "There's some value in that. I don't believe you did peak in high school."

I shrugged.

"I heard how you handled Scooter Stevens the other night. Foolish lunk. He's lucky Marshal Salazar didn't—well, that could have been another body for you."

"Sometimes I think it's my job to just keep things from getting worse."

"You succeeded, at least in that. Even if you did let him loose a few days later."

"His family is suffering, too. No one understands how this happened. Riley was not the kind of person you'd think would end up in something like this, but I don't have to tell you that."

"All of it over that singer, a pint-sized banshee, screaming and shaking her ass in bars for a living. I can't comprehend it. As if she were Ingrid Bergman or Raquel Welch, who I've met, women worthy of such desire. It doesn't make sense that two lives should be ruined. But that's what we're left with."

I took another gulp of brandy. I had no intention of explaining that there was more to this than a conflict over Sally Strummer. He either didn't know or chose to ignore it. I felt as if I was behind enemy lines, waiting to be exposed.

"I have to thank you, Nichols. I wanted you to leave this alone when we first found Alex. Given his history, I was ready to accept that he'd managed to hurt himself. He'd created that aura. But if you'd gone along and I hadn't called in federal assistance, we would have had a murderer in our midst. Who knows what that could have wrought in the future?"

"I've learned to do my job. Whether people like it or not, as you pointed out, can't be a consideration."

"To be honest, I should have known better." Grimes sighed and emptied his snifter in one shot. "I guess we can never really know anyone. I wouldn't have pegged that boy as a morally bankrupt, petty killer. I don't like being fooled, and I was fooled badly."

"You're sure that it was Stevens?" I couldn't help myself.

"Who else could it be?" He put down his drink and gave me the hard stare. "Aren't you the one who first pointed us in his direction?"

"I'd like to be positive, and I'm not quite there yet."

His eyes narrowed. His cheeks flushed red. He breathed through his nose, attempting to quell his anger before responding.

"It is hard to believe, as we've both known the boy. But perhaps you haven't seen all the evidence or been briefed by Marshal Salazar. There can be no doubt."

"It will be hard for you tomorrow," I said. This was not the time or place to air the questions I had. Nor was Randolph Grimes in a position to look at them objectively.

He waved off the thought with one of his big hands.

"Life is hard. You had that case with those girls a few years ago. You found the sisters. And you had to kill that man. Shot him at close range, I heard."

"I had no choice."

"Yes, sometimes circumstances dictate our actions. Does it keep you up at night?"

"It was us or him. I can't say that it does."

"Good for you. I wonder what would have happened if Marshal Salazar had given me the ten minutes with Stevens that I asked for. There might have been no need for a trial."

I nodded. Trout hadn't shared this with me, if he even knew about it.

"Would you like another?" He aimed his eyes at my empty snifter.

"No, thank you," I said. "I better be going."

"Some journeys we make on our own," he said. "I have a long night ahead of me."

"Again, I'm sorry."

"You know the way, Nichols, don't you?" He raised his glass in the direction of the door. I placed mine on his desk and turned, then paused at the threshold.

"Can I ask you a question?" I watched him pour himself another drink. He nodded and swirled it the way people do with wine. "Why didn't you want me looking into it, that Alex's death might not have been an accident?"

"Was I not clear in my appreciation of that? I believe I just thanked you."

After being with Abby, I recognized a politician's answer: a non-answer.

"I'm clear on that. What I don't get is why you didn't want to be sure that's what happened."

He leaned his head back against the dark leather chair, then came forward.

"I wanted to believe that my son's death was an accident. That one of my family could spur another to take his life is not something I wanted to consider. An accident is the universe at work. Otherwise, one has agency. I was hesitant to examine my own. Certainly, you can understand that."

"Thank you," I said, nodding, though I had less than a vague idea of what he meant.

Chapter Twenty-Eight

I wasn't ready to go home. The Rusty Bullet was out of the way behind Cape Laurel Pier and barely larger than a trailer, maybe thirty feet long. It was nearly impossible for a tourist or summer person to stumble in. That's what I liked about it. If I needed a drink to sit and stew over something, it was the place. The lobstermen and laborers there tended to mind their own business. And it was good late at night, because most of the regulars needed to be up early. Even if the place was empty, you could count on Duke never closing before twelve-thirty. He saw me and nodded to empty seats at the end of the bar. Only one of the six booths was occupied. Two guys sat at the other end, near the bathroom. That was it, just about perfect.

I ordered a Bud and settled in. Duke leaned on the back bar across from the door and flipped a quarter, marking down whether he got heads or tails. An anchorman looked serious as he broadcast the eleven o'clock news on the bar's muted, off-color television. Led Zepplin rumbled on the jukebox. I took a breath and tried to concentrate.

I started in again on how to best take my questions to Marshal Salazar. Before I could get anywhere, I found myself circling back to Riley Stevens being the perfect suspect. I was having a hard time arguing with Salazar's conclusions. Meanwhile, the holes in the story that Stevens had exposed wouldn't leave me alone. Halfway through my beer, I didn't know what to think. I ordered a shot of Jack Daniels, hoping that might kick open a pathway in my overloaded brain. Riley had begged me for help, but it seemed that even the best I could do for him would be like pissing into the wind.

I turned, by habit, when I heard the door open. Salazar filled the entrance, looking tall in designer jeans and a white blouse unbuttoned to her navel. This, I told myself, was a sign. Her face was a movie screen: Why's a girl like you thinking about stepping into a shithole like this? I turned back to the bar and watched her in the crusty mirror over the bottles. Her eyes adjusted from the floodlit entrance to the dark interior. Her sweep started left at the bathrooms. She eyed the two men in their green work clothes. Then, her vision settled on me. I waved.

She sighed, making a face as if she had just swallowed a bad oyster. She walked slowly, careful not to touch anything on the way.

"What are you doing here?" I asked.

"I was at another establishment and not really feeling it. This spot was recommended as a good place to get a quiet drink. I don't think the people in this town like me."

"Technically, it is true regarding the drink. Especially if you enjoy the aroma of stale beer and don't mind a little filth."

She shrugged and sat on the stool next to me. I was surprised she didn't first wipe it with a napkin. I waved Duke into action. He moved as if shot with a tranquilizer dart. It could have been that having a stunning woman like Salazar here paralyzed him, but then having any female in the Bullet could have done it.

She looked over at my beer and shot, then up at Duke and his white beard. It retained a few crumbs of what likely had been his dinner.

"I guess getting a cocktail, perhaps a cosmopolitan, would be too much to ask?" she said, smiling at him. I stifled an outbreak of laughter.

"That's right, sugar," Duke said. "You haven't stumbled into the Ritz, just so you know."

"I'll have what he's having," she said. Duke nodded and shuffled to the cooler.

"What the fuck do you people do in this town?" she asked. "I feel like I've been exiled to the Fifties."

"Don't ask me. I'm sitting in our biggest dive, drinking by myself."

"A usual thing?"

"No. Just trying to work something out." I wasn't about to explain that I was alternately questioning and not questioning her investigation.

"So, this," she said, waving her left arm to encompass the entirety of the bar while her face scrunched to communicate disapproval, "is your favorite watering hole?"

"On occasion when I don't want to be bothered."

"Would I be doing that?"

"It depends on what you want."

"Out of this town, and it can't happen fast enough."

"I meant with me."

"This, I can assure you, is an accident. That bitch of a bartender at the Sea Squall sent me here. Quaint, she said. I think she must be a friend of Stevens's brother."

"He's got a lot of them," I said, smiling. "And that's before he threatened you, so his popularity probably went up from there."

She rolled her eyes.

"If Grimes didn't want me hand-holding this case through the grand jury, I'd be long gone. Now I'm stuck. He doesn't trust that clown at the state police to get anything right."

"And he replaced me with him. Because I wasn't sure it was an accident."

Duke put a Bud and a Jack Daniels in front of her.

"You had it right with Riley Stevens." She took a hit off her beer and raised the shot glass for me to toast. It felt good going down, the whiskey, not the irony. "I'll give you that."

"You're sure?" I asked. I was going to share my doubts, but I wasn't blasting through the door with them. "What did you make of Grimes pushing that accidental death scenario?"

"You mean the one that you didn't believe? Which, strangely enough, got me sent here." She laughed. "It's all about the optics."

"You lost me."

"Let me spell it out for you." She sighed. "If it gets out that Alex had an accident, there's no big deal as far as the press goes. It's a simple tragedy.

Anyone could understand. But if Alex was involved in any sort of intrigue, then there's a chance for things to go south and leak out: drugs, violence, whatever. All pieces of meat in election year Washington."

"But if you were Grimes, wouldn't you want to know, without doubt, how your son died?"

"I would. Unless I was more concerned with my Cabinet post being jeopardized."

"You think that's why he called you here?" This was something I'd briefly considered, but it hadn't jibed with the Randolph Grimes that I had known. That was also before I'd heard Abby's description of her father.

"He didn't stop the investigation. He brought in a better investigator. No offense. He accepted my conclusion because it's the only possible result. Whether you would have figured it out is highly questionable."

I must have made a hell of a face, but her point was hard to dispute.

"Grimes didn't trust you on several levels. I can explain, but you might not want to hear it. You decide."

I waved to Duke for another round for us. "Go for it," I said.

"You had the right idea, not buying into the fell-off-the-rocks accident. And you did question Riley Stevens, which put you on the right track. You just didn't carry it through the way you should have. Neither did Wisterman. You didn't find out that they'd had a serious disagreement or that Alex had ridiculed him or that he had a thing for Alex's girlfriend."

"She wasn't his girlfriend."

"A rose by any other name," she said. "It was romantic for Alex. And probably for Stevens, too. That they weren't going at it like a couple of hopped-up monkeys doesn't matter. It was the trigger. The mistake you made was that you didn't go after Stevens hard enough. Maybe because you coached him as a kid. You knew there was reason to, but you saw a twelve-year-old instead of a man. That, my friend, was a fail."

"I didn't know I'd be yanked off the case before I got two hours in."

"You royally fucked up with that reporter, too. Jesus H Christ. Which brings us back to the press. Since I've arrived, you haven't seen anything come out, other than that an arrest has been made. No mention of a romantic triangle, jealousy, a disgruntled employee, nothing. If I fucked this like you did, I could plan on working the airport in Topeka for the rest of my life." She grabbed her new shot and put it down.

She was right. I could have gone harder at Riley. I was wrong thinking I'd said nothing when talking to Sawyer. Salazar had come in and busted the case open in less than twenty-four hours. She was better at her job than I was at mine.

"Don't look so sad, buttercup," she said.

"You're not the one who got shown up on his own turf."

"I'm really good," she said. "At least that's what they say in D.C." She winked.

"I've heard that," I said. "It's all anyone could talk about at the small town chief's convention last year in Wichita."

"I wasn't talking about my investigative skills," she said, smiling.

"Neither were they."

She laughed and put her hand on my shoulder.

"I'm glad you're not taking this personally," she said.

"What makes you think that?"

"You're buying the drinks, aren't you?"

"That's just professional courtesy."

"I don't miss much. You were glad to see me walk in."

"What made you pick up on Riley?" I'd get to my reservations, I promised myself.

"Probably the same things that you did. He was squirrelly. Talking about Strummer, he wouldn't look me in the eye and wouldn't stop moving. He wanted to talk about his connection to her. I talked to the workers at the Dockside. Several of them stated how much of a dick that Alex was to him. His sister admitted as much, herself. And when you have a profile of a guy who doesn't have a lot of self-confidence but does have a great deal of social awkwardness, and who is constantly put down in front of his dream girl, that can be trouble."

"Riley's behavior was dictated by what's in his pants?"

"No. All in his head. Tied to self-image. Being gutted by someone he despised in front of someone he longed for, it would launch plenty of you over the edge."

"You could be right," I said, shaking my head. Psychologically, Stevens was a dead end. Maybe now was not the time to start in on physical evidence.

"You're a little bit cute when you look defeated," she said, taking a deep breath and stretching her hands behind her head, which placed her cleavage right in my line of vision. She smiled as my eyes came up.

"That's a compliment?"

"Look," she said, placing her hand on my arm. "We all have our talents. Some of us more than others. You might be one of those who excel with action. You handled yourself pretty well the other night. And I heard about you putting down some monster a few years ago. You can't be great at everything."

"What's your area of expertise?"

"Wouldn't you like to know," she said, her hand again finding my arm. It wasn't by accident. Apparently, Alex wasn't the only one in town who'd been frustrated. I wasn't a bad-looking guy. My hair had yet to gray, and I was fit. If I wasn't at my wrestling weight, for a man in his late thirties, I could hold my own. But with Salazar, I felt like a mouse getting batted around by a cat. Sooner or later, I was going to get ripped apart.

"You and Mrs. Tubbs. How about that?" Derek Anderson stood off of Salazar's shoulder with a wide smile. I hadn't noticed him come in. Maybe I had become soft.

"How you doing?" he said, nodding to Salazar when she looked to see who was talking. She ignored him and turned back to me. He tugged on the sleeve of his t-shirt and adjusted his Red Man hat.

"Beat it, Derek," I said. Getting schooled on your failures as an investigator would sour anyone, though I'd never experienced a mood that welcomed Suzanne's ex-husband.

"You ain't going to introduce me to your friend?" He smiled.

"No. You can leave."

"Suzy dumps your ass, and you move right on to this tamale. Studly."

I stood. He took a step back.

"You see what's going on here, Tubbs?" he said. "I want to warn you. You're what we call a rebound. LT used to fuck my wife. Then she smartened up."

"If she married you in the first place," Salazar said, "I'd question how smart she was to begin with."

"Funny," he said.

I took a step toward him. Salazar put her arm out, placing her hand on my stomach to stop me.

"Do you remember what happened the last time you bothered me in here?" I asked.

He made a face that communicated he did not. I ran an index finger over the bridge of my nose to remind him. His had wound up broken.

"Take it easy," Derek said, squealing. "I'm just saying hello."

"Try goodbye," Salazar said.

"Why is that?"

"Because you've insulted me. A tamale is Mexican. I'm Cuban. And now I'm angry, as you're attempting to disrupt the lovely time we were having in this beautiful establishment."

She stood. She was as tall as he was. They had four inches on me.

Derek put up his hands. "You people are no fun. Fuck off." He gave us the finger with both hands and walked down the bar to order.

As Duke waited, I called to him: "No way. Not tonight."

"Sorry, Derek," he said.

"You can't let him do that," Derek said.

"See you later, Derek," Duke said, shrugging.

Derek scowled at us, then looked in disbelief at Duke.

"Assholes," he said and left.

"I was hoping I'd get the chance to knock him out," Salazar said as we sat back down. "I never get to have any fun."

"It's not as much fun as you'd think," I said.

"I just thought that a man of action might be impressed by a woman who could act, too."

"I think the missing buttons on your shirt are enough."

"You noticed?" She smiled.

CHAPTER TWENTY-EIGHT

"You're bored here," I said.

"I don't know if that's exactly how I'd put it. Let's just say that insurance men and middle managers from Massachusetts bragging about their golf scores and the small, prestigious, liberal arts colleges they attended don't really get me going. Your town seems to be full of them right now."

"That's unfortunate," I said. "Your luck seems to run hot and cold."

"Why do you say that?"

"Because my place really needs to be cleaned. I'm not going to make a good impression."

"It could be in worse shape after tonight." She turned to Duke. "Do we have a bill, handsome?"

Chapter Twenty-Nine

As I looked up at the ceiling, I considered that it might be the only clean space in the house. I recalled a trail of clothes leading from the kitchen, where we opened beers we didn't drink, to the bottom of the stairs. Underwear was scattered about the second-floor landing. I'd had to get up in the middle of the night to retrieve the sheet and summer comforter from the floor. Salazar hadn't moved.

There are many reasons for having sex. We had not made love. The urgency of connecting with someone you had feelings for could be dreamlike, with corresponding levels of intensity. What we had enacted was the release of two immovable objects freed from the mire of their frustrations. It was also a contest to see who was the alpha. I would have called that a draw, which was far from a bad thing. I must have been fidgeting because Salazar raised her head and looked over at me.

"That's the second time you surprised me this week," she said, smiling.

"Maybe you should stop underestimating me." I considered it lucky that I'd stretched before I ran earlier that evening. Otherwise, I may have pulled a muscle.

"I'd be lying if I said that we're not trending in that direction." She rolled over onto her back and sighed with satisfaction.

It was good to hear.

"You know what would seal that?" she said, rolling toward me. "You, cooking me breakfast."

"If there's one thing that you could overestimate, it would be my cooking skills. I can make coffee, however."

"So you use me, caffeinate me, and then kick me out?"

"Isn't that urban life? I'm trying to make you comfortable."

"Get on it, then," she said. "The coffee, rather than me."

"I hope I can make it down the stairs."

"Suck it up, Romeo."

She came into the kitchen a few minutes later wearing her recovered underwear, the white, a splash of cream against her light brown skin. The blouse was completely unbuttoned. She stopped halfway across the room. Her pants that I'd picked up were folded across one of the kitchen chairs. She looked at them and grinned.

"Keep strolling around in a thong, and we'll never make it out of here," I said. That prompted her to slip on the jeans. She put them on one long leg at a time.

"I think you proved your point," she said. "I'm going to protect myself."

She sat down, and I placed a coffee in front of her.

"Being a fed, I'm sure you take it black, like a tough guy."

"As a matter of fact, yes," she said. I added milk and sugar to mine and sat across from her.

"I needed that," she said.

I smiled and raised my eyebrows. I'd thought it was more obvious that I'd needed it.

'What got you all jazzed up?" I asked.

"Really? I'm banished to the middle of nowhere—no offense—to sort out some rich bastard getting brained by a repressed Boy Scout."

"Won't doing a favor for a Cabinet member pay off?"

"It better, though I'm sure my supervisor will snag most of the credit."

"I'm getting the impression that you don't like Laurel."

"I don't know if it's the widespread aversion to women of authority, a hatred of the federal government, or a racist attitude towards Cubans that I'm enjoying the least."

"I like you, Mrs. Tubbs," I said, laughing.

"Didn't you hear your friend? I'm only a rebound."

"Does that mean I shouldn't ask you to move in?"

"I don't think that would fly at the Grimes compound."

"I didn't mean for the duration of your stay. I thought you might be inclined to put in for a transfer."

"You must still be drunk."

"Yes, because I'm going to tell you something, and you're going to think less of me. Which is no way to spark a budding romance."

"If you have herpes, you're not making it out of this room alive."

"It's worse than that. I'm not sure that Riley Stevens killed Alex Grimes. I was wondering how to talk to you about it. Lucky me, here you are."

"You may be the dumbest man I've ever fucked. And that includes some football players when I was at UMiami. I'm not talking about the quarterbacks, either. I mean linemen, beautiful specimens, but, honestly, a few couldn't count past ten without taking their shoes off. You're giving me those vibes."

"Do you want to hear my reasoning?"

"I don't, but I see you're determined." She took a sip of her coffee and then put the cup down. "Just know words spoken to that effect will eliminate any chance you have of ever getting me in the sack again."

"I know that it looks like Riley is the killer. I was all in with you. Then I talked to him."

"To the actual man or the twelve-year-old you coached in baseball?"

I wasn't biting. She may have had a point.

"There are a few things bothering me," I said.

"I love comedy." She leaned back and crossed her legs.

"First, from the minute he saw his son, Grimes pushed the accident narrative. In my experience with assault and murder, which, granted, is limited, I've found that the victim's family wants someone to blame, to know who did it. Even if your son was an asshole, as you pointed out, you would hope that he wasn't stupid enough to brain himself on a rock. Why would Grimes step on me for asking questions that might suggest another explanation? You started down that road, and he helped you. How does that make sense?"

"If you want to know how these people think," she said, pausing to take a sip of coffee, "consider how something will affect their professional standing. They want to control the story. It's either self-preservation or self-promotion. It cannot reflect poorly on them. In this case, the best scenario to elicit public sympathy for a dead son like Alex is an accident. But once Grimes knew I'd determined that Stevens did it, he accepts the evidence, and it's case closed. Then the energy goes into spinning things to keep Alex noble and the story tragic. Grimes may be friendly enough when you're escorting him around town, but all he's worked for is hanging in the balance. He's not taking chances with the likes of you. No offense."

"Because I could be right about what happened?"

"Hardly. You're small-town, which makes you small time—and dangerous because you don't know the rules he's playing by. It's not about whether you could have figured this out. It's that you couldn't control the narrative. Your quote in that Portland paper was unconscionable to Grimes, whether it was out of context or not. Notice that nothing but the most basic information has surfaced since I arrived. You could be a crime-solving combination of Sonny Crockett and Columbo, and Grimes wouldn't give a damn. He'd rather juggle live grenades than put you with the press again. This is something that needs finesse and a certain acumen. Don't take it personally, but those are things you lack."

"Don't sugarcoat it, Salazar. Tell me what you really think." I got it, but I didn't like it. "That's the thing that matters to him? Shouldn't it be finding out who killed his son?"

"There's the small town coming through. Were you a Boy Scout, too?" She laughed.

"I guess I was under the impression that nailing the criminal, in this case, a murderer, would be the primary objective."

"It's never that simple. But I've accomplished that, too. As you know, I'm the complete package." She smiled and tilted her head. I couldn't argue.

I grimaced and got up to grab another coffee. The day before, Grimes had pointed out that I'd always tried to do what was right, regardless of the consequences. I hadn't realized that he'd seen that quality in me as lethal. I sat back down to make my case, notwithstanding my potential as a detonator.

"Sorry I hurt your delicate feelings," she said. She laughed and put her feet up on my lap. "If it will make you happy, we can ignore that Stevens had means, motive, and opportunity as clear as the sunlight shining through the window and highlighting your need to dust, and you can tell me your lame-ass ideas."

"Okay, here goes." I picked up her feet and placed them on the chair, then began to pace the kitchen. "First, if Riley had killed Alex, why would he have told you that Alex had come down to chew him out and that they'd had an argument? It's like saying, 'Hey, look at me for this.'"

"Would you like me to shoot holes as you go, or nuke everything once you've finished?"

"Let's take it one at a time. That way, I can take notes as needed."

"Grab your pen," she said. "Stevens could have admitted that for a few reasons. One, guilty conscience. Maybe he's not a violent person at heart but got pushed over the line. Though in my experience, Boy Scouts were the ones frying bugs with magnifying glasses. Granted, he didn't mention the confrontation when you questioned him. He and Grimes may have shared an opinion of your investigative skills. He thought he'd be able to get it by you. You didn't go after him, so he didn't see you as a threat. It could be that simple. I, being a US marshal and fantastic, brought more gravity to the situation. He knew he wouldn't get it past me."

"There's no denying that you are a frightening specter, but if that's the case, why doesn't he confess? He could plead self-defense."

"I would if I were him. He's maintaining innocence, as if being honest about that first detail makes him honest about all of it. He's not the clearest thinker, in my estimation. Don't you feel that there's something off about him?"

"To be honest, yes. But not in a violent way."

"People snap every day. Another of the reasons we have jobs. Next?"

She held her cup out for another coffee. I stopped my pacing and filled it.

"The boat hook," I said. "That troubles me."

"You mean the murder weapon that the medical examiner matched to the wound on the victim's skull that has his fingerprints on it?"

"Yeah, that murder weapon. If we believe Riley, which we do in some instances, Alex comes down, calls him out of his apartment, and then starts to ream him because he thinks he got in the way with Sally. This dressing down is so bad that Riley snaps. What would those words be, exactly, that sent him over the edge?"

"Could be anything. Stevens isn't saying much on that, is he? He doesn't want to revisit it. Maybe he never wants to feel that level of degradation again. Or it could be because of what it made him do. You can understand why he wouldn't want to share that humiliation with us."

"If I give you that," I said, watching her dark eyes, "which I don't, then this is what happens. Stevens, instead of going right at Alex, like a normal, enraged psycho, says, 'Wait a minute, Alex. Stay right there while I walk down to one of my boats and grab something to bash your brains in.' And Alex would have stood there, patiently waiting?"

"We don't know that the hook was on the boat. It could have been in the boathouse. Or on the dock."

"Or, being a boat hook, it could have been on a boat. According to Riley, it was kept on the Hinckley."

"Of course, he said that. It supports his story."

"We're not believing that part of it, but are trusting him when he tells us that he and Alex argued?"

"Excellent point. I've never encountered a suspect who lied only on certain details, especially those which would confirm his innocence." She grinned and shook her head. "Is it in your vast experience that they're usually either entirely honest or complete liars? Maybe I should write a white paper on that."

"What made you look for it in the water, anyway?"

"It wasn't easy, but it wasn't hard. I'd talked to the medical examiner and asked him what could have caused a blow like that. To be honest, I thought it might have been a baseball bat. But he said the implement was smaller, something with less surface area and something flat. I suggested a golf club. He said possibly a putter. A high iron or driver might have left a divot. I explained this to Grimes and asked where he kept his clubs. He told me and mentioned there were also similar implements on the boats. We inspected the clubs, my helpers from the state police and I, which were kept in the garage. And, of course, they were all there, and none showed any signs of being used for skull bashing. We headed to check around the boathouse. Secretary Grimes offered to come down to see if anything was missing. He noticed that the hook wasn't on the Hinckley. I thought that if the body went in the drink there, maybe the hook might have followed. I borrowed some shorts and ballparked how far I could pitch a club. I went in at low tide. It was right there in the mud, fifteen yards from the dock. Even submerged, enough of the fingerprints held. Water does not wash away all of one's sins."

"That's pretty lucky, finding it."

"Luck is the residue of good work. He couldn't throw it over that damn yacht. There wasn't much of a field for him to launch it."

"You think he panicked and chucked it, just like he did with Alex?"

"If people didn't do stupid things, we wouldn't have jobs."

"No doubt. But do the fingerprints mean anything? He's the captain who uses it. Of course, his fingerprints are on it."

"If he's such a great captain, how come he needs to use a hook? I'm from Miami. I grew up around boats. You think those old Cubans need a hook to grab a mooring or dock a boat? Please."

I resumed pacing.

"Once Stevens clobbers Alex, he dumps the body in the water. The tide was slack, full-high flooded, which meant the body could go anywhere—or nowhere. This veteran seaman, who knew these waters like the back of his hand, to use a cliche, just drops him in and takes his chances?"

"A shotgun couldn't shoot fewer holes into your theory than I'm going to right now. Perhaps you've heard that people under pressure do not always think logically. There's that, which should not be dismissed. But let's press on. Maybe he does panic and does that exact thing. Entirely plausible. But one could take the opposite argument and still be correct. He knows these waters. Wherever and whenever he dropped Alex in, he was certain that it would take the body out to sea. Which is exactly what happened. It was only a matter of luck, incredibly bad for him, that Alex got hung up on that island. And yes, I did see it. Trout took me out there on the Mako."

"Why then toss the hook after the body? Why not wipe it off and put it back where it goes?"

"Again, panic. It's not like killing the boss's son is an everyday thing for him."

"It's the middle of the night. You've got a Mako at your disposal, which admittedly would make a little noise. But with everyone asleep, maybe no one would hear it running on idle. Plus, there are three sea kayaks and a canoe behind the boathouse. Who knows how many anchors and how much rope? Instead of placing the body in one of those and taking it outside the cove and sinking it somewhere the lobsters would feed on it until it was gone, he just throws it off the dock and assumes the tide is going to make it vanish? I know some idiots, and Riley isn't one of them."

"You're doing more gymnastics than Nadia Comaneci." She gave me a lopsided grin, and her eyebrows formed a questioning arch. "Who is to say he didn't throw him in the canoe and take him out? It doesn't matter. The body ended up where it ended up."

Her arguments were solid. But none definitively closed the gaps in logic that bothered me. On the other hand, my reasoning was equally unproven. That Salazar refused to consider them was the problem. She was satisfied. I was not.

"Does the fact that there were all those people at the Compound and none of them heard or saw anything bother you? Because they were either drunk or asleep? Not to mention that our stone-cold killer, after cracking Alex's skull and tossing him into the cove, claims to have gone to bed at nine-thirty. I'm not buying any of that. Do you know anyone who goes to bed that early on a Saturday night?"

"I don't, but I don't live in Mayberry-by-the-Sea. There's a reason Violet retires early. From what I understand, she and certain fermented agricultural products are well acquainted."

"Randolph wouldn't let me talk to her."

"Well, I did, and she didn't know anything. Two bottles of white Burgundy in the kitchen garbage, both hers."

"And what do you make of Stevens just retreating to his apartment instead of making a run for it? He had the means. He was polishing brass that next morning, as if nothing happened, even after Trout told him that we'd found Alex on Stage."

"Jesus," she said. "Did you really just ask that? First, he never thought the body would be found. So, he's up doing his job, acting normally, following his routine, which is what one would expect from a murderer who thought he was going to get away with it. Then, after Trout talks to him, he keeps doing it so as not to raise suspicion."

"After completely panicking the previous night, now he's calculating and cool? And if he was panicking the night before, why didn't he run then?"

"He thought the body was gone. If not for a one-in-a-million chance, it would have been. That would have been a problem for us. The accident scenario may have become the accepted story. Or perhaps suicide. But that's irrelevant."

"There are too many holes," I said. "Any way you look at it."

"Those aren't holes," Salazar said, sliding her cup into the middle of the table. "They're questions. And they can all be addressed. You just dislike the answers. Think of it from the angle of burden of proof. If we flipped the responsibility, how do you prove that Stevens didn't do it? You can't."

She rose and walked to the sink. She rinsed out her cup and placed it on the counter. She leaned back against it.

"If Stevens didn't do it," she said, smirking, "who did?"

"I don't know."

"That's a problem."

"For sure."

"Who are your suspects?"

"I only have one person without an alibi."

"Sally Strummer, aka Beth Davenport?" she asked.

"Right," I said.

"We'll clear them all, so you don't think I'm high-hatting you." She motioned for me to sit at the table. I was going to get a lecture. She started pacing.

"Do you accept that Alex Grimes was killed at the Compound?"

"Yes," I said.

"That limits our suspect list, doesn't it, if we accept that Mr. Stevens didn't kill Alex Grimes? Someone who we know was there did it, or someone came to the Compound and killed him."

"I'm with you on that." My coffee had gone cold.

"Do we know of anyone coming to the Compound? The answer is no. No one at the house heard anything, not the fight, not a car. When Abby and Ranford returned shortly before one o'clock, they didn't see or hear anything. The time of death, which is estimated at eleven, eliminates them. Even our prime suspect, who would benefit the most from claiming that some mystery assailant showed up on the property, says that he didn't hear anything. And I'm pretty sure the fucking Russians aren't sending frogmen to take out the snotty son of a Cabinet member in an attempt to spur imports of Stoli vodka. So can we rule out those scenarios?"

"As far as we know."

"As far as anyone knows." She paused and folded her arms. "So, if that's true, that means that someone who was at the Compound had to do it, right?"

I nodded.

"Let's look at this list of possible suspects. The least likely: Violet Grimes, passed out, thanks to her wine habit. It happens on a daily basis. Besides, in the number of homicides in this country every year, do you know how many of them involve a mother killing an adult child?"

"No."

"Neither do I, because there aren't enough to count. It's not even worth looking up in the FBI Uniform Crime Statistics. We're eliminating her."

"Agreed."

"Let's move on to his father. Randolph hadn't seen Alex since lunch when they left with, oh yes, Riley Stevens. From your report, you state Grimes didn't know that his son was missing and that he'd asked you what Alex had done. Is that correct?"

"It is."

"And you were sure that he was surprised to find his son on the deck of that boat."

"It looked like he took it pretty hard."

"So either Grimes is Paul Newman or shocked to find out his son was dead."

"True. The only thing I can say about that is that he was quick to assume it was an accident. And he pushed that."

"Of course. But we've addressed that. His son was a party animal, only a poodle instead of a pit bull. While he has a history of drunken exploits and obnoxiousness, there's little reason for Grimes to think Alex would be mixed up in anything violent. The kid was known to buy weed and cocaine, but for personal use. He's not in distribution, which could have put him in contact with some bad actors."

"How would you—and Grimes—know that?"

"If you haven't figured it out yet, I'm very good at my job. And a man in Randolph's position is made aware of what goes on around him. He visits the White House. No surprises."

"Did you know he was at odds with his son?"

"Over?" If she was unaware, her face did not reveal it.

"Career choice. Alex wanted to be an actor. He hated his current job."

"I want to be playing on the Pro Beach Volleyball circuit, yet here I am. We do what we have to do."

"He wanted to quit but was afraid to tell Randolph."

"Likely adding to the frustration he took out on Stevens. And if Randolph didn't know, he wouldn't be upset about it. Regardless, the number of fathers who kill adult sons is also so small as to not be worth looking up in the FBI stats."

"If you say so." I felt like I was banging my head against the wall, though a pleasant one to gaze at. I couldn't help but be impressed with how she'd eliminated so many different possibilities in so little time, leaving me nowhere.

"Let's not overlook that everyone has an alibi. Randolph and Violet are each other's, as are Abby and Ranford. We can eliminate Trout and the maid. They weren't there and are accounted for that evening. Which leaves us with Sally as the only remaining viable suspect. Everyone reported that she was practically incapacitated at the time of death. You interviewed her. What did you think?"

"She's tiny, for one thing. She drank a ton. Everyone I talked to said she could barely speak, never mind walk. On the other hand, she did try to get out of there the next morning after I'd told Trout to make sure that no one left. That's suspicious."

"Sure it is. Or maybe she woke up in a strange house, hungover as hell, not knowing the people and being told that one of her oldest friends had been found dead. What is she supposed to do? Ask for a mimosa?"

"Maybe she wasn't as drunk as everyone thought. Alex could have been fuming because she'd been talking to Stevens, and she had to defend herself. Or she could have been on her way to visit Stevens in the boathouse, and Alex caught her. We don't know."

"That's a whole lot of maybe and 'what if' you got there. Where would this have taken place? In the living room? On the lawn? Her bedroom? His room? Maybe they were on the patio, and her ninety pounds of fury picked up a wrought iron chair, climbed onto another chair, and then clocked him like Hulk Hogan. Afterwards, she muscled up and dragged him over the breakwater or down to the dock. And threw that boat hook in for good luck, only without placing her fingerprints on it. My colleague, who did question her, got the impression that she was a flighty artist who blacked out after leaving the bar. As far as we could determine, she had something like eight rum punches. Her BAC would have been three times the legal limit. She wasn't acting drunk. She was practically in a coma."

"You should talk to her anyway," I said. "Maybe subconsciously she picked up on something important."

"My colleague in Boston makes me look like a cupcake. And you should be happy to know that he came to the same conclusions about her that you did. Prior to this revisionist history."

"Someone could have come to the Compound that night that we're not aware of."

"Who would that be?"

"I don't know. A friend? A dealer?"

"You're reaching. No one heard anything. We searched his room. Nothing there. Some THC in his system, no big concern. Riley Stevens snapped and killed Alex Grimes. It's that simple."

I couldn't argue with any of her logic, even if I questioned her assumptions. I had no alternative theory. I couldn't even conjure a wild guess.

"If you were me," I said, "and still weren't convinced, what would you do?"

"Blow my head off. Because I couldn't live with myself being such a dumbass."

"And if there was a misfire?"

"Go to my backup piece."

"I'm serious."

"If I have to give you those answers, too, maybe you are in the wrong line of work." She laughed so hard she was bent over.

"If I were running the investigation," I said. "I wouldn't quit until I'd eliminated all other possibilities."

"So, what's stopping you? If you want to roust Laurel's dealers and find out no one was within ten miles of the Compound or drive to Boston and hypnotize Sally Strummer, have at it. Just know that those are hours of your life that you'll never get back."

"That's less time than Riley Stevens has already spent locked up."

A serious look came over her face. "Is this coming from guilt? You think you should have made a difference back when he was a kid, and you were teaching him how to hit a baseball? Or do you have something going with his brother, who you were way too easy on? Do you owe that family something?"

"I don't," I said. "I just want to be able to sleep at night."

"A couple of drinks and getting laid seems to take care of that."

I put my empty coffee cup in the sink. Salazar had laid it out for me.

"I'm going to visit a local herb enthusiast and then go to Boston. Do you want to come with me and see how it's done?"

"Oh, no." Her hands came up as she shook her head.

"I'll throw in dinner at a restaurant that won't make you wear a bib."

"However tempting a real date with your bad self might be, you've got to realize something, Nichols. I may not be a government wonk, but I'm close enough that I need to pay attention to my career. I don't want to end up in Des Moines. My track can go one way or another. Maybe in a town like this, you don't have to worry about it. But I'm federal. They don't tolerate coloring outside the lines, especially when you're a woman. If you're crazy or stupid enough to pursue this, you leave me out of it. I'm not kidding. I've done my job here. Correctly, I might add. The likelihood of me getting fucked over if Grimes thinks I'm stirring things up is too great."

"I get it."

"I don't think you do. Unless you're on their level, and by that I mean like Grimes and those who actually run this country, they don't give a shit. We are simply tools, like a hammer or a typewriter. Some of us are capable. As a result, we may be placed on a nice, cushioned shelf. Others are a whim away from the trash. I'm going to give you a piece of advice now, because I like you. Will you listen?"

"Sure."

"I know you think you're doing the right thing by kicking this around out of some warped sense of obligation. It's one thing to mention it to me, because I don't take it as a challenge or a question of my efficacy. But if I were you, I wouldn't be broadcasting this to anyone else, whether it's the state police, another marshal, or the FBI. They won't listen, and you'll be labeled as a malcontent, or a wingnut, or both. You'll be on the outside, and they won't trust you, ever. Even here, it will come back on you. Listen to me. For your own good."

"What about Riley Stevens's good?"

"Riley Stevens is guilty. His good will be determined by the courts."

She buttoned her shirt. Her mouth was closed, and her eyes were downcast. I'd graduated from harmless diversion to potential career killer. I was as dangerous to her as I'd been to Randolph Grimes. None of it seemed right to me.

Chapter Thirty

I gave myself twenty-four hours. If I couldn't come up with anything by then, I'd have exhausted my capabilities and have to accept that Salazar was correct and Riley Stevens had killed Alex Grimes. I called the station and told Crowley that something had come up, and I was taking the day off. He was only too happy to run the town in my absence. According to Salazar, if I didn't watch myself, he'd get the chance to do so on a more regular basis.

After I checked with Laurel's one taxi, which hadn't left its garage the night of the murder, I moved on to the county medical examiner. Fritz Bannon was apparently too busy to take my call, so I drove to Portland. We'd worked together enough so that I imagined he'd supply answers, even if he knew I wasn't officially on the case. Then I saw his face drop when I walked through the door.

"I can't tell you anything," he said.

"About what?"

"You know," he said. "That Alex Grimes business."

"Why not?"

"You know that, too."

"If you don't want to open your mouth, I think the state can afford a photocopy of your report. You could leave it on your desk and go grab a coffee."

He laughed.

"That's not even a good try. I've been instructed that only eyes directly authorized by Marshal Salazar are to gaze upon that work, and you, my friend, do not qualify."

"So, you were able to determine that Alex is dead? Nicely done."

"And you're still wasting my time because…?"

"I'm looking into this."

"Going freelance, are we? That'll go over." He shook his head. "I believe that an arrest has been made and that my report confirms exactly what Marshal Salazar thinks happened."

"If that's the case, what harm would it do to tell me?"

"I'm sure somewhere along the line, a red-hot poker would get shoved up my ass for it."

"You won't help me?"

"Can't." He straightened two pencils on his desktop. The fluorescent light over him hummed.

"I'd consider it a personal favor."

"You owing me a favor does not balance out the prospective wrath of a US marshal and, by proxy, a Cabinet member of the executive branch of our government."

"Will you at least confirm what you told me over the phone a few days ago?"

"I can't remember what I said."

"I'll remind you. Cause of death was a blow to the head. You said he was likely dead before he hit the water, as there wasn't much of it in his lungs."

"I don't recall going into quite that detail, but that is accurate."

"And time of death would have been around eleven?" I'd been told by Salazar, but wanted to be sure I'd been given correct information.

"In that ballpark."

"Toxicology showed marijuana in his system."

"I know I didn't mention that."

"I found a pipe in his pocket. That was in *my* report to the marshal."

"You won't find it in mine."

"Because?"

He cocked his head. "I have a hard time believing you expect me to answer that, considering."

"It would be helpful to know if there was anything else in his bloodstream. I may have some citizens in Laurel who would then need my attention." I hoped this might play to what was hopefully Bannon's sense of duty.

"No cocaine or heroin, if that's what you're after. I was told not to bother testing the hair. You won't find that in the report, either, and you didn't hear it from me."

"Of course not." I raised my eyebrows. "But there's no hiding the alcohol, right?" I guessed that was allowable, as it fed into the accepted story.

"Let's just say that he would have been a danger to the general public had he been behind the wheel."

"And you're confident that the boat hook, the suspected murder weapon, is what caused the fractured skull?"

"You haven't seen it, I take it."

"No."

"This is no normal hook. It's solid brass and four inches long with a ninety-degree right angle. It's thick, and it's attached to a piece of hickory. The brass is heavy. It's like a weaponized golf club. The way the fracture falls in the skull, it goes four inches above the eye, but there's a small crack that runs perpendicular to the main fracture. The base along the vertical axis and the offshoot follow the layout of this particular implement. That is not a coincidence. It's a piece of work, this thing, the murder weapon. You wouldn't need Hank Aaron swinging it to cause damage."

"I appreciate it, Bannon," I said.

"No, you don't," he said.

"I was never here."

Before I left for Boston, there was one last stop I needed to make. The pot Alex had smoked that last night could have been supplied locally. And I knew where to check on that.

Chapter Thirty-One

Torch Harrison was sweating, hunched over the dish machine. A replica of Mt. Washington rose from the dump tray. At one-thirty, he was digging out from the lunch rush. I went past him to find Karen French, one of the sisters who owned the place. I wanted to let her know that I'd be borrowing the backbone of her restaurant for a few minutes and that he hadn't actually done anything wrong. At least, not that I knew of. She offered to get me a sandwich. I declined. Then she walked me back to Torch and told him that I wanted to talk to him and that it was okay with her. He groaned when I motioned him outside.

This was his redemption job, a path to the straight and narrow. He'd worked in the kitchen in his last prison stint—the result of a break and entering in support of a nasty free-basing habit. Karen and Rita, the owners of Allie's, were the only ones in town who'd give him a shot when he told them that he wanted to try the industry for real. Maybe it was because dishwashers were hard to come by. To his credit, he'd been willing to start at the bottom here and had managed to hold the job since spring. Before I put a halo over his head, I had noticed that he was driving a Camaro, even if it was a few years old. My first thought had been that he probably wasn't paying for that on a dishwasher's salary. But one could hope.

Torch and I went into the parking lot. He didn't bother to ask if I minded if he smoked. He lit up a Marlboro.

"What do you want, LT? You know I got a job to do, and I'd like to keep it."

"I'm doing you a favor, Torch. I've washed dishes myself. Looked like you could have used a break."

He stroked his beard the way you'd pet a dog.

"You been dealing at all?" I asked.

"You're joking, right?" He flashed me a wide smile of uneven teeth. He stood in the shadow of the eaves.

"That's a nice car you're driving around in. What are the sisters paying you?"

"I live frugal. At home. Which isn't easy for a man my age." He was thirty. "A guy has to have some enjoyment."

"You weren't out making a delivery to the Compound a few days ago? I don't care if you were. Really. I just want to know what you might have dropped off." The good thing about having a reputation for being reasonable was that people would take you at your word. That allowed one to get away with the occasional lie. I didn't care if he'd sold Alex pot. That he'd been to the Compound would mean something else.

"You trying to put me with Alex Grimes?"

"I'm just asking if you'd been out there. Maybe you saw something? Know something about who he was spending time with?"

"Fuck that and that piece of crap Ford you rode in on. I've been toeing the line since I got my shot here. I'm going to be cooking soon enough. I'm done with that other shit."

"You didn't answer my question, Torch."

"Well, I got you on this one, Chief," he said, laughing and puffing out his chest. "The kid, the other dishwasher, he's off at some baseball camp. I've worked the last ten nights in a row. And days. They let me have a beer after, if you don't mind. Then it's straight home. No bullshit. I get OT. That's how I afford a car like that. You can check my damn timecard or ask Karen."

"If not you, then who?"

"No idea." He nodded solemnly, dropped his cigarette, and ground it into the dirt. "I ain't been paying attention to that. A rock as big as a Pinto could come through town these days. I wouldn't hear about it."

"Did you ever visit the Compound in your previous life?"

He shrugged. "What's it to you?"

"What were you bringing him? Coke? Pot? Anything else?"

"Them are pretty accurate guesses. But it wasn't too often. He usually had his own stash. Sometimes he'd find me around town if he ran out. I wasn't a damn delivery service."

"You or your associates ever have a problem with him?"

"He always paid upfront and never tried to pull that 'All I have is seventy-five bucks' bullshit. A man in my former profession appreciates that. Though if you were only a waitress or a bartender, those folks weren't too fond of G-One. But he never got uppity with me. Guess that might be a supply-and-demand thing. You can get booze anywhere."

"So, you got nothing for me, then?"

"Anyone could tell you, Chief," he said, grinning. "I've been on the straight and narrow. Fully rehabilitated."

"I hope that's the case," I said.

"I thought they had the Boy Scout for it," he said.

"They do."

"Then why are you here?"

"Just tying up a few loose ends," I said.

He gave me a slick little grin.

"Thanks, Torch. Enjoy those dishes."

"You know it, boss," he said.

Torch must have enjoyed seeing someone else on the hook, especially a guy who'd been lauded for his achievements. I wondered how many Eagle Scout killers there had been. Maybe Riley was the first. But I doubted it.

Chapter Thirty-Two

Sally would not answer her phone. I'd called Ranford, too, with the hopes that he might have more to say without Abby standing next to him. I never made it past his secretary. I hoped to be less easy to evade in person.

When you get off the highway in Danvers and start working your way down to Boston—on the same Route One that ran through West Laurel—the tension comes at you as if you've punched it up on the radio. It isn't the volume of traffic. Laurel has plenty for two months a year. It's the intensity. One has to be ready to react to every juke, turn, or dart that some crazed bastard might throw from his Bondo-ed Buick LaSabre. Hesitation at a yellow light would result in the car behind you porking your trunk. This allowed me to imagine that the questions careening around my head weren't the reason my palms were sweating on the vinyl steering wheel.

I only got lost twice after getting off the highway. Chinatown, which I'd been told was the location of the band's loft, was a misnomer. I'd been to Boston enough with Trout to know I was in the Combat Zone, the adjacent area where you'd find Boston's strip joints, dealers, addicts, and, of course, prostitutes. I parked. Though it was four in the afternoon, it looked like I hadn't missed Friday night by much. As I searched for the address, I stumbled across one drunk, stepped over three empty bottles of Gilbey's gin, and dodged two used condoms. The street smelled like piss. One-oh-five was a glass and metal door and transom between an oriental market and an adult bookshop with blacked-out windows. A stocky, goateed man about my age leaned against the storefront, smoking a Camel. He gave me a "What the fuck are you doing here stare?" as I stepped past him and hit the buzzer. No one answered. I waited a few seconds, then pressed it again.

The man looked me over. Despite it being close to eighty degrees, he wore a black leather sports jacket. He held one hand inside it like Napoleon, resting it right where a shoulder-holstered gun would be. I considered that leaving my thirty-eight in the Bronco might have been a mistake.

"You're a long way from Fenway fucking Park," he said.

"Maybe it's the overflowing urinal aroma that's throwing me off," I said. I wore khakis and a short-sleeved collared shirt with the Laurel logo on the chest, which I thought would look official enough. Here, it was out of place. I certainly didn't look cool enough to pass as someone who knew a musician.

He grinned.

"You know those folks?" the man said, nodding at the door.

"Do I look like a traveling salesman?" I was not in the mood to be accosted by a dealer or pimp.

"You should realize this might be the crack of dawn for them."

I hit the buzzer again. He scowled, and his chin came up.

"What do you want with them?" he asked.

"What's it to you?" I leaned on the buzzer for a good thirty seconds.

"They're not going to like that."

"I'll take my chances."

"You a cop? Not from around here, though."

"You a psychic?"

"You haven't told me to move along, and you ain't banging the shit out of that door like you should be."

"Stop with the fucking buzzer." A squeaky voice came out of a dented speaker grill.

"I don't think she wants to talk to you."

I tried to ignore him and failed. "I don't care what you think, Napoleon."

I patted my chest, where his hand rested under his jacket.

"You don't like my threads? Think I should get myself some preppy-ass pants and a shirt with a boat on it?"

A door snapped open. I heard footsteps on the stairs.

"No fucking way, man," Sally said when she saw me through the filthy glass door.

"I don't think the lady wants you around," Mr. Leather Jacket said.

"Take a walk," I said.

He glanced at the door. From where Sally was standing, she couldn't see him. "Keep it real, McCloud," he said, making a crack about a television sheriff from New Mexico who somehow found himself on loan to the NYPD. I waited until the leather jacket disappeared around the corner, then turned to Sally.

"Can I ask you some questions, please? You haven't returned my calls."

"There's a fucking reason for that."

Apparently, I did not only look like a hick, but also like someone who enjoyed being sworn at. She tugged on a button of her red and black flannel shirt. Her hair was all over the place. Maybe she had just gotten up.

"Have you heard what's happened regarding Alex's death?"

"Yeah, the boat guy was arrested. I forget his name."

"That's right, but I'm not sure he did it." I wasn't yet mentioning that she might know more about what happened that night than she'd let on.

"Then why did you arrest him?"

"I didn't. A federal marshal took over the investigation. She did."

"I don't have anything to say. I don't remember anything. Like I told you." She looked down and shook her head. "I told the marshal who came here that, too. I don't fucking remember. And I don't want to. Alex isn't coming back."

"You may know something that you don't realize is important. We didn't get a chance to talk much that morning. You were pretty shaken. Understandably. I just want to ask you a few things. You and your music were important to Riley Stevens, that captain. He told me that your band was for the underdog, that you wrote about important subjects. I've listened to the music. He was right, and now he's the one who has things stacked against him. If someone doesn't help him, he's going away, and he might not be guilty."

It was possible that by helping him, she might also trip up and implicate herself. Another detail that I failed to voice. She exhaled heavily, but the door clicked open. I followed her up the stairs, her footsteps louder than mine as she planted her Chuck Taylors on each step.

I'd never been in a loft that hadn't held hay or fishing gear. This one, the size of an elementary school basketball court, was not any less of a mess, nor did it lack its own distinctive aromas. It smelled like pot and unwashed clothes. Black bed sheets hung from clotheslines at the far end of the room, and a series of amps, wires, and microphones were set up in its center. A row of guitars stood in front of a three-piece drum kit. She led me to a coffee table made from a cable round in front of one of the windows. The plastic chairs surrounding it looked like they'd been liberated from different high schools. She took a blue bong with a Harley-Davidson sticker off the table and put it behind an amp, giving me a "so what" look. She came back and sat down, pulling her knees up in front of her. I landed across from her. I figured my best bet was to start with backstory and work up to that night to get her comfortable talking. She might then be willing to remember and share something important, if only by accident.

"It's my understanding that you and Alex went to college together, Brown. Is that where you know him from?"

"Yes, we were in the same dorm as freshmen. We were both in the drama department. Had a lot of the same classes. We hit it off. He was a sweet guy."

"You were in plays, things like that?"

"Sometimes. He went for the lead in every production, all this experimental Shakespeare shit. I didn't care what I got, especially after I started fronting a band with a few other guys. We were like a bad version of the Talking Heads. As for the plays and student films, Alex *had* to do it. He was driven, and he was great. I found drama interesting. Alex obsessed over it. We had to harass him to go to his other classes. It was all he cared about."

"How many years ago did you graduate?"

"Eight."

"And you stayed in touch?"

"Of course. I moved up to Boston with a guy from the band, and we started the Clap. Alex went to New York. We were pursuing our art. We'd write each other, talk on the phone. Get together occasionally. It's good to have someone trying to do the same thing, more or less. Acting, music, they're not like everyone thinks. It's a fucking struggle."

She put a palm out to stop me from asking a question and took a deep breath. She tried to gather herself.

"Are you okay?" I asked.

"Why? Do you care?" She'd been struck by something. Whether it was about her band or Alex, I couldn't tell. It could have been both. I moved forward.

"Was it too much for Alex? Is that why he gave up and moved to Washington a few years ago?"

She smiled and shook her head. "Granted, starting out, he didn't have an easy time of it. Just a few minor parts in some off-Broadway shit. But it was work. It was his father. He hung him out to dry."

"What do you mean?"

"He eventually stopped paying his rent and shut off his allowance. The starving artist is no cliché." She waved to the room. It was not a luxury penthouse.

"He couldn't get a job waiting tables?"

"That's what you or I might do. I have to work as a secretary three days a week, or I'd be living in a van somewhere. But Alex is from a different world. Those people don't do that. I'm not saying it's better or worse, though it is worse, I guess. It just wasn't something he would have considered an option."

"It sounds like he didn't have the same commitment that you did. You were okay with that?"

"That was him. I can also tell you when the Clap was starting out, there were weeks that I only ate because he'd slip a fifty into a cheesy little greeting card and send it here. He was a huge supporter of the band. And me. It wasn't a one-way street, either. I was there for him emotionally, at least when he was trying to go for it in New York. I kept him off the ledge. I don't think he realized it would be the climb that it was. And then, when he went to Washington, it was even worse. He hated that job, and he hated himself for working it."

"So why did he do it?"

"There are certain perks to being a Grimes, but there's unbelievable pressure that goes with them. He could see that he was going to crack, and he was finally going to do something about it. That's why I had to go to Maine that weekend. He was going to tell his father that he was quitting and going to LA to resume his career. He said that he needed me for moral support. But I was more like his shield. He figured his father wouldn't go ballistic with a guest in the house. When I got here, Alex tried to convince me to move west with him. He said I could start fresh out there, too."

"Were you going?"

"No. the Clap isn't dead."

"How did he take it?"

"He wasn't happy. But what the fuck? We have to do what we have to do."

"How did Randolph react when he told him?"

"He never did. He was saving it for Sunday brunch, at the last possible moment. We were supposed to leave that afternoon. I was going to bring him to Logan. But you know what happened."

"It seems that you were very close. Were you and Alex ever romantic?"

"Never. Of course, he'd made it known every now and then that he'd like to. But I wasn't into him that way. We'd shared so much of our lives and friendship and art. But there was a gulf that wouldn't be right for a life partner, or even a college boyfriend. We saw the world from different places. My dad's a dry cleaner. My mother teaches kindergarten. That's where I come from. I'm not a poseur. I believe in the things that we write and sing about. Alex could only live on his own privileged terms. At heart, he was a good person. But he wasn't someone I could tie myself to in that way."

"And that wasn't an issue for him?"

"You don't have friends who are different from you?"

"I do. What happened that afternoon that made him so upset?"

"He could be a diva, I'm not denying that. The boat captain was a fan. I'm grateful for every one of ours. Alex might have gotten jealous because all my attention wasn't on him. Though I'd come there for him."

"How did he treat Stevens?"

She rolled her eyes. "He was a prick, bossing him around. I don't really remember after we were at the bar. Like I said."

"What happened?"

"You know what happened. I don't want to think about those two days, any of it. Everything that could have gone wrong, went wrong. In all the worst ways. You have no idea. I just wanted out of there."

My first instinct was to think I'd gotten her as far as she was going to go. But the story I needed lay past where she stopped. Salazar would find a way to push through and get to the bottom of what she'd meant. I had to chip away.

"You're right," I said. "I have no idea. Tell me what I'm missing."

She rose and walked to the door, keeping her head down. "I want you to leave. Now."

"Riley Stevens could spend the rest of his life in prison. You just told me there's more to this. What is it? Did you go down to the boathouse? Did something happen?"

"Yes, one of my best friends died." She wouldn't look at me. She opened the door.

"What aren't you telling me?" I asked.

"Nothing," she said, her voice rising. "I've told you everything I can remember."

"You might be the key to understanding all this. Talk to me."

"Please leave."

"No, you're holding back something. I'm not going until you tell me what that is." My voice had risen more than I should have let it. Her face lost its color.

She left the door open and went to the phone on the wall.

"If you don't leave right now, I'm calling the Boston Police. You don't have any authority here. You're no one."

"Did you get into the middle of something between Alex and Stevens?

CHAPTER THIRTY-TWO

Was there something else going on? It wouldn't be your fault."

"What are you talking about? I told you. I was drunk. I don't remember shit. Don't do this to me."

"Does it make sense to you that Riley Stevens could have killed Alex?"

"I don't know." She dialed the nine. She moved her finger to the one.

"Look," I said. "If you change your mind or think of anything, please call me. It's someone's life."

She stared at the floor.

I left, as requested. She knew more than she was saying. And I'd failed to get it out of her. At least when I hit the street, the derelict in the leather jacket was gone.

Chapter Thirty-Three

I went to Jordan Marsh and bought a dress shirt. I assumed anyone in the club business would be less impressed with my town-issued polo than Mr. Leather Jacket had been. I went to Faneuil Hall and got a bite to eat among the other tourists. I killed an hour watching people, none of whom looked twice at me.

At eight o'clock, I stood at the entrance of Foundation, the largest of Ranford's clubs. I assumed that if it opened at ten, he would be there by now. I didn't plan on having to get by the meathead bouncer who was already stationed at the door of what looked like a warehouse with a black-painted brick exterior and lipstick-red door. The living block of concrete with blond hair, black jeans, and a black shirt with a pink liquor bottle logo couldn't be bothered to look up until I was right in front of him.

"I'm here to see Will Ranford," I said, reaching out for the gold-bar door handles. If I acted like I was supposed to be there, I assumed I'd get less resistance.

A hand like a fielder's glove landed on the middle of my chest. He came out of his lean.

"Hold on there, buddy," he said. "Where do you think you're going?"

"In case the music has been taking a toll on your ears, I said I was going to see Ranford."

"What makes you think he's here?"

"He asked me to meet him around this time."

"And your name is?"

"McCloud. Chief Detective McCloud." I pulled out my badge wallet and flipped it in front of him. I snapped it back before his eyes could pull in the clipper ship and realize it wasn't a Boston shield. He made a face like I was bothering him.

"You know where the office is?" he asked, wiping his nose with the cuff of his shirt.

"No, but I can follow directions."

"Cut to the back corner and then up the stairs," he said, opening the door.

I thought the place would be nicer. A black-haired girl at the ticket booth watched me as she loaded a ticket wheel into her stand. The coat check was understandably empty of coats, but full of beer cases. The bar to the right ran the length of the club. Its lacquered orange top shined. Three blondes behind it stocked Rolling Rocks. They ignored me. Opposing murals covered the side walls. One was a black and gray industrial factory nightscape with the pink bottle logo superimposed over it. The other side was the Boston skyline and the Charles River. A band was setting up on the stage. Sally was not among them.

At the top of the stairs was a hallway. Band flyers papered the walls. A naked bulb burned overhead. I passed a liquor room whose walls were a chain link fence. Another room was full of dusty sound equipment. I finally came to an office. A fleet of metal desks like my own crowded the space. Framed concert posters decorated the walls, the Clap's one of them. The mini-skirted singer fronting it barely resembled the disheveled mess I'd been talking to. A long-haired, bearded Jesus looked up as he fed twenties into a money counter and asked if he could help me. Apparently, he was the friendly guy in the place. I told him I was looking for Ranford, and he directed me further down the hall.

The door to Ranford's office was closed. I thought about it and knocked.

"What now?" came bellowing out. I wondered if he had one of those nineteen-year-olds up on his desk.

I opened the door and stepped into the room.

He held a magazine in his hands, not a nubile young girl. He dropped the tabloid and stabbed a Beck's Beer letter opener into the picture of the nightclub on its cover, anchoring it to the desk. I guessed it might not be one of his.

"Can I help you?" he said, his tone implying that if he could he'd be doing me a tremendous favor.

"I hope so. Would you mind answering a few questions?" He seemed to have the only windows in the building. The failing light of dusk dimly lit the space, while a sleek black desk lamp illuminated the offending periodical.

"Who the fuck are you?" he said.

"I'm Chief Nichols, from Laurel, Maine. I interviewed you the day we found Alex Grimes."

"For fuck's sake," he said. "Shut the door behind you and make it quick."

"Thanks." I did what he asked. He did not have chairs for guests. There was a couch to the side. He reached behind him and turned off the music, some electronic beat that I hadn't recognized. If I chose the sofa, it was far enough away that I'd need to yell. I walked up to the black desktop and stood in front of him. I guessed the lack of chairs might have been a power play for his employees. I was surprised that his own chair was not more throne-like.

"What are you doing here?" he asked. "I told you what I knew then and reiterated my ignorance to the marshal who tracked me down, too."

"I just have a few questions. I'm hoping you know something more than you realize."

"Look, man. I'm getting screwed by this fucking rag who refuses to review my clubs, any of which are infinitely better than Madagascar, noted for the syphilitic bridge and tunnel whores who hang there. And once I call my PR firm and ask them why this so-called journalist hasn't been writing about my spots, I'm probably going to have to get the reporter laid when he does come, which I'm also guessing will be no small feat. And, as you can see, I've got a stack of invoices to go over, so I know exactly where I'm getting robbed by my vendors." He pointed to a sizable pile of yellow, pink, and white bills. "So, I ask you, is this really necessary?"

"I believe it is."

"Then I will spare you exactly two minutes—if you'll speak English and get to the point."

"What do you know about the relationship between Sally Strummer and Alex Grimes?"

"I thought that their boat captain did it."

"That's correct," I said, reasoning that my best strategy was to humor him. "But to make a case in court, we need to establish background. Paint a picture of what it was like over there. I really just want to know what you saw that weekend. The dynamic between them."

"I don't know." He sighed and leaned back. "I just heard things from Abby. She and her brother were like a couple of twelve-year-olds, at each other whenever they got the chance. Apparently, Alex had a hard-on for Strummer for years, and she wasn't interested in crossing that line, even drunk. As if there aren't a million more women out there, some of whom can also sing. Abby would tease his ass off about it when she got the chance. Alex, king of the brats, didn't like that one bit. He still had it for Strummer, even after they got dumped by their label. He was fucking fuming that she talked so much to that captain before he dropped them off. Apparently, the guy was a true believer in the Clap. I get it. They're not bad, even if they are on the downside."

"You know Sally from here?"

"Boston is smaller than you'd think. They play at my clubs. She and I are in some of the same places at the same times. We don't hang out, but we are acquaintances. They're playing at one of my smaller places tonight, in fact, the Subwoofer over in Brighton. They used to play here when they were hitting it. Back to the drawing board for them. It's a tough racket."

"That's what I've heard. The four of you got along well that afternoon?"

"Alex bitched, as usual, first about his job, then about his father, then about the captain. Prime Alex. I don't blame Strummer for not getting with him. I don't know how she could stand to listen to his shit on a regular basis. Maybe that's why she got drunk. She weighs about fifty pounds and was putting them away like a champ. They carried her out. Abby and I counted the minutes until we could ditch them."

"Why was that?"

Music started thumping through the floor. Mainly bass and drums. Slow.

It sounded like the blood pulsing in your head with a hangover.

"Those two carried a lot of negative energy. Whether it was all about Sally, I don't know. Alex just had a hard time dealing with anything. My sister wouldn't let my toddler nieces and nephews act out like he did. *He grabbed a waitress's ass.* That gets someone tossed out of here face-first onto the pavement."

"Was Alex nervous about telling his father he wanted to quit his job?"

"Sure. Randolph cut him off once and sent him to D.C. to a real job. He hated the whole idea of it, but he went. Like a fucking kid, he did what his daddy told him. As if he wasn't an adult and couldn't be an actor, if that's what he wanted to do. Zero balls."

"Was there tension between them?"

"Are you kidding? He was afraid of the old man. Probably always had been. He had to be dreading telling him that he was quitting and heading to Hollywood. He probably took that out on Sally, and her talking to one of her fans gave him the excuse to do it. After she passed out, he probably went after the captain, and the guy dropped him. I hate to say it, but he probably got what he deserved."

"Did you get along with him?"

"I didn't have to. He was afraid of me, too."

"Why is that?"

"Because when I started dating his sister a year ago, he made a crack about my business that I didn't care for. I asked him to watch it, and he told me to fuck off. This was here, in front of my staff. I put my arm around him in a brotherly way, walked him away from the group, and told him that I didn't care who his father was; if he didn't watch his step, I'd kick the shit out of him."

"You weren't a fan," I said, wondering just how big of an issue this had been and if I was getting the whole story.

"No, but we never had a problem after that. Abby could handle him, believe me. He was a mental midget compared to her."

"How do you get along with Secretary Grimes?"

"Very well," Ranford said, smiling. "I kiss his ass. He can be a very helpful person to know. The world doesn't end at the Suffolk County line, and I have plans."

Don't we all, I thought.

Chapter Thirty-Four

When I came down the stairs, there were five people hanging around the bar, one for each bartender. If I hadn't had a two-hour drive home, I might have ordered a drink and worked through what I'd learned. It wasn't much. Even so, I walked back to the Bronco, convinced that Sally knew more than she was saying. Either actively or passively, she had to have been part of what happened, and it was tied to Alex. The frustration that he had experienced was greater than I had thought. It not only encompassed unrequited feelings for Sally, but an ongoing life conflict with his father. Ranford had recognized that Alex was riding the edge.

Everywhere he'd turned, there'd been a problem. While many were of his own creation, they existed. That an incident occurred now seemed inevitable. That the result was murder remained astonishing. It called for an explanation that went beyond likely, probably, and "who else could it have been." Under no circumstances could I leave what Sally knew unspoken. I turned around and went back to Foundation. My friend, the bouncer, gladly gave me directions to the Subwoofer. One less dork that he'd have to worry about in his own club.

I was halfway down the block when I noticed the guy in the gray suit. A car had slammed on its brakes and instinctively, I turned, bracing for the crash as it screeched to a halt. As two college kids crossed the street and flipped off the middle-aged woman driver, who gave it right back to them, I noticed him—tall, short black hair, plain face, gray suit—turn to look in the window of a Seven-Eleven. No one looks away from a crash to check out Coke, Pepsi, and Doritos. There weren't many people on the street, and those that were, were not dressed formally. I passed the Bronco and listened for footsteps. Dress shoes clacked on the sidewalk behind me. I considered that I might be paranoid, so when I turned the corner on Friend Street, I shot a quick glance back. He was there.

Only Salazar had known I was coming to Boston to continue an investigation that didn't exist. She'd notified her colleagues. While that didn't make me happy, it did mean that I had to be onto something. Otherwise, why bother with me?

My stomach gurgled as I tried to walk normally and devise a plan to lose my shadow. I could sprint around a corner and, being in shape, probably ditch him, then race back to the Bronco. But they could have someone watching it, too. Instead, I went into the Government Center parking garage and took the stairs to the right of the elevators. I climbed slowly, waiting to hear him following me. When his shoes on the concrete gave him away, I went up to the third-floor landing and loudly opened the metal door. Then I slipped behind it. I hoped we'd have the place to ourselves.

My tracker paused before entering, presumably listening for my footfalls. What he didn't do was check behind the door. As soon as his shadow moved, I swept around and shot the heel of my palm up under his chin. He dropped, and before he could react, I had him. I put him in a half-nelson and rolled him face down. I didn't go as hard as I could have. I wanted him able to answer questions with a certain amount of lucidity. That didn't preclude my knee riding into his back.

"You know I could snap your shoulder right now," I said, establishing who was going to lead this conversation.

"Let go of me, rube. I'm a federal agent."

"And I'm Wade Boggs."

"My badge is in my front coat pocket, which I can't reach at the moment. Because you are assaulting a federal official. Release me before I lose my temper."

"In case you haven't noticed, you're not in a position to be making demands." I patted him down. No gun. I couldn't imagine a marshal operating naked. That had to be against some kind of regulation.

"You're not carrying. Who are you? The Postmaster General?"

"Look, Nichols. I'm with Justice, Department of Commerce Security."

"Never heard of it."

"Because you don't know anything. I need to talk to you. I mistakenly assumed that you wouldn't act like a cornered rat because someone approached you on a public street."

"You didn't approach me. You were following me and doing a poor job. You must be a desk guy."

"I've had enough of this."

The door opened. A family of four, wife first, came through as her husband stepped to the side to hold it. The boys, maybe ten or eleven, followed with cotton candy in front of their faces. When they stopped to look at us, the husband skirted past the wife and swept his arms around the kids to get them moving.

"Call the police," the self-proclaimed fed I had pinned called out.

"I am the police," I said. I pulled out my badge wallet and flipped it open for them.

"I told you we should have stayed at Faneuil Hall," the wife said as they turned up a row of cars. "But, no, you wanted to see the Boston Garden and then got us lost."

"Are we going to sit here all night?" my man asked.

"Who are you, and why are you following me?"

"You're Chief Timothy Nichols from Laurel, Maine. You are down here interviewing witnesses in the Alex Grimes case. You—"

"I know who I am. That wasn't the question." I ground my knee into his back.

"You are going to regret this. I'm with Justice. You went to see Sally Strummer, Beth Davenport, on Kneeland Street. You then came over here to interview Will Ranford. You are operating outside any official law enforcement apparatus. How would I know this otherwise?"

"Let's see your ID, Postmaster. I'm going to slide my knee off your back, but I'm assuming that you can get your wallet with one hand and without any sudden motion. Because a rube like myself might overreact. That wouldn't be good for you."

"Take it easy," he said, grunting.

I slid off him, and he rolled onto his side, moving his left hand up into his jacket pocket. He flipped it onto the cement beside him. He was expecting me to reach for it, putting me in a position where he could have twisted in the direction of his wrenched arm and tried to pull me down. While I hadn't spent much time in parking garages, I'd spent plenty on wrestling mats.

"Nice try. Out of the million to one odds that you are a fed, I'm going to give you the courtesy of telling you that you're going flat down before I reach for that. And, remember, when you're notifying President Bush, please tell him that I treated you with the utmost respect and courtesy."

"I heard what a fucking dope you were. I just didn't believe it. Shows you what I know." He laughed.

I snatched the wallet. Son of a bitch if Edward Osterreich wasn't a member of Commerce Department Security, an agency I hadn't known existed, complete with a Department of Justice seal on the ID.

"You could have walked up to me and asked, if you had a question. I'm going to let you up now." I stood and took a step back to give the agent some room. He got to his feet. He sighed and rolled his shoulders before brushing the lapels of his jacket, covered with grime. A two-inch tear ran across the left knee of his pants. He shook his head and smiled.

"I'm Agent Edward Osterreich, Chief Nichols," he said, holding his hand out to shake. As I took it, the smile left his face and as he yanked me toward him, his right knee thrust forward with no small force. Only a last second dodge saved me from a direct hit to the family jewels. The partial strike connected enough to send me back into a Duster, where I slid down next to a white-walled Uniroyal. My desire to have kids may have been made moot.

Osterreich waited while I gained my breath. He leaned cross-legged against an Olds and looked at me with annoyance. I wasn't as angry at him as I was at myself for letting my guard down. There was probably some unwritten rule mandating that federal authorities exhibit some form of dominance over local law enforcement. He'd initially blown it but had recovered well enough.

"That was a cheap shot," I said, getting to my feet.

"Cry me a river." He approached and offered me a hand.

"What the fuck do you want?" I said, ignoring it.

He laughed. "Let's go somewhere we can talk." He opened the door to the stairs. At this point, I didn't see why I shouldn't follow. I limped after him into the darkening city.

Chapter Thirty-Five

We were in a booth in a place on Beacon Hill. That's as much as I knew. We hadn't moved in a straight line. Osterreich ordered us a couple of Heinekens. The skunkiness of the beer didn't help. He could see that on my face and smiled.

"Why are you following me?" I said, assuming that Salazar and Grimes had sent him. "Shouldn't you be busy ensuring that no counterfeit Tonka Trucks are infiltrating our department stores?"

"Why are you talking to Strummer and Ranford?" he said, calm as could be.

"I'm supposed to answer your questions while you ignore mine?" I'd had enough of federal law enforcement.

"Don't forget, Chief, I'm with Justice."

"I'm for justice, which I've found to be something different."

He grimaced. "You were removed from this case weeks ago. The suspect is in custody. The evidence against him is more than sufficient."

"If that were true, you wouldn't care what I was doing."

He sighed and ran a hand through his hair. "What are you after?"

"Tying up some loose ends for the suspect's family. They're friends of mine. I'm doing them a favor. On my own time. Unofficially." At least this bordered the truth.

He shook his head and exhaled. "Do you know the extent of training that federal agents in Justice receive? Most of us have graduate degrees. We are trained, in language that you may understand, to see through the bullshit. Save us both some time and answer the questions."

I gave him my best fake smile.

"It's my understanding that you identified Stevens as a suspect from the start. What surprises me is that you were actually right about something. Why are you down here?"

Another wave of nausea passed through me. I fought it down.

"If you're right about Stevens, how could I possibly screw it up? Why are you following me? Why plant an undercover outside Strummer's apartment?"

"We are not watching anyone but you. Strummer has cooperated fully. You're the only one running around trying to muck things up. And, this, after you've been ordered to stop."

If they had no inclination that Sally might know more than she was letting on, they wouldn't care if I questioned her. But they did. This only strengthened my belief that I was on the right track.

"How could I be a problem?" I asked.

"We are not taking chances." He took a drink from his bottle in an attempt to be dramatic.

"What does that mean?"

"We don't want this perpetrator getting off on a technicality because you don't follow or know procedure. We can't chance a defense attorney getting testimony thrown out because of the appearance of witness tampering or a due process impropriety executed by a rogue local cop."

"You're afraid I'll find something that may indicate Riley Stevens did not kill Alex Grimes."

"That's absolutely not a concern." He pointed his bottle at me. "You leave this shit alone. Let justice take its course. It's in everyone's best interest."

"Except Riley Stevens."

He sighed and finished his beer.

"Look, Nichols. You are less than an ant, and the only thing you can do here is create havoc. Please remember that you have an appointed position, and a censure from the Department of Justice will get you removed. Think about that when you walk out of here, get into your piece of shit truck, and hightail it back to Maine. You are done bothering Strummer and Ranford.

They will not be talking should they see you again. Go back and tell your friends, that killer's family, that the story is the story. Because it is."

"Thanks for the beer," I said, leaning on the table to get up. I didn't look back and didn't care if he thought I was whipped and crawling home. All this attention told me that whatever happened at that Compound was different than what the US Marshals Service, the Maine State Police, and, most importantly, Randolph Grimes were claiming. I wasn't about to give up now.

When I stepped outside, I started in the direction of the Bronco. Then I thought about it. I was probably being followed. I wasn't sure that I was headed in the right direction anyway. I hopped into the first cab I saw. I told the driver to head to Brighton to the Subwoofer. I watched the back window for a tail. There were too many cars for a rube like me to tell if I had one.

I asked the driver to go past the club and turn at the next block. I stopped him in front of an Irish bar. I went in and had a Harp, watching the door. No one came in who I would have pegged as a fed. I paid and went out through the kitchen. A rat the size of a lap dog eyed me in the alley behind the place. It was the least of my problems as I circled around to the Subwoofer.

Chapter Thirty-Six

I t cost ten bucks to see the Clap. The Subwoofer was a long, thin space with a raised stage at the far end. Sally Strummer was bouncing and belting out a song while her guitar players shook behind her. Her voice was stronger in person than on tape, even though the instruments behind her sounded louder and more chaotic. I recognized the Bullethead song, having listened to the tape a few times now. I hobbled over to the bar and tried not to bump into anyone, my groin still delicate. I ordered a beer and a shot. I thought it might take a bite out of the pain running through my crotch. I scoured the room for possible feds, who I was sure would stand out in this sea of tattered clothes and big hair, while I tried to think of what I was going to say to Sally. When I went to take a piss before the set ended, I was greeted with a red stream. The guy at the next urinal caught a glance, looked at me, and slid in the other direction.

I finished my drink as the Clap closed with *Boo Boo Kat*. The hundred-plus people crowding the room hooted and hollered. I limped to the front. A skinny guy in a Clap t-shirt hopped onto the stage and started rolling up cords. The drummer, hair like a rusted Brillo pad, tossed his sticks into the humanity. I went left, assuming the band would head to a dressing room in the back. I started past the stage to catch Sally as she stepped down. A kid in a Subwoofer shirt stopped me.

"Where do you think you're going, chief?"

I looked to see if I recognized him. Then I realized he was only being a wise ass.

"I need to talk to Sally," I said.

"No one but the band gets back there."

I nodded and carefully slid my hand into my pocket. He smiled, maybe expecting a twenty. I came up with the badge wallet, which I again flipped quickly.

"You're going to need to talk to the manager," he said.

"I'm not arresting anyone. Ranford sent me. What'd you say your name was?"

"I didn't." He looked around for a manager, then sighed and nodded toward the back. "Stay where I can see you."

"You're kidding, right?" I asked.

"Take it easy. I'm just trying to do my job."

"I'll let the boss know. I'm sure he'll appreciate it."

He gave me a look, unable to tell if I was serious or yanking his chain.

The room still had a buzz going through it when Sally came offstage and into the narrow hallway.

"You've got to be fucking kidding me," she said when she saw me. "Get the fuck away." She turned and headed to the back. The bouncer was distracted by four coeds trying to get to the guitar player and bassist. I followed Sally.

"Wait," I said, stopping with her in front of a door. "What's wrong?"

"What's wrong?" she said, her voice loud enough that I thought she still might have a microphone. "Less than an hour after you left, I had some creep from the Department of Justice at my place. And you know what he wanted to know? What you were asking me. And then you know what he told me? That I shouldn't say anything to you. That you can't be trusted. The fucking Justice Department. Like I haven't dealt with enough shit."

"Mid-size guy, grey suit, black hair? Osterreich?"

"Ostrich or something, yes."

"He's not really from Justice. He's with Commerce Security."

"What the fuck is that?"

"I don't know, to be honest, other than that's Randolph Grimes's department."

"Stay away from me." She turned to go into the dressing room, the size of which wouldn't have satisfied my ex-wife as a closet. She started to shut the door behind her, but I got my hand out and followed her in. She sighed.

"I was questioned by Osterreich, too, after I talked to Will Ranford. That was a few hours ago. They're worried that I'm going to uncover something, and you're the only person who may know what that is. If it's not brought to light, an innocent man is headed to jail for a long time."

"How many times do I have to tell you that I don't remember anything? Maybe Ranford knows this mystery clue you think exists. I don't." She avoided looking at me and sat down on a stuffed chair that looked liberated from a town dump. An iced case of beer in a clear plastic bin sat on top of a coffee table made out of a road sign that said Revere Beach. She grabbed one.

"Ranford doesn't know anything."

"Neither do I," she said, flicking the bottle cap into a gray garbage can in the corner of the room. "Did you ever think that maybe Stevens did it and that they don't want you fucking up their case?"

"I put them onto Stevens. But the more I think about it, the less sense it makes."

"I was drunk," she said. "That's all I know. It's all I want to know."

She wouldn't meet my gaze and couldn't keep her hands still. Her feet were sliding and tapping as she talked. She was lying.

"What happened that you're not telling me? Even if you're not sure it matters, or if you aren't one hundred percent certain, it could make a difference."

"I don't have anything for you."

"If that was true, we wouldn't have government agents following us from Laurel to Brighton."

"They're out there now?" she asked, looking up.

"I don't know, to be honest. But I wouldn't doubt it."

"They told me not to talk to you. I'm going to listen to them."

"If you tell me, I can help you."

"Sure, I'll trust a hick sheriff over the US Department of Justice."

"I hate to tell you this, but whatever it is that you may or may not think you're aware of, it's information that some powerful people are afraid is going to get out. If you tell me what you know, or what you think happened, I can piece the rest together. We can make sense of it. If we don't, you are at risk."

"If you will leave me alone, I'll be fine." She finished her beer. "I'll give you ten seconds to get out of here before I scream, and every bouncer in this club comes in to kick the crap out of you."

"They know I'm a cop."

"Pretty sure that since you're not a Boston cop, they won't give a shit. I'm done. I don't know anything. I can't tell you anything. I can't help you." She stood up, grabbed a blaze orange sweatshirt from a hook on the wall, and moved to the door, stopping just before she'd have to cross by me. Her eyes were glassy. "I've got a friend playing the Rat, and you're making me late. Please move."

I shook my head and got out of her way. "You have my card. When your conscience kicks in, and you feel like helping an innocent kid who happens to look up to you and what you're supposed to stand for, call me. We don't have a lot of time."

As I turned to follow her, Sally's bandmates were on their way in with the coeds. We turned sideways so they could pass. "Who's the square, Sally?" one said in a teasing voice.

"Shut up, dickhead," she said.

I slowly ambled to the bar. She worked her way out the door, stopping to talk to a few fans. It had thinned out, so I guessed maybe the group setting up wasn't as good as the Clap. I had no interest in finding out. I had a Bronco to reach across town, and then I would retreat like a whipped dog. A host of federal agencies could rejoice. And Riley Stevens would pay for it.

Outside, there wasn't a cab in sight. I started walking toward the far-off Citgo sign. The Bronco sat miles beyond it.

I'd been shuffling for a few minutes when I spotted Sally in her deer-season sweatshirt a block ahead of me. She was headed to a trolley station where the tracks ran down the center of Commonwealth Ave. I thought about jogging to catch up and giving it one last shot but I knew I'd have better luck trying to put my fist through one of the brick buildings I was passing. And there was that live wire firing in my crotch with every imperfect footfall. Ahead at the corner, Sally waited for the pedestrian sign to switch off its red "Don't Walk" warning. The day I needed a sign to tell me to cross the road was the day I'd know it was time to stay off the streets. I could at least ask her if the trolley would get me to the Boston Garden area. I winced as I jogged across the intersection, passing in front of a maroon Impala. The driver looked familiar. Odd, in Boston. I stopped and took another look.

The black leather sports jacket and goatee slapped me awake. He hadn't noticed me because his eyes were locked in at the end of the block—on that orange sweatshirt, waiting for permission to step into the street. His hands readjusted their grip on the wheel. He revved the engine. Then he shifted. I ran. I needed to reach Sally before the light changed. I ignored the pain rifling my groin.

I had ten yards to go when "WALK" illuminated in white. A green trolley approached, screeching like it had never seen a drop of oil. I yelled, but Sally couldn't hear me. Under the grinding of the streetcar, I heard the grip of tires and the roar of a performance engine. I leapt off the curb and slid over the hood of a parked Datsun B210. I landed in the street and grabbed Sally by the hood, yanking her back as she took her second step into the crosswalk. The Impala swerved toward us, then blew past, its tires squealing onto the cross street to the right. It couldn't have missed her by more than an inch. Sally was propped in front of me, feet on the pavement, with her body suspended by my grip on her well-made shirt. Her glazed eyes looked up at me. I could feel her shaking.

"I almost just died," she said as she tried to get her feet under her.

"I'd say that was the plan."

"Fucking drunk driver."

"That wasn't an accident," I replied.

"Fuck off," she said.

"The driver was staked out in front of your apartment this morning."

"I'm sure," she said, rolling wet eyes.

"I wish I was kidding. I'm not."

She looked at me, lips quivering. Her head tilted to the right. She wiped her eyes, maybe realizing that what I'd been telling her might actually be true.

"I need a drink," she said.

"You and me both."

Chapter Thirty-Seven

I was not unfamiliar with dive bars, but the place Sally brought us to made the Rusty Bullet seem like the Four Seasons. It had the traditional stale-beer-seeped-into-the-floorboards scent but melded it with aromas of puke and sawdust. Sally called the bartender by name and ordered two beers and shots of Cuervo Gold. I paid. I'd finally found a place in this city where I could afford to drink. She led me to a booth at the end of the room. She slid into the back, and I shook my head and asked her to let me sit there. She looked confused for a second and then switched sides. I placed the drinks on the table and sat with my back to the wall and a clear view of the door. No self-respecting fed would be caught dead in a place like this. Maybe we were safe for the time being.

Onstage, she'd looked almost like a teenager. Now, worry lines I hadn't seen, even on the morning we'd found Alex, rose from the corners of her eyes. Her hand shook as she reached for a shot glass. I grabbed mine. It was stuck to the table, which probably hadn't been wiped since Paul Revere drank there.

"What is it?" she said after downing the tequila. "Are they after me because of you? Or are you some kind of fucked-up guardian angel?"

"You didn't notice a goateed guy, maybe in his thirties, brown hair, average size, black leather jacket, hanging out on Kneeland lately?"

She shrugged. "There's always sketchy people around, doing stuff. It's not Newbury Street."

"The guy I described, he chatted me up this morning when he saw me knocking on your door. I thought he might be undercover with the marshals.

He was driving that car tonight. He's no fed or any kind of cop."

"What are you talking about? Like he's a hitman?"

"Sorry, but yeah, something like that." It sure looked like it.

"I think I'm having a heart attack." Her thin chest heaved, and a vein pulsed in her neck. Her hands gripped the edge of the table.

"I'll be right back." I went to the bar and got two more tequilas.

I returned and handed her one of the shots. We locked eyes, clinked the glasses, and downed them.

"Why would someone want to hurt me?" she said, the register of her voice rising. "It's got to be because you're here. I don't know anything. I haven't said shit. What the fuck?" She looked down into her lap, then wiped tears from her eyes. They weren't coming from the alcohol. I had to lay it out for her.

"Someone doesn't believe you. They think you know something. You might not even realize what it is. They're afraid if you get questioned enough, it will come out." Her jaw hung open, her eyes were red, and I was pretty sure she hadn't stopped shaking. I had second thoughts on how much I should tell her. But she'd nearly been run down on a city street and needed to know what she was facing. "If Stevens didn't kill Alex, someone else did. That's what this is all about. Protecting whoever that is."

"Who the fuck is it, then?"

"It could be Randolph Grimes." I'd been refusing to consider the possibility but had finally worked myself into that corner. Only one person had the clout to direct an investigation and bring this level of firepower—marshals, Commerce Security, and what had to be his own operative, the leather-jacketed driver of the Impala. Grimes was doing everything possible to make sure nothing derailed the conviction of Riley Stevens. The question remained: Why, if not to cover himself and protect his position?

"What if it wasn't like that?" Sally said, her breath catching in her throat as panic crossed her face. "What if Randolph is trying to protect Alex?"

"In what way?" What remained of him had been scattered in the Atlantic.

"Like his legacy," she said. She took a deep breath and shuddered. "What if something did happen?"

"With Alex?" She *had been* holding out. I was going to need another shot.

She nodded and looked down as she talked. "It's hazy, to say the least, and with Alex gone, I didn't think it mattered. I didn't want it to matter. I think he did go after Stevens. He was already furious with him, and then…"

She brought her head up. "I didn't want to say anything," she said. "Because it makes me fucking sick."

I nodded, not wanting to stop the flow of words that she'd finally let loose. If I hadn't just seen her almost killed, she'd have been hearing a takedown of how stupid she'd been to stay quiet when someone's life was on the line, and we'd been begging her to talk to us. It wasn't lost on me that this was hard for her. She hadn't realized the magnitude of what she'd become entangled in.

"I wasn't lying when I said I was shitfaced and could barely remember anything. We were at that bar on the water. Like always, Abby and Alex were at each other. She was calling him a pussy for not standing up to his father and quitting his job. He usually didn't take her too seriously, but she must have struck a nerve. And she had a point. He called her a soulless pig for getting into commercial real estate, as if it were continuing some family curse. I guess he was ignoring that he'd spent the last two years working for some bullshit, pro-business think tank. They kept at it all day. I got wrecked."

"Did he give you a hard time, too?"

"Oh, yeah. He was steamed that I'd talked to Stevens. But the guy was a huge fan and got deep into the music. He appreciated the band." She gazed down at the bench next to her. "I'm pretty sure it was Stevens who picked me up in the restaurant and carried me to the car. With Alex directing, of course. That's when I started blacking out."

She looked me in the eye, then dropped her head and talked into her lap.

"The next thing I knew, I was on top of the bed in my room. It must have been later. I don't know who put me there. I'm guessing Alex. It was like a dream, but it wasn't. Like when you're a kid, and you have your tonsils out, and they put you under and have you count backward, and you start doing it, and you're awake but not really, and you don't feel great, you're kind of floating. It was that, but different. Like I was in a pool, but there wasn't a pool. And it wasn't a warm-in-the-sun kind of thing. I felt like I could go under any second. Drowning. It scared the hell out of me."

Her face was twisted, and she refused to look at me as she spoke. Waves of nausea spread through me.

"I was laying there, fighting not to go down. Then I was being talked to, softly. I don't know what the words were. I don't even know if I heard them. They were like background music in a movie. Even though they were trying to make me comfortable, I didn't trust them. Something was wrong. I was just too messed up to figure out what. I didn't understand. Then I felt my cutoffs sliding down my legs. That must have triggered something. I tried to move, but I couldn't. I don't know if it was the alcohol or what. It was like a two-ton blanket of dread was covering me. I had to get out of there but couldn't move."

She stopped and buried her head in her hands. Her shoulders trembled as she cried. I didn't say anything, not out of some psychological strategy but because I didn't know what to say. She took a deep breath and got her breathing back under control.

"Who was it?" I asked.

"I couldn't open my eyes. It was like I was hypnotized. Or maybe I didn't want to. I don't even know. But it felt like I was going down for good, and I knew, with whatever portion of my brain was left working, that I had to do something. So I used my one talent: I screamed as loud as I could.

"Everything stopped. It got quiet. Maybe it was for a minute. It could've been ten. Then there were two voices, and they'd changed. They were loud and angry. Maybe doors opening and closing, too. Then they were gone. I must have passed back out. I woke up in the morning under the comforter, and my shorts were on the corner of the bed, folded."

She looked at me with wet, red eyes.

"You weren't assaulted?"

She shook her head. "Someone stopped it. Someone must have heard me and come in."

"I'm sorry to ask: Are you sure that you didn't dream this?"

"No fucking way. It was real, like being caught in an undertow. As bad off as I was, I knew it was happening. That's why I screamed. And believe me, I'm a drop-the-clothes-to-the-floor girl. Especially when I've been drinking. My folded shorts were on the bed. I didn't do that."

She held out a tremoring hand for me to see.

"Do you have any idea who was there with you? Who stopped it?"

She sighed. "It had to be Alex. Since college, he'd accepted that it wasn't ever going to happen with us, that we were only going to be friends. He'd joke about it every now and then, of course. I never thought it was more than that. But maybe he never gave up on it. I was supposed to be his moral support, because he was going to tell his father he was quitting. I don't believe he invited me to get me drunk and fuck me when I passed out. But the drinking and drama got bad, like the brown acid at Woodstock. It must have been more than he could handle. He must've really snapped because he wasn't violent. Only I was the one who was going to suffer for it. His father must have heard me scream and come in. Thank God I did it."

"Jesus Christ." Her story made sense.

"Alex probably ran out and found the only other target he could get over on, that boat guy. What's that called…displacement? Transference? The captain probably wasn't about to take it, and I don't blame him. He was probably just defending himself."

She gulped her beer.

"You can see why I didn't want to talk about this, right? It doesn't change anything, except to rip me apart every time I think about it, and I can't stop thinking about it."

"You think that Randolph was afraid that if this came out, it would tarnish Alex's reputation?" And by association, his own.

"Why else?" she said.

I could think of several reasons.

"Did he discuss this with you?" I asked.

She nodded. "It was awful, if awful can even describe it." She motioned to me with her empty beer glass. I went up and got a couple more. She could put it away for someone her size. I wondered how much they'd drunk that

Saturday at the Dockside to send her under. I placed the pints on the table.

"How did it play out?" I asked.

"That next morning was the worst of my life. I could laugh about getting dropped by our record label, as there's a certain amount of black humor involved. This was different. He sent that bitchy maid up to my room and had her knocking on the door. I didn't know where I was when I opened my eyes. I just wanted whoever was out there to go away, but she stuck her fat head in and said, 'Miss,' all cheery like she wasn't trying to wake me up. She told me that Secretary Grimes wanted to see me in his office and that she'd wait to bring me down, as it was on the other side of the house." Sally shook her head and rolled her eyes. "The place is big, but not that big."

"I've been subjected to that office myself."

"I was in a fog, like I'd done something stupid but couldn't remember what. Then I saw my shorts on the edge of the bed. It started coming back to me. I could feel them going down my legs. I don't know why that's the only thing that stayed with me, that weird friction against my skin that sparked me to scream. I grabbed sweatpants and two t-shirts out of my bag and told myself I wasn't going to cry. Not with her outside my door. I went to the bathroom and threw up. Partly because of the alcohol and partly because I remembered what was about to be done to me before the old man came in."

"It couldn't have been easy," I said, a dope stating the obvious. She'd had reason to be a mess when I'd intercepted her at the gate. It was also clear why Grimes hadn't wanted her talking to me. "What did he say?"

Her jaw tightened as her expression shifted from shaken to angry.

"I really didn't know what to think when I walked in there. I was a wreck. I felt like shit. He's sitting behind that desk like a one-man Supreme Court. I couldn't look at him. I stared out the window at the water and the flowers. They were so beautiful, and I was garbage. One of my best friends had tried to rape me."

"What did Grimes say?"

"At first, nothing. He sits there looking at me like I'm supposed to explain how it could have happened. As if it were my fault. He just keeps staring. I had to fight to stop from breaking down again. I wasn't going to let myself do it."

"Is that when he told you about Alex?"

"No."

"What was his opener?"

"He didn't ask if I was okay or how I was doing. He didn't apologize for his son being a degenerate rapist. He said, 'I understand that you were somewhat confused last night. Can you tell me what you remember?' I was honest, like a fool. I said, 'Something was about to happen, I think, but it didn't.' He continued to look at me, his face like a fucking stone. 'Tell me exactly,' he said.

"I said, 'I suppose I have you to thank for it not happening.' He nodded and waited. I told him that I remembered being carried out of the bar. That I must have passed out, but then I was kind of aware that I was in my room, on the bed. Of course, I was crying through every word, it being bad enough to remember one of your best friends trying to do that to you, then having to tell someone, his father, for fuck's sake, as he sat there like I was on trial. I said I kind of woke up when someone began pulling my shorts down and that I'd screamed. And that's when he must have come into the room and stopped it, and I must have passed back out after that. That was it."

"What did he say?" Grimes knew what had happened but needed to hear what Sally knew. He'd wanted to frame things from the start—in a way that would maintain that Alex's death had been an accident.

"He asked if I remembered Alex in my room. I shook my head. He asked if I was sure. And I said that he must have been, but that I couldn't even open my eyes. He nodded, an odd look on his face. He asked if I remembered him being in the room. I shook my head again, no. He kept staring at me and said, 'I have something to tell you.' He took a deep breath. 'The police found Alex this morning. It looks like he drowned.' All I could say was, 'What?' I didn't believe him. He repeated it and told me that he'd just come back from some pier where they'd brought his body in."

"That was me," I said.

"I asked how that could be, and Randolph told me that Alex had become unstable, mentally. After what had happened with me—and that's what he kept calling it, 'what happened,' not 'when my son tried to fuck you when you were passed out'—it must have really troubled him. And that when he wanted to reflect, he liked to sit on the seawall. Randolph believed he went out there to think about what he'd done and slipped and fell in. He said that it was also possible that Alex couldn't live with himself and had thrown himself into the ocean. He said that we might never know.

"Guilt broke out over me like sweat. I thought it was my fault. If I hadn't come up there, and Alex hadn't tried what he had, he wouldn't have felt guilty, like he couldn't face that part of himself, and that it only had come out because of me.

"The old man said, 'I'm sorry to have to tell you this.' He told me that when Alex slipped or dove into the water, he'd hit his head, and that's what killed him. That's when I broke down and started sobbing. He said that we couldn't undo things that had been done. That the police would be talking to me. He told me that he didn't want Alex's legacy to involve his son's 'egregious lapse of judgment'—as he called it—that led to this tragedy. He said that as my recollection of the details of the evening was hazy, it would be wise if I didn't mention any of it. That cold fucking bastard said he thought that this result was predictable, that Alex had been declining mentally, and that I shouldn't put any of this on myself. He asked if I would do that for him—and for the Alex that I had known in better times.

"I just sat there. I couldn't speak. I was in fucking shock. Then he cleared his throat and told me there was a selfish reason that I should keep quiet, as well. That if I told anyone what Alex had tried to do to me, that I'd immediately become a suspect. And that, as I couldn't remember the details, while we both knew that I didn't kill him—not directly, anyway, he added— the police would certainly bring me in and put me through the wringer. 'They can be bastards,' he said. 'You've been through enough.' Like I didn't know. And then he gave me the let resting dogs lie bullshit. I promised him I wouldn't say a word to anyone. I just wanted out of there. I asked him if I could leave. Like I had to have permission. So, I ran up to my room crying my ass off, threw up again, gathered my stuff, and got the fuck out. That's when I ran into you."

"Grimes didn't tell you to stay until we talked to you?" Which had been my instructions.

"No. He wanted me to leave. He just forgot to send the guy out to open the gate until you'd already found me."

Randolph had known that either the accident or suicide scenario would have been framed as a tragedy, one that would not have threatened his position and could have even engendered sympathy. He was also aware that sharing what had actually happened would have clarified Alex's behavior and actions, revealing something he didn't want out in public: that his son had been a sexual predator. Randolph had manipulated Sally to think that she'd been the catalyst for Alex's death and took steps to make sure her story remained buried. He'd stayed the course even when Salazar flipped the narrative and determined that Stevens was the killer. While Sally believed that he'd acted to preserve his son's reputation, his actions went well beyond what that would have called for. We'd just survived an attempt on her life.

"You didn't mention any of this to the marshal in Boston?"

"No. Not to the Justice guy, either, and they make you seem like a fucking peach."

"They believed that you didn't remember anything."

"Why not? Everyone in that fucking bar must have seen me carried out. I couldn't even talk."

"Did they push you on it?"

"If you mean did they ask the same question about twenty times in twenty different ways? Then, yes."

"You never mentioned the assault to anyone, your mother, your manager, the guys in the band, a friend?"

"You're the only one who knows about it."

"Do you think you could have been drugged?" There were cases of sedatives being dropped in women's drinks. We hadn't seen it in Laurel, but it wasn't unheard of.

"In my business, we do some drinking, not to mention other things. But those Grimes are professionals. I just went under the table. Way under."

"Was the marshal the one who told you that they thought Stevens had killed Alex?"

"Yes. He asked how Stevens and Alex had gotten along. I told him Alex hadn't been happy with him. When I told him that I thought Alex drowned, he told me to just answer the questions. It wasn't hard to put it together, what was behind it. And it made sense. He didn't like how we'd left him out of the conversation. Alex cared about the band as an entity, but not the music. There's a difference. He must have gone crazy trying to take it out on Stevens. I feel horrible about it. So many things would be different if I hadn't been there. I mean, it's hard to ignore the years he was there for me, even with what he did. It makes it that much worse."

"You believe that Alex went down and tried to take out all this pent-up frustration on Stevens."

"Easily," she said.

I nodded. She thought she was the reason Alex had acted as he had. On the surface, her incident didn't appear to change Salazar's depiction of events and could even support that narrative. But Randolph wasn't willing to let it come to light. There had to be still more to this story.

"I need another shot," she said. I was trying to get my mind in gear. I looked at her, but my vision went to the door. A couple with matching purple haircuts had entered. Not federal agents. "Okay, I guess it's my turn. Though I should know better." She got up and then stopped. "I can trust you, can't I?"

"Of course," I said. She continued to the bar.

Someone, presumably Alex, had attempted to assault Sally while she was incapacitated. Sally never opened her eyes. Maybe she was that drunk, buried at the edge of consciousness. The assault happens in a house where everyone claims they were asleep, undisturbed. We know this is a falsehood for Randolph Grimes, because the assault is interrupted, presumably by him. After being frustrated there, Alex storms out of the room and makes his way down to his only other available target, Stevens. But where does this leave Randolph? It would be hard to believe that he watched Alex take off, said, "Ho, hum," and went back to bed. A father would be torn up over what he'd seen. If he had walked in on his son and pulled him off Sally, there must have been, at minimum, a dressing down and an argument. It could have gotten physical. At the pier, when Crowley pulled back the tarp that revealed his dead son, Grimes had looked angry, not shocked. That was the moment he started protecting himself, because at that point he didn't know what Sally remembered. He could have and should have told us then what had happened but did not. He'd wanted us to accept that it was an accident. It was understandable that a father would not want it revealed that his son tried to assault a house guest, believably to the extent that he'd bury the truth. But that's where things stopped making sense.

If Alex had confronted Stevens, Randolph would have been aware of it. And if he had known that Stevens had killed Alex, it was unimaginable that he would have allowed him to remain free under the accidental death scenario—no matter how much the truth would have tarnished his son's reputation or threatened his own political career. When it came to pass that Stevens could be convicted of the crime, Grimes doesn't stray from that narrative then, either. He took steps to see that it wasn't challenged. I was sidelined for suggesting the accidental death should be verified, then told not to challenge Salazar's subsequent conclusion.

Grimes's actions following Stevens's arrest didn't equate with someone who only wanted to keep his son's issues hidden. I'd been watched, interfered with, and threatened for looking into the details of the case. Of course, Grimes wanted me off it because he knew Stevens was innocent, and Grimes was afraid I'd find something that could prove it. And then there was Sally. She'd given no indication to any law enforcement authority that she knew anything. She wasn't talking. Randolph knew that, but he was also the only one aware that she knew there was more to the story. She could potentially blow things wide open. And, as hard as it was to believe, he'd tried to have her killed. That brought me back to, if Stevens didn't kill Alex, someone else did. Randolph Grimes was the only other person who could have done it. As he had told me, sometimes circumstances dictate our actions. Easy to understand now.

"Are you going to drink that or what?" Sally said. My thoughts returned to the present.

"I'm planning on it."

"Are you drunk? You were gone for like three minutes."

"Someone tried to kill you tonight."

"It could have been a drunk driver. You might have only thought you recognized that guy."

"No. It was him, and he had you lined up."

Randolph would not take a step like that unless he felt he had no choice.

"When Alex was in the room and undressing you, and then he was interrupted, you said the room changed. Could there have been a fight?"

"Honestly, I don't know. It shifted, the atmosphere. I could feel it. But I don't know what happened."

"What are the chances that when Randolph came into the room and found Alex, that when he pulled him out, they could have come to blows?"

"I suppose they could have. But why would Alex have gone down after Riley Stevens then?"

"He wouldn't have. That would have happened before he went to your room. Maybe Stevens added to Alex's frustration by walking away from his tirade."

"You think his father killed Alex and then tried to pin it on Stevens?" Her face paled.

"It makes sense. Alex was frustrated with his father, too. Considerably. You, Abby, and Ranford all remarked on that. He'd gone up there to teach you a lesson. Rape is a violent crime, as well as a sexual one. When his father came in and stopped it, it's logical that Alex would redirect his anger and frustration at Randolph, the original object of the rage. Randolph may have had to defend himself. And killed his son."

"If that were the case, why wouldn't he just call the police?"

Salazar's missives on Washington careerism came back to me.

"It would have been the right thing to do. But it may have threatened his position, a scandal like that. I don't know. An accidental death would have cleared everyone. That's what he wanted from the start. Even Riley Stevens as the killer functions that way—except, of course, for Riley Stevens. But Randolph was aware that you knew different. You have information that could implicate him in a cover-up and obstruction of justice. Manslaughter, if father and son did fight. He must have believed that you knew more than you'd told him. He was afraid that I'd get to you and expose it. I'm sorry."

She looked at me, slack-jawed.

"I wasn't going to let Stevens pay for this," I said, "until I was satisfied that he'd done it. I'm now sure that he didn't."

"Randolph would have thrown his own son into the ocean, after he'd killed him?" She placed her hand on her stomach.

I nodded.

It fit. Stevens said that Alex had approached him just after nine-thirty. Abby and Ranford had arrived home at close to one. Alex would have returned to the main house a little before ten. He's frustrated. Alex goes into Sally's room. Of course, Randolph is not asleep. He hears the scream and comes out to investigate. When he sees what Alex is trying to do and pulls his son out of there, it's the ultimate humiliation. Alex goes after his father. There'd be no choice, seeing red as he must have been. Though Randolph is older, he's fit and athletic and defends himself. It happens.

The hair on the back of my neck was standing up.

Randolph doesn't give up even when Salazar rules out the accidental death that she was brought in to verify. On Monday night, Randolph has time and opportunity to pitch the boat hook into the cove himself. Tuesday, he points Salazar in its direction. Stevens is a dead duck. But as I sat there inhaling the stale beer, I also realized that if I were one hundred percent correct in theory, it would be a monumental task to prove it. I could hear Salazar's throaty laugh as I tried to explain it.

The lights in the bar came on. Grit covered every visible surface, and they were all painted black. Sally's hands shielded her eyes. She was the only one who knew the accepted story was incomplete. It was enough to get her killed. She needed protection. I couldn't just take her home and tell her to lock the door.

"Do you have any friends around here?"

"Sure. Why?"

"Someone tried to kill you. You're not safe if you go to your loft."

"What? Do I have to hide out or something? I've got like ten bucks on me."

"Don't you have a bank card?"

"I do. That doesn't mean there's money in there. We haven't sold a record in a fucking year, and I make six bucks an hour answering phones. I can't afford to run off to Mexico."

"You can't go anywhere like your parents' house, or your best friend's, or stay with the guys in your band. If they come looking for you, you need to be somewhere they're not going to turn you up."

"So, I've got to find some marginal friend and ask if I can crash indefinitely? And maybe borrow a few bucks and some clothes? Do I mention that someone might show up who wants to kill me?"

"I'd leave out that part." I slid my hand into my pocket and handed her some change. "Start making some calls, and I'll get you there."

"You realize that you sound like some whack job from the *Twilight Zone*?"

"I'm aware."

She got up and walked over to the payphone next to the bathroom. This would be okay for tonight. If not Mexico, she'd need to go somewhere. I could get her to my Uncle Hugh's in Vermont. But I couldn't bring her there myself. Someone would be waiting when I got back to the Bronco. It didn't matter if it was a fed or our friend in his leather jacket. Sally came back and stood next to the table. She told me she had a place for the night, and it was only a couple blocks away. I stood up to escort her. It hurt, and I was a little woozy from the booze. I needed to get my thoughts clear. I just wasn't good at it.

Chapter Thirty-Eight

"I'm guessing your new guy isn't a musician."

"He's not, but he's crazier than he looks," Sally said.

I could hear them through the thin walls of the apartment's bathroom. Andrea, the girl questioning Sally's taste in men, had two nose rings, small gold circles that went through her left nostril. It seemed an odd choice for a stunning brunette with brown eyes and smooth skin. But I was too tired to question her choice of jewelry or her evaluation of me. It looked like Sally had made a good choice. The furniture in the apartment was leather. Modern paintings hung on the walls. Andrea was also about Sally's size and wore an expensive-looking silk shirt and black leggings. If Sally borrowed clothes, she'd be upgrading.

Andrea had just returned from a dance club. She and Sally chatted about Ranford's new enterprise. The polar opposite of the Sub-Woofer, it had featured a DJ and had been all strobes and videos and pulsing beats, whatever that meant. Sally told her that the guys were having a party in the loft and that she couldn't deal with them.

"Fucking Brad," she said. She looked over at me. "You know what they call a drummer who gets dumped by his girlfriend?"

"Nope." I took a sip of the beer she'd offered me.

"Homeless." At some point over the previous months, Andrea had kicked Brad, the Clap's drummer, out of this very apartment. He now couch-surfed between band members.

Andrea then told us she was beat and offered us blankets and the couch. We thanked her, and she went to bed. I looked around. Other pieces of furniture included a wicker bench that wasn't much larger than a coffee table and an under-stuffed bean bag chair.

"You can have the couch," I said. She went over and flopped onto it.

"What am I going to do?" she said, sitting up. Her elbows were on her knees, her head in her hands.

"You need to get out of town," I said, starting to pace. "Give me some time to get this into the open. Once your assault isn't a state secret, you'll be okay."

"What do you mean?" She looked sick. "I'm going to have to talk about this? I'm not sure I can do that."

"You may have to. You'll be safer if it comes out in public and people know."

"You can pull this off?" She patted the couch next to her. Her eyes were small, and the lines around them had reemerged. Yet, she probably looked one hundred percent better than I did. I sat down, leaving a cushion between us.

"I'm going to have to," I said.

"You probably don't get paid enough," she said.

"I've heard that before." I leaned back and took a deep breath. It felt good to have clarity on what I needed to do, even though I had no idea how I was going to accomplish it.

"I'm such a moron," she said. "I should have kept my mouth shut and not told Grimes—or you—anything."

"That's a heavy weight to carry, and it wouldn't have mattered. What happened made you dangerous to Randolph Grimes, whether you remembered it or not. Judging by what he's done, I don't think he believed you anyway. Even if he did, he might not have chanced this ever coming back on him. We don't know. If I hadn't pursued it, maybe he believes it's buried for good, and nothing comes of it. But there would have been a cost to that, and Riley Stevens would have paid it. I have to see this through, or we'll all suffer."

She looked up at me and slid closer.

I sunk into the corner of the couch. I closed my eyes and started to drift. Sally nestled under my shoulder. A blanket came over us.

"Am I going to have to go to court and testify about this?" Her voice was quiet, barely over a whisper.

"It's possible." I wondered if I'd be able to find the evidence needed to land Randolph Grimes in one of Laurel's three jail cells, never mind convince a prosecutor to take him on.

"Because I will if I have to," she said.

The girl was tougher than she looked. My arm was wrapped around her when we woke up.

Chapter Thirty-Nine

Despite throbbing temples, I'd come up with a plan to get us off the ledge. I'd offered to send Sally to my Uncle Hugh's in Burlington on a Greyhound. She declined. Instead, she and Andrea decided to visit a friend in Greenwich Village. I told her that would be fine as long as no one knew where they were going. As Andrea and Sally sorted borrowable clothes, Sally made her promise not to tell Brad what they were up to. She was assured that wouldn't be a problem. The Clap's drummer must have been a real winner.

With paranoia in full effect, I wouldn't use Andrea's phone. While they were raiding the closet, I walked down to the Store 24 on the corner and called the station from a payphone. Estelle nearly shouted when she heard my voice but transitioned into an explanation of parking sticker protocols at Gray Gull Beach. Then she said, "Hold, please."

I waited for thirty seconds. Crowley picked up and asked if it was me. I told him that, as far as I knew, it was.

"You assaulted a federal agent?" he said. I could hear him straining to keep his voice low.

"I didn't know he was one when I did it, and he wasn't a real fed. He was from Commerce Security, whatever that is. But how do you know?"

"Salazar was here, and now her supervisor, some stiff named Nigel Dorsett, is in town. Another clown is stationed here, too. They have questions, probably have someone watching your house, too. Where are you?"

"Still in Boston."

"Yeah, I wouldn't be in a hurry to get back. I'm bunkered in your office.

Estelle gave me the nod. I'm guessing that your fed wasn't any more pleasant than the ones here. They make those preppy college kids look like marshmallows when it comes to being entitled. One of them tried to send me for coffee."

I knew how that had gone.

"I'm guessing you came up with something," Crowley said.

"I did. There's more to the story, like I thought. But I'm not sure you want the details."

"These guys are jerks. Give it up."

I had him call me back. My dimes weren't going to last. I started with yesterday's events, then worked my way back to the night of Alex's death at the Compound.

"None of it surprises me," Crowley said. "Fucking privileged assholes. How are we going to prove it, though?"

"That's the problem. Or at least one of them."

Crowley said the marshals told him they just wanted to talk to me, but he wasn't buying it. I agreed. Salazar had proven we couldn't trust them. The problem was, I couldn't do anything if I remained here. I pumped more change into the phone and called Trout at home.

"What the fuck are you doing?" he said. His volume was only slightly lower than the Clap playing the Subwoofer.

"How else was I supposed to get a hold of you?"

"Not that. You punched out an agent in Boston?"

"I did not. I only took him down. Then he tried to kick me in the balls when I let him up."

"Jesus Christ, what the fuck are you up to? Randolph is some hot. He's pissed at me just for knowing you. You went down there chasing that singer, didn't you?"

"Yes. And now I need to get into the Compound."

"You got a better chance of batting cleanup for the Sox."

"I need access to that second floor."

"What the hell does that have to do with anything?"

"Sally was nearly sexually assaulted the night Alex died," I said.

"By Stevens? Sally was at the end of the hall, and Alex's room was next to hers. Randolph and Violet have separate bedrooms, if you must know, so you've got no idea what you're talking about. Abby and her man were in one of the middle rooms. There's no way Stevens walked that gauntlet."

This was new information. Randolph and Violet would not be each other's alibi then. Another detail that had been kept from me.

"No. Not by Stevens. By Alex."

"What happened to her being so shitfaced that she didn't remember anything?"

"She didn't think it mattered once they arrested Stevens. She assumed that Alex had gone after him, and Riley had popped him for it."

"We know that already."

"But that's not what happened. Randolph stopped the assault. Then I think he and Alex went at it."

"You're out of your mind," he said.

"Then he covered it up. Randolph must have taken out Alex himself. Not Stevens."

"For chrissakes, you can't believe this shit. She told you that?"

"She told me about the assault. She's not sure what happened after that."

"Is she making this up, or is it you?"

"That's not all. I'm being followed. And they had someone watching Sally's apartment when I got there. The same guy tried to run her over in the street last night. I pulled her out of the way at the last second. Randolph is doing everything he can to keep her from telling what she knows. He wants it buried for good."

"Christ, if what you claim happened at the Compound, why wouldn't he just say that from the start? He'd be a hero for saving that girl."

"He tried pushing an accidental death at the pier. And when I didn't go right along, he stepped on me. He didn't want this to come out. At first, I thought it was to protect Alex's name. He didn't veer off it until Salazar named Stevens, and then Randolph was happy to let Stevens take the hit. It doesn't look great, politically, if Stevens murdered Alex. But there's no scandal. However, if Randolph did it, even in self-defense or protecting a guest, it's a giant fiasco. Maybe his Cabinet position gets yanked. I don't know. It looks like that's what's most important to him."

"LT, how do you look in your tinfoil hat?"

"You used to say I was as basic as the alphabet. You know I could be right. I want to get into that house and see the layout. I'm sure no one's looked for evidence. Something could still be there."

"No chance. I'm driving them to dinner tonight at the Abenaki. It's their first time out since it happened. They've been really suffering, and I don't want you anywhere near that Compound. It's being guarded, anyway, and those guys won't be friendly like I am, you jackass."

"Why would they guard the place now? What's there to protect?"

"Maybe they want to keep the media out. How do I know?"

"Think about it, Nate. If there's nothing to hide, why all the cloak and dagger?"

"You've lost your shit, Nichols."

He never called me by my last name. I hung up, disappointed for expecting more.

Chapter Forty

Sally left for New York with Andrea, eighty of my dollars, and a backpack of her friend's clothes. She'd be safe there. They'd have no idea where she was. I was heading right where they'd be looking for me.

I had expected someone to grab me as I climbed back into the Bronco. No one did. My next assumption was that I'd be followed. I had little experience trying to shake a tail, never mind identifying one. But I had a plan. I took my time heading up Route One, then jumped on Ninety-five north. Crowley's advice was to avoid the station and my house, as we couldn't trust any of the federal authorities. That was sound thinking. If I let loose with what I'd learned from Sally and declared that Randolph Grimes was involved in his son's death, as well as obstruction, they'd throw everything at me to keep me quiet. I assumed I'd be brought up on assault charges regarding Osterreich. Maybe they'd come up with something worse. I was likely to wind up in one of my own cells if I didn't play this right. I needed to push the truth far enough down the road so that it couldn't be buried. What that strategy entailed, I didn't know.

The other thing concerning me was not knowing exactly what Salazar knew about the night Alex died. Either she believed Stevens was the killer, or she was complicit in Randolph's cover-up. It didn't make sense that Randolph would have compromised himself by telling her the truth unless she had stumbled upon it, and there was no indication that she had. Salazar had wanted to prevent me from talking to Strummer and Ranford, presumably not to screw up her case. But someone wanted Strummer dead, and Osterreich had told me that they didn't have anyone watching her. Maybe it was naive on my part, but I couldn't believe our Department of Justice would kill someone in a cover-up. It made sense that if only Grimes was aware of what Sally could have known, it was he who had aimed Mr. Leather Jacket at her. Even if I couldn't prove that Randolph had killed Alex, obstruction of justice seemed accessible enough. Regardless, I wasn't under the impression that it would be easy.

It had come down to a game of one-on-one between Randolph and me, only he had a full team backing him on the court. As a wrestler, I'd always been matched with an opponent by weight. However, in practice, Coach Holden would have us wrestle out of our class. It would give the heavier wrestler an opportunity to deal with a quicker opponent, and it would give a smaller guy a chance to learn how to deal with superior strength. It was a good training strategy. I was far outclassed here and knew that if I went right at Randolph, I was only going to wind up flat on my back. I needed to work the angles, and I needed to do it quickly.

Despite having my eyes on the rearview seemingly as much as my windshield, it wasn't until I got stuck at the Hampton tolls that I caught a glimpse of Leather Jacket's Impala with him crouched low behind the wheel. The feds knew that I'd have to return home at some point; they could wait. This guy was on a different mission. A wave of sweat broke across my back. I'd have to lose him before I got to Laurel. While my Bronco wasn't fast enough to ditch a garbage truck, it could go places his Chevy could not.

On the long straights of the turnpike, I could see him hanging back. I slowed down as I approached the Laurel turn-off. I wanted to make sure that he didn't miss me when I went past it. I signaled left into the passing lane. He stayed in the right lane. I cruised past the exit, and he stayed with me. I passed the Milltowne exit, too. I got off at Northborough and waited at the stop sign until I could see the Impala. Then I turned left, inland, instead of home to the coast.

Northborough was twice Laurel's size, with half of its population. The Impala had no choice but to fall in behind me. I circled a loop onto Route 35 that took me south. I couldn't see him laughing but imagined him cracking up over this lame attempt at diversion. Then I turned onto County Road 19. After a half mile, the asphalt turned to gravel. There wasn't going to be much traffic. By now, he must have realized that I knew he was behind me. I'm sure he didn't give a shit. I sped up to make it look like I was trying to lose him. He stayed with me. Maybe he liked his chances out here.

The thing about County Road 19 was that it stopped. It emptied into a gravel pit, and at its center back was a man-made sand hill. It was wide enough that you couldn't easily get around it. Behind it was an old logging tote road, lousy with swampy bogs every few hundred yards. I took the Bronco straight into the loose sand and dropped it into four-wheel-drive. To Leather Jacket, it must have looked like I was cruising, but the Bronco was working hard to get through. As I crested the hill, I could see the Impala's front end mired at the bottom. I made for the tote road. The Impala wouldn't be budging anytime soon. It'd be a long walk out for him. I took it slow for the next few miles and came out on Milltowne Road. I hugged the outskirts of Laurel, nothing in the rearview, until I came through the backroads to the West Village, the home of the former residents of Woodman's Village.

Woodman's had been a shantytown that had existed in Laurel for sixty years. A group of interrelated families had lived in a desolate marshland separate from the rest of us in shacks that wouldn't have made good garden sheds. For generations, they'd been ostracized. They'd had zero trust in the government, my department, and others in general. When two teenage sisters went missing from there a few years ago, their mother, Rory Connolly, had come to the station, not to ask for help, but because she assumed we had them locked up. She and I had almost died investigating the disappearance. In the aftermath, we'd worked together to get her people out of those shacks and into some real housing. They slowly had been accepted into the flow of the town. Rory and I had become friends in the process. They were better off than they'd ever been, and I knew they'd help me.

Rory and her husband lived in the middle of the squared-off streets of the West Village. She and Jake were sitting on their ten-by-ten front porch when I parked the mud-covered Bronco next to her Chevelle.

"You been four-wheelin', Chief?" Jake Connolly called out. His thin face was tanned, probably from working the berry farm that they'd been bringing back to life.

"You might say that."

They invited me to sit. Rory pulled out a lawn chair and got me an iced tea. That reminded my stomach that I hadn't eaten since I'd split a bagel with Sally that morning.

Rory looked me over, concern on her face. "What brings you out here?"

"I need a favor," I said.

"Whatever we can do," she said. "You know that." The ordeal with her daughters had taken something out of each of us, but we'd had no choice but to keep going.

"I was wondering if I could borrow your car."

"You sure you don't want the pickup?" Jake said. "I can run down to the barn and fetch it."

"I'm trying to low-key it," I said. "The Chevelle would be great."

"You doing some undercover work?" he asked. I had to give him credit. He wouldn't open his mouth when we'd first met. Over time, whether for compensation or gratitude, he bent over backwards to be friendly.

"Not exactly."

"You're in trouble, aren't you?" Rory was the sharper of the two. She may have been one of the quickest people in Laurel, considering where she'd started from and what she'd been through.

"I wouldn't say that, either."

"Don't lie to me. You look like you haven't slept in a week."

"Thanks," I said.

"I'm just saying."

"Maybe it's part of the undercover get-up," Jake said.

"This isn't over that politician's son, is it?" Rory said, her eyes trying to pull the answer from me.

"Why would you think that?"

"If something horrible happens here, sooner or later you're going to be in the middle of it."

I shrugged. She was correct.

"Here's the thing," I said. "You might want to take the Bronco and put it out behind the barn."

"You are in trouble," she said, gasping.

"Don't worry, Chief," Jake said. "I'll get it so they won't see it even if they bring out a chopper."

"Thanks, Jake. I just need to stay under the radar, that's all."

Rory's eyebrows went up on her forehead as she leaned forward. "When's the last time you ate?"

She must have heard my stomach growling.

"Let me fix you a sandwich."

After I was fed, I swapped keys with Rory. Jake went off in the Bronco, but not before I took my Smith and Wesson out of the glove compartment and grabbed my kit bag. I also borrowed a flannel shirt and a John Deere baseball hat. With sunglasses, I was barely myself.

Chapter Forty-One

It wasn't hard to slip into the room at the Laurel Inn. The locks were ancient and even my rudimentary pick kit opened it in minutes. Now all I had to do was wait. I assumed that Salazar would come back to freshen up before dinner.

I reclined in the lounge chair in the corner and put my feet up on the coffee table. I waited. Salazar had sold me out up the chain, likely providing addresses to make it easier to track me. While I knew where I stood with her—nowhere—I needed to know if she believed in Stevens's guilt or was in on Grimes's cover-up. Then I could be sure of where the pieces fit and just how screwed Sally Strummer and I were.

The key in the lock woke me. I hadn't planned on dozing, but I wasn't going to beat myself up over it. Luckily, I'd taken off the hat and glasses, and enough light came through the windows so that she could see who I was. Otherwise, I might have had a bullet careening around my chest. She was in a slight crouch with her nine-millimeter pointed at my heart.

"Hello, beautiful," I said, slowly raising my hands. "Is that any way to welcome a lover?"

"What the fuck are you doing here?" I was glad to see her lower her gun. She stopped short of holstering it, however.

"We need to talk," I said.

"You think?" she said. "Up against the wall. You know the drill. From the other side, presumably."

"Why don't you relax and sit down?" I motioned to the bed. My own gun was wedged in the back of my jeans. "I'm serious about the talking."

The gun came back up. "Against the wall."

"Sit your ass down, Salazar. I'm no threat to you. And put that fucking pistol away." She sighed, but the pistol didn't move. She wasn't going to like what I had to say, no matter how deep she was in it.

"You assaulted an agent from the Justice Department. You're considered armed and dangerous, and I can't take your word, obviously."

"Are you talking about that joke from Commerce Security who you tipped off, and who was following me and didn't identify himself until I had his face grinding into the cement? That agent?"

She sighed and lowered the Glock.

"Wouldn't you like to hear about what I learned in my twenty-four hours in Boston?"

"Not if you think you're going to fuck my case. You've been off it from the beginning, but you're the only one who doesn't seem to know. You were right about Stevens then, and you're still right. But for some reason, you want to screw that up, and it's causing problems."

"There's more to it than you know. Or maybe you do know. That's what I'd like to find out."

"What are you talking about?"

I motioned to the bed. She holstered her weapon and sat. She did not, however, snap it in.

"Let's start with this. When I arrived at Sally's apartment, there was a man waiting outside, watching her. At first I thought he might be one of you people, poorly disguised. But I ruled that out when he tried to run her over later that night. I figured even your team wouldn't go that far. The same guy was following me today until I dumped him in the woods in Northborough."

Her grin disappeared.

"You're telling me that someone tried to take her out? Are you sure it wasn't a jealous boyfriend? A disappointed record buyer?" If she was surprised, her face hid it well.

"I saved her by an inch."

"You're an action hero. I told you."

"You don't sound like you believe me."

"Someone almost hitting her in a city known for having the worst drivers in the country does not constitute a conspiracy."

"It was the same guy staking out her apartment. The same guy following me today. Those are facts."

Her grin disappeared. "You're sure about this?"

"I am. I don't even understand why, if Riley Stevens is the actual killer, that you'd bother to watch me. What could I do? But—"

"If it were up to me, you could talk to them until your face fell off. Nothing would come of it."

"Funny, then, that you tipped everyone off that I was headed to Boston."

"I pass information on. You know how it works. What they do with it is their decision."

"But I wasn't doing anything wrong or illegal."

"We're under instructions to bring a resolution to this case. It's solid. So yes, they put eyes on you. Big deal."

"That's one thing. What happened to Sally is another. Who is directing this investigation?"

"You know the answer to that. I am. Or I was until Dorsett, my supervisor, got here. Which is thanks to your cowboying bullshit."

"He's here at Grimes's request, right?"

She nodded.

"You're all just jumping through the hoops he tells you to."

Her face flushed. Her eyes blinked.

"There's only one reason that someone would want Sally killed—and there's no denying that was an attempt on her life. I saw it. It's because that person has knowledge that Strummer knows that what you're claiming didn't happen. That there's more to it."

"The reason all this shit is swirling around you and your new friend, the singer who doesn't remember anything, is what then?"

"She does remember something."

"You interviewed her. We interviewed her. The conclusion was the same: She got blackout drunk, and Alex and Stevens didn't get along. Osterreich interviewed her. That was his conclusion, too. Do I have to drive down there myself so she can tell me the same thing?"

"You don't know what happened, do you?"

"Here we go," Salazar said, rising from the bed and taking off her holster, laying it on the far nightstand, away from me but in reach for her. "Let me guess, you took her to a psychic who unraveled a repressed memory."

"It's good, to a point, that you're in the dark."

"Look, Nichols. You're a real All-American. But you've gone off the deep end, and I can't have it. I can't be associated with you. I've got Dorsett sitting in your shitty little office in that shitty little station, waiting for you. If they found out that I talked to you today, never mind fucked you, that would kill my career. Not to mention that you're not making sense with this hitman bullshit. Anything that you found out, I don't want to know. You have more theories than a freshman philosophy class."

"You don't care that an innocent kid is going down for this?"

"Motive, opportunity, physical evidence. Riley Stevens. Can you put two and two together?"

"Sally Strummer was sexually assaulted that night in the Compound."

"Right," Salazar said, whipping around. "And she just happened to remember now?"

"Nearly being killed opened her up to the possibility that it might keep her alive if she told the truth. Yes, she was drunk, nearly incapacitated. Alex tried to take advantage of her, and she screamed. Randolph must have heard her and stopped it. She remembers voices in the room. I believe that the altercation that followed was between Alex and Randolph."

"Wait a minute," Salazar said, arms folded across her chest. "You just said she remembers voices. She didn't see this?"

"Her eyes weren't open. But there's evidence, as well. Her clothes were folded on her bed when she woke up that next morning. She didn't do that."

"Okay," she said, shaking her head. "She doesn't see Alex Grimes in her room, doesn't see them fighting, doesn't see Randolph run down to the dock and get the boat hook and sprint back to club his son. That's some serious Swiss cheese. Much more believable than Riley Stevens walking twenty feet, which you found ludicrous. And how convenient that she suddenly remembers this now and all from only hearing voices. You can't be serious."

"The morning after, Grimes brought her into his office. He asked her what she remembered—before he informed her about Alex. She told him that someone was in there with her, undressing her, that someone had taken off her shorts, and that something was going to happen. She thanked Randolph for hearing her and stopping it. He admitted doing so."

"But, alas," Salazar said, throwing up her hands. "She never opened her eyes and saw any of this."

"Yes. She was terrified, paralyzed."

Salazar sighed and shook her head. "And she didn't mention this because?"

"She felt guilty, as if she caused it. When Randolph told her that Alex had died, he claimed that his son was distraught over what he'd tried to do to her and had gone out to the seawall to think about it and fell accidentally, which is the scenario he pushed from the start. He even told her that Alex may have killed himself, because he was so torn up over what he'd tried to do to her. Grimes asked her to protect his son's legacy and keep it to herself and that if she did mention it to police, she'd become a suspect. She wasn't sure what happened after the assault was stopped, so when you arrested Stevens, it made sense to her. She believed Alex had gone after Stevens for trying to monopolize her on the boat. Typical victim psychology. Sally only wanted to forget that this had ever happened."

"That is some convoluted bullshit. Why did she tell you this if she only wanted to forget it?"

"After I pulled her out from in front of that car, we sat down. I explained that someone was afraid of what she knew and that she could claim all day that she didn't remember anything, but Grimes was afraid she did. He was the only one aware of what that memory could hold. And because of it, she'd been inches from death. That's what it took for her to open up. She realized they were coming after her, and by they, I mean Grimes. He's guilty of obstruction, at the least, and likely, he killed his son, probably in self-defense, after stopping the assault. It makes sense that Alex went after him—the man who'd badgered him since he was a kid, crushed his dreams of being an actor, made him work a job that he hated, and then caught him doing the worst thing he'd ever done in his life."

She laughed. "You are either one paranoid fuck, or you read too many romance novels. Why would Grimes care what she might or might not remember? She wasn't talking."

"That's my point. He knew she was aware of what happened, and when I kept after it because Stevens for this doesn't make sense, he wanted to ensure she didn't talk. He had you working on that officially, but he put his own man on it, too. That's the guy who tried to kill Sally and has been following me. You feds are acting on your own set of assumptions, but Grimes is operating based on what really happened."

"Have you told anyone this fucked-to-the-max theory?"

"Is this where I have to tell you that it's all in a letter, and it will be mailed to the Washington Post if anything happens to me?"

She exhaled. "I can't wait to get out of this fucking town." She sat back down on the bed. "You aren't going to cry when I once again point out all the holes in your stupid theories, are you?"

"You threaten that frequently. It hasn't happened yet."

"One, we have a murder weapon with the killer's fingerprints on it. You have no physical evidence. In fact, all you have is the same kind of conjecture that you accuse me of basing my case on."

"I plan on getting in the house. No one's bothered to look. There's an entire second floor where these events took place. Even now, there could be something there."

She rolled her eyes, believing either that I had no chance of entering the Compound or that the evidence only existed in my head.

"Your witness was," she said, "in your own report, 'drunk and as incapacitated as a tranquilized elephant.' And you just told me she didn't open her eyes during this whole ordeal."

"That doesn't mean—"

"Let me stop the excuse train right there because there's an even larger issue at hand. What makes you think that Randolph Grimes would give a fuck if his son was banging some drunk girl?"

"He was a decent man. Of course, he would try to do something."

"You probably believe that story about George Washington and the cherry tree, too." She took her hair out of its ponytail and shook it. "The decent man that you just accused of killing his kid and covering it up, that girl was nothing to him. Even if he thought Alex was a pussy, he was still his son. That they'd come to blows over him getting over on some tramp is incomprehensible. At most, he might have told him to keep it down before he woke up his mother."

"You're quite the feminist."

"I'm what you would call a realist." She fixed her hair back into its ponytail. "I think I tried to explain this to you before. The Grimes see themselves on one level. And maybe they're right to do so, because they're running the damn country. The rest of us, we're different. Some useful people may be worthy of respect. A slutty rock singer in no way qualifies. He wouldn't have cared what his son was doing to her. He'd have asked if she brought a friend for him."

"He wouldn't go to the extent he has just to guard his son's legacy. But he'd do it to protect himself and his position. Isn't that what you've been trying to tell me?"

"This is too crazy," she said. "Even for you."

I sat there dumbfounded.

"You're okay with Riley Stevens going to jail?" I asked.

"Yes, because he's guilty. I'm going to give you another piece of advice. Go to the station. Talk to Nigel Dorsett, my supervisor. He's in from Washington to put this to bed. Don't tell him anything you've told me. Just tell him that you went down there and talked to Sally and Ranford—"

"I didn't tell you I talked to Ranford."

"But you did. Don't interrupt me. Tell him that you didn't know Oyster was working in association with us. You thought he was a mugger, and that once he identified himself you let him up. Then you say that Ranford and Miss Strummer didn't have anything to say, other than they knew nothing. Then go fishing for a few weeks and don't come back until the trial is over."

"You know I won't do any of that."

"A girl can try, can't she? If you don't back off, it will become your word against Oyster's. They'll find some Boston cop to back him up. It will be trouble. Best case scenario, they'll find a way to take your job. Worst case, I wouldn't want to think about it."

"I'm touched by your caring," I said, trying not to look horrified. It's one thing to think you're up against it. It's another to have it verified.

"Trust me. If you let it slip out about us or that you were here this afternoon, I'll empty a clip into you."

"I may be heartbroken," I said. "But I'm not going to cry."

I got up and walked out of the room. I was tempted to wait at the door and listen to her dial the phone. I knew she'd do it. I was a mile down the road when a Crown Victoria with D.C. plates and a two-way antenna flew by in the opposite direction. I assumed they were looking for a Bronco and not a royal blue Chevelle with a pine tree freshener hanging from the rearview mirror.

Chapter Forty-Two

I drove up to the Reef House, the misnamed restaurant on River Road. It sat on a hill across from the Compound's cove, providing an unparalleled view of the long, black-rock breakwater at the mouth of the river. The owner, Adam Springbrook, was regarded as a carpetbagger because he'd only been in Laurel for five years. He paired the vista with some of the most expensive dishes in town. While locals knew they used frozen seafood and avoided it, tourists couldn't tell and packed the place. The employee parking behind the kitchen looked out over the Compound. I sat in the Chevelle, watching it, breathing in boiling lobster and grilling steaks.

The Suburban left the Compound at seven-fifteen. Trout was driving. The guard shack was manned, either by a state trooper or another fed. He closed the gate behind them. I gave them five minutes to reach the Abenaki Club. Then I walked down the hill.

A sidewalk ran along the coastal road. It was popular with joggers, cyclists, and tourists who liked to climb the Reef House's hill, where benches allowed them to relax and snap pictures of lobster boats plowing into the ocean. Painters also camped there, sometimes in large groups. When I walked past the guard house in my shirt and ball cap, I probably looked like one more dipshit admiring the Atlantic. Grimes still having the place locked down reinforced the thought that there may be something worth finding there. Admittedly, it could have been that he didn't want to face the press and their questions any more than he would have wanted to answer mine.

I went a few hundred yards down the road and around the bend, out of sight. Then I climbed down over the three-foot concrete seawall that ran along the sidewalk and hypothetically stopped tourists from tumbling into the water. I scrambled back to the Compound, hugging the wall Spider-Man style. Even if the guard were standing on the lawn and scanning my direction, his line of sight would shoot well over me.

I hopped the seawall behind the garage, hidden from the main house and guard shack. The only chance for exposure would be a small triangle as I moved to the side of the house. I would've liked to wait until full dark, but I couldn't count on Grimes and Violet staying out. The sun was setting behind the house, casting a blanket of shadow over the grounds. The only cars at the garage were Trout's pickup and Tracey Bolton's Dodge Dart. With Tracey working, the alarm wouldn't be set. I'd just have to avoid her, which likely meant dodging the kitchen. I could do that by slipping in one of the sliders on the back patio.

I stood at the corner of the garage. The guard shack's gate-facing window was barely visible. A light was on in the dining room on the far side of the house in front of the kitchen. The corner closest to me opened up into the living room and patio. The sliders weren't likely to be locked, and once in, I'd sneak upstairs to the second-floor bedrooms. It was a long shot that I'd find anything, but I didn't have many options. At least being at the scene might help me visualize what could have happened.

When a pair of Harleys passed the guard shack roaring like 747s, I took a deep breath and sprinted. I hit the corner of the house and pressed into the weathered shingles. In the shadow, I waited for my heart to slow, then crept below the windows to the back of the house. From the corner, I could see the sliders, screens keeping out the mosquitoes. But I couldn't see into the room. I waited and listened. Water lapped against the seawall. A Fleetwood Mac song played somewhere in the house. As I could barely hear it, I guessed it was coming from the kitchen, where I hoped Tracey was busying herself. I stepped to the edge of the door and looked inside. Lamps burned, but the room was empty. I slid the screen open and went in, then moved to the staircase.

The second-floor landing was clear. I took one soft step at a time to get there and then moved into the hall, out of sight from below. The beige walls were lined with black and white photographs of the Compound in various stages of construction. Wainscotting ran down the hall. From what Sally and Trout had told me, Violet Grimes's bedroom was at the beginning of the hall, and Randolph's was adjacent to it. Abby and Ranford had been on the opposite side, overlooking the cove rather than the ocean. Alex was further down, with Sally at the end of the hall. The doors were painted white, and there were plenty of them. I slipped into the one closest to me.

The room was big and airy. A four-poster king, buried with pillows, sat against the interior wall to the left. There were two bureaus, a fireplace on the left wall, and a door on the right. That led to a bathroom. Makeup and flowers spread across a vanity the size of my kitchen table. Violet's clothes filled a closet larger than my childhood bedroom.

I went back to the hallway, listened, and moved to the next room. This was Randolph's. His cologne hung in the air. The bureau was larger and of a darker wood. No pillows were strewn about the tightly made bed. His bathroom backed up to his wife's, smaller and not quite as opulent. The medicine cabinet revealed nothing unusual. Shaving stuff, aspirin. A television and VCR sat on a stand at the end of the bed. I did not find a journal confessing that he'd bashed his son's head in. All I'd done was verify that the Grimes had separate bedrooms.

After Randolph's room, I went straight to what had been Sally's. I wasn't about to turn any lights on, so I brought out the flashlight I'd grabbed from my kit bag. This was a smaller version of Violet's summer-styled bedroom, with only half the number of decorative pillows. Even if there were a full crime team present, I doubted they would be able to find anything a full week later. This room also had its own fireplace and bathroom. Regardless, I got down on my stomach and looked along the hardwood and under the bed. I checked the armoire. Nothing.

Alex's room next door was not much different than the others, except for the Brown University playbills framed on the walls. If there had been an argument between father and son, it could have taken place here. A closed door could have muffled the sounds, so that Sally, in her drunken state, may have only been able to realize tone rather than words. The bureau was empty. There were a few sweaters, dress shirts, and some I-Zods in the closet, with pairs of chinos and jeans on hangers. Folded towels, fluffy and fresh, were neatly arranged on a shelf in the bathroom. I swung the flashlight around the room. Again, nothing unusual or out of place. There was no telling how many times that Tracey may have run a dry mop over the floor, if they'd even let her in here. Nonetheless, I crawled around checking for droplets, though there'd been barely any blood loss. I stopped when I hit the fireplace.

While the hearths in the other rooms were empty and clean, I found a layer of ashes in this one. I checked the flu, and it was open. This indicated recent use. No one should have had a fire this summer. We hadn't had a day less than seventy degrees. I went to grab the poker from the brass kit to sift the ashes on the chance there'd be something to find amongst them. Only it wasn't there. The poker was missing. My heart jumped.

If there was a piece of equipment on this property that replicated a boat hook and was strong enough to crack a skull, it was a brass fireplace poker. Alex may have retreated here, with Randolph following him. Randolph, furious, begins his rant: 'What the hell were you doing to that girl? What's wrong with you?' It's easy to imagine it escalating from there. Maybe Alex finally reaches his breaking point and swings. Maybe he even lands one. His father, in self-defense, grabs the poker. Alex drops. Then Randolph is the one who panics. He would have shifted straight into covering his ass, carrying the body down to the seawall, maybe Alex's rock, away from his wife's bedroom, hidden from the boathouse and tossed him into the Atlantic. Alex going in from there is a narrative that Randolph endorsed from the start. He even sent us to a specific boulder. When Salazar shifted the investigation to Stevens, Randolph led her to the boat hook, knowing it would have Stevens's fingerprints. He would have had time to pitch it into the cove beforehand. This scenario was as logical as the story that pointed to Stevens.

I grabbed the shovel from the fireplace kit and sifted the ashes. No foreign objects appeared. I took a scoop and put it into a baggie anyway. Maybe a lab could find something, if I could get one to look at it. I ran the flashlight over the walls, searching for signs of an altercation. Again, nothing. Other than the fireplace, the room was pristine.

I went into the hall and checked the walls between Sally and Alex's rooms, looking for a dent, a crack in the plaster, anything that would indicate a fight. I studied the paint for the smallest chip. When the overhead lights came on, it was all I could do not to scream.

"What the hell are you doing, Nichols?" Tracey Bolton stood at the top of the landing, hand on the switch.

"I've been looking for you," I said.

"I'm not in any of the pictures," she said, pointing to the wall. "And you ain't exactly in uniform."

"I'm chasing down some information for the case."

She scowled and curled her lips. "Does the Secretary know you're here? From what I understand, you aren't welcome."

"I called from the front door and didn't hear anything. It was open, so I came in." If I didn't answer and redirected her, I'd have time to conjure a reasonable—if not graceful—exit. "I have some questions. This is an ongoing investigation, as you know."

"I ain't talking to you without the Secretary saying it's okay. I can't believe that dope at the guard house let you in."

"I guess we'll go down to the station then." The best defense is a good offense. I tried not to crack a smile as her brow furrowed and her mouth closed.

"You act like a big man when Secretary Grimes isn't around, but you got your tail between your legs when he is. Don't think I haven't seen it."

I walked over to her and folded my arms across my chest. "What happened when you came in on the morning that Alex died?"

Indignation disappeared from her face.

"Why, we had a party. Jesus, what do you think? It was terrible."

"Can you describe the scene? When did you hear about Alex?"

"I was preparing breakfast when Trout and Secretary Grimes came back."

"And?"

"He went right up to Mrs. Grimes's room. He was in there for quite some time. I'm sure even you can imagine it wasn't the easiest conversation. Then I believe he told Abby after that."

"Who told you about Alex?"

"Trout."

"Did you receive any instructions that morning?"

"When the Secretary came down, he asked me to bring him coffee in his office. When I brought it, he asked me to prepare a shopping list, as he was expecting that there'd be some family and guests with the affairs that would lay ahead. I told him I was sorry and that I'd be available for whatever he needed."

"Anything else?"

"He had me get Alex's lady friend and bring her down."

"What about cleaning?"

"What about it?"

"Were you asked to clean anything?"

"As you can see, the place is spotless. That's my job."

"What about Alex's room?"

"That, I haven't touched."

"Did anyone go in there?"

"Of course, Secretary and Mrs. Grimes have spent time there. Would you expect otherwise?"

"But you haven't cleaned it?"

"Mrs. Tubbs, I mean the marshal, wouldn't allow it until she looked in there. I haven't received instructions, so I've stayed out. Why do you care? I haven't touched that boathouse, either, and I'm not about to. That damn Riley Stevens. That whole family thinks they're something, and I always thought that Riley was a stuck-up bastard, like a few others in town." Her nod indicated that I was in that group.

"Trout is getting a fat head?" I said, to be obstinate.

"I wasn't referring to him." Her hands went to her hips. She must have thought I was a dunce, as well.

"Has anyone taken anything from Alex's room?"

"They did have to dress the boy for his service."

"Did you know there's been a fire in the fireplace?"

"I saw the ashes. When they're ready for me to clean it, I'll clean it."

"Do you know when the fire was?"

She put her hand to her chin. "Sometime between when Alex got here and now. The room was clean before they came. Maybe Secretary or Mrs. Grimes had a fire while they were sitting there this week."

"It hasn't been cool at all. I don't know why someone would light a fire in the middle of August."

"You've heard of grief? People do strange things." Her eyes narrowed over her sharp nose. "Why are you asking? You think Stevens burned something up in there after he killed poor Alex? I thought he did that out on the dock."

"Thanks for your help, Tracey." She'd be receiving a lot of speeding tickets this winter.

I started past her. She stepped to the side. I was halfway down the stairs when she yelled at me to wait. I turned, hopeful that she'd remembered something important.

"I'll walk you out just to make sure you don't get lost."

She shut the door behind me, but I felt her eyes as I started up the walkway. I couldn't very well stroll past the guard house with its sentry, so when I was halfway to the garage, I turned back and waved. If Tracey were still hawking me, she'd be disgusted enough being caught that she'd call it a night. When I reached the garage, I ducked behind it. I waited for the sound of the guard house door opening. There was nothing. I hopped over the rocks and scrambled below the Compound's sight lines to the road, then climbed back up to the Reef. It was a nice night, and I hadn't eaten. But I wasn't sucker enough to pay for frozen fish.

Chapter Forty-Three

I assumed that after going to Milltowne to kill some time and grab a bite to eat at Beefy's, a place where no one would recognize me, and if someone did, they wouldn't care because they were too busy stuffing two-dollar roast beef sandwiches down their throats and then driving by my house twice and seeing no trench-coated agent lingering on the porch, and no full-size government boat in the driveway or on the dirt road I lived on, it would be safe to stow the Chevelle in the garage, go in through the side door, and sleep in my own bed. I'd eventually have to walk back into the office and answer the questions awaiting me. When I did, I wanted my wits about me. I needed this to make sense when I explained it. No one was going to want to believe that a Presidential Cabinet member had killed his son, even if it was an honorable act or in self-defense.

Much remained for me to do. I had to get the ashes under the Chevelle's front seat to the state crime lab, though I wouldn't be telling them they were related to this case. I wanted to question Violet, who'd been in the house when Sally was assaulted and may have heard her scream. Randolph had kept her from me, but I doubted he could keep her from the tennis courts. The Abenaki Club held their women's round-robin every Sunday morning. I hoped she needed a release and wanted to get back to it. I'd have a chance to talk to her there. It wasn't much of a plan, but it was all I had.

I parked and entered through the garage. I'd nearly made it to the kitchen when I felt him. Unfortunately, that was after I'd stashed my thirty-eight on the side table in the hall. I turned in time to see him crack a smile as he snatched my pistol and put it in his belt. I would have taken him right then had it not been for his own gun, which was only slightly smaller than a cannon and pointed at my stomach. He was still sporting his leather.

"Welcome home, Chief."

"Can I get you a beer?" I said, stepping into a kitchen well stocked with knives, if not a backup piece. "I think I'm going to need one."

"I'll pass," he said. "And you will, too. Get your ass in here." He indicated a path to the couch with the barrel of his forty-four.

I did what I was told. Having a gun pointed at my chest was another thing I hadn't much experience with. I didn't like it.

"Are you sure about that beer?" I asked.

"I don't drink at work, Chief."

"I was talking about me," I said. I sat down and leaned back. "I didn't realize that you people had such high job standards."

"Do not confuse me with those marshal fucks."

"What are you? CIA or something?"

"Don't insult me."

"What harm could a beer do? Could be a long night." Any chance to move could provide me with an opening.

"Not for you."

He looked around the room, as if he hadn't already scoped it out. There was nothing in the way of a weapon nearby. An out-of-reach table lamp with a shade the size of a clown hat wasn't going to do much. He stood in front of the wood stove, blocking my own cast iron poker. His finger was on the trigger, anyway, ready to splatter my guts onto the only slightly dusty walls.

We sat there looking at each other for a few minutes.

"That was pretty cute," he said, "that little detour through the gravel pit."

"Glad you enjoyed it."

"Yeah, too bad for you I've spent some time in the desert. A little sand doesn't bother me."

"Didn't look like it."

He shook his head. "Can you tell me something?"

"Sure."

"Is it that you're stubborn, stupid, or have a bug up your ass for Grimes?"

"I'm just trying to get to the bottom of this. Riley Stevens didn't kill Alex Grimes."

"If you say so." He was smiling.

"You know that Grimes killed his son. You might be the only one outside of him and I who knows it."

He shook his head. "I don't know any such thing. I'm an independent contractor, and whatever he may or may not have done is not in the purview of my employment."

"And you've been hired to silence Sally Strummer?"

"You're going to find out, personally, what my job is. Let's leave it at that."

"I'm surprised you still have a job after you botched that hit and run."

"I don't know what you're talking about."

"You missed her. It was a good try, but I'm guessing you don't get bonused for effort."

"You're going to make this more enjoyable than I anticipated," he said.

"Are you one of those cut-rate guys? You can't be at the top of your profession, based on what I've seen. How does someone like Grimes even know where to scrape you up?"

He laughed. The barrel of his gun didn't move.

"You really are that simple," he said, shaking his head. "You know he owns a munitions company or two, right? He was on the Armed Services committee in the House. And there's the foundation he ran in D.C. He knows people who can get things done, and I'm not only referring to raising stock prices."

"And yet he hired you."

"I'll fulfill my contract," he said. "Don't you worry."

"It's okay with you if a kid spends his life in prison for something he didn't do, as long as your guy doesn't go down for it?"

"I'm a well-compensated gear in the machine, not a moralist."

"Do you sleep well?"

"Why wouldn't I? I can only be responsible for my own choices. What others do is up to them. Look at yourself. I believe you were advised to walk away from this. You chose not to. One could say that you're the one who put that singer's life in jeopardy by trying to fuck with Grimes. You may be a small-timer, but you had to see where that would go, right? Trying to take down someone that far up the food chain. Choices have consequences."

"Other people's choices don't matter? Like Grimes killing his son?"

"I don't know anything about that. But can you change what already happened? No. And nothing you do will bring justice—a concept that one could argue doesn't exist, except to half-wits like yourself—to this affair, whatever it may be. All you've done is ensure that the singer will disappear. If you'd left it alone, she might have been allowed to live her shitty life. You could have gone on with your own blissfully ignorant existence. We wouldn't be here right now."

"So if I chose to throw away a kid's life, that would make it okay for me?"

"Sure. Alex Grimes would still be dead. You and Strummer wouldn't be on a list. The Man pulls the strings, and because of the choices you've made, now one's tied to you. That's the way it is, the way it's always been."

"That's the biggest pile of shit I've ever heard," I said.

"I can see you're not a thinker," he said, waving his gun around, legitimately frustrated. "I can't help you in that case. But it doesn't matter. This ends with me putting a bullet through your head, regardless."

"And if I choose not to let you do that."

"Yeah, you're not getting the opportunity to make that choice unless…"

"What?" I couldn't stop myself from taking the bait.

"You tell me where the singer is."

"I don't know where she is. And I don't believe telling you would get you walking out the door, either."

"She didn't come home last night. She's smarter than you. Though you had to return here eventually, the way you think. Where'd you send her?"

"I don't know where she went. I told her not to tell me."

"You'd really be helping me out."

"Why would I do that?"

"Because I'll let you have that beer before I blow your brains out." He grinned.

CHAPTER FORTY-THREE

"You're not going to threaten me with torture?"

I was tough. You don't become a wrestler and not learn discipline and how to handle pain. But I wasn't sure I could sustain my nails being pulled with pliers or having teeth drilled like in *Marathon Man*. I'd have to start preparing myself to get there. Leather Jacket stayed just far enough away that I couldn't reach him in one or two steps. And the canyon that was the barrel of his gun presented every time I thought about trying something.

"I'm not one of those sick fucks," he said. "I'm just doing a job. Strummer or Davenport, whatever she's going by, has the same problem that you did. She'll want to come back to that crappy, has-been band. She might stay hidden for a while. But all I'll have to do is make one call to their manager, say I'm from some record company, and then, like the Stones say, wild horses couldn't keep her away. You, by telling me where she is, only makes my job easier. Then I would choose to give you a beer. Imagine how good that would taste, especially if you knew it was your last."

"Is it a waste of time to tell you that even if I knew where she was, I wouldn't say?"

"I believe so."

"Then I'll spare you."

"Great."

"So, when is this event going to happen?"

"It's a little too busy out there right now, even for this town. We've got some hours to kill, no pun intended."

"You pull the trigger on that forty-four, people are going to hear it. Sound travels here. It's flat."

"This thing," he said, holding up the Dirty Harry gun, "is just for show. This one will be enough for what we need." He patted my Police Special in his belt.

"That's not a cap gun, either."

"Suicides are sad, don't you think?" he said.

It wasn't hard to see where he was going.

"The disgrace of screwing up the Alex Grimes investigation was too much for you. You couldn't live with yourself. Tragic. Imagine what they'll write in the newspapers."

"You won't get close enough to pull that off," I said. "Trust me."

"I thought that might be your response. Your significant other, Suzanne Anderson, lives at 48 Porpoise Creek Road in a Cape Codder, painted white with red shutters. She's quite pleasant to look at, with a nice face and a pretty good rack. She runs the lunch counter at Blink's General Store, and I hear the sandwiches there are quite good. She's a friendly, wonderful small-town girl."

"We broke up a while ago, asshole."

"A week isn't that long, is it? Taking into account the kind of guy you are, I'd think that if you could choose to do something that would prevent me from shoving this forty-four up her twat and pulling the trigger, you might act on that. Because that's what will happen if you don't cooperate. I wonder if that shot would echo all the way over here. You won't be around to hear it, but it's a fascinating question based on what you've told me. Of course, you could tell me where Strummer is, then cooperate with me on this suicide. You can choose to save your girlfriend's life. It really is your choice."

I couldn't even open my mouth.

"Are you seeing the value in my philosophy yet?" he said. His small eyes tried to read me. I stared back, unwilling—or unable—to process what he'd told me.

"It's a lot to consider, I know. Let's find a movie while you think about it. I'm a patient man. I'll give you an hour."

"You're never going to enjoy it if you have to keep one eye on me."

"I'm like an owl, with my vision. I can see two things at once. Very rare." He nodded, as if he weren't bullshitting. He flipped on the television, all the while keeping the barrel trained on me. I thought of rushing him. His threats to Suzanne sat on my instincts along with his gun. He found a movie. Joe Namath was playing a biker on a cable station out of Boston.

I sat there and contemplated what I could do and when I could do it. I had a choice to make, as he said. He was correct in that I wouldn't want to do anything that would put Suzanne in harm's way. He was banking on it.

Maybe that did make the choice for me. I couldn't make a move unless I was sure it would work. I'd already seen him try to kill one innocent woman, and he wouldn't hesitate to do it again. However, after he offed me, would he want to stay in Laurel to do Suzanne? It wouldn't make sense if he needed to get out quickly. If I made it messy, so that it was clearly not a suicide, he'd want to vanish as soon as possible. Then again, if attention was focused here, he could slip unnoticed across town to Suzanne's. It wasn't a chance I wanted to take. Even if I chose to do what he asked, could I trust him to spare Suzanne? I believed so, because he'd have no reason to hurt her, and he wouldn't want to stick around.

As I sat there blankly staring as Namath rode his chopper, punched out guys, and chased Ann-Margaret, I came to a conclusion: if I didn't stop him, Sally would die. That was for sure. I would, too. I had to try to take him down. If I did nothing, two of us would surely be dead. And there was always the chance that his self-preservation would trump teaching me a lesson—as I'd be dead anyway—and he'd leave without hurting Suzanne. Yet, when Joe and Ann-Margaret rode off into the sunset, I still hadn't arrived at an actual course of action. He got up and turned off the television.

"Here's how this is going to go down," he said, standing across from me.

When the screech came howling through the open windows, I stopped thinking. I hit the coffee table with my feet as hard as I could, as if my life depended on it. Which it did. As the table crashed into his knees and staggered him, he whipped the gun around. It exploded. A blizzard of couch stuffing flew through the room. I rolled to the wood stove and came up with the small ash shovel, swinging at him in the same motion. It connected with his wrist just as he got off a second shot. It took out the lamp and splintered the wall behind it, but he lost the gun. My next swing jacked his neck, and he dropped. My ears were ringing as I brought the shovel down on his back and flattened him. He reached for my gun in his pants, but I jumped him and wedged the iron against the front of his neck. He was resisting, but his brain wasn't working fast enough to counter. I took my thirty-eight from him, pulled him up, and whipped him into the wall, unfortunately for a framed picture of my parents in front of my dad's prized T-bird. A right to the stomach had him back on the floor in the entryway. With my knee lodged in his back and my right arm around his throat, I reached with my left and pulled my handcuffs out of the drawer. I wrenched his arm behind him until I heard his humerus crack. That was a choice I'd made.

"What the fuck was that outside?" he asked as soon as he realized he was, more or less, captured.

"A fisher cat," I said. "A simple animal, but dangerous. Not many of them in Washington, I guess."

Chapter Forty-Four

The place was a mess, and company was coming. Couch stuffing covered the floor like snow. Bullet holes cracked the wall and ceiling. A treasured picture sat in a splintered frame. I phoned Crowley at home and told him to get over here. Then I called around town until I tracked Salazar down at the Rusty Bullet. One I could trust, but the other possessed knowledge that might help with my current guest, hogtied on my living room floor.

"You know this is personal now," Leather Jacket said. I'd moved the furniture to the edge of the room and left him in the middle. When he looked up, he saw me enjoying a Budweiser.

"I don't believe I caught your name."

"You broke my fucking arm," he said. "By law, you need to see that I get immediate medical attention."

"I was just thinking about that. According to your philosophy, you broke your arm. You chose to resist the direction that I was carefully moving it in. As a result, it apparently fractured. Unfortunately, medicine isn't my area of expertise. To be honest, I'm not sure it's broken."

"Motherfucker," he said as he wriggled to get a look at me. My belt was around his ankles, a rolled pillowcase connected it to the cuffs. If he were going to escape, he'd have to do so as a worm.

"You might want to find another line of work," I said. "You seem to be really bad at your job."

"There's plenty of witnesses who aren't around to discredit that statement."

"Maybe you can learn how to operate a washing machine or bake bread or something while you're in prison. Clothes are always getting dirty, and people have to eat. Lots of job security in those fields."

"There's not going to be any prison."

"I wouldn't be too sure of that."

"There are people who cannot allow it to happen. You might know one of them."

"Maybe they'll be joining you in the exercise yard."

"Don't count on it."

"It's also possible that you'll be considered a loose end, and they'll hire someone like you, only better, to get rid of both of us."

Crowley's F100 pulled into the driveway. That ended the conversation. He hustled through the door without knocking, only to stop when he noticed the man shackled on the rug. He looked over to me, then took in the entirety of the disarray.

"What do we have here?" he said.

"This fellow was waiting for me when I got home, but he didn't take very good care of the place. I know him from Boston."

"He doesn't look like the toy and game police," Crowley said.

"He's the careless driver who almost hit Sally Strummer."

"No shit. What are we going to do? We've got to take him in, right? Or do you want to get a boat and some big rocks?"

"There is that option, isn't there?" I said.

"Let's go, then," Crowley said.

"It's not that simple."

"The hell it ain't," Crowley said, stomping a size twelve boot close to the man's face. "No one is above the law. Even that bastard across town."

"Why'd you call this guy, Nichols?" Leather Jacket said. "He's as dumb as he is big."

"I ain't the guy on the floor tied like a stuck pig," Crowley said. I was surprised he didn't punt the guy's midsection.

"This asshole," I said, "is claiming that Grimes will sweep this under the rug and screw us. He does have a point. If Grimes was ready to let Stevens go up for murder and send this chump to kill me, we need to watch our backs."

"I haven't given up on that, just so you know," Leather Jacket said.

Another pair of headlights swung through the windows and traced the wall.

"Who is that?" Crowley said.

"Salazar. We need someone with experience in this kind of shit."

"She ain't playing for our team, LT."

"She doesn't want to, but she will," I said.

"Do you know something that I don't?"

"Yup." Our agendas had never been aligned, but she possessed knowledge we did not. If I brought in my assassin, I wasn't sure that I'd be able to keep him. One of these federal outfits was likely to do Grimes's bidding and grab him, no matter what I had to say about it. I couldn't allow that to happen. While I knew that I couldn't trust Salazar with a grocery list, she'd made it clear that any association with me would be a career killer for her. That gave me leverage. She'd help whether she liked it or not.

"Lurch is right," came up from the floor. "You're fucked."

Salazar didn't bother knocking. Maybe that was because I told her that I had a would-be shooter secured in my living room and that she might want to get over here before I made a real federal case of it. I'd added that for her own sake, she'd better come alone.

Her eyes took in the floor, went around the room, then landed on me. Her eyebrows raised onto her forehead, surprised that I had not been exaggerating. Crowley watched. He wasn't smiling.

"Who is this fuck?" she said as she rolled over my guest to see his face. He swore and told her to watch the arm.

"I was hoping you could tell us. It looks like he has something against lamps and couches. But he seems to have left his ID in the car."

"He's not one of ours. You wouldn't get one of us twisted like that."

"If that were true, I wouldn't have your boss camping out at my station and had two more of you racing up River Road as soon as I left your hotel. Thanks for that, by the way. Always enjoy the chance to see upper-level law enforcement in action. They looked really focused when they blew right past me. Of course, I wasn't driving the Bronco so that might have thrown them."

She ignored that dig and nudged her toe into Leather Jacket's ribs. "Are you going to explain this?" she said, turning to me.

I told her how Leather Jacket had been sitting in my Lazy Boy with his forty-four and lousy philosophy, awaiting my return. I added details of his untimely collisions with the coffee table and fireplace equipment and that he'd been driving the car that almost hit Strummer. Her eyes bounced between my face and our prone captive.

"Why don't you tell us who you are?" she asked him. "And save us from having to get it out of you, which, I'll admit, could be fun."

"That would be a no. Because as soon as I make a call, you're going to receive one of your own, and I'm going to be cut loose, and you're not going to have anything to say about it. It's hard to believe, but the only bigger jokes than these backwoods cops are US marshals, otherwise known as FBI rejects. What I'd like to know is how many peckers you had to suck to get your job."

"One thing I forgot to mention," I said, "is that he thinks his left arm may be broken. I'm not sure. Maybe you've had more medical training than I have."

Salazar reached over and ran her hand from his shoulder to his wrist. He sucked in his breath, though he tried to look like he was not bracing himself.

"Last chance," she said.

He didn't speak. When she saw him inhale, she placed her sneaker on his elbow. His eyes got glassy as she leaned in. She looked at us and shrugged.

"He came from Grimes," I said. "He admitted as much. We know why he was sent, though some of us have been slow to realize the extent of what's been going on."

"I'm not going there," Salazar said.

"I told you," Crowley said to me.

"Let's figure out who this guy is before we do anything," Salazar said. "I'm guessing he didn't parachute in. Where's his car?"

I hadn't considered that. But it's not like there were parking lots and garages where he could have hidden it. My guess was that he'd parked on one of the back streets across from the beach. We took his keys, and I gave Crowley a description of the Impala and sent him to look for it. It was almost one o'clock, but I fired up the Mr. Coffee. Salazar followed me into the kitchen. Through the hall, we had a clear view of the living room. We told the Jacket that if we saw him move, we'd be testing his arm for mobility.

We stood across from each other. Her eyes appraised me, glistening like pools of oil after a rainstorm. She shook her head.

"Who is that guy?" I asked. We were careful to be quiet.

"He's not government, of course."

"I told you that yesterday."

She shook her head. "As big as Grimes is, I don't think they'd go black ops for him. It's one thing to send for the calvary, me, but this is something else. Entirely."

"So where does he come from?"

"Grimes was Armed Services. He's a big shot in the defense industry, besides. With the connections he's made, he probably has access to a hundred guys like this—washed-up Army or some shit. You've kicked up quite a fucking problem."

"You have this backwards. You see me as the problem."

"Yeah, I do. There are larger forces at work, and we need to take that into consideration or we're all going to be collateral damage."

"Getting screwed in service of a royal family who thinks they're above the law is not something I'm interested in experiencing."

"I'm pleased," she said. "You're learning. You're just behind on the application of that knowledge."

"That guy came to put a bullet in my head. He wouldn't be here if I wasn't right about Grimes killing Alex." I stopped and threw my hands in the air. "You've got to see that by now."

"No, I don't."

"Him sending someone to kill Strummer and me doesn't tell you anything?" I was having trouble keeping my voice down.

"This is so far up the chain, even if you were able to prove it to someone, and I don't know who that would be, it will never surface. They'll bury it or spin it into something unrecognizable. You need to go into survival mode, not law enforcement mode. Do you get that? That's where this is at. It isn't truth, justice, and the American way. It's 'how do I come out of this with my ass intact?'"

"That's bullshit," I said.

"I've seen it. I could give you examples. But I can't. You know what I mean? You should have left me out of this. I sold you out once already."

"Just realize that if I go down, everyone's going to know that you were with me all the way."

Her mouth opened. No words came out.

"There's a kid," I said, "that's looking at years in prison, and he's not a consideration to anyone except for me and Crowley. This guy tried to kill me. You've got to draw the line somewhere, Salazar."

"Jesus Christ, Nichols. Survival of the fittest. The truth doesn't matter."

"I've heard enough nonsense for one night," I said.

"You asked," she said, shrugging.

"Leave, then," I said.

"I can't now. He knows I've been here." She nodded to the living room. "What do we do with him?"

"You're not going to like my recommendation."

"What's new?"

"I assume you have access to a boat. Take him and do what Stevens should have done to Alex. Anchor him and drop him somewhere deep. If you bring him in, the pressure is going to come down like you've never felt it. Grimes will go apeshit, and somehow this asshole will skate. I'm not kidding."

"As much as I'd like to, I'm not poisoning the local bottom feeders with the likes of him."

"Your choice." She held up her hands in surrender.

"What about you?" I asked.

"What about me?"

"Grimes called you here, set you up with a false crime scene, and then helped you frame Stevens. He's tried to have two people killed. You're in it the same as me. By now, he knows that you're aware of what he's done."

"That's wrong. I never thought that anyone but Stevens killed Alex. I'm still not otherwise convinced."

"Grimes won't chance that with you. Strummer wasn't talking, either. Look what happened to her."

"Do you need me to take this guy out for you?" she said, nodding to the lump on the floor. "Because I'll do it."

"Of course, you would. Then you could finish off Stevens and walk away."

"I'll screw something up with Stevens, some technicality, and then your boy will walk. No one gets hurt that way, including us."

"We both know you won't. Your precious career."

"Eat me, Nichols."

"I'm playing this straight. It's the only way. Because if you're right about Grimes, he won't stop at this clown. He knows a thousand of these guys, right? He'll send another, and one for you, too."

"No. If we get rid of this asshole, he'll never know I was here."

"I'll wind up in a hunting accident. Strummer will get clipped by a drunk driver, and you'll walk into an ambush disguised as a drug bust." I shook my head. "You don't even see it. You're the patsy."

She took a deep breath. Rage passed through her face in a crimson wave. The skin around her jaw tightened as she thought about what I'd said.

"Even if you're right, we can't prove anything. It's all conjecture. The stiff in your living room isn't going to talk. And if he does, it'll be crap. He says anything, he knows he'll get popped."

"We haven't even put it to him."

"We can try." She shrugged. "But it will be a waste of energy, and he doesn't solve our problem. It's Grimes. He's the one with all the juice."

"I've been saying that for a week," I said. "Maybe we lean on him, too."

"You think you could get him in for an interview? He's in the damn Cabinet. And, if by some miracle you did get to talk to him, he'd have a lawyer who gets paid more per hour than you make in a year. The last thing you'll get from him is any kind of confession."

"We've got what happened to Sally Strummer."

"Any half-assed suit will expose her testimony as a drunk girl's dream."

"Then we rely on physical evidence. We find that poker. Get the ashes analyzed."

"Where do you think that poker is? On the other side of the cove?"

"Why not? He sent you in one direction. Maybe he sent it in the other."

"It's been in the water for two weeks now. There's zero chance for a fingerprint, which wouldn't prove anything anyway. And what do you expect to find in those ashes?"

"I don't know."

"Your witness was in a coma. She didn't open her eyes. Stevens said he didn't see or hear anything. How much of nothing can one cop have?"

"There's Violet," I said. "No one has talked to her."

"I interviewed her. She was devastated and positive that Stevens killed her son. She didn't know anything happened in that house."

"Did you push her?"

"I didn't have to. She confirmed what we believed happened. She'd be the last to know anything, the way she drinks."

"I'd like to talk to her."

"They won't let you within a mile of her. From what I've seen, she hasn't made it to sundown in weeks. The chardonnay comes out at lunch and doesn't stop."

"Maybe there's a reason for that."

"Like her son dying?"

"From what I understand, this behavior preceded his death. What about the separate bedrooms? What does that mean?"

"That one of them snores?" Salazar said.

"You're telling me that even though we know what happened, there's no way that we can get there?"

"Exactly. And it's what you think happened, not me."

"So, what do we do?"

"Take off to the Caribbean, where we open our own version of the Rusty Bullet."

"I do have bartending experience," I said. There was zero chance that we wouldn't be at each other's throats like wolves before we could agree on a name for the place.

"Look," she said. "We can think we know what happened, but there's no way to prove it. There's no prosecutor on earth who would drop the case against Stevens and go after Grimes, especially anyone up here. You can do everything right and still come out on the losing end. Be smart and get rid of the mutt on the floor. We keep our jobs. Let Grimes go back to Washington. He'll have to live with his conscience. That's the best we can hope for. Don't tell me it's not right. It's reality."

Crowley came through the front door carrying a blue duffel bag. We went into the living room. Crowley jerked his head. The maroon Impala sat in the driveway.

"This asshole's name is Roger Franklin, or it could be Miles Winthrop. He's got two IDs in one wallet. Each with its own Visa Card. He's got a folio with business cards that say everything from IRS agent to insurance investigator." He tossed the wallet to me and the business card holder to Salazar. "One license says he's from Virginia, the other from Maryland."

"We've got us the lamest covert operative in the greater beltway," Salazar said.

"The car is a rental from Hertz. Under the Franklin name. Handcuffs, garbage bags, bleach, three-eighths inch nylon rope, and a sniper rifle with a tripod in the trunk. There's also a camera. But I don't think that's illegal." Crowley laughed.

"You guys are dead meat," Franklin said. "You can't imagine how this is going to come back on you. Take these cuffs off, and let me walk. We'll forget this ever happened. You don't have a snowball's chance in hell of it going anywhere. The marshal knows that, even if you don't, Opie."

"I will admit," I said, "you've got us right where you want us."

Crowley put the canvas duffel on the coffee table. It didn't have much in it besides four of the same gray t-shirts, four pairs of black socks, some Fruit of the Looms, and ten thousand in cash, all twenties. There were also three boxes of ammo for each of his weapons.

"I don't see any other recourse but to bring him in and start working on him," I said.

"You're fucked if you think I'm talking. Listen to the bitch."

I laughed. "I think he has a crush on you."

"From what I see," Crowley said, "we've got him for breaking and entering, attempted murder, false identity. And I wouldn't bet all his guns are legal."

"That's not the way to go," Salazar said.

"It's a start."

"If you insist on doing that," Salazar said, "I'll take him to the state police barracks. That's the most secure location."

"Secure in what way?" I asked. I knew that Salazar's trip would take a detour. She'd made that clear. "If one of us isn't there, your associates show, and away he goes. We put him in a cell at the station and take the keys, so they can't grab him even if they want to."

"I'll move in if it's called for," Crowley said.

"I don't like it," Salazar said. I had expected her to put up more of a fight. She was ceding control, or appeared to be.

"Once Mr. Franklin is settled in," I said, "I'm going to the women's tennis round-robin at the Abenaki Club at nine o'clock."

"You're going to need to shave if you want to get in that tournament," Salazar said.

"That's where Violet will be. The question is, will she be accompanied by security?"

"You bet she will," Salazar said. "Grimes has everyone on red alert after your trip to Boston."

"Is there a way that you could be that security? You act surprised to see me, outraged even. But I talk you into letting me interview her. She might not object if I allow you to be present."

"You do ask some ridiculous questions, and so earnestly."

"Then take me to your supervisor, and I start greasing the wheels with what we know."

"We don't know anything," she said, shaking her head. "*You* have some theories that I do not wish to be attached to."

Salazar was one foot in, one foot out. In a boat, that usually landed you in the drink.

"Then you can leave. But you need to keep quiet and make sure your friends aren't looking for me. If I feel any heat from your camp, I'll make sure they know you're in this up to your neck."

"You wouldn't."

"You can't make me cry, but you sure could piss me off. And that would be bad for you." Crowley's eyebrows came down, confused by the conversation. Salazar sighed and wished us luck. She was still shaking her head as she went out the door.

I made some calls. I woke Dr. Lindsey and asked him to come to the station in an hour, as we'd apprehended a suspect who'd been hurt, but that we couldn't risk taking to the hospital. I warned him that he may have to splint or set an arm. Then I phoned the DA, Laurent. He wasn't happy, either, but at least I hadn't interrupted his morning round at the country club. I told him he could come after golf but warned him that we had some heavy lifting in front of us.

Crowley and I convoyed to the station. I drove the Chevelle with Franklin in the back seat, and my sergeant followed. There wasn't even a marshal waiting for us. We were that early. After securing Franklin in a cell, I took one key and gave the other to Crowley. The third we buried in a potted fern in the lobby. We questioned him from the adjacent cell. After the first few hours, I let Crowley go home to grab some sleep. I did not let the prisoner near a phone. I worked on him from different angles and logic. It didn't make a difference. True to his word, and as Salazar had warned us, Franklin wouldn't talk, not even after we let the doctor set his arm. I finally gave up.

I went into my office and found the business card that my new friend Sawyer at the Press Herald had left me. We needed cover, and none was coming from a government agency. I called him at home and gave him the basics—that I believed Randolph Grimes was involved in his son's death— and promised to provide the details in person. He didn't start questioning me, but asked when we could meet, the sooner the better. I told him to give me two hours, and I'd get back to him. He double-checked that I had his number right, even though I'd just called it. Undoubtedly, he saw another headline in his future.

When Crowley came back at eight, I went home to take a shower before going to Pearl Harbor Violet Grimes. Things were foul enough.

Chapter Forty-Five

After threatening Salazar that I'd tie her to me, I was counting on the federal government's interest in me diminishing. And with Franklin locked up, I assumed that it was again safe to drive through my own town. I filled the Chevelle's tank and returned it to Rory. Then I went to find Violet Grimes.

From the road, the Abenaki Club didn't look like anything special. A low-slung building with weather-beaten shingles across from the river, it could have been an oversized lobster pound. Once inside, however, you stepped onto gleaming yellow pine flooring and found a white-tableclothed dining room and glistening mahogany bar. The waiters and bartenders wore burgundy serving jackets and never failed to have a pristine black dinner napkin draped over a forearm. A tidal pool provided the view on one side, with a stone pathway leading to the groomed croquet lawn and clay tennis courts that stretched behind it. It wasn't that Laurel was flooded with those requiring such a place, but come summer, there were just enough of them to sustain it. I wasn't sure what a membership cost, though I was fairly certain I'd have to sell my house to afford a season of Lobster Thermidor, Baked Alaska, and properly stirred martinis—which, of course, would have defeated the purpose.

I bypassed the club's front parking area and went to the employee lot behind the courts, hidden by a row of bushy hemlocks. A few women were already rallying on the clay. None of them were Violet. From the looks of it, the near-Olympian would have an easy time with the competition, most of whom appeared better suited for croquet. I was in uniform for the first time in days. If the Grimes didn't care about the authority it projected, the staff at the club would.

I went in through the kitchen. Fred Baker, a high school kid who pitched and played right field, was doing dishes. He nodded hello. Two cooks in chef coats and houndstooth pants worked the line, emptying an institutional-sized egg carton into stainless mixing pans. Omelet hell, I presumed. They looked up and at each other before returning to their cracking.

I stepped through the service doors into the dining room. It was eight-thirty, and the round-robin started at nine. I didn't think it was a coincidence that St Adrianne's, the small church on the bluff at Bishop's Beach, didn't hold their Sunday service until noon. I went over to the bar, where I'd be able to see everyone entering the club. A man my age was shoveling horseradish and shaking Worcestershire sauce into a pitcher of tomato juice.

"Whatever it is, I didn't do it," he said, picking up a peppermill and working it over the concoction.

"I'm just here to watch the tennis," I said. "I heard Chris Everett is playing."

"Really?" He stopped grinding, and his eyes went to the windows. I guess it was possible. Celebrities did pass through on occasion.

"No, not really. Where's the manager?"

"That's me for the moment. The dining room guy, Harvey Whetmore, comes in at ten. We don't serve until eleven, after the first casualties from the tennis."

"I'm sure you know it's illegal to serve a drink before noon on a Sunday," I said.

"News to some of our guests," he said. "But of course, we'd never do anything like that." The wink I expected to follow didn't come.

"I'm going to need a place to talk to one of your members."

"Seriously?" Panic flashed on his face. I could imagine him trying to explain to the real manager how he allowed one of the members to get grilled on the premises.

"Yes," I said.

"I guess you could use the private dining room."

"Where's that?"

He came out from behind the bar and took me to a room tucked into a front corner of the building. A picture window faced the tidal pool. There was a table for twelve with high-backed chairs and a candelabra. I told him it would be fine.

"Great," he said. "It's where the Grimes family dined after their son's service last week."

Not great. As we left the room, we ran into Trout and Violet Grimes entering the club, headed to the bar. She wore a determined game face, which, considering the circumstances, I assumed wasn't part of readying herself for competition. She had a sizable Wilson racquet bag slung over her shoulder. Her grip on the strap was tight. Trout stopped short when he saw me. Violet nearly walked into him. The bartender watched, apparently afraid to let me loose while he was in charge.

"What are you doing here?" Trout said. He widened his stance, remaining squarely between Violet and me.

"I'd like to talk to you for a moment, Mrs. Grimes," I said, looking past him. Pale blue eyes stared back. "About Alex."

"What could you possibly have to say?" she said, her voice cool and even. "It's my understanding that your efforts have been incomprehensibly focused on clouding the guilt of the man who killed him."

"That's not exactly the case," I said. "I just have a few questions. I promise I won't take more than two minutes of your time."

"James," she said to the bartender, ignoring me. "I'd like a Bloody Mary, please."

He looked at me, recalling our discussion five minutes earlier. I nodded okay.

"Mrs. Grimes," Trout said, "you don't need to do anything."

"I certainly don't, Nathan," she said, taking the drink from James. "You can tell your friend he can leave."

"LT, you heard her," he said.

"Mrs. Grimes," I said. "There are certain details that I'm not sure you're aware of. But that you should be." She looked at me and sighed, her eyes focusing as she appraised me. "Nate is welcome to be present, if you'd like."

"I'll give you one minute," she said, looking over my shoulder to the courts. "Then I have to warm up. Nathan can wait here."

Trout gave me the hard stare. He wasn't happy with the ambush.

"Fair enough," I said. I turned to the bartender and asked if there was a place outside where we could have some privacy. I wasn't bringing her back to that room.

He placed us at a marble umbrella table on the patio next to the empty croquet lawn. I sat facing the courts, and she positioned herself opposite me. Racquets thwomped tennis balls as the women hit behind us. Green windscreens blocked our view of them.

"First of all, I'm sorry for your loss."

She raised her right hand and flipped her wrist at me. Get on with it.

"You were home the night that Alex passed, is that correct?"

"Let me ask you something, Chief Nichols. Do you think I'm a delicate flower?" She sat back in her chair. Lines crossed her forehead.

"Excuse me?" I asked. Her hair was pulled back in an athletic ponytail. Her arms were well-toned and tanned brown.

"My son did not pass. He was killed. True?"

"It is."

"Then be accurate with your words. If you're here to whitewash me, I'm done."

I nodded.

"But you are correct," she continued. "I was home. And as you may have heard from Marshal Salazar, I didn't hear or see anything. If I had, I may have shot Stevens myself that evening. So, I'm not sure what you're doing here."

"There are things that happened that night that you may not be aware of."

"I'm aware that my son was killed," she said. "By Riley Stevens. If you have a point, please get to it. I'd like to loosen up properly."

"I talked to your houseguest this week, Sally Strummer. There are circumstances which I'm going to explain to you, and I'll let you know why I think they're true. You will not be treated like a daisy."

"Have you discussed these things with my husband?"

CHAPTER FORTY-FIVE

"I have not. There's a reason for that, however."

She tapped her fingers on the stone tabletop.

"The accepted narrative that Riley Stevens killed your son outside the boathouse is flawed."

Her eyes flickered. "You're trying my patience."

"We know that Alex and Stevens had a disagreement that took place there not long after he and Sally returned from the Dockside. Stevens admitted it, which did not do much to help his case. I think he was being honest, because he didn't have anything to do with what happened to Alex. That Stevens went down to a boat, grabbed that brass hook, returned to the patio, clubbed your son with it, and then pitched it and Alex into the cove makes very little sense."

"Have you known many logical, clear-thinking killers, Chief?"

"I have not."

"You, whose experience in law enforcement is basically handing out parking tickets, are at odds with what one of the best US Marshals available to us, and the state police, have determined. And I'm expected to listen to this?" She asked it as if it were a real question, and not the verbal swatting of a mosquito.

"Yes, and I'll explain why."

"The next words out of your mouth better do just that, or I will be on those courts before you finish your sentence."

"As I said, the accepted narrative didn't make sense to me, and I'm the one who initially pointed the investigation to Stevens. I've talked with everyone present in the house that night, except you. At the time, Secretary Grimes indicated that you were having a rough go of it and asked that I respect your privacy. I accommodated that request. Maybe I shouldn't have."

"Because?" she said.

"I found that your husband and son were often at odds. The reason that Alex was there that weekend was to tell Randolph that he was leaving the job the Secretary had secured for him to resume his acting career. He'd invited Miss Strummer for moral support. Were you aware that Alex planned to discuss this with Randolph?"

She did not react. Rather, she looked impatient to swing her racquet.

"I was. My son and I had a more communicative relationship than he and his father."

"Did this conversation take place between father and son?"

"It had not, as of Saturday when they went out for the afternoon. I imagine Alex would have left it for Sunday, prior to his departure."

"I talked to Abby the night before the funeral. She informed me of the ongoing professional unrest between Alex and his father."

"How considerate of her. If you're going somewhere, get there."

"I let Marshall Salazar know of my doubts on the Stevens narrative and told her that I was going to Boston to re-interview Strummer and Will Ranford. I went to Strummer's apartment. There was a man outside. He eyeballed me as I pressed her buzzer. I believe he was watching her. She eventually let me in, though she had little desire to talk to me. At that point, her story remained unchanged. You know it, I'm sure: She was drunk, passed out, and didn't remember anything after being carried out of the Dockside by Stevens. She'd mentioned that Alex and Stevens hadn't gotten along, Alex being angered by the attention that she gave Stevens, who was a fan of her music. These were all things we'd known. After I left her, I went to Will Ranford's office to talk to him. His story didn't change, either."

"You're here to tell me that you learned nothing?"

"When I left Ranford's office, I was being followed. I ducked into a parking garage and took down the man tailing me. It turns out he was Commerce Security. I asked myself, if the Stevens-as-the-killer narrative was spot on, why was I being followed? Why was Strummer being watched? What did they think I would find that could disrupt their case?"

"I can answer that for you. They, and when you say they, you obviously mean my husband, had tasked himself with making sure that my son's killer is not let off on a technicality—something that you are apparently working toward. Also, if you recall how our legal system functions, only one juror needs a seed of doubt, and a killer can go free. I believe, out of some loyalty to one of your own in Laurel, you are trying to help these people—and at our expense. Randolph won't have it, and neither will I." She stood and heaved the racquet bag to her shoulder. I stood with her.

"If there was nothing there to be found, there would be no reason to have me followed or Sally watched. There had to be something that they—your husband—did not want me to find. Sally had to have been the key, whether she realized it or not, or she would have been left alone. I couldn't let that thought go. After leaving Ranford, I tracked down Sally at the bar where her band was playing. She still denied knowing or remembering anything. She left. I followed. I was twenty yards behind her on Commonwealth Ave when I cut in front of an Impala revving at the corner, waiting for traffic to pass. The driver was the man who'd been watching her apartment. He didn't notice me because his eyes were locked on her. She was about to cross the street. I saw what was going to happen and was able to pull her back just as she stepped off the curb. He missed her by inches. He'd tried to kill her."

She raised her right hand to stop me. A gold and diamond bracelet dangled from her wrist.

"And you're positive this driver was intentionally trying to hit her and the same man who was outside her apartment? You couldn't possibly be mistaken?"

"I'm certain."

Violet's head leaned forward. Her mouth, which had been pressed shut, opened.

"I got Sally off the street. As you can imagine, she was shaking. She was scared enough to finally tell me what happened that night at the Compound."

As we stood there, I gave Violet a word-for-word description of how her son, frustrated by Riley's flirtation and angry with Sally, attempted to take advantage of her as she appeared to be unconscious, how her husband must have walked in and prevented it, and how Sally remembered voices. I explained that there must have been an altercation between father and son. Violet's face dropped as she lowered herself back into her chair. It was hard to tell whether she was shocked that I'd even propose this or that it could possibly be true.

"It's my belief that as a result of that altercation, your husband harmed

Alex. It may have been self-defense."

She raised the tennis bag to her chest, as if it would shield her. Her eyes locked on mine. The denial that I had prepared for didn't come. I asked again if she heard or saw anything that night.

"You didn't know my son, did you?" she finally said, her voice a whisper above the breeze.

"I'd met him a few times. Arranged for rides home. The DWI. That was it."

"If you had made the effort, you'd be certain that he could never do something like that to a woman. Especially one he valued as a friend."

"From what I understand, it was an unrequited love."

The hand that had urged me on earlier waved that sentiment away. "Hardly."

"Alex may have been quite drunk himself, and his emotions got away from him."

"It doesn't matter how intoxicated he may have been. He doesn't have that kind of violence in him, and that is a violent act, is it not?" The symmetry of her face went askew, her bottom lip crooked.

I nodded. No mother would want to think her son capable of such a thing. What she was not doubting was the possibility of a clash between father and son.

"This is what she claims happened?" she said.

"This is what she thinks happened. Her intoxication level was quite high. She was in and out of consciousness. She remembers voices and tones, noises, a few details. But unfortunately, nothing concrete."

"What are you saying?" This was not uttered defensively, but for clarification. "She thinks Alex was in the room with her, but she's not sure? How did she know what was happening?"

"Her clothes were being removed. She felt that."

"But she didn't see Alex doing it? How am I to believe this?"

"She was practically comatose. She couldn't manage to open her eyes. Completely overwhelmed."

"I can sympathize with a woman in that condition being taken advantage of, but I'm not following this. She doesn't awaken? She just imagines or assumes it was Alex?"

"She was aware enough to scream. Your husband heard her and came to her aid."

"And you believe her," she said, her hand going to her forehead, "that it was Alex preparing to assault her and Randolph stopping him, based on her feeling that's what happened?"

"I do. Who else was present in the house? When Randolph entered the room, she felt the atmosphere change. That's when the confrontation between father and son could have started. They left the room, and I believe they came to blows."

Violet's hand went to her chin as she thought this over.

"My son wasn't a fighter like that."

"Even if his back were against the wall? I don't imagine your husband would have taken something like this lightly. Randolph may have followed him into his room. Alex could have felt threatened. I'm not saying the ultimate result was intentional. Perhaps far from it. But the fireplace poker from Alex's room is missing. It could have been the murder weapon."

Her jaw clenched, and a storm crossed her face as she ran this through her head. I waited.

"My husband would…," she said, then stopped, practically choking on the words. She pressed her lips together, and her eyes closed for a five count. When they opened, she began running her palms over their opposite biceps. She stopped when she noticed me watching her do it. "Do you have evidence of any of this?"

"As of the moment, I do not. But I'm not done. I know this might be difficult to hear. Your husband has tried to keep me from pursuing this from the get-go. He wanted Alex's death to be seen as an accident. But then he accepted it when Marshal Salazar settled on Stevens as the murderer. When I started questioning that assessment, he placed barriers in front of me. This only strengthened my belief that Riley Stevens didn't add up as the killer. And the closer I got, the more he raised the stakes. He tried to have Sally killed. The man driving that car was waiting for me at my house last night, sent to kill me. I was lucky to subdue him. Only a person with something considerable at stake would go to these lengths to hide the truth. That's your husband's Cabinet position. I'd like your permission to search the Compound. I may be able to turn something up."

She shook her head. "You think my husband is behind all this?"

"Yes."

"And this man, the hired killer, he confessed and told you that my husband sent him?" The grin left her face.

"He said enough before I took his gun from him."

Violet took a deep breath, then exhaled slowly. She looked at the ground, then up into the sun. Her eyes came back across the table to me. She had reached some conclusion.

"Maybe you are somewhat capable, Chief Nichols, but that's not really an answer, is it? Let me guess what your assailant has to say now: Nothing. That's why you're here talking to me instead of arresting Randolph. Because you aren't sure. Because you have no proof. It's guesswork."

"I wouldn't say that."

"Of course not," she said calmly, as if stating another fact. "But any sane person would realize that you don't know what happened. You also don't know what kind of people we are and how hurtful this is. I don't know what your reason for doing this is, but you can leave now. Go find yourself a less hateful windmill, Chief Nichols." She stood.

"Excuse me?"

"Are you not familiar with Don Quixote?"

"I know of it." I'd heard the name and knew it was a book or movie.

She shook her head. A hint of a smile flashed and vanished.

"Well, maybe you should look into it. I'm going to play tennis now. I'd appreciate it if you could see fit to leave us alone. We've been through enough. Go read that book." She stood and hoisted the racquet bag to her shoulder.

"Riley Stevens as a killer doesn't make sense, Mrs. Grimes. Your husband could have told us what happened from the start, if it was self-defense. I'm sure he could have kept certain details from the press. Instead, federal agents and hired operatives have tried to keep me from the truth. He chose to protect his position over all else, and many of us are in line to pay for it, one way or another."

"I can't believe you could think that of a man like Randolph." She rested the tennis bag on the arm of the chair.

"I've always had the greatest respect for your husband. But all I've done is try to do what's right, and he tried to have me killed. That's a fact. If you know anything, you need to tell me."

"The mythical quest always ends in failure, Chief Nichols. It's a lost cause. You can thank me. I just saved you some reading. You should forget this and go back to doing whatever it is you do around here."

She heaved her bag onto her shoulder and walked off toward the court. I would not have wanted to be her opponent.

Chapter Forty-Six

I sat down to think things through. Violet had not burst with anger or wept with grief. I hadn't anticipated a contemplative reaction, even though she hadn't considered what I'd proposed as plausible. Maybe it was too much for any wife to believe her husband could kill their son; no more than a mother would believe her son would assault a woman. She'd denied it all. I supposed I was lucky that I hadn't wound up wearing her Bloody Mary.

I was screwed. Franklin, sitting in one of my cells, was my best hope. But not much of one. He'd laughed when we threatened to work him over and smiled when we'd stated lengths of prison sentences. This could have resulted from some sort of professional code, but more likely, he counted on being protected from above. Of course, he'd denied everything he'd said while holding me captive. That left me to find the missing fireplace poker. A search would not be easy. The Grimes wouldn't let us on their property, and no judge would sign a search warrant that targeted a member of the Cabinet, especially based on what I had to admit sounded like a far-fetched story. I could only hope that Grimes's planting of the boat hook was a repeat of what he'd done to get rid of the poker. I could summon my rookies and their bathing suits, and we could wade the oceanside of the Compound at low tide looking for it. My last resort was to go at Grimes himself. But even if I could fight my way through the army he'd surrounded himself with, he'd probably laugh harder than his man Franklin had.

I went into the Abenaki club to call the station. I was going to have the rookies pick up their surf shorts and meet me at Cape Laurel Pier. Trout gave me a look from the bar. He was watching the tennis courts, a third down into his own Bloody Mary.

"You fucking moron," he said, jabbing his drink with a celery stalk. "You told her your stupid theory, didn't you?"

"I did." I was not in the mood for this.

"How far did she tell you to stick it up your ass?"

"She was nice about it."

Trout nodded. "You're lucky. She's not having the best day. She just went home to get a different racquet. Broke a string or something. Told me to enjoy my drink and not worry about it, that she wasn't a teenager and could drive herself. I told her it was my job, but she wasn't having it. I think she needed some time to herself. You haven't helped matters."

Something didn't make sense. I'd watched Violet exert herself picking up her pro-sized gear bag. It probably held five or six racquets. And Trout always drove her.

"You ever carry her tennis bag?" I asked.

"Sure."

"Heavy?"

"A hair less than a ton."

"Doesn't it seem like she'd have a backup racquet in there?"

"I don't know. Maybe she didn't have the one she wanted. She's got a million of them."

If she wasn't making a trip for a Wilson, she was going back for something else. The picture of her choking out "My husband..." and stopping short came back to me. She'd gone dark then, and she'd had to work to correct it. Maybe she hadn't dismissed what I'd said.

"Violet," I said. "Would you consider her confrontational?"

"She's the only person on earth who scares Tracey Bolton, let's put it that way." Trout leaned into his cocktail and took it down to halfway.

"Is Randolph home?" I asked.

Trout nodded.

"Let's go," I said. "Now."

"For what?"

"She could be going after him."

"Based on what you told her?" Trout laughed. "That's a good one."

"She put something together when I was talking to her. I'm sure of it."

"No fucking way," he said. "You leave me out of this. She told me to wait here, and that's what I'm doing. She'll be back in two minutes."

"Sure," I said and started for the door. I could hear Trout swearing behind me, but he wasn't moving. I stopped at the front desk and borrowed the phone. Then I ran to the Bronco.

Chapter Forty-Seven

From the gate, I could see the Suburban parked in front of the house. The statie stationed in the guard shack opened his window. I told him that Violet had left her pocketbook at the Abenaki Club and they'd asked me to return it. Plausible, as I was in uniform. An eyebrow arched up, but so did the gate. I guided the Bronco to a spot behind the Suburban.

"Hello," I called from the front door. "It's Chief Nichols."

"In here." It was Violet's voice, this time breathless and unsteady. It had come from the back, Grimes's office. I ran. The door was open. Randolph, standing at the edge of his desk, straightened as I entered. A lock of hair had broken free from the death grip of product. Violet was half-sprawled on the couch at the window, fifteen feet away. Her face had brightened, as if she'd just finished on the courts. But lipstick was smeared across one side of her mouth, and her lip was bleeding. Spots of crimson dotted the chest of her white tennis dress.

"What's going on?" I asked.

"I think you should tell us that, Chief Nichols, having burst in here like the proverbial bull," Randolph said, haughtiness dripping from his voice. He stepped toward the front of the desk, closer to me.

"Mrs. Grimes, are you okay?"

"Of course she is," Randolph said.

"I asked her."

"I'm fine," she said, her lip raising.

"You don't look fine," I said.

"Is there a reason that you're here, Chief, and if so, could you please enlighten us?" Randolph folded his arms across his chest. The question was a demand, and his tone made sure I would not confuse that.

"Mrs. Grimes, I'd like to speak to you outside."

"She doesn't want to talk to you." Her eyes locked on me.

"She can speak for herself, Randolph."

"She will not be talking to you. Do I need to call someone of authority to have you removed?"

"I have all the authority I need. Mrs. Grimes is bleeding. She and I will be going into the living room."

Randolph gave her a look that would have stopped a rabid Doberman, had she any intention of joining me.

I stepped toward her, but Randolph slid into my path like a basketball player ready to take a charge. That's when I saw the gun on the desk. When I'd appeared at the door, he'd positioned himself to block my view of it, a small caliber, single-shot target pistol with a long barrel and rounded sight. I unsnapped my holster and rested my hand on my Smith and Wesson. I hoped that would be enough. A mistake here could be devastating for all of us.

"Get away from the desk," I said to Randolph.

"What the hell are you doing, Nichols?" he said, not moving.

"Step the fuck away," I said.

He raised his hands as if I had my gun pointed at him. "Do you have any idea of what you're doing? Did you forget who I am?"

"I know who you are. You're the bastard who sent someone to kill me. You're the one who tried to have Sally Strummer run down in the street, and you're the man who killed his son. You're also the one who's going to pay for it. I think that should cover it. Get over there." I brought out my pistol and directed him to one of his office chairs. My hand was steady. "Now."

"You're out of your mind. You're imagining things that never happened." He shuffled away from the desk but remained standing.

"Why is there a gun on your desk?" I asked.

"I was cleaning it for Violet. I thought that after tennis, she might enjoy some target shooting. It relaxes her, and no thanks to you, she's extremely troubled."

"What happened to you, Mrs. Grimes?" I asked.

"I walked into a door." She avoided my eyes. I didn't believe her, either.

"I don't think you realize the extent of the trouble you're in," Randolph said. "I'm glad your father isn't around. He'd be mortified at the bumbling jackass you've become. Threatening us like this, he must be spinning."

"Nichols, what are you doing?" It was Salazar. She filled the doorway. Her hand moved slowly under the dress shirt she wore untucked. She was reaching for her Glock.

"I'm sorting out what went on here," I said.

"What are you talking about?" Salazar said. "Put the gun down, Chief."

"There's a pistol on the desk, Marshal Salazar. Until that's secured, I'm not moving a muscle. You might want to take a look at Violet, too."

"My wife's target pistol," Randolph said, turning toward it. "It's barely a BB gun. I had to take it from her. I was afraid she was going to use it on herself. After what you told her, Nichols." He shook his head. "Your irresponsibility is beyond comprehension."

"You just told me you were cleaning it."

"I was trying to keep our family business private, as it should be."

"I've heard enough," I said. "You're coming in."

He laughed. "I hope you're enjoying this, because your next job for this town will be collecting trash."

"I'll secure the pistol," Salazar said. "Lower your weapon, Chief."

She stepped beside me and grabbed the target pistol by its barrel. She didn't use anything to keep her prints off it. She broke the action and removed its twenty-two-caliber cartridge. That went into her pocket. She placed the gun on a shelf behind her.

"Nichols, why don't you just head out," she said. "I'll take it from here. I'll make sure this doesn't come back on you. It's over."

"Does it look like it's over?" I said, nodding to Violet. Then I turned back to Salazar. "Did you forget about the animal sitting in my jail?"

"This is a family matter," Randolph said. "That you should have stayed out of. This never happened."

"This isn't all that happened, Randolph," I said.

"Nichols," Salazar said. "Be smart."

"Don't you go, Chief Nichols," Violet said. "My husband striking me is the least of his transgressions. I was going to use that gun. But not on myself. You leave, and they'll fuck me first and you later."

"Quiet, Vi." Randolph started toward her. I holstered my gun and stepped between them, hoping he'd swing so I could act. "You don't know what you're saying."

"You were right to think the worst of him, Nichols," Violet said. "He's the one who did that to Alex. I'm sure of it."

"Violet, enough."

"But you had it backwards," she said. "It wasn't Alex trying to rape that girl."

"You frigid bitch," Randolph snarled. He lunged for her, and I dropped him with a right to the stomach. He was on his knees on the oriental rug, struggling for air. That wasn't a problem. That Salazar had her Glock trained on me sure seemed like one, however.

"It was Alex, then, who found his father with Strummer?" I asked.

"Of course, it was," Violet said, her tongue tracing her split lip. She bit down and spit blood in front of Randolph as he tried to get to his feet. "He's lucky I didn't get a bullet through his head."

"You failed at that, too," Randolph said, unsteady as he crouched, hands on his knees.

Violet went to kick him in the face, and I almost let her do it, pulling her back just in time. Salazar helped Grimes into a chair.

He turned to Violet. "Your son, the rapist. He's a twat, just like you. I saved that girl from him."

"Liar," she screamed.

"I'm taking you in," I said, stepping toward Randolph. "You're under arrest for the murder of Alex Grimes, conspiracy to commit murder, obstruction of justice, and domestic violence."

He smiled at me. "You, my friend, are in well over your head."

"That may be true, but I've got a guy in my jail who's ready to roll on you. Your best-case scenario is one of those federal country club penitentiaries. Embrace it."

"None of this can be proven," he said, his voice confident. "Straighten him out, Salazar."

"If you believed that, you wouldn't have sent that spook after me and Sally." I turned to Salazar. "We are not letting this go."

"His man won't talk for anything," Salazar said. "It's all impossible to prove. We've gone over this."

"Then you're out of luck, Marshal," I said. "Because I'm taking him in."

"Let's come to our senses," Grimes said, standing. "Because if we don't, Marshal Salazar will find something to put you away for, Nichols. I'll take care of Violet myself. She'll come around, I guarantee that. The marshal just explained it. You're in no position to dictate anything."

"He's right, Nichols," Salazar said. "You're up against something you can't beat. It's a machine. It chews up people like us and spits us out."

"I'm not like you," I said.

She sighed and shook her head. "Think it through. You must have learned something these last few weeks. You were in here illegally yesterday. That's enough to cost you your job, if not put you away."

"You also maniacally harassed my family, which will not be tolerated," Randolph said.

"You're fucked, Nichols," Salazar said.

"But there's a deal to be made," Randolph said. "There always is."

Violet looked to me. "Don't listen to this."

"For example," Randolph said. "You can bring your story out, that I walked in on my son as he was engaged in some untoward activity toward a female house guest. An altercation resulted. I'll prepare a statement. Stevens will be released as a result, which I believe was your goal from the start. I will pay. I'll admit publicly that, though I'd done the right thing at the time, I could no longer live with the guilt and the chance that Stevens might get falsely convicted. I'll be forced to resign from the Cabinet. I'll be ostracized from the circles I live my life in. I won't even be welcome at this town's July

Fourth celebration. You'll have what you want, and I'll be finished. That's the best you can hope for. We all know that you'll never be able to prove anything. Your potential witnesses are drunks who neither remember nor know. All you have are unprovable theories, which my lawyers will turn to confetti. Then they'll shred your reputation."

"He's right, Nichols," Salazar said. "Take the deal."

"Are you kidding?" I pivoted to face her. "You know differently."

"Legally, this will never go anywhere," she said. "For many reasons."

She looked me in the eye when she said it. I wanted to throttle her. The Glock in her hand was reason not to.

"It's what's best for all of us," she said.

I turned to Randolph and tried to keep the fury out of my voice.

"I'm supposed to forget about the man you sent after Sally and me? The guy who threatened to kill Suzanne Anderson, who had nothing to do with any of this, if I didn't cooperate?"

"That will all go away. It was business, not personal."

I'd finally heard a reference I could place.

"I'm not taking guidance from *The Godfather*, no matter how you frame it."

Randolph didn't answer. He watched me.

"I take this deal," I said, "and you get to play golf and tennis and drink martinis at the Abenaki Club. You keep selling millions of cardboard boxes and ammo and whatever else you make. A rapist and a murderer. No fucking way."

"Disgrace is the true punishment for someone like me. Granted, it may seem a shallow victory for you. But consider what I could've been, where I was destined to be. I could've made it to the White House myself, one day."

"Your disgrace is not justice," I said.

"It's not your job to decide justice. You told me that you just look to do the best you can." A sheen of sweat covered his face, his veneer cracking. "This is the best you can do here. We all see it."

"I can do better than to sell out my principles for a fraud like you."

He cocked his head and sighed.

"Marshal Salazar, what are we going to do with the last honest man in America?" he said, forcing a chuckle.

"How do you like it, Randolph, when the cock's in your mouth for a change," Violet said.

He grinned at her.

"I give up," he said, raising and dropping his hands. "Do what you have to do, Salazar."

I didn't know what that meant, but I wasn't encouraged by it. The Glock remained out. I wasn't taking chances.

"Okay, Randolph," I said. "We have a deal."

"No, Nichols," Violet said. "Don't you dare."

I stepped toward Randolph and extended my hand. When he reached to shake it, I grabbed his arm and whipped him around, launching him into Salazar. I jumped sideways and followed him, tackling her from the side. Her gun hit the floor. I leapt on Salazar and snagged the Glock at the same time. In seconds, I had my former lover in a knot. She yelped as I wrenched her shoulder. Randolph hurdled us and broke for the door. As my cuffs were going on Salazar, Violet took off after her husband. The target pistol was in one hand, shells from a box on the desk in the other.

I sat Salazar up, then helped her to her feet. She wouldn't even look at me. I told her I was glad she wasn't taking this personally and hustled her to the bathroom. I emptied her pockets and used her own cuffs to attach her to a five-hundred-pound antique iron bathtub. From the phone in the kitchen, I called Crowley at the station and told him to bring everyone we had. Then I ran outside.

Randolph was at the helm of the Mako. The strain of the Mercury cranking but not turning over drifted across the grass. Apparently, Riley hadn't gotten the chance to work on the engine. I didn't know if Randolph was running from panic or had an escape plan. He could have had a car stashed somewhere or even a helicopter on standby. I started toward the dock, then spotted Violet. She stood at the edge of the lawn, pistol trained on the boat.

"Don't do it," I yelled as I ran toward her.

The outboard caught, but it was low tide and Randolph buried the propeller in the mud trying to back out of the slip. Violet had a clear shot now. Randolph saw it and ducked behind the console. The boat lurched forward. A wake of mud sprayed behind it. He wasn't drawing enough water to get up to speed.

Violet rested her gun hand on her left palm. She took aim. I stopped ten yards from her.

"Put it down, Violet," I said.

"Nothing will happen to him," she said, lowering the gun and turning to me. "You know that." She calmly spread her feet and took a breath. She raised the pistol. The Mako must have caught deeper water. It gained speed to quarter throttle.

"That's not true," I said. "Trust me. Take out the engine. I'll bring him in. The engine, Violet." I took off running behind her, at an angle to catch the Mako at the end of the channel before it hit open ocean. I counted on her doing the right thing. Whatever she aimed at, I was sure she'd hit.

Randolph had to hug the outlet along the property to reach the Atlantic. I hopped on the boulders at the far corner of the lawn. I was going to have to jump from there onto the boat. The Mako had found water and was starting to plane. I heard the shot. I thought she'd missed, but then the engine coughed and sputtered. Black smoke poured from the Merc, at first a thin stream, then a full contrail. The boat lost speed but didn't stop. By the time it approached, it wasn't any faster than Gus Brown's dory. But that gave Randolph time to spot me waiting for him.

I leapt from the seawall as a comet of orange phosphorus rocketed past me. I hit the deck ten feet below and rolled, crashing shoulder-first into the far rail. I ignored the pain and scrambled to my feet. A grin spread across Randolph's thin lips. He loaded another flare. I didn't want to think of what that could do to my gut. I was plenty tired of having guns aimed at me.

I lunged and planted my good shoulder into his stomach. As I flipped him over my hip, a green fire sizzled and swooshed over us. He landed flat on his back on the deck. The boat careened into the exposed low-tide mud of the cove. The engine whined. Black smoke engulfed us. I gripped Randolph's arm and pulled him up, then drove him into the captain's chair. He gasped.

I'd taken his air.

I pushed him back against the console with my good arm, wishing I had another set of handcuffs. He looked at me and caught his breath.

"Fuck you, Nichols," he said. "I'll be having my usual martini by five o'clock."

I ignored the burning oil searing my lungs and grabbed the collar of his button-down shirt. He could very well be right, but I wasn't having it. With my good hand on his neck and disabled left on his belt, I ran him face-first into the dying outboard. The cartilage in his nose crunched. Teeth scattered onto the deck. So much for evening cocktails.

Epilogue

For the first time in my career, I'd been able to fill all three cells of the Laurel police station at once. Randolph Grimes, Franklin, and Salazar had made quite a collection. A week later, I was painting my house. At least I was getting paid for it.

The Attorney General of the State of Maine, Nelson Cooley, had walked into my office the day after I'd apprehended Grimes, along with Nigel Dorsett and Colonel William Porter, head of the Maine State Police. Link Johnson, Laurel's lead selectman, tagged along behind them. The first thing Cooley did was ask for the reports I'd written regarding the death of Alex Grimes. Then he asked for everything I'd recorded separately on Randolph. After I gave them to him, he asked for all the copies. I provided the carbons, as well, except for those stowed under the rear mat in the Bronco. I had been learning, just as Marshal Salazar had hoped.

Cooley informed us that the Maine State Police would be conducting a full inquiry into what had gone wrong in the original and subsequent investigations that had implicated Riley Stevens. Byron Wisterman and I would have no role in either, other than to answer questions asked by the officer in charge, and only those questions. This was fine by me. I'd had enough.

Johnson then congratulated me on being instantly approved for my annual vacation, one I hadn't put in for. It would cover the rest of the summer, usually a blackout period for time off. Cooley stood behind him, nodding as Link told me. If he hadn't coached Johnson on how to present it, I would have been surprised. They weren't calling it a suspension, which I wouldn't have accepted so gracefully. I hated to think what would have happened to me had Riley Stevens actually killed Alex Grimes.

The smartest thing I may have ever done was call Mike Sawyer from the Abenaki Club. He'd gone straight to the Compound and arrived at the gate in time to watch Randolph's attempted escape. There was no denying that the press, no matter what headline they wanted to write, had ultimately saved us. It became impossible for Grimes or anyone to bury the story.

Dorsett let me know that Salazar had been suspended indefinitely, pending further review. I imagined she could start looking for apartments in Peoria or Wichita, if she wasn't fired outright. In my reports, her incompetence and compromised position came across mostly as a result of Secretary Grimes's influence. I guess she could have considered that a win.

After they filed out, she came in. The white sling she wore on her right arm contrasted nicely with her gray slacks and black shirt. It also matched the one on my separated left shoulder. She was lucky she wasn't again in cuffs.

"You do know that this investigation is just a formality, right?" she said, sitting in one of the metal chairs across from my desk and straightening her legs out in front of her. "He'll be at a country club federal spot, like you said. And for not long enough."

"I guess we can hope that Violet takes him to the cleaners in the divorce."

"That won't happen, either."

"How could it not?"

"You still don't know those people." She smiled. "Enjoy your vacation. I'm out, too. I'll be surprised if they take me back."

"That's a cryptic way of asking me to run off to Jamaica with you," I said.

"Another thing that will never happen." She had several smiles, this was the crooked, not funny version.

"It's not like we can hug each other." I raised my one good wing but didn't rise from my seat.

"I think you covered for me some," she said.

"I just wrote what happened. You should have known better, but he did take advantage. Anyway, Des Moines is probably a very nice place."

She nodded, frowning. "Be ready when the court shit comes. What happened and the real story are going to be two different things. Accept it. Don't go off the rails."

"Would it be small of me to point out that from the start, your advice has been less than stellar?"

"I guess not, considering," she said, offering a barely perceptible grin.

"I've got a question for you," I said.

"Shoot."

"Is everyone out there corrupt?" I asked.

"That's the wrong way to look at it," she said, the smile expanding. "It's not necessarily corruption. Everyone's human. Motivated by self-interest. Think of it that way."

"That's not exactly comforting," I said. "Or true."

She gave me a cute little wave, like a girlfriend going off to college while the dope she was leaving was staying behind because of his great job at the fish processing plant. She was another person paying for Randolph Grimes's mistakes. Something I had chosen not to do myself.

* * *

I was at the top of a ladder, in my sling, brush in my good hand. Sweat and drops of Benjamin Moore exterior white fell like rain beneath me. It wasn't just the heat. I was a lousy painter, and I had a fear of heights. I cursed myself for declining Riley and Scooter Stevens's offer to help with the project. When a red Mercedes coupe pulled into the driveway, I hoped it would provide an excuse for me to stop.

Abby Grimes stepped out. She stood in front of the car, looking up at me. She put her hands in the pockets of her cut-offs, which extended beyond the fabric of the faded jeans.

"Is it wise to be up there when you can only use one arm?" she said.

"I've never been known for my intelligence."

She shrugged and waited as I crept down the ladder.

"You ruined my father's face," she said. "It's so bad it won't even look the same when it heals."

"Yeah," I said. "Sorry about that." I wasn't.

"I came to thank you." She reached through the open passenger window and pulled out a case of Budweiser. She looked at my sling. "Where do you want it?"

"You can throw it on the porch," I said, putting down my brush and following.

"They're cold."

"Convenient. I'm thirsty."

She grinned and placed them at the top of the stairs. She opened one and handed it to me. Then she popped one for herself. We sat down next to each other on the top step.

"Where is he now?" I asked.

"House arrest, in Washington, though. Resigning and all that."

I sighed.

"I hate him," she said, taking a drink. "He won't nearly pay enough."

"No," I said, shaking my head.

"That's why you did it, right? Smashed his face like that, because you knew that would happen in the end."

"Your father once told me that sometimes circumstances dictate our actions. So, you may be giving me too much credit."

"I think you haven't been getting the credit you deserve."

I shrugged. "How's your mother?"

"She doesn't know what end is up. They're not pressing charges for her shooting at him, which might be the only thing that makes sense in any of this. She's at our Santa Barbara place, which is as far away as she can get and still be in the United States."

"That's good. How are you doing?"

"I've got an enormous waterfront estate to myself. Violet's claiming she'll never set foot in it again. I don't blame her. Mr. Trout is watching it. Fired as security, hired as caretaker. The easiest money he'll ever make, if he can handle the ghosts."

"Are you staying there?"

"For a few days. I'm an existentialist. I don't think I believe in ghosts."

"You're going to have to explain that to me." I'd had a summer of references I didn't get.

"Sure. How about over dinner tonight?"

"I don't know if that would look good."

"Are *you* scared of ghosts?" Her eyes drilled into me.

"I don't think so," I said, hoping it was true.

"Then who cares?" she said.

That was a question I'd been asking for weeks.

A Note from the Author

The places, organizations, businesses, names, characters, and events described in this book are either products of the author's imagination or are used fictitiously. Any resemblance to actual persons, living or dead, is entirely coincidental.

Acknowledgements

I have much gratitude for my wife Kim, daughter Sydney, and son Aaron for their understanding and unlimited patience with me, as well as their continued support. I'm grateful for the time invested by my initial readers, Rob O'Regan, Dan Healy, and Ray Bartlett. Their feedback never fails to help. I'd also like to thank my longtime friend and marketing guru, Doug Quintal, for his guidance.

THE WRITER IN RUINS NEWSLETTER

Scan below to sign up for Albert Waitt's "Writer in Ruins Newsletter." You'll receive book release and event information; notices for special offers and discounts; bonus content; answers to reader questions; movie, television, and book recommendations; and the occasional cocktail recipe. All usually delivered with humor.

About the Author

Albert Waitt is the author of *Flood Tide*, *The Ruins of Woodman's Village*, and *Summer to Fall*. *Flood Tide*, published by Level Best Books in March of 2024, is the second book of a series featuring Laurel, Maine, police chief, LT Nichols. Waitt's short fiction has appeared in *The Literary Review*, *Third Coast*, *The Beloit Fiction Journal*, *Words and Images*, *Stymie: A Journal of Sport and Literature*, and other publications. Waitt is a graduate of Bates College and the Creative Writing Program at Boston University. Experiences ranging from tending bar, teaching creative writing, playing guitar for the Syphlloids, and frying clams can be found bleeding through his work.

SOCIAL MEDIA HANDLES:
  FaceBook: @Albert Waitt
  Twitter: @albertwaitt
  Instagram: @albertwaitt

AUTHOR WEBSITE: Albertwaitt.com

Also by Albert Waitt

The Ruins of Woodman's Village

Summer to Fall